BA...

'Knowledgeable and s... ...it matters most'

Observer

'Mr Kabal ... has demonstrated an Ancient Mariner's hold and an eye for those sulphurous twists that keep a plot boiling'

Guardian

'Gripping tale ... startling finale'

Sunday Express

What the critics said about A. M. Kabal's
THE ADVERSARY

'An exciting and fast-moving thriller ... deserves to be read'

Jeffrey Archer

'A new talent in the chase-and-chills department'

Guardian

'As brutal as comes, but good ... first class'

Listener

Also by A. M. Kabal in Sphere Books

THE ADVERSARY

BAD MONEY

A. M. Kabal

SPHERE BOOKS LIMITED

SPHERE BOOKS LTD

Published by the Penguin Group
27 Wrights Lane, London w8 5tz, England
Viking Penguin Inc., 40 West 23rd Street, New York, New York 10010, USA
Penguin Books Australia Ltd, Ringwood, Victoria, Australia
Penguin Books Canada Ltd, 2801 John Street, Markham, Ontario, Canada l3r 1b4
Penguin Books (NZ) Ltd, 182–190 Wairau Road, Auckland 10, New Zealand

Penguin Books Ltd, Registered Offices: Harmondsworth, Middlesex, England

First published in Great Britain by Allison and Busby 1986
Published by Sphere Books Ltd 1989

Printed and bound in Great Britain by
Richard Clay Ltd, Bungay, Suffolk

for
Quentin Guirdham and Candace Siegle
il maestro e la prima donna

'Bad money drives out good.'
Sir Thos. Gresham, his Law

ACKNOWLEDGEMENTS

Lady Empson, Chatto & Windus and Harcourt Brace Jovano-vich for the line from 'Aubade', from the *Collected Poems of William Empson* (p. 48), on page 42.

Faber and Faber for the lines from 'Song' by W. H. Auden, *Collected Poems*, on page 65.

Pattern Music Limited for the lines from the song 'Run that Body Down', by Paul Simon (from the album *Paul Simon*, 1971), on page 80.

The Society of Authors as the literary representative of the Estate of A. E. Housman for the quote from his poem 'An Epitaph' (*Collected Poems*, Jonathan Cape, p. 149) on page 322.

AUTHOR'S NOTE

Prologue:

A SHORT NIGHT'S MURDERS

Midsummer's Eve, the hard men moved.

It was weeks before any of the murders was explained. It was longer before anyone put them all together.

By then, it was almost too late.

In Rome, Tom Wellbeck, senior Italian correspondent for the *Examiner* of London, had returned to his flat close by the Spanish Steps rather later than usual, after supper with friends. He had been at his desk, making notes about what he had learnt over dinner, off the record, with a banker, a civil servant and a priest, when he heard the knock at the door. A gentle tap. Almost mild.

Thinking it might be his young mistress, Zara Francchetti (though, to be sure, he had not been expecting her tonight), he had gone to the door with a self-satisfied smile on his lips.

He was still smiling as the first .22-calibre bullet punched his left eye and cut through his brain to the back of his skull.

The second killer, the one with the .45, shouldered the door open while the first one grabbed the falling journalist under the arms and dragged him back across the room to the chair by the desk. By the time the second gunman had locked them into the apartment, the first had forced the muzzle of his pocket Beretta into Tom Wellbeck's mouth and fired one neat, clean .22-calibre hole through Wellbeck's tongue. Clean at the point of entry. On exit it tore away most of the Englishman's throat.

The second killer walked across the room to look in sour satisfaction at what was left of a larynx which would speak no further about his bloody-handed masters. Then the first killer nodded, and the second man raised the big .45 with its thick bolt of a silencer, and finished the job.

They waited for silence before forcing the desk, scattering

3

its contents till they found what they were looking for. Then they were gone into the happy crowds of a warm Roman night, dropping the surgical gloves they had worn down the first drain they passed.

They had been in the flat for ninety-six seconds.

In Panama City, the same evening, Colonel Enrico Perez, exiled military adviser, confidant, bagman, torturer, to the former Somoza regime in Nicaragua, sat in his hotel bedroom waiting for a telephone call from Mobile, Alabama.

He was not in the least surprised to hear the knock at his door. He had told the bell-captain to bring him his usual room service, a bottle of Old Forrester and a woman. One of those tight little Puerto Ricans the *yanquis* brought in their wake, ones who wriggled and hollered and called him their general.

But the woman waiting at the door when he opened it was not the one he had been expecting, nor even Puerto Rican. She was a slight, high-blonde with a cream complexion, and if she had spoken at all it would have been in the distinctive accent of the South of the USA.

She did not speak, however. Instead, she struck the Colonel one stunning blow, straight-fingered, to the throat. As Perez crumpled, she made her hands into fists, pushing forward the knuckles of her middle fingers, making bony points, and cracked them, hard and twisting, into the Colonel's temples.

Then she stepped aside, to let the big black man with her through the door.

He swept the fallen Colonel up by the ankles and dragged him into the bathroom, leaving the blonde to close the main door behind them.

It was one of those anonymous, antiseptic bathrooms, built to American specifications for American travellers, but it had all they needed.

The black man picked their victim up by the ankles and smashed him down, head first, into the toilet pan, cracking his skull and breaking his nose. As the Colonel began dimly to struggle, the woman came through and took him by the right wrist, forcing his arm away from his body, placed a knee between arm and trunk, then leaned down hard against the arm. Then she walked casually round her partner to the other side and broke the Nicaraguan's other arm in exactly the same fashion.

Then she flushed the toilet.

Again. And again. And again. Till the water soaked her colleague's trousers and his new, Italian shoes.

A few miles away, to either side, lay two great oceans. But Colonel Enrico Perez died by drowning in the comfort of his own hotel.

The following morning, in London, Detective Inspector Mike Thomas of the City of London Police looked down on the sodden body beneath its canvas mortuary cover, looked across at the grey young men from the Foreign Office and the Bank of England talking to the grey middle-aged man from the Home Office and thought, eloquently, to himself, *Oh, fuck*.

The body had been seen hanging below Blackfriars Bridge by a railwayman on the early shift just before dawn. As soon as he reported it, alarm bells had gone off everywhere, even in quiet England, even in the City, underpopulated out of office hours.

So why did this have to happen to him, why did he have to be the duty officer this time?

It was only six-thirty in the morning now, but they had already identified the body, from Interpol's Confidential Missing Persons list (the secret list, the one for the people for whose arrest no warrant had been issued, but who were wanted for questioning, urgently, without fuss). The identification had been easy. All the man's papers were still in his pockets. Along with half a dozen household bricks.

Teach him to wear such extravagant overcoats.

Inspector Thomas squirmed in his cheap, light coat, sticky in the drizzle of a June morning, and wondered, *But why a winter coat? Even in an English summer?* He filed the thought away as the grey man from the Home Office came over to talk to him. Further off, he could see the young journalist from the *Standard* looking up, and looked interested.

Errol Hart, the dead man's name had been. American.

5

Banker. Executive Vice-President of the First Manhattan Bank, recently vanished in New York, and the fraud boys in the Apple wanted to talk to him. Badly. Bit late for that now.

But the identification had set the alarm bells ringing, had meant they had to notify the powers that be. Which was why the four of them were standing around under Blackfriars Bridge in the rain, Home Office, Foreign Office, Bank of England and City Police all trying not to mention the name of the last banker to die like this: Roberto Calvi, of Banco Ambrosiano, Italy.

None of them wanted another multi-billion-dollar bank fraud and murder scandal played out in court in London.

The grey man from the Home Office was trying to sound casual. 'A little discretion would be welcome, Inspector,' he said, nodding towards the journalist. 'Don't want this one all over the evening paper. Any of the papers in fact. So no announcements, if you don't mind. No telling the local radio stations.'

Mike Thomas stiffened at the implied doubt about his reliability. He could not resist a taunting reply. 'Bit extreme, isn't it, Mr Hawkins? State censorship about an ordinary murder investigation?'

The grey man stopped smiling. 'Don't be so bloody naïve, Inspector.' Then he added what was almost an apology: 'Not that I think you are.' Then he ruined it all by explaining, 'But if you bring me a banker found hanging under a bridge with bricks in his pockets, blood all over his trousers and his prick stuffed into his mouth, I at least want the time to get hold of New York to find out if we have problems out of Sicily to deal with, on top of everything else.'

That same morning, in Gdansk, Stanislaw Pidulski, caretaker of Saint Ada's, arrived at the church to find the doors already unbolted. Frowning, he wondered why Father Zbigniew had forgotten to tell him he would be holding a special early mass, as he so often did, for those who would not have been safe attending the regular masses, watched as they always were by the secret police.

Stanislaw's question was answered as he pushed open the doors, letting the thin morning light leak into the building.

Father Zbigniew was not holding an early mass.

Father Zbigniew had been beaten to death with meat hooks and was hanging, chained and nailed above the altar of his church.

No one put the murders together at the time. No one knew enough to do so. They remained, for the time being, four separate, brutal, apparently pointless killings.

But if anyone had known enough to link the murders, they might have noticed, once the autopsy reports, the initial investigations, were in, that all the attacks had begun at 01.01 Greenwich Mean Time.

They might, in time, even have noticed that the only thing the four victims had had in common was that all of them, in one way or another, had had dealings with a man called David Medina.

But if that hypothetical anyone had known about David Medina, or even known of him of old, they would, if they had any sense, have kept their mouth shut.

Part One:

THE HEART OF
STANDING

CHAPTER ONE

'You have to be out of your fucking minds.'

Caro Kilkenny looked down the long editorial boardroom table of the London *Examiner*, and glared.

She was angry. Angry with the Old Man, the editor. Angry with the departmental heads. Angry with the pious stiffs who wrote the editorials. Angry most of all with Iain MacKinnon, who should have known better than to make so stupid a suggestion.

The red-faced Scotsman, his scalp glowing through the short blond mat of his hair, tried vainly to pacify her now. 'I don't see what you're so upset about, lassie . . .'

'Don't patronize me, MacKinnon,' she interrupted.

He threw up his hands in exasperation. 'I don't know what's got into you since your husband stopped a bullet.'

You scum! Caro thought. But all she said was, 'Ex-husband.' Everyone on the paper knew she had been hit harder than she could have expected when the news came through of Tom Wellbeck's murder. She tried to calm herself and start again. She fingered a Camel from the soft pack in front of her, and lit it, buying a few seconds of calm.

'This has nothing,' she started again, 'to do with Tom's death. What this has to do with is the contract between this paper, my publishers and me.' She saw the editor stir uneasily. The Old Man always got nervous when contracts came up. He had an old-fashioned respect for the written word. She had to hand it to MacKinnon, though. He was still trying to outface her. 'That contract,' she continued, 'is very simple. In return for first serial rights on my book, the *Examiner* undertook to allow me an unpaid sabbatical, to supply me with a decent research assistant, and to cover both our expenses within pre-set limits . . .'

MacKinnon cut in. 'And that is exactly what we are proposing.'

She leaned back and blew a long column of smoke into his eyes. Not a flicker. He was good. 'No,' she said, quietly, and paused before continuing. 'There is no definition by which John Standing is a decent research assistant.'

At the other end of the long table, a look of anguish flickered across the Old Man's face. Twenty years he had been editor. He had seen the beginning, the triumphs, and the sudden end of Standing's career. 'You used to say he was the best,' he whispered.

She turned from the editor's pained expression to where Iain MacKinnon sat stony-faced. She knew what they were thinking. She knew how they felt. She felt the same herself. But this was no time to be weak.

'Was,' she said at last. 'The operative word. But come on, Iain, you were his boss. You loved him. There wasn't anything you wouldn't do for him. And have you used him since he quit?' MacKinnon made no reply. 'I mean, for Christ's sake, what's he been doing these past few years? Financial advice columns for the professional trade press. Tax relief for dentists. Insurance policies for undertakers . . .'

MacKinnon tapped his pencil against the table-top. They all played with their pencils. She had often noticed it. Perhaps it was their way of proving, in the age of computer typesetting, of single-key access and VDUs, that their first allegiance was to the written word. Perhaps they all owed too much to the past. Perhaps that was why they wanted her to take on John Standing now, and why she felt the sudden tug of ancient loyalties. Loyalty to Standing, above all, who had been all their pasts. MacKinnon returned them to an idealized present.

'He has been doing more, of late,' he said, not looking at Caro. 'Some good leg-work. Desk research. The odd piece for the *Financial Times*. Some other stuff for *Private Eye*. And the fact is, Caro, who else is there?'

She let out a sigh of weariness. 'So that's it.' She drew on her cigarette again. 'I'd been thinking of young Alan Clarke.'

MacKinnon shook his head and lay his pencil on the table. 'I can't do that. You know damn well you're taking this sabbatical at the height of the summer holiday season . . .'

'You knew that would be the case when you signed the contract,' Caro interrupted.

'I know, I know,' he answered, putting up his hands again, his red sweaty scalp positively radiating through his hair now. 'But it does mean I'm understaffed, just at the point when there's a raft of public companies reporting their half-yearly results. Why journalists have to have children I'll never know.'

Caro grinned shyly and said, 'They can't drink all the time, Iain.' She could feel everyone round the table relax.

MacKinnon nodded his head in acquiescence. 'Maybe. Anyway, on top of that, young Clarke has the best leads we have on the Errol Hart murder story . . .'

'But that's a news story, not City and Financial.'

'Oh, come on, lassie.' She let it pass this time. 'You can't expect those slobs to understand the banking background to a case like this one.'

The Old Etonian news editor stirred uneasily, fingering his polka-dot silk bow-tie. Like most people, he was frightened of the Glaswegian City Editor. 'I say, Iain . . .'

The Scotsman thrust a long red finger at his colleague. 'And you can shut up, you over-educated git.' The Old Man bleated idly at the head of the table. MacKinnon turned back to Caro. 'So I can't spare you any of the regular staff. So I had to find you an alternative. So I thought we might give the Long Fellow a try.'

Caro shook her head, her eyes closed. 'Is he still drinking, Iain?'

There was a long pause before the answer came: 'Less.'

She looked him in the eyes; eyes so pale a blue they were almost no colour at all, twin vacancies in his over-florid face. 'It has to be a lot less. I want him dry if he's to work with me.'

MacKinnon licked his lower lip. They all knew how much she was asking. They all knew it was only fair. 'Go talk to him,' he said at last. 'Ask him. Tell him.'

'You tell him.'

A crooked little grin spread over the Scotsman's face, as if in embarrassment. Then Caro understood. 'When did you talk to him?' she asked.

13

'Over the weekend.'

She ground her cigarette out in the heavy glass ashtray before her and considered, for a moment, heaving it into MacKinnon's face. She let the idea pass.

'You conniving shit,' she said.

She went out into the newsroom. It had been refitted for the new technology – new for England, out of date in most of the rest of the industrial world. Still, all the journos faced a computer VDU now, and inputted their copy directly. It could lead to problems in sub-editing, some articles slipped through unread and uncorrected. A number of the sub-editors, some of the best in fact, still refused to work from the screens, calling up hard-copy print-outs and working through them laboriously in the old way, a blue pencil in one hand, a cigarette burning down to the stub and their nicotine-stained fingers in the other. But it was the new technology and the City and Financial pages which had turned the newspaper into profit. The paper was the result of a merger in the early Sixties, of a financial and a national daily, which was why its City editor was also its Deputy Editor. The Financial pages attracted a well-heeled readership which was an up-market advertiser's dream, and the technology had freed up funds (by laying off compositors and print-workers) for the single development which had most contributed to the recent surge in circulation. The *Examiner* had always prided itself on its Saturday edition, with the first and best of Lifestyle sections, from the time before the word was coined. The addition of a weekly colour magazine had transformed a nice little earner into a goldmine.

Caro drifted past the magazine department, through the main news team, turning here and there to acknowledge a greeting or to tease a friend, coming at last to the City and Financial section, its journalists newly arranged with their hi-tech white desks facing each other in pentagons. Beyond the big picture window, the traffic flowed relentlessly down Queen Victoria Street. The *Examiner* had got out of Fleet Street years before, snarled up as it was, hour after hour, by lorries delivering great rolls of newsprint. It was convenient for Caro and her colleagues to be further into the City, but she missed the grime and grubbiness, the drunkenness and depravity of Fleet Street itself, the Street of Shame.

At the pentagons, young Alan Clarke, the paper's newest recruit, a bright aristocratic young man, sat with his long legs up on the desk before him and a look like thunder on his face.

'Trouble?' she asked. *A looker*, she thought, not for the first time. And he knows it. The same long good looks as Tom when he was that age. Had been that age. Death changed all the tenses.

Clarke breathed in deeply and let out a long, explosive sigh. 'It's that bastard Mike Thomas,' he explained.

Caro arched an eyebrow. 'Mike? He's not usually a problem. One of the more helpful people on the City Police. What've you been up to?'

Alan smiled shyly, and Caro suddenly realized what he always reminded her of. He reminded her of that first day, in this building, on this floor, in the age of manual typewriters and carbon paper, thirteen years before, when she had first clapped eyes on Tom Wellbeck, then also a new recruit to the *Examiner*, talking to the man who was to teach them their business. Talking to John Standing. Tom had had just such a shy smile, self-deprecating and confident at once. She remembered how they had looked that morning, two tall good-looking men against the sunlight. She had wondered who they were. She had wondered how to get one of them to ask her out.

Alan Clarke swung his legs off the desk and rose to his feet, plunging his hands into the pockets of his jeans. Jeans and a hand-made shirt. The classic combination. 'You wouldn't guess it,' he said, 'from the way he's been warning me off.'

'The Hart Affair?'

Alan nodded. 'It's bad enough ‚eporting restrictions weren't lifted on the inquest. And there was pressure not to say anything from day one. But what pisses me off is the shoddiness of the police investigation.'

'You have something?'

'I think so. I think I have a trace on Hart's movements in those last few hours. The hours in which the police told the coroner Hart was simply missing. I don't believe that if I could make the connections the City Police didn't, so I thought I'd try flying a few of my notes in front of Mike Thomas, and got the most terrific bawling out for my pains. It's as though they didn't want to know the truth. He told me very firmly the whole affair was dead and buried.'

His enthusiasm was attractive, though his scowl now was more that of a spoilt child than a frustrated writer.

'And it isn't?' Caro asked.

Clarke was certain. 'No. Hart is. It isn't.'

'Then get on with it.' She slipped on her Italian cardigan. A present from Tom, years ago, after the divorce, after he had taken up the Rome posting. 'Today's my last day before my sabbatical. I'll be back later. We can go over it then.'

'You going somewhere?'

'Yes,' she said, with only a little irony, 'I'm going to pick up a legend.'

The Underground out to Standing's flat in Bethnal Green was hot, congested and sour with sweat. The pleasures of the brief English summer. They did not trouble Caro, however. She was thinking of the past. It seemed half a lifetime now since she and Tom and Standing had met. Both she and Tom had come to the *Examiner* from provincial training grounds, the *Glasgow Herald* and the *Yorkshire Post*. Standing was only six years their senior but already, under MacKinnon's watchful eye, a by-line and a name.

Perhaps it was being an American which had done it. He had had the inestimable advantage of not being placeable, and he had never been frightened by the English establishment. Not that that was surprising for the son of an American ambassador and an aristocratic English mother. To this day Caro did not really know what had brought him to England. He had been educated on both sides of the Atlantic, of course (his diplomat parents had compromised on everything): Groton and Westminster, New College, Oxford, and Harvard Law School. And then the break. The first male Standing in five generations not to enter the Foreign Service. Why? Was there a woman involved? With John there usually was.

When she and Tom had first known him it had been common knowledge that his second marriage was falling apart. Perhaps that was why he had been so pleased when she and Tom had taken up together, fallen in love and married. Perhaps it bolstered some incorrigible hope in him. He had taken them up, and taught them. More than anyone, he made journalists of them.

He had an American, a poker-player's, refusal to be panicked into defeat. Almost alone he had sat through the Stock Market and property market crashes of '73 and '74 refusing to believe the talk of impending revolution, waiting for the market to turn. Perhaps it was because he had helped to precipitate the crashes. He never had had any faith in the Happy Hour of easy money, the Barber Boom under the Heath government. He had pointed out the myriad crooks, the weaklings and weaknesses brought to sudden prominence by the government's easy-money policy. He had predicted the 'readjustment' which inevitably followed on saner policies and the oil-price rise. He had pursued the wheelers, the dealers, the movers and the shakers. He watched Slater tumble and Bentley fall. He was in on the end for Poulson when that local-government corruption scandal broke. It was why he had first taken up Tom, who came from Yorkshire where the architect's operations were centred.

But even then John had warned them, 'Look abroad. The besetting English weakness is parochialism.' He was one of the first journalists to see and understand the significance of the Euromarkets, the great deposits of US dollars overseas which, especially after the two big oil-price rises fuelled a spate of international lending syndicated out among groups of banks, had kept the Third World afloat, and in the process created the banking crises of the Eighties, as countries from Brazil to Zambia discovered they could not support their overseas debts. And it was the Euromarkets which had broken John Standing.

That was later, however; much later, after the years in which she had been happy. What had happened to them? What had gone wrong?

Something happened. The world turned, and caught them

unawares. Yet she could not blame the world. She and Tom had been the *Examiner* couple. What broke them was that the world afforded them opportunities no generation had had before. For her, the opportunity not to have children. Tom had wanted them so badly. She had never really been able to forgive him for assuming she should be prepared to put her work second. Why should any woman?

So they had drifted apart, and finally parted. MacKinnon had been curiously sympathetic. It was the season everything had gone wrong; he had to pull Oliver Ireton out of Italy, the best Rome correspondent the paper ever had, when the death threats became unignorable; John Standing had gone to pieces, for any number of reasons; and so, when Tom and Caro split up, he did everything in his power to give them what they needed. For Caro, that had been the chance to move from the grind of daily reporting to longer, analytic pieces. For Tom it had been transfer to Rome, and new sensations, a new life.

But now Tom was dead.

There was no denying her grief, and her anger at that grief. Worst of all was the nagging pain that came with the thought that if she had been ordinary, normal, if she had wanted children, he might still be alive.

She refused to think of it. She thought instead of John Standing and of David Medina.

John had always had an obsession with the secretive billionaire. No one knew why. He seemed to resent the man's existence – his power, his wealth, and most of all the fact that no one understood how either worked. And in those last months John had seemed so sure. She could not remember all of it. Syndicated Eurodollar loans had been at the heart of it. Illegal loans through Medina's shell companies, the funds rerouted to South Africa and behind the Iron Curtain. She remembered the manic intensity of John's pursuit, his savage delight in the chase. But the chase had gone sour. The final evidence simply had not been there. MacKinnon spiked the story. Standing cracked up.

It had been coming for years; everyone could see that now. How long could it be for anyone before drinking, gambling, fornication stopped being attributes and became the man himself? Before a hell of a fellow became simply unreliable, alcoholic, untrustworthy?

Yet she could not help but feel some sympathy for him. His was a common fate in their business, and there was a sense in which the depth of the fall was the measure of his former virtues. If others had been saved, it was perhaps a sign that both their strengths and their weaknesses were so much less than his.

And though he did not speak of them much, and did not choose to plead, there had been other reasons. He had watched his daughter die. Emily. There had been a time when he could not even bear to hear strangers speak the name. Fate, with its arbitrary exaggeration, had dealt the child a double blow. She had been born microcephalic, with only enough brain to keep her alive and provide her with the fringes of a consciousness. And she had leukaemia. Her mother had been unable to cope, and had pleaded with John for their rights, their lives, and the life and fortunes of Eleanor, their older daughter. But there was something in John which made him unable to let go, which would not allow him to put flesh of his flesh into a home and simply walk away. It had broken his marriage, and it had broken his heart. His wife had gone back to America with Eleanor, and he had stayed, with Emily, who was never able to live outside hospital, and watched her die. She had been eight years old.

Caro stepped blinking out of the Underground into the bright dusty streets of Bethnal Green. It was almost a year since she had visited him here. She had to pick the path out of her memory, down past crumbling Victorian terraces, Asian-run corner shops with protective grilles up in their windows against casual attack, the shabby look and the musty smell of poverty everywhere.

His flat was in the basement of a terrace house, exposed to the streets. Black plastic rubbish bags were piled up against the railings, one of them split and stinking. The debris of the outer world drifted down the steps on the wind. There was broken glass underfoot, cigarette ends, spent roaches, bird droppings. A box of empty bottles, cheap two-litre bottles of supermarket wine, sat outside the door. She had to ring four times.

He looked worse than she remembered. He always did. His tall, once-athletic frame was permanently stooped now. His skin was sallow. He had not shaved, the stubble glinting silver. His long fine hair, entirely grey, hung down into his eyes. His trousers were baggy at the knees and spattered with paint. He was wearing a nylon shirt yellow with age, its collar frayed, and a three-inch rip at the left elbow. He said nothing, and there was a look of infinite weariness in those once-wise eyes.

Caro could not bring herself to speak, and pushed past him into the flat.

The one big room, with a kitchen and bathroom off it, was covered in gutted newspapers. The desk was piled with library books well past the due return date, unpaid bills skewered on a sub-editor's spike, the remnants of a takeaway Chinese meal. Dead bottles were scattered about the room, their tops long since vanished, their necks gaping as though they gasped for breath. There were orange-juice cartons everywhere too. They explained the sticky pool at her feet: orange juice mingled with years of ground-in cigarette ash in the landlord's horrible electric-blue nylon carpet. A half-full bottle of vodka stood on the white laminate table by the bed. Caro went over, lifted it by the neck, looked about her a little theatrically, identified the green metal office wastepaper basket in the corner of the room and threw the bottle into it. Vodka gushed from its neck as it fell, then the bottle splintered with a crash.

'They told me you'd be expecting me,' she said. 'Is this what they meant?' She was picking through the mess of papers on the table, apparently counting the final reminders.

For once, he really did feel apologetic, something different from his generalized self-loathing. 'Sorry. Bit of a celebration yesterday, after I heard.'

She was sharp, but he could not tell if she was genuinely angry. 'Heard what?' she asked. 'The final decision's mine, John, and I haven't made my mind up yet.'

A naked girl came out of the bathroom, ignoring them

both. Incongruously, Caro stood with her arms crossed, as though waiting for some explanation. He gave her none. The girl got dressed slowly, almost carelessly, as though taunting them to say something, but neither of them spoke.

When she had done, the girl stood before them in her slinky pink shift, jutting one hip forward and jutting her tongue into her cheek as though cleaning out a fragment of food from her teeth. 'Could do with some money for a cab. Late for my agent.'

It figured. She had the look of the over-ambitious, under-employable would-be model. John rolled a tenner from a fold of banknotes, thought better of it, and handed her a twenty.

She was sarcastic, 'Well, thank you,' and headed for the door, saying: 'See you around.'

Caro replied for both of them. 'I doubt it.'

'Fuck you.' The girl turned. 'Come to think of it, don't bother. He isn't worth the effort,' and she was gone.

Caro turned on Standing in something like despair. 'Picking them a bit young these days, aren't you?'

He shook his head sadly. 'Not really. It's just me that's getting older.'

'How old are you now?'

'You know damn well. I'm forty-two. You sent me a card. Two weeks ago. Thank you.'

She shrugged, dismissing his thanks. 'You look twenty years older.' It was almost true. He looked like a forty-year-old so burnt out he might as well be sixty.

He did not seem at all abashed by the thought or angered by its utterance, merely resigned. 'Well, thanks. Grab a chair. I'll nip out and get in some coffee.'

'Don't bother. I've had enough instant for one morning.' She paused and looked him in his deep brown eyes. There was no denying it. Under the greying collapse it was still possible to see the outlines of the manner of man he had been, and he had been magnificent. And he was still kind, whenever he was not careless. 'Thank you for your letter about Tom's death. It really wasn't necessary.'

He half-smiled, almost brightened. 'That's why I sent it. I reckoned you needed solidarity more than you needed the grieving widow crap. I take it you've had quite enough of that already?'

She looked almost surprised, at what was left of his sensitivity, and nodded.

It was his turn to shrug, picking up his scattered clothes and saying, 'He was all right. I miss him.'

'So do I.'

They stood looking ineffectually at each other, he with his hands in his pockets, she wondering what to do with hers, finally saying, 'Oh, hell, John. Get dressed. Let's go into the office and sort this nonsense out.'

CHAPTER TWO

As they stepped into the *Examiner*'s newsroom, she felt him tense. It was four years since his resignation, since the old cry went up: 'Did he fall or was he pushed?' To someone who had been reduced to eking out a miserable living as a freelance, the newsroom, with its new equipment, probably looked like paradise.

What she had not expected was the reaction of the longer-established staff to John's unannounced appearance. His presence ignored; the ghastly reminder of the mighty fallen. Caro had the impression that if she turned round suddenly she would find someone behind them crouching, squinting, making the sign of the Evil Eye. She shot a nervous glance at John. He had relaxed again, but he was absolutely still. He did not mind. He knew he still had the rotten smell of failure on him, a bringer of bad luck. Even the sub-editor who called to Caro, 'They said to keep an eye out for you, Caro. They want you in the editorial conference as soon as you arrive . . .' acknowledged Standing's presence only by adding: 'On your own.'

She shrugged at her unwanted new colleague and showed him to her desk. As she collected a notepad she said, 'There's something you can do while you're waiting, John. I promised Tom's parents I'd collect his effects from the Foreign Office. Ring the Duty Officer. Fix us an appointment for tomorrow.'

'Us?' John queried.

Caro licked her lower lip, hesitating. 'I could do with the support,' she said. Then she went in to the conference.

Iain MacKinnon was chairing it. The editor had doubtless had to slip out to one of his customary grand lunches. Very grand indeed, by the look of it, for the senior editorial writer was missing too. Iain was bringing the meeting to a close when Caro came in, talking to the Foreign News Editor.

'OK, then, that's agreed. We keep your pages fluid. Keep it down to two people working on it, lock them away. We'll set it once and late. The rest of you know how it might affect you. No word of it, please, till we're out on the street. And the best of luck.'

The rest of the editorial team dispersed, some with quizzical looks at Caro, leaving her with MacKinnon. He closed the door on them and turned to her.

She was interested. 'Sounds big.'

'I think it is. In the day of the electronic media . . .' He said it with a wry smile which concealed a real frustration. 'It isn't often given to a newspaper to get an exclusive on a straight news story, which is why, God help us, we have investigative reporters . . .'

'Cut it, Iain. I know the deadlines and the schedules are always against us. What's the story?'

He looked cunning for a moment, but it was merely for effect. He would not have asked for her if he had not learnt to trust her over twelve years. 'The Szkrypecki murder.'

Caro was puzzled. 'The priest? In Gdansk last week? Old hat.'

The Scotsman grinned. 'It's not the murder, lassie. It's something bigger than that. I need someone to write it. Do you fancy the challenge?'

She was more mocking than she meant to be. 'I'm not working today, remember?'

Iain was sterner. 'Oh, yes you are. I checked with salaries. They booked you out for three calendar months, not thirteen weeks, starting the first of July, tomorrow. You're still on duty, girl, and you've been malingering with a known drunkard.' He softened, very slightly, at the mention of John Standing, asking, 'Did you bring him with you?'

'I did, but I warn you he's the worse for wear.'

'Most men are. Will you take him?' She nodded. 'In that case,' Ian continued, 'if I tell you what this is all about I can leave you to it and sort the old piss-artist out.'

Caro smiled, 'Sounds good.' Then she paused. 'I'm waiting.'

The Scotsman sat her down and began explaining. 'Everyone knows the Szkrypecki murder is big, bad news. Well, the

24

army turned out in force in Gdansk today. There's been rioting and fighting in the streets. It *could* turn into a full-scale rising.'

Caro shrugged. 'The radio and the wire-services will have it already. It'll be cold by morning. At least anything we can put to bed in the course of our runs will be. How far can you push back the last London edition? Midnight? Latest.'

Iain agreed with her assessment, as far as it went. 'Ay, but the TV people won't get pictures out tonight.'

'And neither will we. They'll have them for the breakfast programmes, though.'

Once again he agreed with her. 'All true. But what none of them have is the background pieces waiting to go.' He paused, looking cunning again. 'And nor do they have the details on independent action by the secret police, or of a meeting going on in Warsaw now of the Politburo members called over the General's head. It looks as though the General may be for the high jump. Our stringers are getting it out to us in dribs and drabs . . .'

'But how . . .?'

'Don't ask. The Foreign Desk have been working on these links for months. If the timing goes our way we could be the only people with the story, whatever the story is. I'm keeping tomorrow's paper as fluid as I can, and the Old Man and chief leader are waiting to go on a special leader page if we have to.'

So that was where they were. 'And me?'

Iain sat down facing her. 'I don't want this one leaking down the street. I'm keeping it all at editorial level only and away from the main news people. But I need at least fifteen hundred as a cracker of a wrap for the front page. If we lock you away where no one can get at you, and feed you what comes in as it comes in, how do you fancy writing it?'

She felt like asking, *Is the Pope a Catholic? Do Russian marshals wear lots of medals? Is John Standing the drunkest man in Europe?* But what she did was to flex her fingers in the air, as though before a typewriter, and say, 'Cigarette me, boss.'

*

It was past five o'clock when Iain MacKinnon marked up Caro's copy and sent it down to composition and the camera. She found herself feeling nervous about it. The information was that the General was hanging on, despite a serious attempt by secret-service colonels to oust him, with the support of some of his Politburo colleagues. The operations in Gdansk (and there were fires, and firing, in some of its suburbs) were at once a show of strength and a cover for the power-play in the south. If they were right (and the Foreign Desk sources looked solid) it was a hell of a story and, based on old-fashioned infiltration, one none of their competitors, even in other media, could rival. But if it went wrong they would look like fools. And there was a whole night to get through, in which the situation might change completely, leaving their story high and dry, and the day to the radio news services.

'Are you sure about this?' she asked the Scotsman. 'We still have time to pull it. Run the same stories as everyone else.'

Iain shook his head, but he was looking tired and wary. 'Everyone has to take a big risk sometimes. I guess this is mine. Anyway, we'd have to remake the whole paper, or half of it – wrap, foreign, editorial, the lot.'

'We've done it before. We've still got an hour before you have to pull the first edition together. We do more every Budget Day.'

'True. But then we have all the staff geared up for it. This time seven of us did it.'

'I know. We did all right. I liked the editorial. And the background pieces stitched in well. Better than some of our special surveys.'

'Don't talk dirty, lassie.'

She smiled and stretched her arms, her back stiff from an afternoon's typing and revisions as each new piece of information came in. 'What if it goes wrong?' she asked between yawns. 'Could be another Munich.'

She was referring to the seizure of Israeli athletes at the Munich Olympics by a Palestinian group. The West Germans sent the army in. At the time of the newspaper deadlines it still looked like a completely successful operation with none of the athletes harmed. Which was why, the following morning, the breakfast tables of Britain were loaded with papers welcoming a triumphant operation, while the radio news programmes were able to tell the British public it had, in fact, been a bloodbath. More than any other event in Caro's working life it had revealed the advantages of electronic media in getting instant updates over the daily schedules of papers. She suspected it had done more than any other thing to turn the majority of the population to radio and television as their principal sources of news, using papers for comment or information. Only specialization and investigation were holding a market for the quality press. Those and habit.

Iain was still thinking about Munich. At last he threw his pencil into the corner of the room and swept up his jacket saying, 'The hell with it, Caro. We can always go back to the *Glasgow Herald*.'

Caro grinned. It was a proud newspaper. 'What makes you think they'd have us?'

Then she remembered Standing.

She was furious, mainly with Iain. 'I don't believe it, I really don't believe it, Iain. I mean, whose idea was all this? Fine, I don't care about what you're paying him. I don't even want to know. He's happy, you're happy, I'm happy. But you offered me a legman, Iain, you said the more feet in more doors the better . . .' He tried to protest vainly that it had been the editor. She ignored him. 'You suggest John for the job, you set it all up, and now tell me you're cutting his legs off by not paying his expenses. What is this? I mean, who dreamt this one up?'

MacKinnon was trying to calm her down, embarrassed for John as well as himself, with half the newsroom listening. John alone seemed unabashed and unconcerned. His voice was calm and reasoning as he tried to take Caro by the arm and turn her to him, though she shied away.

'I don't think that's what Iain means, Caro. I think he's prepared to pay my expenses. It's just that he's not prepared to pay them to me, or give me a cash float or credit cards. Isn't that right, Iain?' MacKinnon nodded. John tried to turn

27

her to him again, succeeding this time, though she still looked away, angry with him for not supporting her when she was defending him.

'So what's the bloody difference?'

'The difference is that I have to draw my expenses from you and give you my receipts and then they pay you for both of us.'

'And where does that leave me?'

John slumped, and turned to Iain. 'Why don't you just double her credit-card limits and her float? That way she's covered for us both. Can you get that done tonight?'

The little Scotsman nodded emphatically, glad to be off the hook. 'I'll sort it out right away.'

Caro remained dissatisfied. 'I don't know what the problem is, John. It was their idea to hire you. Why can't they do it in the usual way?' She felt tired and angry and frustrated.

He took her by both arms and stared down into her eyes, his mop of fine grey hair falling over the grey skin of his forehead, his own eyes looking weary, and said in the quiet dry voice of a man who smoked too many cigarettes, 'But you do know, love. You know what they're frightened of. They're scared I'd only piss it all away.'

Before she could say anything Alan Clarke was bleating into earshot.

'I'm sorry to trouble you,' he said, rolling down his shirt-sleeves and plainly wondering who John might be, 'but I need some advice.' He looked at Standing frankly now, but MacKinnon waved him on. 'Well, you know I've found this Panamanian finance house Hart telephoned in London? There's something very, very weird about it. It's almost as though it never actually existed. Even its cancelled cheques have vanished at the bank. Whenever I talk to anyone about it, they clam up, and I don't know how to shake it out of them.'

He threw up his long hands in despair, and John Standing positively grinned. Caro and Iain glanced at each other. They both smelt trouble.

John went on smiling as he asked, 'Can you make it sound like possible fraud?'

Alan pointed at MacKinnon. 'Not enough to satisfy him or

our libel lawyers, but enough for anyone else. I think it is fraud.'

'Then get on to Fraud Squad at the City Police,' John said, 'Tell them what you know, spin it out a little. There'll still be someone there. They'll accept it from the *Examiner* if you say you have to protect your sources, but coming from here it's serious information. They're obliged to investigate it. Which means you can legitimately write a story about "Fraud Squad to Investigate Panamanian Finance House in City." If that doesn't cause enough panic to flush someone into the open, nothing will. It'll be an exclusive, too.'

Alan looked doubtful. He glanced towards Caro, pleading for advice.

She hesitated, shrugging her shoulders in uncertainty. 'Well, I've known it work before.'

'Who for?'

She pointed towards John. 'Him.'

Alan refrained from asking who the burnt out case might be, turning to Iain instead. But Iain was fleeing across the newsroom, his Glasgow accent thickening as he said, 'I didna hear a word he uttered.'

Alan thought it over, for several seconds. Then he picked up the nearest phone.

Hours later, past eleven o'clock, the last edition locked and rolling, Iain, Caro and John sat alone in the editorial office. All phone and telex lines from Poland had been cut an hour before and the borders were closed. They had a radio tuned to the BBC World Service playing in the background, but as far as they could work out they were still ahead of the competition. Caro was apologizing to John, explaining at last her part in the story, and the need for her to sit out the evening doing the rewrites for each edition as a few new facts came through. But John hadn't minded.

'It doesn't matter, Caro. I needn't have stayed. It just felt good to be back.'

Iain was brutal with him. 'You're not back, Standing. You're just a tourist here. You may never be back while you're still on the sauce. Even without it you may never be back.'

John got up to go. 'There are some things I know already, friend.' He must have been very tired, for he suddenly sounded very American. But he wasn't really paying attention to them. He was listening to the radio. 'If they've got anyone good editing tonight,' he muttered, 'they'll kill to get more news out before the morning. They'll have your first edition by now. They all will.'

Iain nodded. 'And the Polish authorities will kill to stop news getting out.'

Standing smiled wryly. 'I know. It's the best break you've had all night.' He patted them on the back. 'It was bloody well handled, Iain. And that was a hell of a wrap. Better every edition.'

Alan Clarke put his head round the door. The survivors in the newsroom were watching television. 'We're on *Newsnight*. They're taking the story straight off our first edition.'

Iain was heading for the door as he asked: 'Are we getting a credit?'

'Every other sentence.'

John held out a hand. Caro did not take it. 'Can I get you a cab, Kilkenny?'

'Sure can, Standing.'

In the lift he asked if he should come to her flat or to Examiner House in the morning. She remembered Tom Wellbeck for the first time since her arrival in the newsroom with John.

'Did you call the Foreign Office?' she asked.

He nodded. 'They're expecting us between eleven and twelve.'

As they came out into the last deep-blue light of the late summer's evening she said, 'The flat. At ten. And, John . . .'

'Yes?'

'Be sober.'

CHAPTER THREE

It was well past eleven before they found somewhere to park in one of the side streets from Whitehall to the river, then walked back to the Foreign Office building. They cut through to the entrance by the statue of Sir Robert Clive, victor of Plassey and founder of the Empire in India which made up for the loss of thirteen colonies in the Americas, on the steps down into St James's Park. Even in the summer sunshine the high courtyard was gloomy as they waited by the barrier to be cleared by the casual, uncomfortably uniformed security guard.

At last he ticked them off his list and let them through, and they picked their way between official cars to the main lobby and Great Staircase. There was another wait at the desk as the Duty Officer was called. He proved to be a fresh-faced young man in his twenties with a barrister's collar, who came down the stairs with his hand extended and a look of oily sympathy on his face, saying, 'Mrs Wellbeck?'

'No,' said Caro firmly, shaking his hand, 'Caroline Kilkenny. We were divorced.'

'I do apologize.'

'Don't. We didn't. Tom's father asked me to collect his effects.'

'Ah, yes, of course. And this is . . .?' He waved a languid hand at John.

'John Standing, an old friend of Tom's.'

'Yes, I see.' Caro guessed he was over-interpreting, a constant danger in the profession of diplomacy. It was the main way foreign services got things wrong. They took their own assumptions for the truth. 'Please come with me.'

The Duty Officer led them up the marble stairs, past the looming portraits of former Foreign Secretaries, down high, wide corridors which clicked echoing under their heels. He brought them to a large office overlooking the Park, where two big reproduction antique desks sat facing each other across bare floors. The second desk, further from the door (presumably for those busy times in war or other catastrophes when a second Duty Officer was required), was piled with Tom Wellbeck's jumbled effects. The Duty Officer leafed through a manila file, producing several flimsy sheets of paper.

'The Italian authorities sent a schedule of Mr Wellbeck's effects, with a note of those they were withholding pending the completion of judicial inquiries. I've had a translation prepared.'

Caro took the papers, placing the translation on the desk. It wasn't possible to have been married to Tom for nine years and have lived with him for eleven without having picked up a working knowledge of Italian. Perhaps if he'd aimed for the Foreign Desk when they were first married, when she was young enough to be flexible, everything would have been different. Perhaps.

John Standing was puzzled by something. '*Judicial* inquiry?' he asked.

Before the Duty Officer could reply, Caro said, 'Yes. That's customary in Italy. Investigation of major crimes is managed by an investigating magistrate. And murder still counts as a major crime.'

The Duty Officer nodded, Caro obviously rising in his estimation, adding, 'Which is why, in a country with so many gangland murders to investigate, so many magistrates end up dead.'

Caro looked up sharply. 'Are you saying Tom Wellbeck was murdered by gangsters?'

The young civil servant hesitated. 'I'm not suggesting anything, Miss Kilkenny. Just making an observation.'

Caro smiled shrewdly and turned to Standing, who was staring vacantly out of the window. He looked terrible. Was it because he had a hangover or because he was thinking of Tom? He looked worse than she felt. It made her feel a little guilty.

She took the papers over to the desk where Tom's things

lay. The clothes, still packaged up in a couple of battered suitcases, she would take as read. It was the files which interested her. She moved some of them, slamming them down heavily on the desk to win back Standing's attention, and told, rather than asked, the civil servant, 'I'd like to check the files before I sign for all this, if you don't mind.'

He looked doubtful, suspicious that she might pull some fast journalistic trick. Journalists always made him feel uneasy. They kept wanting him to reveal the things it was his function to keep hidden. But it seemed a reasonable request. The contents of the dead man's cabinets had been listed by the Italian authorities merely as files and papers. He hardly imagined they were important. 'Go ahead,' he said decisively. The important thing, he believed, was to be prepared to make a decision. (Caro might have disputed that, had she known what he was thinking. Sometimes she thought that diplomats made far too many decisions. Quite often the best thing of all to do was nothing.) 'You're welcome to use this office.'

After all, it couldn't take them long.

It took three hours. They even asked to use his telephone, to postpone some meeting at the *Examiner*. He had expected them merely to flick through the files, but they went through them as carefully as though they were an ambassador's final briefing paper for a Foreign Secretary's meeting. The man Standing seemed to grow more ashen as the morning wore on. Whatever the matter with him was, he looked too sick to do any active harm, so the Duty Officer left them to his alternate while he went out to lunch.

They were waiting for him when he returned.

'These files are incomplete,' she said, matter-of-factly, as though she expected him to do something about what could only be an irritation. 'Mr Standing and I worked with Tom Wellbeck for a long time. We know how he organized his files, and at least two major sections are missing. Maybe some individual papers as well. That's harder to say without going through everything here in detail and sorting out the blanks. But there's no reference in the paperwork to any files being kept back by the magistrate. Which is strange in any case. If

I were investigating this, the files would be the only things I'd keep.'

The Duty Officer was growing weary of these people. It was a lovely summer's afternoon, when he could have been doing nothing but watching the walkers, derelicts and lovers in the park, instead of dealing with their petty inquiries. 'Are you sure?' he asked. 'Can you be sure?'

The woman was positive. 'If they were his personal files I couldn't be. But with his working files I know, he cross-referenced everything. There ought to be a whole set of papers on IOR, the Vatican Bank, here, and a complete file marked Liechtenstein, and there aren't. If the magistrate didn't hold them back, then they've been stolen, either before or after Tom's death. Either way I'd like to know. I think it could be quite important.'

The young civil servant was polite. It was his job, even more than his duty, to be polite. 'If you'd wait here for a few moments I'll look into it.'

During the twenty minutes he was gone, John sat with his head in his hands, shielding his eyes from the light from the windows. His face had gone a faintly jaundiced white and he was shaking in a cold sweat. Caro hardly knew if she should ask him about it, he looked so desolate, so distant, so alone. In the end silence defeated her. She wanted him to talk, to tell her he was all right. She wanted him to be all right, if he was going to work for her.

'John?' she asked gently, moved by simple curiosity as well as concern. 'What is it?'

He shook his head wearily out of his hands and looked at her. His eyes had fined down to thin lines, his big eyelids drooping, his long eyelashes crossed in tiny networks. 'It's nothing.' And then, realizing it was an inadequate explanation, he added, 'It's physical withdrawal. It lasts three days when you come off the bottle. Then it's over, and you only have the habit to fight. That and the bad dreams.'

She was surprised to find him so well informed about his own affliction. 'What's it doing to you?' she could not help asking.

He sat back with his eyes closed saying, 'Mainly what you

34

can see. It takes seventy-two hours for your body to work out it can live without a drink inside it. Till then it's quite convinced it's sick and it throws everything it's got at you, because you're the only enemy it can see. You, without a glass in your hand.'

'So how come you got through yesterday?'

He grinned and reached into the depths of his jacket pocket, but it was as though all movement hurt him, because he was no longer smiling as he hoisted the battered half-bottle hip-flask.

She could have kicked herself, but she almost felt sympathetic as she asked, 'Why not use it now?'

He flicked open the hip-flask's top and slowly turned the whole thing upside down, empty. He looked grave.

'How will you cope?'

'I'll manage. I've done it before. It's just prolonging it I can't bear. I end up getting bored. You even get used to the hallucinations after a while.'

She felt both appalled and intrigued. 'You get hallucinations?'

'Getting them now.' He was sombre, and pointed to the carved stucco above the picture-rail. 'See that cornice?' It was a kind of respectable Victorian Art Nouveau. Stylized reeds and ferns folding round the wall on to the ceiling. 'Been dancing every time I've looked up for an hour. Like grasses blowing in the wind. And growing. Elongated across the ceiling, towards the chandelier. Doing it now. Every so often grows so long the ends look as though they're going to break off and shoot towards the chandelier. But each time that happens they fall back, into the cornice and start growing and waving all over again. I think it must be me that makes them do that. Makes them fall back. If they broke away towards the centre I think I might go mad.'

'That's why you've been reading so slowly?' He nodded, very slightly, as though even such small actions hurt him. 'How did you manage to read at all?'

He smiled, the sweat on his upper lip glistening, his whole face with a slight sheen on it. 'The same way I keep on walking when I'm pissed out of my mind. By extraordinary acts of will.'

The Duty Officer had no real news for them when he returned. 'I'm sorry, but that is everything the Italian authorities handed over to our people in Rome. It all went into one diplomatic pouch and wasn't unsealed until it got to us here. If there are any papers missing – and I find it difficult to understand how you could really know – then they are presumably still in Italy, perhaps with the authorities. I can ask for that to be checked with the investigating magistrate's office, if you would like.'

Caro was business-like. 'Yes. I would like that, very much. We may have been divorced, but I still want to know who murdered him.'

The young man looked pained. 'We don't know for certain he was murdered, Miss Kilkenny. That's for the investigating magistrate to decide.'

Standing answered him, quietly ironic: 'Oh, really. And what do you think Tom did? Rise from the dead after he'd shot himself in the brain, just to do it again? Twice? Because it made him feel good?'

The civil servant stood with his hands behind his back, trying to look judicious, but looking only officious. 'As you wish. I'll have it taken up in Rome but I wouldn't hold out much hope.'

'Then you'd better just do the best you can,' said Caro. 'In the meantime I've noted that I think there are missing files on the manifest and that I'm signing for receipt of an incomplete set of my ex-husband's effects. I'll need a photocopy of that for my own records.'

They made him help them pack Tom's things into the dustbinliners John had brought with him in a Harrods carrier bag.

As they ferried the sacks down to the car, a Foreign Officer messenger following with the suitcases, Caro asked John, 'Well, what do you think?'

His eyes were screwed up against the afternoon sun. 'I think it stinks,' he said. 'I think it smells badly like a story.'

Even before he opened the door into Iain MacKinnon's office, John could hear Alan Clarke's highly educated vowels straining into disillusionment. It did not stop him. He went straight in.

36

Alan was saying, 'I don't see it, Iain. I really don't. Last night you were all in favour of pressing ahead with the story, as long as I kept away from anything covered by the reporting restrictions on the coroner's inquest. Now you're trying to tie me up in multiple sources and infinite checks. What's happened? Why are you trying to kill a good story?'

Iain did not look away from Alan as he said sidelong to John, 'Fuck off, Standing,' and went on without missing a beat: 'Don't give me the journalist-as-hero bullshit, laddie. I want the story as badly as you do, but I don't want to spend the next ten months in and out of the courts. You have to make it stand.' Then he turned to John to say, 'I told you to get out of here.'

John got. A few minutes later Clarke emerged from the office with disgust all over his face, looked once at the older hack as though asking vainly for support, and headed for his desk. Standing went back in to see the editor.

MacKinnon was standing with his back to the door, looking out of the window on to the soft refracted City light.

'What do you want? Where's Caro?' he asked without turning.

But Standing wasn't taking that. 'Look at me when you're talking to me, Iain.'

The Scotsman turned, still furious, his scalp salmon-red under his almost albino hair.

'That's better. She's with Accounts, getting the additional cash float.' He was calmer now, but not by much. 'Don't screw me around, Iain. I'm halfway out of my mind for want of a drink and though I'm grateful for the job I'd just as soon snap the neck off you as off a bottle.'

MacKinnon shrugged and sat down. 'I'm sorry. It was just the lad. I'll not be told I let people kill my stories.'

'Don't you?'

MacKinnon flared up again, pointing the longest finger of his right hand at John accusingly. 'I didn't kill that story, John. You did it yourself. We could've run it if you'd only listened.'

Standing hung his head, shaking it. There was so much he felt ashamed about. 'I know, Iain, I know.'

'What is it you want?'

John sat down, his long legs crushed up against the desk in the little office. 'It's Caro.' He hesitated, looking out of the window, feeling guilty again. He was no one to be giving anyone advice. He had made enough of a mess of his own life without mixing in others', but she was a good woman, and a good friend. 'She's all right. She's going to be all right, as long as she keeps working. I think she hurts without any need at all at the moment, and knows it, but doesn't know how to stop it. If she keeps on working it'll stop in any case. And now she has the smell of a story on her.'

Iain was sympathetic. 'I'm glad to hear it. But what does that have to do with me? She's off the paper for three months.'

John eased his chair to one side, to give himself more legroom. 'Yes, I know. And as I understand it, you have first serial rights.' MacKinnon nodded. 'Then if you're like any other editor I've known you'll be buggering about and interfering every ten minutes to make sure you get the series you're after. All I'm asking is that you trust her. She's good. She knows what she's doing. And there will be things she wants to do in her own way.'

MacKinnon, with the newsman's natural suspicion, was not prepared to let it go at that. 'Like?'

John wondered if he should tell him or if he should leave it to Caro. They had all known each other a long time. It might as well come from him. 'I think she'll want to go to Rome.'

MacKinnon looked unhappy. 'I thought she planned to start in Brussels.'

'So did she. But we've just picked up Tom's things from the Foreign Office. That's why we were late. And some of his files are missing. It doesn't look good. In fact it smells. Will you pick up her expenses?'

Iain sat back, pushing his chair against the wall, rocking like a schoolboy and punching slowly at the edge of the desk, looking deeply embittered. 'I hate the Italians,' he said at last. 'Three years ago I had to pull Ireton out of Italy, the best head of station this paper ever had there, before they got

38

to him with concrete overshoes. Now someone blows the head off Tom. And you tell me Caro wants to find them, though the Lord knows what it might have to do with a book on government corruption . . .'

'Everything in Italy has to do with government corruption, Iain,' John admonished him gently. 'It's the way they run the place.'

MacKinnon raised his eyebrows in baffled agreement. It had been a frustrating day. It could do no harm to tell the old drunkard. 'And on top of it all, I have the Home and Foreign Offices trying to close down on Alan's story, which looks too much like the Calvi killing not to have an Italian connection.'

'So that's what all that was about.'

MacKinnon nodded. 'I'm not taking that kind of Old Boy pressure, John. I never have and I never will. But Clarke's too much the old-school type himself to see it. What I *have* got to have is a story that runs, that could hold up in a court of law, so I can fend off our own lawyers and keep the Old Man quiet.'

'Don't worry about it. He was just blowing off steam. He'll see it himself when he thinks about it. Right now he's just feeling the righteous young journalist. All of us have done it.'

'You more than most.'

'Granted.' He might have been angry with anyone else, but he could not deny it to MacKinnon. 'On that basis, would you like me to talk to the boy?'

'If I agree to play along with Caro?'

'Something like that.'

'Look after her.'

'I don't suppose she'll let me.' He got up, smoothing down the battered jacket of his aged suit. 'Is the boy good?' he wanted to know.

MacKinnon's eyes lightened. 'He will be. When I'm through with him. He's pretty damn good already.

'As good as I was at his age?'

'That was a long, long time ago.'

When Caro came down from Accounts, John and Alan were

39

standing in the middle of the newsroom having what looked like an argument. It was odd. John, the older and marginally taller of the two, was the one who looked more vulnerable, more defensive, like a junior supplicating for some favour from a powerful superior. Was it just the contrast between broken middle-age and the confidence of youth? What was it that John wanted the young man so urgently to understand? Whatever it was, Alan was holding his own.

'I really don't believe that,' Clarke was saying. 'If you must know, I think he plans to spike the story. Mike Thomas of the City Police was in his office this morning. I gather from the secretaries that the Home Office has been on to the Old Man, who is still lunching at the Athenaeum. What do you think it looks like?'

John was unusually patient. Perhaps he was just too unwell to manage arrogance or anger. 'I think it looks like a bright young man with a cracker of a story forgetting the basics of his business in all the excitement. You have to check and check and check again. A story isn't any good unless you make it stick.'

Alan was looking at him as though he was some kind of traitor. 'I'm surprised at you. I thought you'd understand. After some of the stories you lost.'

'You heard about that?'

'I asked around.'

Looking more powerful now, John stared him down, and Caro realized what Standing's old attraction had always been. It wasn't the old, once-dazzling, tennis-player still locked inside him, or the quick intelligence. It was the attentiveness they had not been able to withstand. He had a gift of suddenly focusing all his attention on one person as though they alone existed. The gift had faded over the years, but he still had it in some degree. He was using it now. It made people feel safe. It made them feel he was a man who could be trusted. He was asking Alan to trust him.

'Then you ought to know,' John said gently, 'that Iain didn't kill the story you've been told about. He would have run it. He could have run it, if I hadn't been too pig-headed to refuse to cut or change the things I couldn't prove. If Iain had run the series as it stood, Medina would have crucified us.' It was the first time since it happened that Caro had heard him speak of the series which had broken him, the series on David Medina. He went on talking, trying to make Alan understand.

'Have you any idea how long his lawyers can tie up any paper? It would only have been worth it if we were certain we could make it stick. And Iain was right. We couldn't. At least you've got an excuse. You're a damn sight younger than I was. I should have known better. But I promise you that kilted bastard will run anything you write, as long as you do the necessary work.'

She almost wanted to laugh, almost purely out of pleasure. There, in the middle of the newsroom, stooping and sounding off, he sounded almost like the John Standing she had used to know, the man he was in the days when you could have forgiven him anything, and all too often had to.

She had let him rattle on enough. It was time to break his spell on Alan, and there was something she had to tell him.

'John?'

He looked across at her, noticing her for the first time and switching all his attention to her. Alan seemed to deflate, released from his intensity. She noticed that John's eyes were horribly bloodshot as he said:

'I know. I've told Iain already.'

She felt annoyed, for an instant, at his presumption in daring to know her so well, but as he held her in his gaze he looked so weary and concerned she could say nothing.

'I think you ought to wait,' he said, 'at least until we've been through every clause and comma of Tom's files. I think you should know exactly what you're looking for.'

She shook her head. She had been thinking it through all the way back from the Foreign Office, waiting as Accounts reluctantly prepared a fat brown envelope of money. 'What for?' she asked, sounding and feeling sardonic. 'To give who-ever's got the files more time to alter or destroy them?'

'They've probably done it already.'

'Well, at least I'm going to try.'

Alan was still angry, still trying to find someone to blame

41

and, listening to Caro get the same advice as he was getting, thought he had a scapegoat. He turned on Standing: 'What happened to you? Why are you, of all people, lining up behind the cowardice of editors? From what I hear, you weren't like that at all when you were a serious journalist. Is it envy you're taking out on us now?'

Caro wanted to hit him, an ignorant little pillock who would never understand. But she did not get the chance. John turned on him, so gravely only those who knew him well would ever have guessed how incensed he had become.

'*She* doesn't have to,' he was say, 'she has me to do it for her. To dig, to check, to read, to think, to check and check again. But you aren't Caroline Kilkenny. You aren't a grown-up yet. You have to do it yourself. She can run because I'm here to do her walking for her. But you, you have to learn the only rule that counts. Your work has to stand alone, without the benefit of your passion or curiosity. And nothing you write will ever stand up until you learn . . .'

Caro finished the sentence off for him, she had heard it so often before, so long ago, when John taught the likes of her and Tom their business, their craft. She told young Alan Clarke, 'The heart of standing is you cannot fly.'

He made her stay. She found herself wanting to stay. They had sat down with Alan Clarke and his Errol Hart file and, when they had been through every inch of it with him, they hit the phones. She found herself filled with something like gaiety, the darknesses of the past week cancelled, now that she was back at her business, being a working journalist, with the half-forgotten sounds of John Standing in her ears, as he whined, cajoled, blustered and insinuated. When Iain came out to find out why they were still in the building, and what John was doing using the office phones, Standing had stared him down and the Scotsman backed away in unaccustomed and defeated silence. They sent Alan down to the Graveyard to check a short list of names in the Cuttings Files. They filled ashtrays and they filled notepads. And by five o'clock they were ready. They called for the editorial conference room, and Iain MacKinnon's attention. He was uncompromising.

'I'm not paying you for newspaper work, Standing, and I'm not paying you at all today, Caro. So what do you have for me?'

Alan was looking on attentively, silent, a little puzzled, learning. His blue eyes were so soft they were almost grey. Caro almost regretted being angry with him, he seemed so patient now, so eager to be good, and to get even better. John waved the editor silent.

'Not yet, Iain. First, are you re-running Alan's first piece in tomorrow's paper?'

'Plan to, in the first two editions at least. They missed it last outing. I've told make-up we can drop it after that if another story grows big enough to need the space, but we might end up running it through the night.'

John tapped his notebook with a pencil saying, 'Good, because this stuff shouldn't run tonight. It has to go to the Fraud Squad first. Whatever Mike Thomas says, I guarantee they've been investigating this ever since Hart's body was discovered. Better they be with you than against you, and a re-run of this morning's piece will be enough to keep the story alive until we've tried to get their comments on all this. Second, we've got some good stuff here, but there are still gaps all over it. The walls of silence are beginning to break, though, and another twenty-four hours may give us a better piece.'

Iain nodded, taking all this for granted. But Caro was surprised and happy. It had been years since John had seemed so completely in control. She wished, with a lost surge of regret, that Tom could be here to see it.

'So, again,' Iain asked, 'what have you got?'

'OK. Alan, your stuff first.'

He looked taken aback, like a student at a seminar who had expected the class's star to be called on first and now felt naked in the spotlight. 'Er, right.' He flicked quickly through his file till he reached the notes he was looking for. 'It came out at the inquest, though we can't say that, that Hart had spent the two nights before the murder in the Great Eastern Hotel. Usual place for American bankers, so he obviously needed to be in the City, or away from anywhere he might

43

run into people he knew. He wasn't there the night he died, though he hadn't checked out.'

'What name was the reservation in?' MacKinnon asked.

Alan smiled. 'Johnson. But he used his own Mastercharge card. It was a double room. It seems they thought he was expecting a woman called Johnson, so they didn't query the reservation name. Anyway, at the hotel we get lucky. It seems he couldn't understand the direct-dialling system the night he arrived. Maybe he was tired. Whatever happened, he had the operator put a call through for him. I got the number and had a friendly engineer trace it.'

Iain was making notes, and looked across at Alan. 'Good, but I don't know this. If I'm asked, I trust to your judgement and sources.'

All of them smiled. 'Understood,' Alan said, and continued: 'The telephone number he rang – at eleven o'clock on the Friday night, remember, so someone must have been expecting him – was Panamari Finance, behind the Baltic Exchange. I went there. It's a one-room office. Just a desk, a couple of chairs, and a telex machine.'

Iain stopped him again. 'No filing-cabinet?'

'No filing-cabinet. But on the walls, framed, are half a dozen tombstone advertisements. You know, the kind which just announce that so-and-so has just borrowed so much and so-and-so organized the financing. Well, anyway, these claimed to be financings arranged over the last two years. Half a dozen, in all, totalling ninety-six million dollars.'

'Small potatoes.'

'Granted. But the borrowers were all stated as British or French companies. I checked the British ones in Companies House. I had our Paris office do the same in France. None of the companies are registered. Oh, and yes, the Bank of England has never granted any sort of licence to take deposits or conduct financing operations to any outfit called Panamari.'

MacKinnon broke in, interested now. 'This is good, but it all derives from information which came out of the inquest, which we're not allowed to cover. We need at least another source tying Errol Hart into what is otherwise a straight fraud story, which by the way, I will run.'

Alan grinned. 'Thank you. It was John's idea to check the Register of Companies, under the borrowers' names.'

MacKinnon pursed his lips, acknowledging Standing's perception. 'Always,' he said, 'always, look in the obvious places. But I still need another source linking Hart and Panamari. Something we can use.' He looked around the table, wondering which of them would break him out of the editorial straitjacket he was in. Alan pointed casually down to Caro, who flicked back through the pages of her notepad.

'Right, we haven't been able to run an effective trace on Panamari in Panama yet, but I had a word with some friends at the Baltic Exchange who said they'd had no dealings with the company but I could try a couple of names in New York.'

'So they'd heard of Panamari then?' MacKinnon asked, interrupting his own note-taking.

Caro smiled again. 'Well, all but one of them denied it. The one who didn't only said he thought he might have heard of it. He thought it might be one of the less-than-honest outfits that masquerades as a shipping company. You know, like import–export companies almost anywhere. No, they suggested trying New York; they said it was the best place to start trying to track down suspect Panamanians, unless you speak Spanish and know your way around Miami.' Iain nodded and waved her on. 'Right, well, we've got our lines open to New York now but nothing's come back so far. That's one of the gaps John was talking about, because I think we ought to be able to shake something out of the American side. The reporting restrictions don't apply there and the Hart murder is building into a proper little scandal.'

John interrupted her. 'On that point, Iain, I've been thinking. Now that the *Examiner*'s printing its overseas edition in Frankfurt, is there any way we could drop a fuller story into the Frankfurt edition? That way at least we'd be seen to be covering the story by our American readers, who must be wondering what we're up to, and could claim in court that it was a European, devolved editorial decision. We'd also have the advantage that quite a few copies of the Frankfurt edition get brought back into Britain one way or another.'

MacKinnon had been trying to get a word in since almost as soon as Standing started, but John had given him no chance. Now he said, 'You know that's out of the question. The Frankfurt edition's edited in London, and everybody knows it. We could pull a fast one on a European story, but not a British one. We'd just be inviting prosecution, so don't be flashy, John.'

Alan smiled to himself and murmured, 'Nice try.'

'And you can shut up too, laddie,' MacKinnon fumed.

Caro defused the situation. 'The point is, I think John was right to say we ought to try to panic information into the open. We ought to be able to make it work in New York, where the story's getting much more play, at least the Hart murder is, because it's already working in London.'

'Tell me.'

'Well, John's little gambit, running the fraud investigation story, worked. The people it's panicking are the honest ones. Inevitably, I suppose. Fraud's sticky. They're frightened of what they might be accused of being party to. Anyway, I got back in touch with the owners of the building Panamari's in, who put me on to the head-leaseholders. After this morning's paper they were jumpy enough to talk. They'd never subleased to Panamari. They had sub-leased to an outfit called Reinsurance Venturers, registered in Nassau. If any further lease existed with Panamari – anything in writing, that it – it must have been, illegally, from them.'

Iain looked impatient. 'Fine, so we know that shipping, and marine insurance and reinsurance can be a very shady business, but how does this get us back into our story?'

Caro turned another page of her notepad and said, quietly, with evident pleasure, 'I asked the head-leaseholders if I could pick up a copy of their agreement with Reinsurance Venturers. They said yes. I think they were quite relieved I'd stopped asking after Panamari, that I'd accepted they had no direct involvement.'

'And?'

'And the agreement was signed on behalf of Reinsurance Venturers by Errol Hart III, Director.'

Iain clapped his hands together, crying, 'Housey, bloody housey. When was it signed?'

'Eighteen months ago. No trouble ever with the rent. Paid by monthly banker's draft on First Manhattan's Nassau Branch.'

'Careless,' added MacKinnon, suddenly pensive, 'using his own bank. Dangerously close to home.'

'That's what I thought. I've got a string of calls out to New York trying to find out if First Manhattan knew Hart was moonlighting. No word yet. But I'm waiting.'

MacKinnon looked more pleased than he had in days. 'It stands up. We can run it.' Then he turned to Standing and asked in a voice thick with irony, 'And what have you been doing while these two have been working?'

John lit up another cigarette, uncoiled his long frame, pushed the grey hair out of his eyes and said, in a gross parody of the Deep South accent of his youth, 'Well, y'all know I'm just a down-home country boy, but I got some big-city friends way up in New York still awhiles.'

'And?'

John paused, producing a couple of pages of flimsy typescript and sliding them towards the Scotsman. 'Well, it took some time,' he said, speaking in English again, 'but that's an on-the-record statement by the Deputy Head of the New York Police Department's Corporate Fraud Squad, linking Hart with investigations into illegal import operations through Panama and the Caribbean.'

'How did you get this?' MacKinnon asked suspiciously.

John smiled. 'The hard part was tracking down the right man in the right department. I wasted a lot of time with the Department of Trade in DC. Once I'd found him, all I had to do was ask.' He placed his right hand across his heart and said, 'God Bless America. They won't love us for it here in London, but we haven't done anything they can nail us for.'

MacKinnon stood up. 'OK, it's looking good. I'm half-inclined to run it as it stands, but let's wait another day to see what else you can shake loose. I want what you've got already put in draft. John, we're paying you. How do you fancy writing it?'

Standing shook his head. 'Oh, no. Caro and I won't be in here after tonight. And anyway it's Alan's story. He can write it.'

47

The young man bowed slightly in acknowledgement of John's gesture. MacKinnon, however, looked almost unhappy. 'OK, Alan. Do it. I want an up-date before tomorrow's conference, and another at five o'clock. Sooner if anything important comes up.' He turned to Caro and Standing. 'Are you two going to stick around? We could slide out for a quick one before I wrap the first edition up.'

Caro looked uncertainly at John, who simply held his right hand out in front of him. He had relaxed, and it was shaking, violently. The others felt resentful at being involved, and somehow faintly disgusted, as well as sad for Standing. But none of them knew what to say, and it was John who broke the silence, gently.

'No, thank you, Iain. I couldn't even hold the glass. And, Caro, if you're really going to Rome tomorrow . . .'

'First available flight.'

'Then I need all Tom's files. Someone has to do the deskwork.'

CHAPTER FOUR

The day after Caro left for Rome, John sat at the desk in her Fulham flat, gnawing a cheese roll and trying to make sense of the files in front of him. He didn't want a cheese roll. He didn't want paperwork. What he wanted was a bottle of vodka. If he couldn't have that, and he knew he could not, then what was so terrible about dying? It had to be better than being sober. He slapped the roll down as another hot flush seized and shook him. He had a headache, the worst headache he had had since the last time he stopped drinking, but he could not work and drink, so he forced his bleary eyes to open, his anxious mind to work and his limp hand to write.

He was stopped by an urgent desire to check the locks on the door and all the windows, to open all the cupboard doors. He forced himself to ignore it. He knew it was paranoia, the desperate hatred of his mind for a world which was obliging it to endure without its customary, comfortable alcohol, a fearful attempt to drive him on, out, anywhere, in the hope he might stumble on a bottle. He waited for it to fade. He sat in the chair with his eyes screwed tight, telling himself over and over again there was no mad axe-man lurking behind his chair, no burglar with murderous intent in the kitchen. When the impulse had finally passed there were only the random, arbitrary physical symptoms to cope with, the hot and cold sweats, the stomach cramps, the aching head, the sense that some loathsome parasite had somehow got into his bones and was breaking them all at once, slowly, from the inside out. Those and the conviction that the right side of his scalp was somehow coming away from his skull and shrinking, wrinkling, up to the top of his weary, hurting head.

He told himself he was already half-way through the physical effects. He tried not to think of the others which followed, the mental ones. He tried not to think of the harrowing hours avoiding anywhere he might come across a drink. He tried not to think of the endless empty boredom of time usually spent indoors. He tried not to think about the bad dreams.

He returned to the files. He had worked through them once already, that morning, but now he made himself do it all over again. He forced himself to check his list of every cross-reference which did not, in fact, refer. He wanted as exact a profile as possible of the papers which must be missing. It took him all the afternoon.

When it was done he lay down in the bedroom, remembering, for once, to take his shoes off first. This was Caro's apartment. He mustn't mess it up.

It was a small reminder he was sober, he realized, that he had noticed what he should and should not do. It was one of the great reliefs of drink to free him from the constant pressure of deciding what was right and what was wrong. As long as he kept himself afloat on vodka, anything was tolerable, anything allowed. It freed him from the burden of the shady, shifting, complex ethics of the always-changing world. It helped him not to care.

Somehow, for the first time in two days, he fell asleep.

His clothes felt heavy with sweat. His mouth and throat were parched. His eyes were heavy with sleep. He had been crying in his sleep. From the sticky wetness on his cheek and neck he knew he had been dribbling as well. He felt a wave of self-disgust. He tried to get up, off the bed, but he had turned and tossed so violently when unconscious, caught up in dreams he could not remember, that his legs were tangled in the bed-clothes. As he tried to put his feet down on the floor he fell, heavily, hitting his head against the bedside table, opening a shallow graze on his nose. He lay on the floor, his eyes closed, wanting to cry, wanting to find some way of losing the pain. Slowly, unreflectingly, he began to curl up, pulling all the covers off the bed after him, trying to fold his head beneath his arms, blocking out the late summer light, pulling the bedspread about him.

But the pain in his bones, the deep internal ache would

not go away. Then the screaming began inside him, but no sound came out of his open, grimacing mouth.

When the attack was over he clumsily remade the bed. It seemed to take hours, but he knew that was only the effort any concentration took him. It was ridiculous that it took so much thinking to make a bed. He would have laughed, but he felt as though anything so violent would hurt, would start the ringing in his bones.

Afterwards he stumbled out into the kitchen to make some coffee. It took him twenty minutes, just trying to remember why he was in there. All the instructions contradicted each other – water, kettle, plug, mug, milk – so that he found himself at one stage putting cold water in the mug, at another looking wonderingly at the inactive kettle, until he re-membered he had to switch it on, and, at the last, standing fuddle-brained in front of an open refrigerator door, unable to remember what he was doing, although he already had the milk-carton in his hand.

Back in the study he nursed the mug of coffee, sitting with his eyes closed, touching the papers on the desk before him lightly with the fingers of his left hand to remind himself by the faintest contact that the world existed, that there was some-thing else outside the wrinkling scalp upon his head.

He was trying to remember something, something which had seemed important, something which had come to him back there, there in the nightmare bedroom, where the night-time monsters roamed.

He could not quite recall it. He knew that it was in there, waiting to come out, some time when he was not looking and would miss it as it passed. But he would not let it go. He would drag it into daylight from the messy luggage of his dreams.

One thing he had not forgotten. He had to make a tele-phone call. He opened his eyes and the light beyond the drawn curtains was still bright enough to hurt. He could not have been out for long, though it felt like hours. It was time that he stood up.

The coffee-mug tumbled from his nerveless hand, spilling on his lap and scalding him. He bent over, to pull at his trousers, but felt himself falling, his eyes blacking out, so he sat down, as quickly as he could, before the shooting stars could start, and even almost missed the chair. But the pain had cleared his head for a vital instant and though his body was still exhausted and shaking, though it still rebelled at everything he wanted it to do, he knew what it was he had wanted to remember and why he had to use the phone. It took a long time, cleaning himself up, wiping the floor, clearing away the fragments of the mug. Even dialling the *Examiner*'s number turned into a test of will. He knew the number as well as he knew his name, he spoke it out loud as he dialled, but three times he made mistakes, till finally he was through.

'Foreign Desk, please.' His address-book was at home with the direct-line numbers in it, which would have allowed him to call straight through to the foreign sub-editors. Perhaps it was as well. Those numbers were reserved for journalists calling in with stories. He would not have wanted it said the *Examiner* missed an item because John Standing had kept the line engaged.

'Hello, who is that, please? Hi, Mary, I don't think you'd know me. I'm John Standing, I'm doing some work for Caroline Kilkenny and Iain MacKinnon ... Yes, that's right. All I want to know is are you expecting Oliver Ireton back from Switzerland in the near future and do you have an address and telephone number where I can reach him? He's in Basel these days, I think ... That's terrific ... For his daughter's wedding? I didn't even know he was married ... Oh, I see. Could you give me the address and phone number anyway? ... Great. Yes, yes. Got that. If he calls in at all could you ask him to call me at Caro's? I'm working here while she's away ... That's right, just in case I can't get hold of him. Thank you very, very much, Mary ... That's right, John Standing. Don't worry, Iain will confirm it. Thanks so much. Have a nice day.'

He could not resist that final ironic parting, as much at his own expense as the world's. They should have thought of it earlier, all of them. If it had anything to do with Italy, then Oliver Ireton would know.

*

52

He went through the files again. There was no doubt about it; they had been wrong. Three whole files were missing, not just two. There seemed to be nothing missing in the files which still remained. No cross-reference within those files had been damaged or tampered with. Which meant the thieves were either amateurs, who had panicked and grabbed only the obvious files, or the very opposite of that. They could be good enough to have been watching Tom for months, to know his methods, and to have taken only what was strictly necessary. He knew from long experience that it seemed less suspicious when complete files were missing than when an existing file had been weeded of vulnerable material (he had, on occasion, stolen files himself, not that he would ever have admitted it).

Three files missing. Liechtenstein. I O R. Camorra. It was time for him to think. It was evening now, and later, when the pubs were closed, he would allow himself a walk, down to the river and along the Embankment, to clear his head, if anything could, before he slept, if he could sleep. Now, however, he had to think. He had to try to remember. What could he remember?

Liechtenstein. All he had to go on was a short list of names. Nine in all. Italian companies whose names meant nothing to him, but all of which were cross-referenced Liechtenstein in Tom Wellbeck's files. The inference was obvious. Either they were registered there or had some association with another company which was registered there. Which company? No, it had to be the first option. If it had been an associate Tom had meant, he would have put the name into the cross-reference too. Wouldn't he? Wasn't that how he worked? Unless there was something about an associate company he didn't want to leave scattered in the other files. Something kept specifically to the Liechtenstein file. But if it was that, perhaps the file wasn't missing, except to them. Perhaps Tom had hidden it, frightened of some attempt on his papers, instead of on his life. But no, that was too fanciful for Tom, wasn't it? He was too level-headed, too much the Yorkshireman. Wasn't he? Only these nine names could tell.

He would check them all anyway, in Companies House

and with the Bank of England, looking in the obvious places, just in case they had affiliates registered or licensed here. It was an outside chance, but anything was worth trying, because otherwise he was only left with Liechtenstein, and there was only one reason people registered a company in Liechtenstein. Secrecy.

True, the little state on the eastern edge of Switzerland levied no taxes on corporations, but there were other tax-havens in the world which offered the same advantage. What Liechtenstein offered as well was a guarantee of secrecy. No information on the registration ledger of a Liechtenstein company (and hardly any was required) would ever be made available to any third party. That guarantee of anonymity, added to having Switzerland for a neighbour, made the place a magnet for people who did not want their affairs made public. It was a standing joke in Fleet Street that no one really knew who owned the *Daily Mirror*, once it had been acquired by Robert Maxwell, because the Maxwell parent trusts were all registered in Liechtenstein. The beneficial owners of those trusts might have been Maxwell, the Mormons, or the Man in the Moon, for all anyone would ever know. So he had to find another line on these nine companies somewhere, or the first missing file would tell them nothing, and Tom's murderers would have won.

Yes, murderers. He admitted that now. He, at least, no longer believed it might have been some common, squalid killing by disturbed burglars or a forsaken lover, for what would they have cared about the little state of Liechtenstein?

Or IOR? The Istituto per le Opere di Religione, the Institute for Religious Affairs. Or, put more crudely, the Vatican Bank. It had been set up in 1942 by Papal Decree, to manage the assets of the Holy Roman and Catholic Church. The commercial assets, that is. It did not look after the unsaleable wealth of the Church. It was not responsible for the Sistine Chapel or the Aldobrandini Wedding. It had no control over the Holy Shroud or Santiago de Compostella. But the little Vatican state, and the greater Roman Church, had revenues and expenses and sometimes cash-flow problems. So it had set up a bank, to deal with them, at a time when the nations of the world had made it difficult to trot around the corner to take the advice of a friendly local manager, in Rome, in the City, in Wall Street, Tokyo or Frankfurt.

Officially, the management of the bank was responsible to a committee of five cardinals, including its chairman. In reality, effective control of the bank was left to the chairman alone. His ineffective control, some of the crueller commentators had said. For the current chairman, the Chicagoan Archbishop Paul Marcinkus, who had been put in charge in 1971, had seemed to bring it closer than could ever be comfortable to complete financial disaster. It was a completely secret organization, reporting, for all practical purposes, to no one. Which was probably how it had become entangled in the affairs of Michele Sindona, the corrupt financier who had died of poison in his prison cell, and of his protégé Roberto Calvi, the corrupt General Manager of the Banco Ambrosiano, who had ended his days swinging at the end of a rope from Blackfriars Bridge. Just like Errol Hart. It had been, as far as anyone could piece together, a woeful tale of incompetence and stupidity, with IOR being manipulated to provide a cover for Calvi's operations in return for who-knows-what promised assurances (for the Banco Ambrosiano was known in Italy as a very Catholic bank). There were others, however, who doubted that the Gentlemen in Black had been as stupid as they seemed in the Ambrosiano Affair, who suggested that any organization which could last two thousand years had to have intelligent men in its company, and who suggested those intelligent men had used Roberto Calvi in unknown and unknowable ways, that it was not the Ambrosiano Affair the scandal had uncovered, but merely the smallest iceberg edge of the affairs of the Roman Church. If asked to explain, they could not, for all their surmise and innuendo. All they could do was shrug their shoulders and suggest that the Church, like its supposed boss, moved in mysterious ways.

In any case, John could hope to tell nothing from the files cross-referenced to the missing one on IOR without the help of an Italian specialist. He would have to wait for Oliver Ireton, the best such man there was.

And Camorra? Camorra. It made him feel stupid, unbelievably, unforgivably stupid. He cursed his aching head. He cursed the vagaries of a memory half shot to death by drink. The third file. The one they had missed on their first skim through. He knew he knew the name. He knew he had read it before, somewhere, quite recently. But what was it? What did it mean?

And why did he feel, uneasily in the pit of his belly, that he would live a great deal longer if he did not ask such questions?

CHAPTER FIVE

Two days later, John Standing sat in the café a few doors up from Companies House nursing a big white cup of stewed tea. He felt terrible, but the slice of apple pie and gelatinized custard he had just eaten might have had something to do with that. Whenever he stopped drinking he felt these cravings for sweet foods. A medical student had once told him something about alcohol mimicking sugar and the body having to make up the deficiency. Anything was possible, in a world with vodka taken out of it.

Without a drink inside him he had had too much of what he most dreaded: time. Without pubs, bars, bottles, parties, there were too many hours in the day to fill, and now that he was avoiding places where he might stumble over alcohol he had only himself to fill them with. Loneliness and self-disgust drove him to keep working. Perhaps that was why sober people were so often successful, he thought: they had nothing better to do.

He had spent the previous morning going through the principal banking works of reference. Though the Banker's Almanac, the International Banking Directory, and the major American and European abstracts. He had called into the *Examiner*'s library to check the cuttings files under the nine names he had. Nothing. But he had also checked the name Camorra while he was there. He wished that he had not.

It all came back to him as soon as he saw the cuttings. Articles bearing Tom's initials in *Examiner* Italy Surveys. No wonder Caro had thought nothing of the cross-references in the files. Or perhaps it had been his incompetence, that morning in the Foreign Office, when he could hardly see, and what he could see did not really exist.

Camorra. Naples. Everyone knew about the Mafia, or thought they did. The confederation of criminal families which, starting as a landlords' unofficial police force, had grown up over centuries in the bandit-land of Sicily. Which had emigrated to the United States and created a greater, separate, collateral empire there. Gambling, prostitution and, since the end of Prohibition, drugs. Vast cash-rich milking-cows of criminal empires, whose money had nowhere to go but legitimate industry and politics, so that now, in both the USA and Italy, it was impossible to tell where their tentacles might not spread. All that power, all that money, built on a bizarre, medieval code of family loyalty and honour, so that even their endless, internecine murders took on an epic, ritual air.

But the Camorra? Fewer people knew of that. Even John had managed to forget. It was newer, for a start. As far as anyone could be certain, it had not yet spread out of Italy, though there were some rumours growing in places like New York and Marseilles. Most of all, they had not had the advantage of a half-century's attention from a self-glorifying FBI and a fascinated Hollywood. But it was organized, it was dangerous, and it was powerful.

It was also the extraordinary creation of one extraordinary man.

For centuries Naples had been known as the most violent city in Italy, a great big bruising sea-port ruled, if it was ruled at all, by fists and iron. Three hundred years ago, painters from the north invited down to work in Naples would make a supply of bodyguards against the revenge of the local Painters' Union a condition of their contract. Otherwise canvasses might be slashed, pigments burned, thumbs broken, and, if you happened to annoy the likes of the great Master Caravaggio, throats slit. What went for art went for everything. On the simplest level, where smugglers in the rest of Italy worked, like smugglers everywhere, secretively, at the dead of night, the Neapolitans (and almost all the cheap cigarettes on sale all over Italy came in through the Bay of Naples) simply put their money into bigger, faster, showier power-boats and ostentatiously outran the Excise boats in the bright hours of the afternoon.

It was the home of arrogant individualism. The characteristic Italian strut must have started there. And no one, not Napoleon, not the Kingdom of the Two Sicilies, not the Hapsburgs or Bourbon-Parmas, and certainly not the modern Italian state, had ever been able to organize it, to bring it under control.

Until Raffaele Cutullo came along.

At some time in his youth he must have looked down from the residential quarter of the modern city on the Vomerò, down on Castel Nuovo and the great Hohenstaufen Emperor's Castel dell'Ovo, on the teeming avenues and bustling docks of his native city, on past the palm-lined shore out to the industrial district and, far away, Pompeii and Vesuvius and the rocky full-stop of Capri, and seen, like God before him, that it was good.

As Cutullo grew older, he took a little from the Mafia's family organization, more from the remnants of ancient feudalism, and bound them together into a context within which the Neapolitans' individuality could flourish. By force of will, and by expedient murder, he had provided the warring clans, the recalcitrant tribes, of Naples' illegal economy with finance and distribution. He had set up entire industries in the city which never bothered the Revenue Service once. He had, for instance, taken the output of Naples' cottage leather industry, fine goods worked in tenements and slums, and as a bulk purchaser organized the distribution lines to the north, improving both the supply and prices, to the benefit of both parties. And, an intelligent man, he had taken care to buy the politicians too.

So now the Camorra, his organization, was the effective government, not only of Naples and Sorrento, but much of the rest of southern Italy. Nothing moved, nothing happened, here without the Camorra's blessing, without it taking its share.

But the most extraordinary thing of all about this genius for administration was that he had achieved the bulk of it from behind his prison bars. For Raffaele Cutullo had spent twenty years in prison. He was still there, sentenced to life, for murder.

For seventeen years the Camorra had grown, prospered,

flourished under his expert guidance, managed from his office in the city's high-security prison. Not that it was so very secure for him; his visitors came and went as he decided, and he had made the occasional foray to family weddings. But most of the time he appeared the model prisoner, for a very simple reason: it was safe.

Then, in the early 1980s, Naples erupted, in scenes which rivalled anything the great volcano down the coast might have produced. Gang-war had broken out within the Camorra. Two hundred corpses splattered about the streets, the restaurants and churches of the city. Things were a little quieter now. And there was no doubt still the Camorra ran Naples and the South.

But who, some people were asking, ran the Camorra these days?

Was that the question Tom had asked himself? Did that explain the missing files? John shuddered, despite the heat of the afternoon. He did not want to know.

He had set aside the Camorra cuttings and returned to his list of nine names. He had come up with nothing. In the end he tried the Bank of England. Nothing again. So, whatever the companies were, they were not banks or finance houses. Not legitimate ones anyway, thinking of Panamari and young Alan Clarke's investigation. So today John Standing had gone into Companies House, to discover if they were registered in England at all, these nebulous Liechtenstein entities.

He had taken the Tube, getting himself confused as usual, even after so many years, by the modern station's multiple underground exits, ending up on the wrong, the northern, side of City Road. He had walked the short distance to where, a little before the Honourable Artillery Company barracks, by the unconsecrated graveyard where great Nonconformists like John Wesley, William Blake and the sons of Oliver Cromwell lay, with the edges of the City, of Finsbury Square and Moorgate, hoving into view, there was a pedestrian crossing over to a low, modern, unprepossessing building where the nation's corporate archives were kept filed.

It was a shabby corner of the world, just beyond the fringes of the hustle and bustle of the nation's financial capital, in the curious, lifeless hinterland where the City gave out into Hackney and the offices of security typesetters and printers, and company search and formation agents. On a sleepy summer's day in the pubs and cafés here it was hard to imagine that not ten minutes' walk away billions were being turned over by the hour, by the minute. The dividing line between the two worlds, of power and patronage, of scavenging and services, was almost tangible. And he stood on the wrong side of it, looking wistfully back on the wonderland where he had spent his earlier years, inhabited by the creatures of fable, by bulls and bears and stags, by wolves, by sharks, its gates apparently for ever barred against him, chained with his lost innocence and the fragments of his dreams.

He had let Security check his carrier bag, smoked a final cigarette, and walked through into the big, too-brightly-lit Search Room with its banks of microfiche readers and its hideous formica and tubular aluminium tables. Here every company registered in the country was listed alphabetically on rolls of microfiche, just a name and a six- or seven-digit number. The alphabet was split across groups of four machines. He began at the beginning, pressing the button which would spin the film back towards the letter A, its great speed making a blur of the blue screen and a high insistent hum. It always helped to begin at the beginning.

Fifteen minutes later, he had checked all nine names on his list. (He had to wait a few minutes for one of the S–Z machines to come free.) In six cases nothing was registered which could possibly be what he was looking for. There was the same, or a similar combination of letters, but there was, after all, a limit to the permutations of the alphabet and human ingenuity, but no limit at all to the number of companies which might be registered. With one of his names, for instance, he had found an exact correspondence on the index, except that that company's name ended in the formula "(Wigan) Limited" and he did not believe that international financiers, especially those using a haven like Liechtenstein, were likely to establish subsidiaries or associates in Wigan or in Slough. But in three cases he had found companies registered which, on the basis of their names alone, might have some link with his list and with Liechtenstein. He made a note of the numbers and went to the glassed-in booth at the corner of the room.

Somehow, in what must have been one of the dreariest jobs in the world, in tacky, prefabricated surroundings, they usually managed to be quite friendly here. The woman behind the counter had even smiled as she slid over the six search tickets he had asked for (there was more than one possible correspondence for each of his three names) and he parted with a grubby five-pound note and an already faded coin. Did he look so vulnerable or uncertain, he wondered? She had not even seemed to mind when he asked for a receipt. He filled in the forms with the full names of the companies he wanted searched, their numbers, and his own name and address (as usual, he could not have said why, he took the precaution of giving a false name and address) and took the forms past the public telephones beyond open swing doors into the main Search and Reading Hall. He had to queue to hand in his six tickets and be given another number. It would take another hour at least, and possibly more, on a busy morning, for the microfiches to arrive. He could not wait in here, where smoking was disallowed.

There were padded plastic benches in the entrance hall. He waited there, smoking, and trying not to think of drink. Eventually boredom, and a definite shortage of pretty clerks trotting their way into the search room, drove him to work through his battered address book, carefully putting the fat elastic band which was the only thing which kept his most important information intact into his jacket pocket. He went through the book slowly trying to think if any of these names, the collected sources of twenty years of working journalism, might be able to help him find what he was looking for, even though he did not know what it was.

For twenty minutes he looked in vain, till finally, the ache beginning in his head again, he held the book's loose pages tightly in his lap and closed his eyes and tried to remember what it was, the other thing, which had been worrying him for days.

Something had not been right. Something had smelt faked.

Something he had to see the Scotsman about. Something to do with MacKinnon.

That was it. The silence. The absolute silence from Poland since the reopening of communications. It had been a good story, the one the *Examiner* ran the night they closed the borders and cut all communications. It had been a scoop. Infighting at the very top in Poland, accurately reported. A struggle the General must have won, for when, after sixteen hours, without any statement or comment, Poland had opened its doors to the world again, he was still in power. What was the story on that? That was the important question. And yet the sources who had fed the Foreign Desk the story of the week, the month, had remained silent since the borders opened. They must have done. There had been no further exclusives in the paper since then. But why were they silent? They clearly had had access to communications in the past. Good communications. So they must be close in to the very centres of power. So why were they silent now? Unless they had been silenced. Unless they were themselves members of the apparently failed conspiracy against the General. But that had been a Secret Police conspiracy. Why would the Polish Police talk to the *Examiner*?

No, that didn't make sense either. But something wasn't right. Something smelt very, very wrong. He would have to talk to the Scot.

It was time to go check for his microfiches. John gave his number to the clerk behind the high banks of pigeon-holes.

'How many?' he asked.

'Six.'

The clerk took the ticket and handed over six brown envelopes. John took them over to the nearest available microfiche reader. He had been lucky. Sometimes they came down in dribs and drabs and researchers had to be forever checking with the desk, but today he had them all together. He opened the first envelope, slid the first stiff plastic sheet into the tray and into the reader, moving it about and refocusing until its first page came clearly into view.

He made himself go through every page of every microfiche, just in case, even though he knew within minutes that his search was hopeless. He checked the original registrations, the articles of association and the memoranda, he noted every change of director, shareholding and auditor. He studied the accounts for the last three years. He checked each mortgage and directors' guarantee. But they were six entirely respectable private British companies in different manufacturing and distribution sectors. Nothing to do with Italy. Nothing to do with Liechtenstein. Nothing to do with Tom Wellbeck's death. Nothing, nothing, nothing.

He made one last effort, re-checking the names of directors and shareholders in each case. Nothing suspicious, nothing unusual, nothing which rang any bells. Another morning of wasted effort.

He could have murdered a drink.

But as he was heading for the door, out to the pub around the corner, he could have kicked himself for his own stupidity. He had been through the main index, it was true. But he had not checked the Recent Registration file, of companies too new to have been transferred to the main microfiche rolls.

He went back into the Search Room and headed for the Recent Registration index.

One. One out of the nine. The last but one. T I A Investments Limited. He went to the booth for a form.

The fiche had not come through till after lunch. He had sat it out in the entrance hall, smoking cigarette after cigarette, no longer thinking of drink. When it did come through, as he expected, it was only the thinnest of envelopes. A single sheet of microfiche. Like most companies they were slow in reporting to Companies House, perhaps deliberately so. But there was enough here. There was what he needed.

First, came the original registration, by a company registration agent, as Y Y Y Y Y Limited, a shell they could sell off the shelf to anyone who wanted a company without having to do the paperwork himself. Then there were the Articles of Association. Irrelevant until the company started trading. Then there was the change of name. And then there were the shareholders and directors, the new directors, the real directors, who replaced the agents when they bought the shell. There were four names altogether: three directors, who were

64

also shareholders, and a fourth shareholder. Two of the directors' names meant nothing to him. But one of them did: Ismail abu-Sa'id. As did the name of the fourth shareholder: Genassets (Liechtenstein). Together they meant one other thing. They meant the cover of the man who was his oldest adversary. They were tools of David Medina.

Which was why John was sitting in the café now, Companies House having closed as usual at four, waiting for the minutes to tick away to half-past five when he was due to meet MacKinnon and Oliver Ireton in El Vino's, when he would show them the heavy, shiny-surfaced photostats he had made himself from the original microfiche.

He had feared he would feel impatient. He had feared he would need a celebratory drink. But he was not impatient at all. He felt curiously fulfilled, and even happy. He would not have minded now if the door had opened and an angel entered saying, 'You must hand these papers over to others. Your time on earth is done.' He would have gone with the angel willingly, blessing MacKinnon for having let him come so far, blessing Caro for being patient with him.

It was almost enough, this distant prospect of his enemy, glimpsed from beyond the shining towers of one of the financial centres where he roamed. It was almost enough to know that Medina was not, quite, impregnable.

He almost burst out laughing with simple pleasure at the thought but contented himself instead with murmuring, to the astonishment of the café's owner:

'Underneath an abject willow,
Lover, sulk no more:
Act from thought should quickly follow.
What is thinking for?'

CHAPTER SIX

Caro Kilkenny lay in the arms of Ezzo Spaccamonti, the man who was investigating the murder of her former husband, stroking the rough skin of his long back as the cool draught under the door fanned them in the aftermath of their heat. This time they had only just made it through the door, tugging at each other, hands roaming under clothes in their desperate desire to touch each others' flesh. They had pulled each other to the floor, he kicking the door shut behind them, before they found each other and crashed together and she could think of nothing any more. Afterwards he had undressed her above the waist and she had undressed him and now they lay naked on the floor, touching each other gently and pausing only to kiss.

She had enjoyed the violence of their mutual desire. It had attacked them both, at once, in a glance, as they came in through the street-door, with two flights of stairs to get up, kissing and touching each other desperately, before they were safely in his apartment. Once it was over, he was as gentle as he had been the previous night, their first time, when as her orgasm had built to the edge of endurance he had withdrawn himself, leaving her hollow and empty until a few long strokes, rubbing the whole length of himself backwards and forward along the lips of her sex, had toppled her into exquisite ecstasy before he came in puddles of semen glistening on her belly in the moonlight.

'You didn't have to do that,' she had told him as they lay together, before the laughter in the shower which had brought them to bed again, 'I'm fitted with an IUD.'

He had smiled at her in the birch-leaf light of the Roman moon, his almond eyes half-shaded, saying, 'But I was not to know that.'

She had felt a sudden wave of tenderness for his thoughtfulness and care, and it made her want him even more, again, inside her till the end.

Here, this afternoon, he sat up in a single sweep of his powerful dark body and, before she had time to complain of his absence, swept a cushion from the nearest chair and placed it underneath her head, propping himself up on his elbow to look down into her shining smiling face.

'Cara,' he whispered and blew in her ear so she crinkled up her nose and laughed because it tickled. 'Not Caro. Not in Italian. It does not,' he hesitated, searching for the right grammatical term, and found it, 'agree. Caro is for a man. Cara for a woman. And you are very much,' he stopped, to kiss her throat and her belly, and to lick the insides of her thighs, before saying, 'a woman.'

He made her laugh. She could not remember how long it had been since she had laughed. He made her feel safe. He made her feel desired. He made her feel, for the first time in months, desirable. He made her, simply, happy.

'All right,' she told him, 'Cara, but only alone together, when we are being Italian.'

He unshielded his almond eyes and taking her by the shoulders laid her down on the hard cold floor. She closed her eyes, as he kissed her forehead, her ears, her eyelids, her cheek, her mouth, lingering over it, kissing each of her lips, alone, together, alone. She reached up to stroke the base of his head where the short coarse hair joined to the lighter hair of his neck and back; she gripped him to keep him there, but he shook her loose, to continue his downward journey, covering her in little petals of kisses. When she felt his tongue flirting inside her, scratching her deep endless itch, she stroked herself down towards him, down her breasts, across her nipples, down her belly to his head and held him there, as she braced her feet against the floor to raise her back and buttocks, taking the strain on her shoulders to mould him deeper inside her. She started to come in little grateful whimpers, but as the walls of her vagina heaved, he unflexed himself like a snake and, looming down upon her, kissed her deeply, cancelling the day, and was inside her with a single unassisted stroke which made her feel as though she would dissolve.

*

67

She did not think it had been planned. He had simply come to her hotel because he had a message from the British Consulate. He had not known what to expect, and had more than half expected to be faced by a grieving widow, which was why he had not waited till morning. He was glad, he told her, to have discovered someone younger, more beautiful, less involved, for he had dreaded the embarrassment of telling her what he knew.

He had not known how she might take the news that Tom had had a mistress, who had been missing since the day before the murder and who had to be his first, main suspect. It had at once relieved him and surprised him to discover that not only did she not mind, she also seemed almost pleased. It was then that he had told her he could not imagine what Tom had been doing leaving her, even for an Italian mistress. What sort of world was this, where it was the wives who looked like mistresses, the mistresses like wives? She had mentioned the apparently missing files, and he looked puzzled and invited her to his office the following afternoon, behind the Palazzo Senatorio. That was how they had parted, that first evening in the lounge at the Raffaele, thirty hours before they had become lovers.

She had passed most of the following day calling on old contacts, for journalism still remained, like politics in many ways, a 'touch and feel' profession. They were old friends, some of them, many of them friends of Tom, and had looked sorrowful on her behalf, but not too sorrowful, for, better than the English, they responded to her mood. She had been right, the previous day, to suspect they were waiting to see her face to face before they would tell her the scandal of the summer. Journalists and their sources were by their nature gossips, and the story which most delighted those who were not Christian Democrats this season was that the financial links between the party and the Vatican were finally coming apart, in the long-delayed (nearly two decades' delayed) aftermath of the Vatican's disposal of its Italian industrial and property assets. She knew what that might mean, if it was true (so very little in Rome was true). It would mean the unquiet ghost of Roberto Calvi and the imprisoned spectre of

68

Michele Sindona were finally rising up for vengeance. She would have to re-acquaint herself with that epic of fraud and dissimulation if she was to make sense of what the summer might bring.

But that could come later. That she might even leave to John. What she wanted now was for Ezzo to reassure her, as he had begun to do the previous evening, that, whatever the cause of Tom Wellbeck's death, she was not to blame, and the case would soon be closed. She wanted them, she wanted herself and John and Iain and even Ezzo, rid of that responsibility.

She sat in his office that afternoon, a small bright cubby-hole tucked into a corner of the city's judicial administration building, watching the pouter pigeons flirting on the window-ledge beyond as his deep gentle voice explained what he had learnt.

'None of this is pleasant, Miss Kilkenny.' She was still Miss Kilkenny then, and he Signor Spaccamonti. 'I would advise you not to ask to see the photographs.'

He had been right, but she had insisted, and had ended weeping for what seemed a very long time. It was the first time that he held her in his arms.

'The pathologist,' he explained, 'found the remains of two bullets in Mr Wellbeck's skull. Point two-two calibre, a very small pistol. He calls it a woman's gun.'

'But how, how,' she had almost sobbed, 'could it do that to him?' remembering the shapeless jelly most of the head had become.

Spaccamonti had calmed her again, trying to explain. 'He was shot at very close quarters, always in the head. Even a small weapon can do very much damage at such range. And we cannot be certain how many shots were fired. We found two bullets, enough to shatter the skull. Enough to kill. But what if the murderer, or murderess, in an excess of passion fired the whole pistol into him? That would cause the kind of destruction we have here. And he was sitting at the window. We know, it was broken, at least one other bullet must have gone that way. So, a small bullet, or bullets, out through the window, all force spent, the bullet drops, into a busy street, much traffic, many passing feet, many gutters, we would never see them again.'

'So it was one person who killed him?'

'I think so.'

'And was anyone seen going into or coming out of the building?'

'Not as far as we can establish. It is something we might never know. Who notices who comes and goes in a busy street? Do you?'

Caro shook her head forlornly. 'But you think the murderer was a woman?' she made herself ask at last.

Spaccamonti nodded, sadly, looking sympathetic, before reaching into a large manila envelope.

'These were among his papers,' he said, handing her three photographs. One was a ten-by-seven studio portrait of a young, pretty dark-blonde girl of about nineteen or twenty. The other two were snapshots, one of the girl on the Ponte Umberto I with the Castel Sant'Angelo and the Vatican behind her, the other of the girl with Tom at the Baths of Caracalla.

'She's pretty,' she said.

'She's also very young. A student at the university here . . .'

'A real one?' Caro interrupted. There were over a million students registered at the University of Rome, which had been designed for perhaps ten thousand. Few of them actually studied, though most of them arrived high in hope, for few of them could get into the lectures. Significant numbers of them were just along for the ride. Others graduated into terrorism.

Ezzo nodded. 'As far as we can tell. Studying English and Economics. Well-liked by her class-mates.'

'How long had she and Tom . . .?'

'A couple of months. They met when he was asked to speak to an Economics seminar.' The magistrate looked thoughtful, wondering if he should continue. Finally he faced her across the desk. 'Miss Kilkenny, you do know, I take it, Signor Wellbeck had something of a reputation?'

She had managed to smile at that, a little wanly. 'Oh, yes. Rumours had reached us in London. Visitors from the paper

70

would get back to London with news of yet another teenager on Tom's arm every time we sent someone over. It came as something of a shock, at first. He wasn't anything like that in all the years I knew him.'

'Are you sure?'

'I'm sure. Contrary to popular expectations, I would have been the first to know. He would have shambled around in shame and despair for weeks if he'd so much as kissed a secretary at an office party. There was a very Yorkshire moral streak in him.' The magistrate looked puzzled. She did not bother to explain about Yorkshire. 'Perhaps it was Italian women who changed him.'

Spaccamonti looked away as he said, 'Looking at his former wife, I would guess it was more a case of being unable to find an adequate replacement.'

She had been grateful for that. She should have known better. Gratitude was a dangerous emotion.

'Does the mistress have a name?' she asked, as much out of embarrassment as any desire for information.

'Zara Franccchetti, from Naples.'

'Any family?'

'Mother. Two sisters.'

'Father?'

'Dead.'

'Money?'

'Moderately wealthy family.'

'And she's missing?'

He nodded again. 'And she had good reason to be jealous.'

'And what about Tom's missing files?'

'Tell me about them.'

She told him about going through Tom's files, speaking on as afternoon lengthened into evening. When she was finished, he sat frowning in his chair, a silhouette of a thinking man set out against the sinking sun, low on the false horizon of the rooftops on the city's seven hills. He sat with his face in his hands and said:

'I am sorry to have to tell you it could simply have been incompetence. Two files, in a mass of papers. IOR and Liechtenstein. They could have been adjacent files. The letters J

71

and K are rare in Italian. Alternatively, they may not have been in the apartment at all. Did Signore Wellbeck never deposit important files in safe places? It is customary in Italy.'

It was possible, she supposed.

'But I cannot believe,' he continued, 'it is significant. Not, at least, until we find and speak to Zara Francchetti.'

Caro found herself having to agree with him. He was a reasonable man, and she knew that, even in Italy, murders were more often private and personal than public and political. Perhaps they had all been simply over-reacting.

'I suppose you're right,' she had said. 'I'm likely to be in Rome a few days yet. I have some work to do. Could you keep me informed of any developments? I will, in any case, make sure to see you before leaving Rome. Would you like me to tell the Consulate that we've had this meeting and I'm satisfied with the course of your inquiries?'

He had smiled at that, and said, 'Miss Kilkenny, all I want from you is your company at dinner this evening.'

That was how it had started. She had gone to have dinner at his flat, and stayed to have him as well. She had wondered what the staff at her hotel might make of it, but they had raised no eyebrows when she returned the following morning. It amused her that she might end with as scandalous a reputation in Rome as Tom. She supposed there ought to be something strange about sleeping with the man investigating her former husband's murder, but she did not feel it. She was only aware how happy she was to be touched, and to touch, again.

That Saturday he drove her out into the Alban Hills, to Frascati and on five miles or so to the ruins of medieval Tusculum, sacked by the Pope in 1191. They walked amidst tumbled stone walls already leeched by the coarse grass of this volcanic landscape under a heady mix of mid-Italian trees, of poplars, beeches, olives and palms. The wild thyme dipped and rattled in the cool hillside winds and the light swelled to the miracle of blue the centuries of painters Rome had gathered about her had always celebrated. Here the sky was a fragile membrane, softly filled with liquid air, smoothing out the complex, cracked surfaces of modern Italian life.

He took her back into Frascati for lunch, picking up tickets for the Villa Aldobrandini before wandering through the high winding flagstoned streets of the mountain-top castello to the baroque cathedral and medieval fortress. She found it hard to believe that anything very much mattered here, in a country which had seen conquerors come and conquerors go, leaving remains like the looming fortress of this celebrated little vineyard town, without changing very much. Life went on here, much as it had always done, whatever arguments and compromises, whatever vicious fighting, might be the squalid entertainment of the ruling class. He had told her how ancient Tusculum was supposed to have been founded by the son of Odysseus and Circe; but this region did not make her think of the city on the Tiber's classical, brutal heroes claiming descent from Troy, but of the old fox, Ulysses himself, and his enchanting mistress, preserved by her enduring powers safe from the swinish snuffling of mortals obsessed by paltry greeds and lusts.

They had a light lunch on the summer terrace of the Ristorante Spartaco, in Via Letizia Buonaparte, and Caro could not help noticing how the street-name itself was another reminder of the passing whims and fancies and the dark, frustrated dreams of the world of public and political power, but softened here, to the feminine, and the Italian, Corsican, version of the little Emperor's family name, safe from the grandeur and ambition of the kingdoms to the north.

In the afternoon, as they wandered through the gardens of the Villa Aldobrandini, still owned by that enduring family, down the box-lined avenue, beside the fountains and follies of its fantastic grotto-filled park, having trailed coolly already under the frescoes within, he turned to her and said, 'There is something I must tell you.'

She had been expecting something of the kind all day, for even on the brief drive out of the capital already beginning to swelter this early summer day she had noticed a certain hesitance about his manner. She had found it attractive, the slight sense of distance, and flirted with it, watching his large eyes darken as she did so. So she smiled, and said matter-of-factly, genuinely not minding at all, 'You have a wife.'

Then he laughed, holding her bare shoulders above the neckline of her peasant blouse, and told her, 'As a matter of fact I haven't,' and it had been her turn to be surprised, and they held hands, and walked deeper into the shade of a plane-tree at the edges of the park.

She said, 'I thought all Italian men were married at your age. Even some of the priests. I shouldn't have minded if you had been. You would have had nothing to fear.'

But she found herself glad, in a calm way, that he was not entangled elsewhere. He had merely smiled agreement at her point, playing with his signet ring and saying, 'You're right, of course. I suppose it's just I've always been too busy.'

She could imagine it. He was very young to be a magistrate, even in Italy, where the investigating judiciary was almost a separate career, parallel with that of ordinary lawyers, but separate. She wondered how much he owed his current position to patronage, and graft, to family connections, but she put the thought aside, as unworthy of the hour.

'No,' he told her, 'what I wanted to say is that I know you have your work to do, but I wonder if you are going about it the right way.'

'How do you know about my work?' she asked, not really minding. 'I've only ever talked to you about my former husband.'

He shrugged his shoulders. 'Rome is a city of gossips. Things get known. I know you have a book to write, and that you have not so very much time before you must leave us, leave me, to look at other things in other places.' She did not know what to say. He seemed to understand and continued without expecting any statement from her. 'And yet you are acting like a journalist, looking for the story of the day. It will be old by the time your book is printed. Why not just take an older, but important, story, and explain it better than anyone has done before? Wouldn't that be better, for a book?'

She could see the sense of what he was saying, and

suspected her editor would agree. It was hard to get out of the habit of mind of someone whose life was governed by the daily rolling of the presses.

He held her hand in his. 'And you must understand our Italy. Most of the gossip here is lies, spread for political advantage. The outside world gets upset about the way we deal with public matters here, but it works. Our checks and balances are personal, private, shifting. Can you look about you and tell me our people are unhappy? Can you tell me the system does not work?'

Somehow, listening to him made her feel a stab of guilty conscience, of bad faith. 'What is it you are asking of me?'

'Nothing,' he replied. 'I am telling you that people might tell you the truth about the scandals of the past. And this would be better . . .' he groped for the word, 'copy, for you. Why punish yourself with rumours which will be dead by the time your book is published? Why waste time on the impossible? On things even Italians do not understand?'

She felt obscurely guilty listening to him. She also felt that he was right. So she slipped into his arms, into his routine, and she let a fortnight slip away.

CHAPTER SEVEN

They were two of the worst weeks in John Standing's life. They began badly, at his meeting with Oliver Ireton at El Vino's (Iain MacKinnon had not shown; five-thirty was the middle of his working day, and he had a paper to put to bed). Oliver, back for the wedding of his daughter by his first wife, was in no mood for poring over files. Their meeting had been frosty. All he would do was give John some salutary advice: to have nothing to do with anything which might involve the Camorra (Oliver had good cause to give it; it was an open secret that there was a price on his head if he ever returned to Italy). To give up any hope of getting anything out of Liechtenstein. And not to entangle himself in the affairs of IOR, the Vatican Bank.

'No one understands the Vatican's financial affairs, John,' he had said. 'Most members of the Curia, the Vatican Civil Service , are permanently confused. Everything's done by mirrors there. And because they never say anything about their operations they're the perfect candidates for lies and slander. If you want to start a scandal in Italy, all you have to do is make up a story about the Vatican. The country splits down the middle, for and against the clergy. And the anti-clerical half will believe any crap you feed it about the Church's evil ways. I spent eleven years there, John, and I never even began to understand what went through the minds of the Gentlemen in Black.'

He had had only one other piece of advice. 'It isn't a link, you know,' he said. 'You've established no link between Tom Wellbeck and David Medina. All you've got is a coincidence. You'd only have a link if you could tie Genassets to the TIA in Liechtenstein, which might have nothing at all to do with the one registered here. It's just a coincidence of letters, unless you prove a link in Liechtenstein. And Liechtenstein's impenetrable.'

He had drunk down the last of his seven stiff gins and tonic and added, 'And aren't you tired of Medina yet? No one's ever going to break him, John. Especially not you. He's proved that once already. Frankly, I don't think there is a link with him. I think you're making bricks without straw. You want him badly enough to fantasize about his operations. But don't involve us. Don't involve Caro. She must hurt enough already.'

He had gone back to the grubby flat in Bethnal Green, desperate for a drink. Desperate, at least, to talk to Caro. But when he lifted the telephone hand-set he discovered he had been disconnected and would have to wait till the morning and Caro's flat in Fulham.

She wasn't in that Friday morning, and the *Examiner* office didn't hear from her all day. She wasn't in on Saturday either, and on Sunday evening he was told she had checked out of the hotel leaving no forwarding address. He supposed she had borrowed a flat somewhere. It was how most of them managed their longer stays, leaning on the curious free-masonry of journalism. Wrong term, he thought, in an Italian context, freemasonry, thinking of the scandals surrounding the all-powerful P2 Lodge. She was bound to make contact again when she was ready. In the meantime he had work to do, preparing the background digests she had requested, on scandals all the way from Baudouin and Lockheed to banana republics and Watergate. But he also wanted to know why three files were missing from Tom Wellbeck's collected papers.

He had called on Iain MacKinnon on the Monday, and received a cold reception. He had been told he was working for Caro, not the paper, and was not expected in the news-room. He could deal with Caro direct. MacKinnon had refused to be perturbed about the silences from Poland, telling him to mind his own infernal business, but had admitted that the Errol Hart story seemed to have collapsed, because of lack of further information. What they had run on Panamari had been good, but they had had nothing they could follow it with.

John went to see young Clarke.

Alan was desolate. 'The hard fact is,' he told the older man, 'we don't know what Panamari was for. The only thing the police, or I, have to work with is one unpaid shipping bill with a Southampton company. But why should a finance company act as a shipping agent? Panamari chartered hold-space on a vessel bound from Mobile to Limon in Costa Rica. The cargo never showed up and the firm put in a bill regardless. It's still outstanding. But that's the only commercial dealing for Panamari that's shown up. Its files are gone. We have no evidence it had any other commercial dealings in this country.'

That had come as no surprise. If it had had other dealings, and if its suppliers had known there was something suspect about it, they would not be stepping forward now, with information, especially if they had, unlike the company in Southampton, been paid. Nor did it surprise him that space on a vessel in Central American waters should be chartered from this side of the Atlantic. Half the cargo-space around the world was booked through London's Baltic Exchange.

'If you can think of anything,' Alan said, 'let me know, because otherwise I think we're stuck with whatever comes out of the US inquiry. MacKinnon's said in principle I can go over when something more is known.'

That at least made sense, and showed the Scotsman had not lost all faith in the story. John promised to think about it.

He had much to think about.

He admired the way Caro had put together the outline of her book. It asked two simple questions. How widespread was government corruption? How big a part did it play in international trade? Much of her evidence was what a daily journalist would dismiss as historical, gathered over the last ten years. She had taken the major corruption scandals of a decade and investigated them more deeply than the pressures of newspaper and magazine deadlines allowed. She had leavened them with original research. She had made intelligent estimates of the frequency and size of covert payments in major international markets and industries. And now she was looking at the great Western corporations and institutions which paid the price of corruption, or countenanced it. That was what she needed him for, an extra pair of investigating hands, to check how many of the conclusions she had come to in her study of the developing world were borne out by the experience of the developed. It would make good reading, and it would be a first. So why could he not interest himself in the preparatory work for it now?

What was there about the events of the past few days which gave him the gut-feeling he had always trusted that, by accident, he and Caro were looking at the biggest story either of them had ever faced and missing it and its significance?

Was it fantasy, as Oliver suggested, as Iain implied? Was it the deluded hope of a has-been hack? He knew what his colleagues thought of him, and he suspected they were right. He knew he was a broken, untrustworthy drunk. He knew he was unreliable, selfish and in despair. He blamed himself for all of it. He blamed himself for everything. He never expected to be redeemed. But some forlorn nostalgia for a time when things were otherwise, and the world seemed full of hope and promise, made him want, once, at least, to make up for all his years of broken promises and unaccomplished dreams. His instincts told him that the time had come. That here, in this strange welter of disconnected papers and stories, lay a single thread, a solitary conspiracy winding back upon itself again and again so often that it looked like many things, instead of only one.

But he could not allow himself to believe that. It was the stuff conspiracy theories were made on, the mad delusions of the frightened few who wanted to put a name and shape to the unknown Them who haunted the paranoid visions of their endless anxieties and fears. If there was a story, if there were any stories, he could only find them by working through the implications of the material he had, the material which had alerted his suspicions from the start.

What did he know? He knew Tom Wellbeck had been murdered. He knew Errol Hart had been murdered. No. He must not link the two. It was an arbitrary trick of the mind. There was no link between them. They were quite separate stories. But again his instincts told him to stop, told him not to turn away, that it was here, the link he wanted. That even though the mad were victims of conspiracy fears, sometimes the conspiracies were real.

This was insane. This was his body punishing him for years of alcohol abuse. He lit another cigarette, and a line from a song came into his head, a sweet voice singing, 'How long you think that you can run that body down? How many nights you think that you can do what you been doing?'

He didn't know. He didn't know. He just wanted the ringing in his head to stop, the constant anxiety, the crippling sense of guilt. He wanted to know what was real, how much was his imagination.

Stop, he told himself. *Stop*. There was something he could do, something practical, to try to break the current deadlock. It might not work, but at least it meant doing something, instead of sitting here, vainly thinking, trying to make sense of something which might have no meaning at all. He sat looking out over the dull empty streets of Fulham and picked up Caro's phone. It was not a number he was likely to forget.

'Good morning,' the voice said, in a bright Essex accent, 'First Manhattan Bank.'

'Good morning. Could I speak to Stefan Altberg in your Transport Financing Division?'

He waited for the call to be put through. He waited for the woman's voice to say, 'Mr Altberg's office. Can I help you?'

'I do hope so,' he answered, as casually as he could manage. 'Is Stefan there, please?'

'I'm afraid he's in a meeting at the moment. Can I help or take a message?'

He knew what would happen if he left his name. He knew his call would never be returned and that, each time he called again, the secretary would suddenly discover that Stefan was in a meeting or on his way to Kuala Lumpur.

'I'm afraid I don't think you can. It's a rather delicate matter,' he explained, 'and I'm only in town a couple of days,' lying fluently, helped by what was left of the lift of his American accent. 'I won't be easily available. Can you tell me when he's likely to be in so I can try and catch him?'

The secretary hesitated. Important bankers did not like being tied down, did not like their office staff inadvertently making them available. 'I couldn't really say,' she tried at last. 'Their meeting could go on all day. Stefan's only just back from Scandinavia and there's a lot to catch up on.'

So Stefan was still keeping Finland to himself. He had always had a weakness for small dark Finnish women.

'Are you sure you don't want to leave a message?'

'I think I'd better not. I'm not even sure where I'll be this evening. I'll try again a little later.'

He put the phone down quickly, realizing he had nearly slipped. He had nearly given her the opportunity to ask for the name of his hotel. His best bet was to try again later, just at the start of lunchtime, when the secretary might have been replaced by her cover, someone who might not know enough to keep calls from strangers away from her boss, who might even be persuaded to go and look for him.

That did not work either, but his fourth call, in the afternoon, the third through Stefan's secretary, had brought him better luck. She put him on hold, presumably while talking to Stefan to tell him the stranger had called again. Then there was a click, and he heard a familiar voice, a voice out of the past, saying, 'Altberg here.'

'Hello, Stefan,' he said, trying to keep the cold sweat out of his voice, 'John Standing here.'

'Are you out of your fucking mind?'

'Don't hang up,' he got out quickly, 'or I start phoning in and leaving messages for you to call me. So far no one knows it's me trying to get hold of you, but I could change all that in fifteen minutes.'

'Are you threatening me?'

'Yes.'

'I don't want anything to do with you. You are the kiss of death. People's careers curl up and die when you walk past in the street.'

'Yours didn't.'

'That's history.'

'Well, you still owe me, Stefan, so why don't we get this over?'

'What do you want?'

'To see you.'

81

'That's impossible.'

'Don't talk balls. It isn't for me in any case. It's for a young lad on the *Examiner*. Bright man. You ought to get to know him.'

'Where?'

'Not in town, as you're so frightened. There's a meeting at Sandown this Saturday. None of your Yankee banker friends are likely to be there. Can you make it?'

'What time?'

'One-thirty, on the rails, in the Members' Enclosure.'

John noted, with professional satisfaction, that they had got through their conversation without Stefan ever having to acknowledge his caller's name.

The intervening days passed in the slow grind of milling down Caro's researches into manageable form, fine-tuning her references and suggesting areas where up-dates might be beneficial, and in trying, unsuccessfully, to get hold of Caro herself. He wasn't too worried. The *Examiner's* Rome office reported she had called in a couple of times and seemed to be keeping busy and well. If she never returned his calls, that only meant she was busy. Like many other journalists she was never off the phone if she found herself in straitened circumstances, at a loose end for a story. But when she was working she would become as uncommunicative as he was now, hiding from the world in Fulham, living on take-away sandwiches and Chinese meals, avoiding company, excitement, drink.

He had contact with only three people that week. He telephoned Alan Clarke, to confirm the meeting with Stefan, but not, at this stage, telling him who they were meeting. He telephoned Iain, asking him to kick the Library, which was being slow in getting him some of the cuttings he needed. And he got a call from Oliver Ireton, before his return to Switzerland.

Olly was apologetic. John couldn't blame him for his reaction the previous Friday. To him, John must have seemed a bleary old hack using a private tragedy to muscle into the territory Oliver had called his own for eleven years and from which in the end, he had had to flee in order to save his own skin. He was a good man, with a fine nose, and the inexorable patience an Italian correspondent required, and it was no secret he found Switzerland, by comparison, too bland, too straightforward, too safe. Besides, he had had a wedding to attend. After it, he had the time to give advice.

'Look, old love,' he had said, 'if you and Caro are serious about Italy, there are some things you ought to know. The first is to pass your papers in front of me. I know I've been out of the old hell-hole for three years, but I'm not dead yet, nor yet senile.'

'I tried to, Olly.'

'I know. I'm sorry. I had other things on my mind. The second thing you ought to know is that I very much doubt Tom was killed for professional reasons. I don't want to speak ill of the dead, and he was good, but to be honest he wasn't me. I don't see anyone had sufficient cause yet to take him out. Third, forget Medina. Even if you're right – which I doubt – you know damn well he's always been your maddest obsession. No one will listen to you if you try to keep involving him. I didn't, and I knew you in the days when you were human.'

John had laughed at that, not that he had much cause to, but it was true there were things which could be said by those who had known each other many years that others could not presume to. Friends were the people you didn't have to be polite to.

'Fourth, and last,' Oliver had concluded, 'if you're so smart, how come you're such a clown? From what you were telling me, Tom's papers sound like so much old hat. God knows why he kept raking over old coals. But if you are right about the missing files, and he might well just have hidden them (I used to), why haven't you noticed the obvious thing about them? Screw Camorra. Who needs to die? But if you put the IOR together with Liechtenstein, what do you get?'

John had been silenced by his own stupidity, before saying, 'You're right. Why am I such a clown?'

It had been obvious. It had been staring them in the face from the beginning. The Vatican was an independent sovereign state within the geographic bounds of Italy. It was not covered by Italian banking law, which meant it could move its money (and other people's if they could carry it through the streets and, if they had contacts, deposit it at a bank within the Vatican walls) wherever it pleased. And if it didn't want prying outsiders to find out where the money was bound for, if it didn't want the money-trail tracked back to the Holy See, what better place to launder it than through the impenetrably secret corporate laws of Liechtenstein? You could track money into the Grand Duchy. You could track it out again. But you could never tell what happened to it there. You could never prove the money going in was the same stuff as came out.

If there was a story there, if Tom really had been on to something, then it would be perfect for Caro's book. There had never been a successful attempt to trace the movement of Vatican funds. If that could be done, it would almost inevitably uncover the strange illicit relations between the Roman Church and Catholic Italian politicians.

Oliver had not finished. 'If Caro's serious, John, and you can stay sober, I can give you some advice. Don't bother trying to trace it from scratch. You have to start with paperwork uncovered by judicial investigators. Which means you have to start with Calvi and Ambrosiano. It's the only affair involving the Church which is anything like properly documented. You have to do the paperwork, John.'

John smiled. 'The heart of standing.'

'I know, old love, if you can only keep your head together. The other thing you have to do is try some inspirational guesswork. You know the ramifications of the banking system. You know how easy it is to hide millions in it with a couple of telexed instructions or stuff squirted down computer cables. If you're going to get anywhere – and I never did, and I'm a damn sight better than you are – then you have to guess where the money's going and try to trace it back. It's the only chance you have.'

John thanked him, as best as he knew how. He had had too many reasons to be grateful over the years to be comfortable with gratitude. He could not help hoping that Oliver

84

had some ulterior motive for his help. He could not help asking, 'Why are you doing this, Olly?'

Ireton had paused unhappily before replying. 'Because it's a crazy bloody country. Because it's the story I always wanted to write. And because they'll kill me if I try to do the work on it.'

'I'm sorry. I hadn't realized it had been that bad.'

'Worse. There's a limit to how many enemies any one man can afford. On which subject, I gather you worked with young Clarke on the Panamari story. Will you try to talk some sense into him? Tell him to be careful. The penis-in-the-mouth job precludes any kind of suicide.'

'I'd rather gathered that.'

'Don't patronize me, John. It was Mafia or Camorra. Only they kill like that. And I know Mike Thomas knows it. Anyway, next few weeks, you can reach me at the Basel office. Call me if you need a fact, or feel like talking sense about the Madhouse in the Sun.'

It was his nickname, justified over the years, for the Italian Republic.

'One last thing, John. Honestly the last. Remember, and tell Caro to remember, the only institution you can trust in the whole crazy country is the Central Bank. Don't take anything else as gospel, even if it's on paper.'

'I'll remember.'

'Do that.'

'Dream good, Olly. Thanks.'

'Put it down to auld lang syne. Dream well, you pathetic old lush.'

But John did not dream well. Sleep was a torment to him. He could not remember all of them, could only judge them by their side-effects, the migraine-headaches, the dehydration, the constant lowering paranoia, the sweaty tangle of bed-clothes. But some he could remember. Old dreams. Bad dreams. Recurrent dreams through all his adult life.

Sometimes he was falling. But more often during this period he dreamed he was on trains. Trains boarded in mysterious night-time stations far away in Eastern Europe where small dark men, heavy with muscles and moustaches, spoke a tongue he could not understand. They were steam trains, always, a kind he had hardly known outside museums. Big shiny monsters with faded, once-luxurious carriages, smelling of steel and oil, leather, French polish and coal. It was always night, the murky wasted hinterland of Europe interrupted only occasionally by the lights of farms or the sudden acid electric glare of stations. He did not know where he was going, or why. He did not know where he was. He was only aware of constant pressing fear, but he did not know what he was afraid of. He would try to rationalize his anxiety, wondering if, in his dream – for he knew that these were dreams, though as concrete as the daylight world – his suitcases contained contraband, or something was wrong with his papers. Was it border guards, customs officials, he was afraid of? Something he could explain, explain away, somehow find a way to deal with. But it was none of these. It was merely fear, in its purest most unending form, sapping all will, all certainty, all reason or desire. He would sit in the carriage filled with face-less souls, or in the corridor where soot and smuts and steam blew back into his face through the open windows, and listen to the mournful chanting of the wheels and the thin hysterical whistle of the locomotive as it entered tunnels and know, with an appalling certainty, that he was bound to die.

Saturday morning, and the certainty of a day at the races, came as a relief. He had fallen in love with racing in his childhood, when the Ambassador, whose one weakness was for an occasional gamble to offset the careful, precise restraint of a diplomat's life, had taken him to minor meetings and, once, as the great treat of his fourteenth birthday, to the Kentucky Sales. It was there and at that age John had par-ticularly realized the curious mix of satisfactions the sport afforded. Like his father before him, what he took to was not merely the big-money, born-to-the-country manners of the very rich who made up the racehorse-owning class, but the whole mixed and raffish society the sport drew in its wake. Especially since coming to England and finding his schoolboy certainties bewildered by its class structure (no harsher, per-haps, than that of his native States, but very different), he had delighted in the chance to slip into the enchanted world of racecourses, where size of personality still mattered more than size of wallet, and lines of credit more than the length of your family tree. Like most journalists, in the end, he loved the company of scoundrels, being more than half a knave himself.

On this fine morning, a little overcast but promising fair, he knew a moment of panic as, walking in Fulham rather than Bethnal Green, he realized he did not know where to pick up a copy of *Sporting Life*. He always got the *Sporting Life*, and the *Morning Star* because the Communist newspaper's racing tipster was so often right, and *The Times* because it was almost always wrong. (Like a marksman, he thought of it as bracketing his target.)

He picked up young Alan Clarke at the meeting point at a hideously renovated Victoria Station, from where trains left for Sandown; he had found the newspapers he needed at the big news-seller's stand at the Buckingham Palace Road entrance. He hated what they had done to the station (never one of his favourites), putting up electronic indicator boards, prefabricated plastic buffets and shops and generally masking the Victorian structure, half cathedral, half barn, which was what a station ought to look like. Most of all he hated the modern notion of a meeting point. He missed the old wrought-iron clock. He missed the romantic, half-hopeless ring of saying, 'I'll see you underneath the clock at Victoria Station,' and he missed the youth in which he had said it, to girlfriends coming up to spend the day with the interesting new American Westminster schoolboy.

The two men – physically of similar build, but the younger one dressed in the smart country casuals of his background, the older in the worn-out remnants of a suit – walked the short distance from the suburban railway station to the racecourse. The roads were already thick with traffic, from the runabouts and family saloons of people out for a day of fun, to the BMWs and Mercedes of the dedicated punters. Every few yards along the pavement were groups of alert local men talking earnestly of the day's races, making their way steadily forward as they examined the racing pages of the tabloid press and shared half-truthful information about horses' form and their own previous winnings. By the time they got to the course, its big, open-field car-parks were already almost full, and it took them ten minutes to cut through the crowds milling like pilgrims up the gentle slopes to the gates beyond which the grandstand stood.

John led Alan round to the left, to a side entrance for Members' Enclosure ticket-holders. As they approached the window and John reached for his wallet Alan said kindly, 'It would be simpler if these went through on my expenses, wouldn't it?'

John nodded. 'Don't forget to put a claim in for the money you gamble while entertaining a source. And remember that, for your expenses, you always lose. No point in troubling them with your winnings.'

'Are there going to be any winnings?'

John looked at him sidelong. 'Ever been to Sandown before?' Alan shook his head. Standing looked almost sad as he said, 'Bound to be then. Beginner's luck.' Then he had looked seriously disgruntled as he said, 'I don't know what journalism is coming to. Fine young man like you never been to Sandown. So close to London too. In my day you could hardly get young journalists, any journalists, out of a bookie's. One summer we ran a land line over from the phone system in the *Examiner* to the pub and to the bookie's in Queen Victoria Street. I can remember Iain MacKinnon, when he was still the senior sub, putting one whole issue to bed from the public bar, with the Main News Editor passed out under a table and the Foreign Editor weeping in the bathroom because he'd put the money for his wife's anniversary trip to Paris on a certainty in the 3.45 at Haydock which was still running when the others were back in the stables eating their oats and hay.'

Alan said nothing. He was used to older journalists mourning the passing of the high old days they used to know. Like most people, he thought it was just the ritual whining of the ageing. He could not know that this was a generation which had truly seen times change, from the high-rolling certainties of the Fifties and Sixties when they were in their youth, to the dour deflationary Eighties when the world had been inherited by serious-minded graduates and young fogies on the make. Like Alan Clarke, in fact.

What Alan was surprised by was the ease with which he found himself liking the older man and, in a curious way, almost respecting him, though he had been warned by MacKinnon that John was utterly unreliable and given to flying by the seat of his pants. A dangerous example for a journalist fresh from his three years' provincial training to the hazardous byways of the City. But what Alan found attractive, without realizing it, was the combination which charmed almost everyone who had ever known John Standing: the combination of intense attentiveness with a kind of baffled frivolity, a sense that nothing, in the end, really mattered at all. When he was younger he had used to say self-mockingly, 'The game really isn't worth the candle, but the candle is the only light we have.' If he sometimes seemed desperate, it was perhaps only because he was out of the price of wax.

'What time are we supposed to be meeting this chap?' Alan asked once they were through the gate and John had picked up a couple of copies of the day's race-card. Standing took him by the elbow and steered him towards the stand, past a wildly blowing jazz band.

'One-thirty,' he replied, under the frantic brass, 'at the rails. But he will be late, as a matter of principle, to show that he is more important to us than he thinks we are to him, so we shall be even later. Anyway, I want to get a tote bet on for the one-forty-five.'

They walked up the stairs to the main hall under the body of the stand, an area as large as the departure lounge of a medium-sized airport, one wall lined with Tote booths in front of which lines of willing gamblers were permanently formed, another lined with a row of public telephones, and scattered with bars. The two men showed their temporary Members' Passes at the barriers which bisected the hall and walked past the Champagne Bar, already doing flourishing business, thanks to a group of Surrey businessmen showing off to their girlfriends. Alan thought they looked like a works outing of airline stewardesses and aircraft engineers. Not his type at all. John, however, seemed to be enchanted and even managed to keep even-tempered as they stood in the long queue for coffee. Alan suddenly realized that he felt cold. The glass doors out on to the course were open, and a stiff breeze was blowing in across the Downs.

'Are you going to tell me who he is?' Alan asked as they sat at last over their black coffees. He noticed the china in the Members' Enclosure was no better than that used out in the grandstand bars and buffets. He had found himself surprised to find real cups in the main areas at all. Like almost every Englishman he expected some sort of class distinction even in tableware.

'Stefan Altberg,' Standing said, as though that ought to be sufficient explanation. Seeing Alan still looking baffled, he elaborated. 'German–American. Banker. First Manhattan. (Yes, I thought that would interest you.) My age. We were at Harvard together till I quit. His specialty is aircraft financing, on a very large scale. He did a stint at the Export–Import Bank in the States before moving out into commercial banking. He now heads the Transport Financing Division of First Manhattan's Merchant Banking Group. Which makes him a powerful man in the world of airlines, railways, mass transit systems and, most importantly for you, shipping finance.'

'So why's he seeing us?' Alan almost blushed as soon as he said it. He realized he might as well have asked: *What has a broken old hack like you got on a man like Stefan Altberg?*

Standing did not reply at once. He was thinking, almost happily, about better days. He had looked up Stefan when he first worked on an Aerospace Survey for the *Examiner* sixteen years ago. He had also talked to the Ambassador, his father, to ask him to make introductions to the aerospace lobby in Washington. He knew perfectly well he had been chosen for the assignment because he was an American, with good Washington connections, and the aerospace industry was US-dominated. He was intelligent enough to give his editors what they wanted, except for one item he suppressed. The item which gave him his influence (he would not put it more strongly than that, even to himself) over Stefan Altberg.

The Export–Import Bank for which Altberg had worked

was a government-funded institution. It financed American exports at preferential rates of interest, and it was one of the main reasons that the US aircraft business had come to dominate the world market. While it was true that American manufacturers, and in particular Boeing, had shown a startling gift for predicting customer requirements (as had been proved by the development of the 747, to carry large numbers of people cheaply, at a time when the European industry was wasting time and money on Concorde, a beautiful monolith of an aeroplane whose market was destroyed by the oil-price rises and the advent of the age of mass air travel), aircraft were expensive. Airlines around the world were forever looking for aeroplanes which were not only cheap to run but also relatively cheap to buy (if anything which could cost up to seventy million dollars could ever be called cheap). Time and again, American manufacturers had waited to see the financing terms on which their overseas rivals offered their aircraft, and then gone to the Export–Import Bank to arrange a cheaper loan. Money talked, and it had gone a long way towards persuading the world to buy American-built airliners.

Stefan was good at such operations, very good indeed, and the manufacturers had been duly grateful. That was not unusual. The successful sale of such expensive items, by any manufacturer anywhere in the world, would always be likely to result in the spreading of a certain amount of gratitude around those who had helped to put the deal together. But Stefan had been careless. Sometimes he had accepted such tokens of gratitude before the deal was struck, and John was able to come up with hard documentary evidence of several such occasions. In a suspicious world – Washington and the aerospace industry were nothing if not suspicious – an unkind soul might have been tempted to think of such gifts as bribery. It would have made a wonderful story, and still would today, it had occurred to John, thinking of the deals involved and Caro's book on government corruption, but he had suppressed it. Just that single item. Because, being young, although he needed a scoop or two to further his career, he needed good contacts more. He needed people who owed him things. He did not write the story.

But he did mention it to a few contacts in commercial banks, for banking was a strange business, built on unusual kinds of trust. Behaviour which could destroy the trust in which a man was held within a government-sponsored institution was very often exactly the kind of behaviour which persuaded hard-headed commercial bankers that the man concerned understood his business and the market sector involved. It had not been long before Stefan was head-hunted away from the Ex–Im Bank by a major Wall Street house. He knew he had John to thank for that, though what he felt could hardly be called gratitude. But it had paid off in the end, for he had been able and intelligent enough in the world of commercial banking to make the right moves and noises, moves which had brought him to his current uneasy eminence. It could be said he was one of those not altogether unusual men who owed his eminence to the weakness of his character.

John gulped back his coffee and said, 'Let's just say he owes me a couple of favours.' He got up, slapping the bundle of newspapers and racing-card against his thigh. 'Now, I fancy a little something on number five this race, just to get the wallet moving.'

Standing placed his bet, and they went out into the crisp summer air just as the horses for the 1.45 cantered out to the starting-boxes, a voice on the tannoy identifying them as they loped on beyond the stand. The race-course lay in a broad shallow hollow in the Downs, stretching out almost as far as the eye could see. Beyond it lay a train-line and a straggle of houses, diminished to a pale unimportant grey beside the vast green bubble of the course. The sheer brightness of the turf took Alan's breath away and, as they forced their way through the crowd gathered before the on-course bookies' stands towards the Members' Enclosure, he began to feel the lift which racing gave men like Standing, in the presence of clean air, green grass, clear light, high-strung animals and a happy mob. He found himself struggling towards one of the bookies' stands to hand over a five-pound note and shout, 'Five on number five to win.'

The man at the side of the stand, calculating odds, cried,

'Take the man's money. Five to one,' as the man actually on the stand swooped down to take the note. Alan was about to complain at the odds, but the first man was already signalling to other bookies to shift their odds while the second one changed the chalked figures beside his horse's name. He was pushed out of the way as other punters struggled forward to get their money on to a horse which had suddenly seized the fancy of the crowd before the odds started falling even further.

'What is that thing I've put my money on?' he asked John as the Enclosure steward waved them through, seeing the Day Passes looped through their buttonholes.

'Nice little filly,' Standing replied, 'out of good stock. Only her third outing. Unplaced the first time but second time out a respectable second to a horse which is already looking like a candidate for next year's Classics. Word out of the stable is that the harder going here should suit her better than it suits the favourite. How much did you have on her?'

'Five.'

Standing nodded. It was the minimum bet with the on-course bookies, unlike the state-run Tote, which would accept stakes as low as fifty pence each way. 'Sensible. Save the tens till later.'

He was scanning the crowd, which was already pressing down towards the rails at the finishing post. As the day progressed, fewer and fewer would stand down there, as more punters pulled back to be closer to the bookies and the comfort of the bars. 'That's him,' he said, pointing.

Alan was surprised to see a man who looked much younger than Standing. Which was to say he looked much more like a normal forty-year-old these days, when people seemed to age less quickly than in the past. He looked Prussian, thought Alan (though the family were in fact Bavarian Catholics), tall with short precisely cut blond hair, rimless spectacles and an expensive blue overcoat with velvet lapels, which made him look all too much like a secret policeman. They pushed their way forward to the rails and stood beside Stefan Altberg.

Without looking at them, he said to Standing, 'You're late.'

'So were you.'

'We are like-minded people.'

Alan wondered if he was laughing at them under his light American accent, but realized that in one sense at least what Altberg said was true. He had never been so aware of Standing's being an American as he was when these two tall men stood side by side being hard with each other. He was about to introduce himself when he heard the voice on the tannoy saying, 'And they're off!'

Suddenly the whole character of the crowd changed. Even he changed. Everyone's attention focused on the horses beginning their five-furlong sprint. They were coming out in a pack and the names the race-commentator kept mentioning meant nothing to Alan. Where was Dosvedanya, the favourite? Where was Cable Queen, which had risen in the past ten minutes, odds shortening by the second, to the second favourite slot on the board over by the finishing line?

A low, thrilling hum was growing round the course as the horses went into the second furlong, a buzzing like the lowest strings of an orchestra's double-basses. It was people. It was the crowd, under its collective breath, urging on its selections. Alan wished he had checked the colours of his horse's jockey's silks, the only way he could have identified at a distance how Cable Queen was doing now that the steady rumble of the crowd was building to something like a roar. He faintly heard the commentator crying, 'And it's Dosvedanya on the far side holding off from Cable Queen,' before all he could hear was voices shouting, 'Come on, Dosvedanya,' or 'Come on, Cable Queen,' and realized with a shock that one of them was his.

As the small field, spreading out now, combed outwards like a horse's tail, came in to the final furlong mark, he could see that two horses were racing head to head for home, and could feel the ground shaking almost as much from the roar of the crowd as from the horses' hooves, the noise a purely physical pressure. Then as they coursed into the line he saw that one of the two horses had broken free and was charging in a length, a length and a half, ahead. He saw that Standing was leaning back and mouthing, 'Yes, yes, yes!'

94

Altberg was throwing away his bookie's ticket in disgust and saying, 'Only five furlongs. Doesn't prove anything about her stamina,' but Standing was too busy smiling to pay him any attention. Alan realized, watching them, that the two men enjoyed gambling together quite as much as they disliked each other personally. It occurred to him that bankers must find it difficult to lay their hands on partners who did not mind them betting.

Perhaps that was why it was not until he returned from collecting their winnings (Altberg had played safe, with an each-way bet, so he had something coming for Dosvedanya's second place) and placing their bets for the next race – for which Alan felt lucky enough to place ten pounds of his winnings on the favourite, to the consolation of the bookie – that Standing introduced him to the banker, saying, 'If I were you I'd bet with him today. He has beginner's luck.'

Altberg was stony-faced. 'Beginner's luck never lasts.'

But it did. Alan picked the winner and two seconds in the remaining races of the afternoon, and Altberg's look got stonier as Standing relentlessly refused to tell him why they had wanted to see him until they had done some serious gaming.

'It's the three-fifteen I'm interested in,' he explained without explaining anything.

They could not imagine why. The 3.15 looked as though it was hardly worth running. It was a big field, of sixteen horses, but only one of them, the favourite, Stoneman's Bluff, looked anything like a contender. Even so, Standing insisted on dragging them back into the paddock to watch the horses being walked before they were taken off to be saddled.

Alan was enjoying himself. He liked the mixed odours of the course, of cut grass and greed, of human and horsey sweat, the faint tang of horse-shit and the pallid bitter scent of spilt champagne. He liked the complete mixture of the crowd, composed of everything from gentlemen to jailbirds, all intent on making money, all having a damn good time. And standing at the paddock, he noticed again the faint undercurrent of sex that seemed to hum under every aspect of the course. He noted with satisfaction the stable-girls' tight, denimmed rumps moving in unison with their powerful, uncannily erotic

95

charges. He noted with equal satisfaction that there were stable-lads too for the entertainment of the women in the crowd. He had noted holiday couples studded through the crowd, and he had noted well-dressed women on the public phones, doubtless fobbing off their husbands or their official boyfriends with some seemly-sounding excuse. *It must be the horses*, he thought. *No wonder cavalrymen have always had such a gallant reputation.*

Altberg could not see what all the fuss was about. To his practised eye Stoneman's Bluff seemed easily the handsomest, best-conformed horse entered for the race, but Standing was looking cunning.

He turned to Altberg and said, 'You're down on the day. Quite badly, knowing you. Put fifty on the Irish colt, to win.'

Altberg looked suspicious, but as they headed back to the enclosure he peeled off at the same bookie's stand that Alan had been using. 'Ah,' said John with real satisfaction, 'Mr Cohen, and Mr Cohen's son, whom Stefan and I have kept in hot dinners for longer than either of us care to remember.'

The banker affected not to have heard the remark, paused as he was handing over his money, plainly wondering if the journalist had tricked him, but Alan noticed that the old man calculating odds tipped his cap to Standing.

Altberg began to head to the rails again, but Standing took him by the elbow of his expensive coat and steered both of them towards the bar high in the stand looking down over the enclosure.

'You don't need to watch the race,' he explained. 'All you have to do is trust me. And anyway we have things to talk about.' Alan could see that Altberg was torn between protecting his investment and finding out why he had been summoned here. The latter desire won.

John bought them both stiff whiskies but took no drink himself, sitting with his back to the picture windows on to the course, enjoying the sight of the banker trying to snatch glimpses of what was going on without looking inattentive.

'Errol Hart, Stefan,' Standing began.

'Never heard of him.'

'Then I'd better tell you all about him.' Both Altberg and

Alan looked up at that. Was Standing bluffing? Or did he really know more than the rest of them?

'Errol Hart was a Texan, and a banker, in Manhattan. In First Manhattan. Your bank, Stefan, in New York. I expect that he got lonesome. Homesick for the Lone Star State. Those Texan boys do, you know, if they're away from down-home cooking for too long.'

Altberg looked at Standing with a stare which spoke of infinite contempt. He was plainly more interested in his fifty pounds and the race commentary which had just begun over the loudspeaker-system. Standing leaned forward and interrupted his listening, and Alan's just as he heard it confirmed that the r e was long, over a mile and three furlongs.

'But he was good, Stefan, the way some of those country-folks can be, with their natural low-born cunning, so he made it to Executive Vice-President, of your Central American Trade Division. So good he could authorize up to nine million without recourse to any other officer. Which was fine by all of you as long as he went on turning in good profits. Don't look out the window, there's a good boy. Your money is quite safe. That horse will come in first with three or four lengths to spare.'

Standing sat back and reached for a cigarette, lighting it slowly before resuming. 'He was much too smart, when the time came to help out his good ol' Southern buddies, just to make loans out to third parties. After all, new loans have to go up one rank higher than usual to be authorized, and he didn't want this taken out of his oh-so-careful hands. So he did something very much smarter than that. He authorized deposits, large deposits, from his friends down in the South, because – I'm right in thinking, am I not? – an honest bank like your own won't simply allow big deposits from anywhere. You have to know the money's clean. He promised you all it was and gave you some cock-a-mamie story to help you forget that big cash money from the South is almost always out of drugs. Am I right so far?'

Altberg said nothing, but looked the purest murder. Standing ignored him and continued.

'Once that was going nicely – deposits coming in, I guess,

97

by way of some nice respectable nominee, another bank, say, in the South – once that was going, he started nominating deposits by your bank with that nice bank in the South. Good interest he earned, I expect, as well, on short-term money. Good enough to make you overlook the fact that he was depositing more with them than they were depositing with you. After all, that way you were making a nice healthy profit on the big interest your dollars were earning down in the South. And because it was a bank you were putting your money in, you didn't have to ask too closely what they might be using all that money for. Because to pay you all that nice big interest they had to be lending it on to someone else at even higher rates.'

There was a shiny line of sweat on Altberg's upper lip. Standing smiled at him and said, 'You can cheer now, Stefan. Didn't you hear that on the tannoy? Our horse just came in first by five lengths. I knew he would. He hasn't got much form. The stable's had temperament problems with him. Very headstrong. But I saw the one race he had in Dublin last year, in conditions just like these, and there wasn't anything in a strong field as came anywhere near him. Those are the ones you have to watch, my friend. The ones with hidden talents.'

Altberg tried to look uninterested. 'I don't know what you're talking about, John.'

'I rather think you do, Stefan. Shall I tell you why?'

'I would find that very amusing.'

'Good. Because whatever Errol's down-home friends were financing was very, very illegal. Which was why he had to launder the money through another bank down in the South. They were too many checks at First Manhattan to allow him to lend himself, direct. But dear Errol got greedy. Whatever it was his friends were financing had to be shipped to its destination, and he wanted a piece of the action for himself. Which is why he set up a shipping-company, masked as a finance house, safely away in London, to try to increase his personal take. Only, before he could really get that going, when he'd made only one, unsuccessful, try, the people his friends were financing got angry with him and said, This is no man of honour. So they chased him, all the way to London, and hanged him under Blackfriars Bridge. Which leaves you with a horrible mess, because marine finance comes under your jurisdiction, and your bosses want you to sort this whole mess out.'

Altberg stopped bluffing. 'All right, John. What are you offering?'

Standing smiled and bobbed his head. 'That's better, Stefan. Alan here is a very talented young man. He wrote the Panamari stories which have appeared in the *Examiner* already. Now, neither he nor I have any desire to spread any dirt about First Manhattan. It was Hart who was the crook, not you. Even if he wasn't, it's in the interests of you all to make damn sure it looks as though he was. So, we're not after you, we're after the people he was dealing with, and the people they were financing. We want to know what all this is about. You tell us that, and I guarantee your bank comes out of it smelling as sweet as daisies in a trash-can full of shit.'

Altberg seemed on the point of breaking, but pointed at Alan instead. 'What about him? He looks all fresh-faced and schoolboy-honest. How can I trust him?'

John turned his hands palm upwards, looking like a farmer regretting the spiralling price of eggs. 'You can't,' he said, 'not really. But if you don't, we are going through our friends in the investigating office in New York and I swear that we will hound you till your collective nuts drop off. Oh, and by the way, Stefan, tell your secretary to stop telling lies. First Manhattan and the *Examiner* use the same travel agents. You weren't in Finland last week. You were in Mobile.'

Altberg was about to speak, thought better of it, buttoned his coat, explained, 'I have to collect my winnings. Will you join me?' Standing nodded. 'He can stay.'

John came back ten minutes later, on his own.

'Where is he?' Alan asked.

'He had to go.'

'And?'

'And it is, understandably, too complicated merely to explain. And they haven't finished looking. He will send a photostat of his papers to me, anonymously, at Caro's flat. In return we keep his bank clean and promise him absolute security. Which does mean you and I may have to go to jail to protect our, charming, source.'

'Do they have deadlines in jail?'

'Every ten years or so.'

'I wish you hadn't told me.'

'I had to. You're going to write it.'

Alan looked, and felt, surprised. 'I don't see why. I didn't get any of the Southern banking stuff. That's all your angle. And how did you get your hands on that?'

Standing smiled. 'I didn't.'

'I don't understand.'

'I mean I didn't. I know the way large American banks work. I know the restrictions they place on both borrowing and lending. And I assumed that whatever Errol Hart was up to had to include handing out money in the area of his own jurisdiction, which was funding business growth in Central America. So I worked out how I'd have done it if I'd been him, made a couple of intelligent guesses and . . .'

'You mean you were lying to Altberg just then?'

'Completely.'

'But what if you'd got it wrong? What if you'd got everything upside down? You would have been a laughing-stock.'

Standing looked genuinely surprised at Alan's reaction. 'No, I wouldn't. It wouldn't have mattered what I said to him, though it's flattering to be right. No, he'd already made his decision to talk, or he would never have come. All I was doing was giving him an excuse. Rather a good one, I thought. And anyway, he was grateful.'

'Grateful!'

'Oh, yes. We've been gambling partners far too long for him to ignore my handing him a twenty-to-one outsider.'

CHAPTER EIGHT

She was happy, she realized. Simply happy. Her work had been going well. She had been absolved of her sense of guilt for her former husband's death. And she held Ezzo in her arms each night. She knew it was not made to last, but she was glad to be reminded of what happiness was like, how good it was to feel no pain.

She had taken Ezzo Spaccamonti's advice. She had confined her researches to Italy's best documented recent scandal, the Calvi–Ambrosiano affair, and tried to fill in its many remaining blanks and mysteries. Even if no one could get to the bottom of it, and even the Bank of Italy had failed, there would be enough to trace the extent and range of corruption in the state. What was more, since Calvi was safely dead, she found that people were willing to talk to her. She knew that most of what they told her was untrue, part of the constant dissimulation of the country and its hundreds of fragmented, shifting, political clans and alliances, but she was beginning to sift through what she had learned, in order to evaluate it. She knew she would have to talk the whole thing over soon with an impartial outsider. She would have to talk to Oliver Ireton.

Only one duty remained to her, before she would be rid of all her guilt about Tom Wellbeck. She had to make sure nothing he was working on was left unfinished. She owed it to him as a journalist to establish if any of his last researches had any mileage in them. What she could do now was to go through Tom's diary for the weeks before his death, to see whom he had been talking to, to check if any of them was a stone beneath which a story lay unturned.

It proved a largely fruitless exercise. Most of his calls in those last few weeks had been the regular 'touching base' of journalists round the world, keeping his contacts fresh and sounding out the gossip. The rest had been the bread and butter of reporting, attending press briefings, on and off the record, press conferences, and picking up the hard data even Italian public companies put out, providing a paper like the *Examiner* with the facts about foreign companies' results, activities and future plans.

There were only two people she had left to see, both of them contacts Tom had spent time with on his last day alive. There was Bartolomeo Montevarchi at the Central Bank, known to everyone simply as the Dottore, who had spent two hours with Tom that morning. And Father Tomasso Falmi – a name which meant nothing to Caro – of the Vatican Secretary of State's department, who had been one of Tom's guests at dinner. She had already spoken to the other guests, old friends, a civil servant and banker Tom saw regularly, who told her, and who had no cause to lie, that the evening had been spent in idle gossip.

She had appointments with both Montevarchi and Falmi today. Once those were done, she would be well rid of her responsibilities to Tom. She could go to Basel to talk to Oliver Ireton. And she could catch up with the work she was supposed to be doing.

One thing she would have to do, however. There had been a message for her this morning from MacKinnon, asking her to call, and another from Alan Clarke. He wanted her to find out anything she could about a company called Istituto della Protezione Popolari. All he could tell her was that it had subsidiaries in Panama and Nassau. She had noted down the name. She had made notes on so many Italian companies with overseas subsidiaries since working on the Ambrosiano affair that she had to be careful not to get them confused. Not the easiest thing in the world when most of them existed solely to confuse the authorities, concealing illicit activities from over-attentive eyes. Perhaps the Dottore might know something? Otherwise she was stuck with searching the Company Registration Files, which left something to be desired, in the low Roman fashion. She wondered idly why Alan wanted to know about this company.

It was time for her to make her way to the Central Bank.

She had known Dottore Bartolomeo Montevarchi for nearly a decade. They had never become friends. It was doubtful he had any friends amongst his working acquaintances. His spare time was spent with old friends from his college days, playing chess or reading poems. No one minded the distance he kept, however, for everyone knew that the great concern of his life was tending to the wife he loved and who had been struck down by multiple sclerosis while they were both still in their early thirties. Now he was in his sixties and there was talk of his retirement. There must be many who would have welcomed his immediate departure, for in the thirty-five years he had worked at the Banca d'Italia the Dottore had become known as that most dangerous thing, an honest man.

They were not uncommon at the Bank, and sometimes they would die for it, as would the Milanese magistrates they preferred to use to investigate trouble in Rome, as Giorgio Ambrosoli had done when he was investigating the Sindona and Calvi affairs. But the Dottore was too public a man to kill, too obvious and important a target, for his name had been before the delightedly scandalized Italian public as long as anyone could remember.

His job (not one he would have chosen, he often claimed) was to pursue and prosecute, under Law 159, illegal currency exports by private individuals. He himself had always hoped to run the Corporate Currency Export Department, in which his career had begun, for it was companies not individuals, he rightly pointed out, who were the biggest offenders against the country's stringent exchange-control legislation.

Law 159 existed to control the movement of money out of Italy. The intention was twofold. First, by stopping the export of hard currencies like the dollar, it was meant to make those currencies available to productive Italian industry. Second, by preventing the export of lire, to areas where they could be sold uncontrolled for hard currency at any rate they would fetch, the Central Bank hoped to manage the exchange rate of Italy's money. In the process, they hoped to trap the export of illegal earnings undeclared to the Revenue Department. Historically, the law, and those it had superseded, had failed. Not a day passed when Italians did not drive north into Switzerland or France, or, if they were very well favoured, within the Vatican walls, carrying suitcases filled with cash, and the Italian lira had fallen so far over thirty years against every other major currency that there was now serious talk of a massive hundred-fold revaluation, lopping a couple of noughts off the price of everything, as De Gaulle had once done in France. It was impossible to take a currency seriously if anything worth buying needed thousands, often millions, of its units. And as the currency weakened, so the flood of money over the borders, into harder currencies, pushing the lira down yet further, had quickened to catastrophic proportions. Nor was it merely large companies that played the international currency game. Private citizens did so, whenever they had an opportunity. It was said there was not a film-star, footballer or musician in Italy who did not make sure to salt away as much as possible in untaxed dollars in Monaco or Switzerland. The Dottore's job, or rather that of his department, as he was always at pains to point out, little loving scandal himself, was to catch them at it and bring them to court. Such occasions were blissful open-days for Italy's popular press, and so it was that gentle, shy, retiring Dottore Bartolomeo Montevarchi was probably the only one of their Central Bankers every Italian could name.

Caro had often thought that Banca d'Italia had chosen wisely in selecting him for the job, however much he might hate the attendant publicity. It was the very hatred of the high life and the world of the paparazzi which placed him above suspicion. Other men might easily have been dazzled by the world of film-stars and jet-setters he had to investigate. Other men might have succumbed to the beautiful women and numbered bank accounts which were offered to him daily. But he only wanted to look after his wife in peace and play a little chess in the evenings, and that made him incorruptible.

He was not, in fact, a Doctor of Philosophy, or a doctor of anything at all. What had begun as an affectionate nickname for his slow and scholarly manner had become an honorary title and an emblem of respect. For though he was a mild, soft-spoken man he was, as many languishing in jail had discovered to their cost, remorseless in ways showier investigators hardly ever aspired to, and he extracted prices for his department's connivance higher than any other investigator dared.

For there was no doubt that his department did sometimes look the other way as prominent politicians, financiers and industrialists exported currency worth billions of lire. They had to. The practice was too widespread in Italy to avoid it. Even the honest Dottore could not countenance throwing almost all the Italian establishment into jail. But he had used his participation in such blindnesses in a way those who took him at face value would never have thought possible. He knew more about the financial irregularities of the country's leading figures than any other man alive, and he used such knowledge against them to win their consent to prosecutions others would have said were politically impossible to bring. The work against famous faces which so delighted the tabloid-reading public was only the glittering surface of his labours. Though he was no longer of the Corporate Currency Department he was the best ally it possessed. He knew the damage corporate offenders did to Italy's foreign exchange and, quietly, without fuss, he used his secret knowledge to ensure that major prosecutions were not halted or entangled in political stalling operations. He worked behind the scenes, deftly, shyly, to bring great corporate culprits to book. It was work undertaken with such little fuss but so much suave cunning that one exasperated Socialist politician (Socialists shipped their money overseas at every opportunity, too) had once described him as 'the last Jesuit employed by the secular Italian state'.

He was a short, stout man who always wore a three-piece suit, shiny at the elbows but immaculately cut. He was almost entirely bald and the thin fringe of hair around his domed head did indeed make him look more like a monk than a banker, except for the fact that he shared one physical characteristic with the greatest financial figure of modern times. Like the late great Pierpont Morgan he had the ugliest nose in the world. It was vast, pimpled and permanently red, though everyone knew the little banker drank only sparingly. It dominated any room he was in, shining like a beacon in a stormy sea. There were times he seemed only an appendage to it, rather than the other way round. And, perhaps to try to distract attention from it, he seemed almost always to be smiling. Caro tried to concentrate on the smile as she sat in his office on the third floor of the Bank's beautiful nineteenth-century neoclassical building in Via Nazionale (the best-looking Central Bank in the world, she thought), overlooking the palm trees, unable to help noticing the incongruous way his great lighthouse of a nose divided the smile from the sadness in his eyes.

'You must know how sad I was to hear of Tom's murder, and how ashamed, that it should happen in my country.' She nodded, trying not to fake a grief she did not really feel. Her silence prompted him to ask, 'Is there any news in the investigation?'

'A little. It seems Tom's mistress is missing. A young woman called Zara Francchetti. The magistrate wants to speak to her urgently.'

He seemed relieved at the news, so she could not help raising the question she would most have liked to forget. 'You don't think, do you, Dottore, that there might have been anything political about his murder? I know he saw you on the day he died. It would help to know what he was investigating.'

The Dottore understood all too well what and why she was asking, and though the little smile under the lighthouse remained unchanged the sad eyes looked yet sadder. 'It isn't easy to be certain,' he said. 'Not here, where anything may be political, even the appointment of magistrates.'

She wondered if he meant it as a warning, but his eyes remained unchanged.

'I have to say, however,' he continued, 'that I doubt it. Tom sometimes didn't seem very concerned with Italy. He was a good correspondent, it is true, but his real passion was the Vatican. I think he saw himself as being the man who revealed the Church's financial dealings to the world. To the best of my knowledge the Gentlemen in Black do not normally murder people who are investigating them. They simply breathe incense on them till they run away.'

Caro was relieved, and even more reassured when she saw the smile had spread to the eyes.

'But you wanted to know what Tom and I talked about the last time we met.'

'Yes. Please.'

'It was nothing very exciting. But if I tell you it has to be off the record, as it was with him. It was only a preliminary briefing.'

Caro understood, and nodded.

'Say it, please,' the old man insisted softly.

'Anything you say to me in this room on this occasion is completely off-the-record, and will not be quoted by me without your express permission.'

The huge nose turned a satisfied shade of purple. 'Good. You know, I imagine – it is the most open secret in Rome – that we are pressing, we in the Banca d'Italia, for a major revaluation of the lira. Of course, the effect of knocking two zeroes off the price of everything would be purely psychological. We would be announcing to the world at large that we intend to make the lira a strong currency again. And the strength of currencies is in any case largely a matter of psychology. Only faith and interest rates move the international exchanges.'

Caro smiled politely. It was one of the little Jesuit's favourite sayings.

'All of us in the bank are agreed, however, that we cannot create faith in the lira abroad if Italians continue to do everything in their power to get their money overseas and into dollars or Swiss francs. A number of my colleagues are suggesting that we institute a purge on currency smugglers as soon as the revaluation is announced. I happen to believe that would be futile. It would simply show the world Italians did not even trust the new revalued lira. I am also aware that there are many in all political parties who do not wish to see either revaluation or any further efforts to curb the export of currency, by their own immediate circle at least. That fact had not a little to do with the fall of the Craxi government. That and the Mafia trials in Sicily.'

Even Caro was surprised by that. 'Are you serious?' she asked.

'After four years in office, in Italy, Craxi was beginning to look like ... like Gladstone. If he had stayed in office it is possible he might have been able to effect much. Much was already in hand. Much that many powerful people in Italy could only disapprove of.'

It was a sad story, but it made sense in modern Italy. 'So what do you want to do?' Caro asked.

The nose positively beamed. 'What I want to do and what I can do are very different things. Personally, I would like to prosecute every currency smuggler I know, but that is politically impossible. Failing that, I would like to conduct a huge purge of smugglers immediately before the revaluation, to show that we mean business. Then after revaluation, the fall-off in prosecutions will show how much more Italians trust the new lira. That is something we can easily arrange. Even if the smuggling continues, we simply avoid prosecuting too many of those involved, to make it look as though smuggling has fallen off. But that, too, is politically highly sensitive.'

'So what did you propose to Tom?'

'What I proposed to Tom and several other journalists was that they carry stories suggesting that was what I proposed to do. That I intended to conduct a purge until the lira was revalued, without any allowances for persons. That includes the politicians. I would deny the story, of course, which would only make the politicians believe it more. Which might, in turn, make some of those who are holding back on the revaluation change their minds.'

'It's very elegant, Dottore,' said Caro, who meant it. 'I thought you didn't like the press. It seems you know how to use it.'

'A man must dine with the devil if he wants to eat at all in hell.'

'I hope it works. I hope you'll mention it to our new Head of Station whenever one is appointed.'

'I had hoped it might be you.'

She shook her head, troubled again for the first time in days. 'No,' she said simply, 'too many memories.'

He looked sad, above the nose, again. 'I'm sorry. But have I put your mind at rest?'

'Oh, yes. Perfectly, thank you. I only hope they find this Francchetti woman quickly.'

'I hope so too. And I hope we will still see you often.' He was rising to show her to the door. She remembered in time she had another question.

'One last thing, Dottore.' His little eyebrows rose questioningly on his high bald forehead. 'Does a company called Istituto della Protezione Popolari mean anything to you?'

His eyes went expressionless, though the smile continued under the nose. She could not tell what he was thinking, nor what he might be withholding. 'It means something,' he replied, 'but I can only tell you what I told Tom when he asked the same question six or seven months ago. I told him to ask the Gentlemen in Black. To the best of my knowledge, it is Vatican-controlled.'

She had time for a long lunch with Ezzo that day, for she was not due to see Father Tomasso till five in the evening at his office in the Vatican. She felt better just being with him, in the cool shade of the plane trees of a garden-restaurant close to the magistrate's offices. Most of what they had to say to each other was the small change of conversation between two people comfortable with one another. He was glad that she had become so calm and had chosen sensibly to work on things which could be achieved, instead of burning herself to ash trying to do his job, or chasing the current Roman gossip. Besides his feelings as a magistrate, his feelings as a man were reassured that she found him sufficient in himself to cancel out the guilt Tom's death had filled her with. He was glad of her, as well as for her, for his own vanity's sake.

He asked her if she was still seeing the priest at five, careful about the time, wanting to know when she might be finished, and where they ought to meet. They settled on dinner in the tiny, delightful Papa Giovanni, her favourite Roman restaurant, in Via dei Sediari near the Piazza Navona (she wondered a little guiltily if she should pay a visit to her former hotel) and Ezzo went off to telephone their reservation. He was gone so long she had only time to kiss him once before heading off to the *Examiner* office to check for any telephoned messages.

Emilia, the secretary, was a little sour with her, from

spending too much time alone. Caro also guessed that Roman gossip about the magistrate had reached the secretary's active ears. It was not that Emilia would mind or disapprove. It was merely that she would not easily forgive Caro for not having told her first, so that she, as was only fit and proper, could be the centre of any gossip in the city about the newspaper, rather than leaving the duty to some stranger. Her self-esteem was wounded. Caro, unlike Tom, had robbed her of one of the innocent perks of her job.

The only message was a further request from Alan Clarke to look into Popolari. She wondered what could be so pressing about a Vatican-controlled corporation. Was the pretty boy getting involved in the mystique of the Gentlemen in Black, the way that Tom had done? But why had the Dottore been so backward with information about it? He usually took delight in savaging the currency loophole the Church provided right in the centre of the city. She would have to ask Father Tomasso, if she could get him to talk.

The telephone rang. Emilia interrupted her studious examination of the current issue of *Vogue* to answer it.

'It's for you,' she told Caro flatly.

'Hello, Caroline Kilkenny speaking.'

'Signorina Kilkenny . . .' Father Tomasso's heavily accented voice had trouble with her name.

Caro switched into Italian, thinking Emilia should have warned her it wasn't a call from London. 'Padre Tomasso, *che . . .*' she began, but he cut her off, rather rudely she thought.

'Signorina, could I ask one favour of you? Could we meet at four instead of five, at my office? I am sorry to change the hour so late, but it gives you half an hour to get there.'

She swore to herself. If she had only known at lunch, she could have arranged to meet Ezzo after work. Was there time to call him now? No. Damn, damn, damn.

'Yes, Padre. I will be there. I will be at your office at four.'

She wondered where would be best to get a taxi from at this hour.

Her driver took the slowest route available through the dense smoggy summer traffic, idling up the Via della Conciliazione to drop her at St Peter's with only a few minutes to spare. She pushed her way through the dawdling crowd of tourists and pilgrims filling the main entrance to the great Piazza and ran round the southern semi-circular colonnade, cursing her ill-luck that her route lay along the path to the Vatican museums. She cut through the Borgia courtyard into the Belvedere Court, then out through the side gate into the garden, leaving the crowds behind her as she explained her business to a bored Swiss Guard. (They were, she had often thought, the worst security force in the world, despite their charming hose-and-doublet Renaissance uniforms. They never knew what was going on, and would let anyone through any door which was not firmly bolted.) It was hot in the garden as she half-trotted into the Vatican City proper, the warren of offices and living-quarters tucked around the basilica of St Peter, to the Secretary of State's Department. It always seemed hotter in the Vatican than in the rest of Rome (even the public drinking fountains dribbled out warmer water than the Italian ones beyond), as though to remind the Church's politicians of the fires of hell they were working to avoid.

At the main desk in the small lobby of the Department, in a small stone jewel of a baroque palazzo, she was told that Father Tomasso had only just returned himself. His office was at the end of the corridor on the second floor.

There was no lift in this building, so she had to walk, but she was grateful for the cool, pale marble of the spiral staircase. She had made sure she was properly dressed for a visit to the Vatican, wearing a long-sleeved, below-the-knee dress and a cashmere cardigan. She had begun to regret it in her dash through the highest heat of the afternoon, but here in the high vault of the offices she began to feel comfortable at last.

As she climbed she thought she could hear footsteps beside her own echoing round the stairs before her, and wondered idly if she could catch up with the priest if she ran up the stairs. But women, except for nuns (some would say even nuns), were only allowed here on sufferance and it would have been thought unseemly to run, as well as being far too tiring in the heat of a summer's day. Running was a vulgar,

Northern, probably Protestant, practice, so she gave up the idea.

When she entered the short corridor off the second-floor landing there seemed to be a sort of expectation in the air, as though the marble floor might still be slightly ringing with the echo of the priest's steel-quartered boots. She realized, though, that it must have been the welcome the open door at the end of the corridor seemed to give, at the end of unbroken walls of solid, shut, mahogany doors. Light was flowing into the corridor through the open door from a window in the room beyond and she set off happily towards it and her meeting with Father Tomasso.

She saw and felt what happened what seemed an age before she heard it. In fact she never heard it at all, the explosion, already unconscious beneath the door blown off by the bomb which tore Tomasso Falmi quite literally, limb from limb.

CHAPTER NINE

When she finally came round, from the drugged hallucinatory sleep her mind had stumbled through since the explosion, she was lying in cool linen sheets in a cool white room where the Roman sunlight filtered through Venetian blinds. There was a vase of irises by her bedside. There was someone sitting just within the periphery of her vision, but she could not move her head to get a better look.

He got up and walked round to the other side of the bed. It was Alan Clarke. She could not focus on him properly. He swam in and out of her vision like something on a burnt-out television tube. He sat down carefully on the edge of the bed and took her right hand in his.

'Caro?' he whispered.

She could not speak. She was too tired. She felt as though she had been inflated like a balloon. All her body felt painfully filled with air. But it was blood her skin was filled with, with bruises and contusions.

Alan smiled at her and squeezed her hand, stopping when he saw the frown of pain wince across her face. 'Welcome back.'

She tried to speak, but she could not make her mouth and tongue work properly. All that happened was that her breathing deepened to something like a smoker's wheeze.

He stroked her hair with his long delicate hand and told her not to speak. 'You're going to be all right. The mahogany door saved you. You're bruised, and you've had concussion. There's a broken bone in your left wrist, and your ribs and neck have taken a beating, but you're going to be OK.'

She tried to form the question, 'What happened?' and though no sound came out he could interpret the vague movements of her lips.

'There was a bomb,' he told her, 'in the Vatican, in the

office of the man you were going to meet. Father Tomasso's dead, but you're going to be all right. There isn't anything to worry about. We're with you now. We've come to take you home.'

There was so much she wanted to ask him, but even her mind would not work, as the drugs reasserted their control. So much she wanted to know, as she edged back under the shifting shroud of sleep.

When she came round again, about ninety minutes later by the little-changed look of the light in the room, she remembered what had happened, and her mind and mouth both worked.

For some reason her first question was, 'Where's John?'

Alan smiled his boyish, charmed smile. 'If he's still in the mood he's been in the past two days, he's busy beating shit out of Dottore Montevarchi.'

'What for?'

Alan shrugged. 'He wouldn't say. He hasn't been saying a lot of late. He just muttered that Montevarchi must know. Don't ask me what. He's been half-demented since he heard.'

'How long have I been out?'

'It happened Friday. It's Monday morning now.'

'When did you get here?'

'Friday night. Rome office phoned the paper with the news. John was in to see me . . .'

'How's he been?' She did not know why she cared.

'He's been all right.' The young man crinkled his small nose, pausing to think about what he had said and looking shyly anxious. 'Well, actually, Caro, he's been looking like death. I don't know what's the matter with him.' Caro knew. 'When we got the news he went insane. I've never seen anything like it. I've never seen MacKinnon terrorized like that before.'

Caro tried to smile, but the effort hurt too much. She had seen MacKinnon running scared before. Occasionally, in the past. When God and John were boys.

'He stood in the middle of the newsroom,' Alan continued, 'and just yelled and yelled till he got his way. Brought the whole of the Saturday edition grinding to a halt till they gave him what he wanted.'

She felt strangely safe to hear it. Nothing could ever be too bad if Standing still had the energy for one of his celebrated rages.

'Anyway, he insisted we had to pull you out. He all but held Accounts to gunpoint to get them to book the tickets. They weren't going to clear the money, but by the time he'd finished they were virtually begging him to go.'

'I suppose,' Caro guessed, 'they sent you along to hold the money.'

Alan looked bashful. He almost blushed. 'Well, MacKinnon did mention it, yes. But it was Standing who insisted. He wouldn't tell me why. At the height of it he vanished into the editorial conference room with the Old Man and MacKinnon. All we got in the newsroom was the occasional gargled cry. When they came out the Old Man and Iain both looked as though they'd had a spike shoved up their arse and John was telling me to buy a shirt and toothbrush at the airport. MacKinnon just told me to go along and do whatever Standing told me.'

'What has he told you?'

'Fuck all. Just to sit here with you and guard you from the crazies while he got on with his work. He called in again this morning. He's looking absolutely knackered.'

It would be all right. She was safe as long as Standing stayed demented. She did not believe anyone could hurt her while his rage remained intact. For the first time since coming round she thought of Spaccamonti.

'Has Ezzo . . .'

The boyish grin returned. 'Your magistrate friend? He's come in a couple of times each day to see you. Good-looking fellow. He's been running around looking hideously anxious. You know, with that tight-arsed Italian wiggle . . .'

'Shut up, Alan.'

He squeezed her hand again, more gently this time, the lightest pressure in the palm. 'No, sorry. He looks all right. Though I don't think he and John hit it off too well. He's said that if he can lever the case out of the Vatican, who seem to want to handle it themselves, he'll conduct the investigation personally. He should be here soon. He said he'd come in again at lunchtime. I hope we'll see John back then too.' He looked down on her with blue eyes filled with tender amusement and said, 'You're a very pretty lady, Caro, even when you've been bombed, but I wouldn't mind leaving you to them for an hour, and let them sit looking at you. I'm getting pretty sick of Italian hospital pasta.'

She smiled, despite the pain, and drifted back to sleep.

Ezzo was standing over her, stroking her forehead and hair. He stood with his back against the light. She could not see what lay within his almond eyes.

'Don't talk,' he told her. 'It is all right. I am so sorry for what has happened to you, and while you were under my protection. I have spoken to your friend John Standing. We do not agree about much, but we agree you should be taken somewhere safe. He is going to take you home.'

She closed her eyes and lay back against the pillows, the soft light glowing pink through her eyelids, and heard him whisper, 'I don't want you to be in danger ever again. There is always danger here.' He paused, trying to find the right words for what he wanted to say. All he could say was, 'Think of me in the times when you are happy. Happiness is rare.'

She was herself again. She hurt, all over, but she was in control. The heat of her angry body had passed, as had the heat of afternoon. It was early evening, and John Standing sat beside her.'

'My God, but you look terrible,' she said.

'You don't look so great yourself, kid.'

'Well, thanks. There's nothing like giving a woman confidence, and that was nothing like it.'

'The hell with that. You've got every nurse in this hospital wondering who the Englishwoman is who has two men like Clarke and Spaccamonti with the hots for her. They're asking if you can't spare one of them at least.'

'What about you, you old bullshitter?'

He threw back his aching head, stretching the muscles in

his neck, and said, addressing the ceiling, 'Well, it's true I'm off the sauce. But this is Italy, remember, and they can't abide my clothes.'

It hurt horribly, but she, like John, began to laugh.

The next morning she could walk, she could move, and she could be herself. The doctors said it would take her a few weeks to recover from all the internal and external bruising, and her wrist would have to remain in plaster (she gave thanks it was not her right wrist); but the concussion had worn off. There was nothing wrong with her brain.

Ezzo, Alan and John stood about her bed like a personal vision of heaven and she began to believe at last that her body would get well. It would have to, as long as men like these existed.

John, sitting on the radiator by the window (*He'll get piles*, she thought to herself foolishly), took charge of their proceedings.

'You'd better tell her, Spaccamonti.' Alan had been right. They did not like each other. She put it down to infantile male envy, though that was not at all like John.

Ezzo uncoiled his long legs and smoothed down the jacket of his pale grey double-breasted suit. He looked magnificent, she thought.

'We've found Zara Francchetti, Caro, in a flat in Naples. The neighbours called in the authorities because of the smell from her rooms. She had been dead about two weeks, the coroner said.'

A wave of nausea swept through Caro, bearing with it wild, half-formed thoughts.

'She still had the gun in her hand,' Ezzo went on, trying to be distant, judicial. 'A point two–two Beretta. Only the ballistics test will tell us for certain, but I am assuming she committed suicide, with the same gun she used to kill Tom Wellbeck.'

Caro felt relieved, released from the thoughts which had first come to her. She had to believe that Ezzo was right, for it would rid her of her memories. She had to have him confirm it.

'So it was suicide, then?'

Ezzo nodded, but John was looking at the floor. After an uneasy silence he said, 'I think we have to assume that.' He added, inconsequentially: 'She didn't leave a note.'

Ezzo stilled the particle of doubt. 'It isn't all that unusual, whatever the detective novels say.' Then, after holding back for an instant: 'We will never be certain, the pathologists say, because of the condition the body was in . . . in Naples in the summer heat . . . but it seems likely she was in the early stages of pregnancy. She was a Neapolitan. This is Italy. It makes a certain kind of sense.'

He stood up, getting ready to go. 'I have to go to my office, Cara.' She did not mind the slip. She did not try to correct him. 'But I hope to wrap it up as soon as the ballistics report comes through. Then it will be over and you will have done a great deal more than your duty. I am taking over the bombing case myself. In the meantime, it is best if you are returned to safety. I think your being hurt was accidental. It happened because you were early. But I cannot take any risks. These gentlemen will take you home on this evening's flight.'

He turned in the doorway, looking unhappy, and said, 'I will see you all at the airport.'

When he had left, John settled briskly to business. 'Two questions only, Caro. Can you walk? Can you work?'

She nodded. 'Yes. I can.'

John looked away. 'Well, it's a hell of a lot more than you've been doing these past two weeks.'

Caro was outraged. 'Who do you think you are?' was the only rational thing she could manage to say.

John frowned. 'I'll tell you that one day. Meantime we have been wandering like clowns around the edges of the mother and father of a story. I wanted Alan here as well because he is a part of it. The only serious question is: Are we going to see it through?'

She did not know what he was talking about but she was prepared to hear him out. 'What is there to stop us?' she asked.

'My . . .' he took a deep breath, 'reputation. There are people who no longer trust my journalistic judgement. Most times I'm one of them myself.'

Caro sighed. 'Why don't you just tell us what you think you've got? Then we'll decide.'

John stood up, his hands plunged deep into the pockets of his baggy suit jacket. There were times he looked more like a circus clown than a journalist, his clothes billowed out by years of over-use. He began to pace slowly up and down the room, pausing sometimes at the window to look down into the quiet gardens below. He always preferred to move around when he was thinking and explaining aloud. He was too tall, too shapeless, to be comfortable confined to desks and chairs.

'The first thing to say,' he began, 'is that I nearly screwed it up. I wasted days in London looking through Tom's files . . .'

'Stop right there,' Caro said. 'I need to know. Do you think Tom was murdered by his mistress?'

John paused, considering the question. 'I don't suppose we'll ever really know,' he said softly at last. 'I think we have to assume he was, otherwise we'll go mad. It's as likely as anything. We have to, you have to, Caro, let Tom go.'

She nodded her head sadly. At least he understood. She was glad that someone did. She was glad that Ezzo had been there to take away the pain. But that led to another question she had to ask.

'Do you think he's playing straight with this investigation?'

Standing sounded infinitely weary in reply. He sounded as though he ached. 'Who knows? He's a Roman magistrate, which probably means he's crooked one way or another. The straight ones end up dead. But we've no reason to disbelieve him. What matters is whether you believe him or not.'

She could hear the strain in her own voice as she said: 'I believe him.'

'Then let Tom, and Zara Francchetti, rest in peace. The best thing we can do is finish off this story.'

'I'm sorry. I interrupted.'

He knew she knew he was right. He continued his slow pacing. 'I told you I wasted a lot of time in London, before I realized that the only thing that mattered was where the Vatican's money was going. It was Oliver Ireton who put me right.'

She opened her eyes. 'You spoke to Olly?'

'Yup. He was in London for his daughter's wedding. We would have got there in the end, but he saved me wasting a lot more time. I've briefed Alan on the missing files, by the way.'

That made sense. She wondered what the new boy made of it. There would be time to ask him later.

'Olly pointed out,' John continued, 'that if both the IOR and Liechtenstein files were missing, the chances were that Tom was looking at the way the Vatican Bank shifts money out of Italy.'

'That makes sense,' Caro interrupted. 'The Dottore told me Tom had got obsessed with the Vatican's finances.'

'I know. He told me that too, along with a lot of other things. But one thing at a time. The reason Tom wouldn't have got anywhere is Liechtenstein. Once the money's over the border, it can be transferred into another name. No one would be able to prove the money coming out of the Duchy was really the Church's funds.'

'The same dodge Calvi used,' Caro interrupted again, 'laundering money overseas so that it looked as though independent foreign companies were buying up Ambrosiano shares and driving up the price, when all the time it was Ambrosiano money.'

'Precisely. But it was only the collapse of Ambrosiano and the sequestration of its records that allowed anyone to prove that. You can't just walk into the Vatican and ask to see the books. So we might never have known where the money was going if we hadn't got lucky and the Vatican hadn't been careless. The first part of that is Alan's story.'

She opened her eyes again, watching the young man trying to put everything in order. His seriousness looked charming, packaged in his long good looks. John stood by the window motionless as Alan took his turn to explain. 'Yes, well, it came out of looking into the Hart murder case in London.' Caro wondered what on earth the American had to do with Italy. She waited for Alan to explain. 'The Hart affair looks like a bit of a side issue in this. It looks as though he got killed because he got greedy. His Panamanian outfit was an attempt to make an extra profit on the side. What is relevant is that we now know, unattributably, from within Hart's own bank . . .'

'John,' Caro said warningly, 'what have you been up to?'

'Nothing illegal, love. Let him go on.'

Alan looked from one to the other and continued. 'We know that Hart was authorizing large deposits, at good rates of interest for short-term money, in a little bank in Alabama. The speculation is that the Alabamans were using the short-term funds to finance something rather less than legal.'

'Such as?'

'Well,' Alan answered uncertainly, 'John says in that part of the States it would be drugs or guns. He reckons guns.'

'Why, John?'

'Hell, missie,' he replied in his deep-South accent, 'those Alabamans, they been runnin' guns since before the war between the states.'

Caro smiled to herself. He was right. He was also right that no true-bred southerner would ever refer to it as the Civil War.

'Anyway,' Alan went on, 'First Manhattan's own investigators have turned out a list of the Alabamans' largest recent borrowers. Almost all of them were trade-financing deals for exports to Latin America. Two of the borrowers have remained impenetrable to investigation. But both of them when their loans were set up gave matching funds in Popolari accounts in Panama as their security. Popolari issued letters of comfort.'

'And did any money change hands?'

'No,' said Alan, 'that's what's got everybody puzzled. The trade deals must have gone through all right, because the companies concerned got paid amounts which showed them a sizeable profit. But none of it came from Popolari.'

Caro looked at John again. 'John, explain.'

He stood up and started walking. 'I think somebody in Rome got careless. I wouldn't mind betting that the money that did finally come into Alabama was ultimately Vatican money. But we still have to prove it. The Popolari connection gives us the excuse to look.'

She remained unconvinced. 'Are we sure that Popolari is a Vatican connection? The Dottore told me he thought it was, but he wouldn't tell me anything about it.'

Standing gave a wolfish grin. 'I know. He was a little more amenable after the bomb got you, though, and after I'd talked to him. He told me how it works.'

Well, at least being blown up had helped accomplish something, she thought. 'What did he say?'

'He told me that Popolari is an Italian-registered company. It has to be. It's the ultimate beneficiary of the sale over the past fifteen years of enormous numbers of Italian assets. Those proceeds cannot be exported, under Italian law.'

She had to stop him there. She wanted this part done slowly. 'The beneficiary of what assets, John?'

He smiled again. 'Of the sale of the Vatican's holdings in Italian industrial and property companies over the past decade and a half.'

Caro looked at him as though he was insane. He was insane. He had to be. No one could know that.

He knew what she was thinking. 'The Dottore knows. He's been working on it for years.'

Caro lay back against her pillows. She knew the Vatican had been selling its assets, of course. Everyone knew that. The Church had got embarrassed about being seen to be involved in capitalism and Italy's grand commercial corruption. 'Do you mean the profits like the ones out of the deal with Calvi? In 1972. The one where he paid way over the odds for their share in the property company SGI?'

'That is exactly what I mean. And he didn't pay over the odds, considering the deal had a secret clause allowing him to buy their share in the Banca Cattolica del Veneto as well. The Vatican is turning assets into cash and holding them in Popolari, which is, officially, a charitable trust. It just happens to be run by members of Opus Dei, the Roman Church's very own bunch of ultra-right-wing loonies.'

Caro could still hardly believe it. 'You can prove all this?'

'The Dottore can.'

She left the question of getting him to prove it to one side for the moment. The more immediate question was, 'OK, how do they get the money out? To places like Panama? How do they launder it?'

'It's beautifully simple. The Dottore hates it, because it looks quite legal. There's nothing he can do about it. The money is held in Italian banks. It therefore doesn't breach the currency export regulations. But it's held in IOR accounts, the special accounts that Vatican Bank is allowed to maintain in mainstream Italian banks. It is then loaned to the Vatican, through IOR itself. IOR repays the money not to the accounts in Italian banks but to separate accounts held within the Vatican. Each year the accounts are aggregated, as is valid under Italian company law, to show Popolari is still financially healthy, but it's the Vatican which has the use of the money, and can funnel it as it likes through Liechtenstein. All it has to produce for the authorities here are consolidated balances stating the money is still safe and available for use in Italy. But it isn't and Popolari never tries to draw it.'

One detail still puzzled Caro. 'Isn't there, technically, an export of currency in the loan from Popolari's Vatican Bank accounts to the IOR itself? Isn't that illegal?'

John shook his head. 'Not under the Concordat between Church and State. IOR accounts are specifically exempted. They are simultaneously in Italy and outside it, under the current law. And the Vatican helps out too many politicians by giving them IOR accounts for that to be easily changed.'

Caro understood at last. 'So that's why the Dottore talked.'

'Yes, simply. But he can't just publish. He wouldn't survive if he did. What he wants us to do is to find out where the money goes, to prove the Latin-American connection. If we can do that, he'll give us all the paperwork he has.'

It sounded as though it might be true. It sounded as though it might work. But there was one thing she still found almost impossible to believe. 'Are you seriously saying, John, that the Vatican is buying arms in South America?'

He laughed and nodded his head. 'It's a cracker, ain't it?'

Somehow the very thought repelled her. 'But why?' she cried.

He leaned across the end of the bed. 'I don't suppose that

anyone will tell us here. We're also single-sourced on the American story and it's all unattributable. I think Alan needs to get in on the ground with the Hart investigation. I think it's time you brushed off what you know about the American defence industry. And I think it's about time I went back home to Washington, where the real power-brokers roam. But I need your approval for all of that, after we've taken you home. What do you say?'

He was always so persuasive. It sounded so much fun. She knew it shouldn't. She knew it was serious. She knew it might be dangerous. But if he had already worked his way alone and sober through Tom's files, the First Manhattan, Oliver Ireton and the Dottore, wasn't it worth a try? But it was not her decision alone. There were three of them involved.

'What do you think, Alan?' she asked, almost in a whisper.

The young man looked serious. 'I don't know, Caro. I don't pretend to understand all of it. All I know is that John's got me further into the Hart case than I'd ever have got on my own, and deeper than any other journalist I know could have managed. I'm inclined to think it's worth a try. I think, this time, the old fellow may know what he's doing.'

Why not? she wondered. *Why the hell not?* Why not, as John's countrymen would say, just go for it? If he was right, if he was himself again, then why not ride the wave? And if he was wrong, she was due to go to the States in any case. She could go on with her work while he drew all the hostile fire.

'OK,' she said, 'let's do it.'

She interrupted John's rebel yell and Alan's boyish smile with a warning wave of her hand.

'But first, let's get me home. And last, one question. Who killed Father Tomasso Falmi, and why?'

John closed his eyes. He looked so tired. 'I don't know,' he whispered. 'I wish I did. I wish I could tie it in. Maybe Spaccamonti can. I can't. It would make a kind of sense if he worked on the Central or Latin American desks. But he didn't.'

'What did he work on?'

John looked surprised. 'You didn't know?' Caro shook her head. John let out a long deep breath.

'Oh, Jesus.' His brown eyes seemed to be telling her not to read anything into it. It was only coincidental. It was peripheral.

'It was Poland.'

Part Two:
FROM SEA TO SHINING SEA

CHAPTER ONE

As they sat back in adjacent aisle seats in the Tourist Section of the Air India 747 (currently, through any decent agent, the lowest scheduled fare across the Atlantic, especially since they lost a plane near Shannon the summer before last), John Standing closed his eyes and tried to think. It was difficult to think. He had been drinking.

He had seen the look of despair flicker across Caro's eyes as he greeted her with a kiss at Terminal Three Heathrow. She could smell the vodka on his breath, he knew. It wasn't true that vodka didn't have a smell, it was just that the junk most people had to put in it to make it palatable disguised it. Not the same thing at all.

But the hell with it. He had been working hard. Too hard. He had been working well. He knew uneasily that Caro was giving him rope, assuming that, whatever came, she would pick up something worth using out of the Hart affair and its ramifications. He knew that he had sold her the concept of the story despite considerable gaps. Gaps which needed to be closed quickly. It was why he had insisted that Alan Clarke should go on ahead, while he took Caro home for a few days' rest. And they were lucky. They had the perfect cover for being in the States. The preparatory session for the annual autumn International Monetary Fund conference began in Washington DC in a few days. Where else should the *Examiner*'s people be? And if he was no longer accredited to the paper, who'd care? He was only going home.

And what about his drinking? He was working. He could handle it. It was like the old saying: most people begin each morning two stiff whiskies under par. He was only catching up. He had been under-strength for over a fortnight. Still, he knew she worried, if only because she wanted to protect her and the paper's investment. But he wouldn't let them down, he told himself. Not this time. He could not bear the blame.

He was glad she was with him. He was glad it was someone who knew his ways. He had always scared his editors, who always thought he flew by the seat of his pants. It was not that he was not a good hard news journalist. He put in as much time as any at the brutally boring business of accumulating facts. He had always been good at it, and when he was sober he knew he was incomparable. But where most journalists seemed almost to work in the dark, having to turn their undigested raw material over to sub-editors to refine, evaluate and polish, Standing had an editorial nose. What frightened people was that he seemed uncannily to be able to guess which avenues were worth investigating, which a waste of time. He put stories together by intuition and then set about checking the facts needed to prove his hunches right. He was not a proud man. If the evidence simply was not there, he would think again. He did not pursue his intuitions in the face of reason and of fact. But it meant his editors had always had to trust his judgement. And in the end they had decided that it was lost, somewhere at the bottom of a bar-room glass.

She, at least, was trusting him for the moment, though he could not tell her why he was so certain he was right. He tried not to think about it for the moment. He tuned his earphones to the classical channel, coming in on the slow movement of Beethoven's Second Symphony. Why was it, he wondered, every airline classical music channel seemed to have Beethoven's Second on it, rather than one of its more famous brethren? Did the airlines think the others would get the passengers too excitable? In which case why not the Sixth, the Pastoral? Perhaps it was too long. The film in their section of the aircraft was an Indian one, so there was little point in listening in. He had always wondered why Air India, while providing both Indian and European food and apparently segregating passengers on racial grounds in rows, never bothered to ask which film you might want to see. As it was, he had no desire to see *Rocky XXVII* or *Star Trek 33*, or whatever else it was they might be showing. But it would have been nice to be given the choice. He didn't mind watching the Indian one, in any case, so long as he didn't have to hear it. There was something innocent about the random sequences of images Indian popular directors put together. Nut-crunching kung-fu duels, followed by lovers mooning amongst trees or in endless mountainsides in flower, then cut to jiggling disco dancers or the inevitable dance-duet-and-chorus sequence for the two main leads. The narrative lines, with their tragic lovers doomed never even to kiss, betrayals, random violence, and constant breaking off for songs and parties were, in a strange way, almost truer to life than was real art. That was what made them so funny. *Most human life is a farce*, he thought, *where the final joke is death.*

But the word 'innocence' had troubled him. It was the word Medina had used about him what seemed endless years before. 'You have,' he had said, 'the innocence of all our compatriots. They want the world to be perfect, and believe it can be, and for them. I am uniquely unAmerican, Mr Standing, in not believing in perfection. So I make of the world only what I can. Your tragedy is that you do not have the gift most Americans are born with. Only to want what people like them also want. They think it is individuality. They think they are finding themselves. And in a way they are. They are finding individual happiness by only wanting what other people want, by wanting what is available. You have too much imagination to do that. Your vision of the world is personal, and you have not the power to make it. It is your imagination that will destroy you, Mr Standing. Unless you come to me. It is so little to give up. Only hope. Only freedom. Not much to ask to ensure that anything else you can imagine can come true.'

Was Medina right? Was that what the world was like? Was that why John seemed so often, without understanding why, to be running himself towards the edges of destruction? Had he always wanted more than anyone could have?

He did not know. Perhaps he never would. He only hoped (and it *was* only hope) that he had been right in what he said, rejecting Medina's offer. He had said no, because, 'Although all things end, not all things fail.'

131

Medina had not even laughed.

Now, John could only ask himself if he had been right. Perhaps some things always failed. He had failed himself, so many times. Was he going to fail again?

He had not been able to tell Caro or Alan that he smelt the sour track of David Medina along the tortuous path they were unravelling. They would have told him he was obsessed, he was ridiculous. And he was. But he had followed Medina's spoor so often he was certain he was right, though he could not tell them why. To think of TIA in England as being proof was proof only of mental sickness or possession.

Nor had he mentioned Camorra to them either. He felt less guilty about that. He was not ashamed of being afraid. He did not know exactly what part Cutullo's organization played in this whole affair, and he did not propose to discover. Even he did not want to die just yet. Of one thing he was certain. He would keep Caro out of Italy until long after this was all over. He was prepared to lie, or to conceal evidence, and if necessary kill this story, to keep her away from both the potential danger and the actual danger of her guilt over Tom. It was why he had agreed that Spaccamonti was probably right to think Zara Franccchetti had murdered her lover. But he had to keep Caro out of Italy, however happy she had been. He would tie up that aspect of the story himself if necessary (he could always telephone the Dotorre) or send out Alan Clarke, who looked as though he might yet prove to be as good as Iain MacKinnon hoped.

Yes, he would do that. Because an image of Medina, with smiling pale green eyes, kept coming back into his mind. And the thought of Medina, a Roman magistrate, and Raffaele Cutullo's Camorra, the implications of such a connection, were too horrible to contemplate.

He pressed the call-button on the arm of his seat. He needed another drink.

It must have been a new film. It took some time for a stewardess to disengage herself from the vision of two lovers dancing like demented children round a peepul-tree. He saw the look of warning in Caro's eyes as he ordered another vodka and tonic.

132

Caro took her headphones off. 'I wish you wouldn't,' she said, still looking tired and unwell, and sounding plaintive.

He found himself feeling suddenly angry. Offended and rejected. Who was she, after all, to talk? She'd let her work slide for a fortnight in the arms of a prancing Roman judge, while he had been working himself half-insane. But he knew it was not the work which had been gnawing at his sanity, so he kept his anger to himself and said, 'The last one, I promise you, till we're safely mid-town.'

He knew what she wanted him to say. She wanted him to promise not to drink until the job was done. But he could not do that. Not honestly. This was the best he could do.

An hour later the aircraft began its long descent into Kennedy Airport. Caro felt her stomach-muscles tighten with anticipation. It was strange that, after all the travelling she had done, coming into New York still made her feel everything was fresh and new. She was looking forward to being in the city with Alan and John. She hoped Standing still possessed the ability he had had all those years ago to hit the street already running. He always seemed more expansive in New York, not only because the years of unconsciously acquired English reticence and understatement slid away, but also because he too claimed to be a foreigner in this town, though one who spoke the language. 'You have to remember,' he had told her once, 'New York is not America. Hell, I know people in the South who think we ought to cut Manhattan free and sail it back to Europe where the other fags and weirdoes roam.' Then he had grinned his old irresistible smile and added, 'This ain't a city, lady. It's a zoo. They even make you pay to get in.'

She found herself surprised when they finally got on the ground, having swung in low over suburban Queens where each scrubby patch of garden seemed to be filled by the pin-bright jewel of a tiny swimming-pool. She had never liked JFK as an airport much, and had usually found the officials the rudest in the world, with the possible exception of Montreal on a filthy winter's night or any internal border within the mighty USSR. Today, however, all of them seemed to have been through charm school. She noticed that John, having left London on a British passport, produced an American one here. He winked at her as he left her for the US Citizens' entrance saying, 'I bless my parents all the time.' Weren't twin passports illegal, in Britain at least? They left the queues of Indians behind them, trying to explain the complexities of Indian given names to worn-out immigration officials, and came out into one of the small refurbished arrival halls. She felt her stomach-muscles tighten again, and knew it for the onset of incipient paranoia. She always spent her first few hours here in a whirlwind of anxiety, half-expecting to be mugged, raped and left for dead by a priest or a policeman, by any damn one in this violent town. She knew it was irrational. She knew that it would pass and that by the middle of the evening (it was nearly five-thirty now) she would only take the usual precautions (well-lit streets, large thoroughfares and taxis) and settle into having a good time, but for the moment she was glad that she had company.

'Got dollars?' she asked him, knowing the answer, having given them to him herself.

'Got dollars,' he concurred, and swung their cases out into the brilliant, humid, sunshine of a hot summer's afternoon.

The Yellow Cab they climbed into had kitchen-rolls instead of sun-visors. Three bullets with their sleeves beaten out into flat crosses swung from the rear-view mirror. And the windscreen split in three long cracks like a tripod round the mirror.

The big black driver shouted over the insistent thrumming of the ghetto-blaster on the seat beside him, 'OK, where you folks heading?'

Caro tried to make herself heard over the pounding, but it was John who got the man to hear the words, 'Manhattan, Plaza Hotel.'

The roads were filling up with rush-hour traffic, even into the city. There was the usual jam outside La Guardia. They sat in it in the dazzling light while all about them car interiors filled with the heavy fumes of ganja.

'You mind the music?' the driver cried. 'Me I love the music.'

She minded the music very much, but the paranoia took

her over again. She had a momentary vision of being clubbed to death by a big black man using his ghetto-blaster. Foolish, but it silenced her. John was no use either. He just sat back on the dirty plastic seat, pulling at the No Smoking sign taped to the seat before him and grinning.

As they came to the Triboro approaches the driver hit his horn, startling Caro with the noise. 'Will you look at that crazy woman? Hey, lady, lady, this ain't no subway.'

But the woman driving the Toyota beside them merely accelerated, her window still wound down so she could prop up the *New York Post* on the wing-mirror and read it while she was driving.

Their driver hit the horn again as the Toyota pulled away, shouting, 'Looky the lady's tail. That rear-end look like an AIDS case ass on a heavy night in Frisco.'

Then they swung out towards the Triboro bridge and to their left the blank western towers of Citadel Manhattan came into view. She loved it. She loved the long slim slip of an island where the crazy people roamed.

She turned smiling to John, whose eyes were shining as he whispered, 'Well, I guess I'm home. Or something.'

CHAPTER TWO

The doorman at the Plaza did not bat an eyelid as their cab drew up, blasting out street-sounds on the early evening air. Back in London, they had bullied themselves access to the suite permanently reserved for the *Examiner*'s most senior management, for even in the height of a hot humid summer the city had no hotel rooms to spare. As they checked in, Caro asked if there were any messages. The only one was from Alan Clarke, saying he would see them in the Oak Room Bar.

'I thought you said this was his first time in New York,' John said, surprised.

'It is.'

John shrugged his shoulders as a bell-hop took their luggage. 'The boy is learning fast.'

They went up to the suite to shower and change and investigate their several bedrooms. To be honest, Caro preferred the Pierre across the street. But beggars could not be choosers and she counted herself lucky to have the suite. She had stayed in some slums in her time.

They went down through the Palm Court where the string band played each afternoon to the Park side of the big free-standing building. The long Oak Room Bar was dark and cool, with its windows thrown open to what little breeze there was. The Yuppie after-office-hours crowd were in, barking to each other. Alan sat alone in the corner, looking very much at home. He rose to greet them as they struggled their way through the press of solid oak furniture and baying credit-card owners. His eyes and blond hair were bright in the darkness of the room, and one half of his face stood traced by the fringe of a beam of sunlight. He looked enchanted, Caro thought.

'Why didn't someone send me to this city sooner?' he asked

smiling, before pumping John's hand in both of his and stooping to kiss Caro. He summoned over a red-jacketed waiter.

'Er, Dick,' the young man announced, in a curious blend of emphatic hesitation, 'I'll have another dry martini and . . .'

'Whisky sour,' John said, helping Caro to a chair.

Alan looked uncertain, but Caro let it pass. It was too early to fight. But she added, 'A Perrier,' firmly.

'Is it just me,' Alan asked as they all sat down, 'or does this place make everyone feel alive? I keep hoping it doesn't only happen the first time that you come.'

John was about to answer, but Caro interrupted. 'It's like sex, or drinking,' she explained. 'It gets better every time, but as you get older, you find you need it less.'

John disagreed. 'It's because you get it or need it less that you end up feeling older.'

Even Alan, the most charming of the paper's younger bloods, found it difficult to think of any remark which might soothe his older colleagues' tension. He was saved by the returning waiter, but only for an instant. As the waiter began to back off, John flung out his right arm. His left was supporting the big tumbler of sours he was drinking down in one. He set the glass down with a sigh of satisfaction and said to the waiter, whose jacket hem he was now holding, 'Bring me another.'

Caro issued a word of warning by speaking his name softly, once. John smiled at her with innocent open eyes and said, 'Just getting myself acclimatized. Just getting the taste of home.'

She surrendered. 'And bring me a bourbon with iced water on the side.'

Alan savoured his dry martini. 'How do they make these things so perfectly?' he wondered to no one in particular, although aloud. Caro wished they could get off the subject, but John was not to be denied.

'The Ambassador . . .' seeing the puzzlement on Alan's face he explained, 'my father, always used to say you needed servants and room to make the perfect martini. You have to swill water round the glasses, then set them upside down on a block of ice till the droplets freeze. Then you take 'em out on the estate with a bottle of vermouth, a bottle of London gin that's sat in a cavity cut in ice for two and a quarter hours, and a twelve-gauge. Then you get one of the servants to throw the vermouth in the air, as far away as he can get it, and you blast it with the twelve-gauge. When all the rumpus is settled, you pour the gin into the glasses and drink it in a swallow. Course, you make too many in one afternoon, you end up losing some of your servants, but perfection always costs.'

As Alan laughed Caro said, 'I've heard it too often before.'

John was courteously blunt. 'It is a sign of getting old.'

'It is a sign of being sober when too many others weren't. But I didn't know it ran in your family.'

John's voice had slowed to a southern drawl. 'It doesn't, my dear,' he told her. 'I am our only authenticated lush.'

Enough, she thought. They had too much to talk about. John was well enough in control to realize it too. He insisted that they did not talk about it here.

'I know these guys,' he gestured to the room about them, 'or the crowd at the Sherry –' he was referring to Happy Hour in the bar at the Sherry-Netherland Hotel across the road – 'don't look as though they've got a couple of brain-cells between them, but talking about our business here is about as sensible as whispering Stephen Spielberg's private telephone number to a crowd of hopefuls up for an audition, or trying to hand a cheese sandwich to a shark.'

They finished their drinks and went back up to the suite, both Alan and Caro refusing John's offer of a whisky or, better, bourbon. He helped himself to a ten-ounce glass of Jack Daniels. It occurred to Caro he was just coasting, just reacquainting himself with the tastes. Only time would let him settle down with one, in excess or moderation.

'What do you have?' he asked Alan, unfolding his baggily clad legs on the nearest coffee-table.

The young man reached for his notepad, his files having become too bulky, and flicked back through its pages. 'Well, the first thing to say is that there's been a hell of a lot more liaison between London and New York than anyone was letting on back at home. I went to see your friend Mr Chew in the NYPD Fraud Investigation Department, and discovered Inspector Mike Thomas was with him.'

'Mike Thomas is here?' John interrupted, simultaneously startled and pleased.

Alan nodded. 'City Police flew him out specially. Seems that now the coroner's court has brought in a verdict of unlawful killing on Errol Hart's death, they don't want to be snowed under by all the criticism and speculation they got after the Calvi inquests. The reporting restrictions still stand, though. They don't intend to unleash this one on our side of the Atlantic until it's been sorted out.'

'I'm not sure which is my side of the Atlantic,' John said, smiling and taking another swig of his bourbon. 'Let's just say my loyalties are divided. How did Mikey react to seeing you?'

'It was all right. He isn't a proud man, and he's taken so much crap from the Home and Foreign Offices over this one that he'll listen to anyone who might help him sort it out.'

There was something which puzzled Caro. 'Did he say what the Home and Foreign Offices are afraid of?'

Alan flicked on through his notepad. 'He wouldn't really talk about that, but if you want to know what I think . . . I think he thinks they know more about it than they're letting on. Mr Chew at the NYPD thinks so too. He had a visitor from Langley.'

Caro and John both sat up at once. They both listened when people mentioned the headquarters of the CIA. 'Who said?' Caro asked for them both.

Alan laughed to himself. 'Well, it goes back to John having been right, on one count at least. This thing involves something to do with Central America. Apparently he tried to persuade them that the Agency had an investigation of its own going on in that area, were doing it for the FBI. He asked them – very politely, it seems – not to bother themselves with anything outside the continental United States.'

'What did Chew say?' Caro asked.

'Well, that's the funny thing. He claims they weren't even worried about the Central American connection till the CIA came along.'

139

John and Caro both clapped their hands and laughed. Alan looked at them in bewilderment. John explained. 'It's all right, Alan. If you get to work here a little more you'll understand that the one great law of American life is that the Agency always screws it up.'

Alan frowned. 'Maybe. But the thing that puzzled me is that I was certain from London that Mike Thomas knew about the Panamanian connection, and I didn't know where he could've got it from except the same place as us – Mr Chew.'

'Did you ask them about it?' Caro wanted to know.

'Well, yes, as a matter of fact I did. And they fed me what sounded like a pack of lies.'

'Tell us,' John instructed this time.

Alan found his place in his notepad. 'They said that they were satisfied the real investigation ought to centre on the mainland. They said the causes might lie overseas, but they thought the people behind the whole affair were here.'

'That's perfectly possible,' Caro said.

'I agree. And they said it was the warning by the Agency which made them look that much harder at Hart's dealings in the border and coastal states. They're sure the bank's internal investigators are right, and that the answer's in Alabama. I told them, by the way, what I knew about the bank's investigation, though I didn't tell them how I knew and I told them it off the record.'

He looked at the two older journalists anxiously, wondering if he had done right, or if he had jeopardized his sources.

John reassured him. 'There wasn't much else you could do in the circumstances. We came out here without any leverage. You had to give them something to get them on your side.'

'Does that foul things up between you and Stefan Altberg?'

John shook his head. 'No more than they were already.'

But Caro was intrigued. 'Stefan? Stefan Altberg? I didn't know he was one of yours, John. I've been trying to get him off the record for years.'

Standing was not to be further drawn. 'We go back a long way. What I still don't understand is why you're so suspicious of Chew and Thomas. Why should they be overly worried by the Caribbean connection? After all, on drugs cases they'd mainly be concerned about what was going on here. They couldn't spend too much time on detailed investigation of the Mob in, say, Bolivia, though others might. Aren't they just writing off what they can't hope to deal with or track down? Out of all the dealings of this very busy banker only the Panamanian ones seemed to smell at first. If anything, the Agency helped them by refocusing their minds on Alabama.'

Alan disagreed. 'But they know that it goes further. They know there's a tie-in with the Italian funds . . .'

Caro sat up and stared at him hard. 'Do they? Oh, sure, they know by now there's something very tricky about the Alabaman arrangements, but how could they track them down? Aren't we the only people who know about the Italians? And don't we only know because we started, by accident, at both ends? They haven't had time to put it all together. Time, if nothing else.'

John's voice was barely audible even in the uncertain silence of the room: 'How much did you tell them, Alan?'

The young man looked at Caro first, then John. He was blinking. He was trying to remember. 'Nothing,' he said at last, 'I'm sure that I said nothing. Not about Italy or the Vatican.'

John and Caro looked at each other. They were silent for what seemed an age to Clarke. Finally, John spoke for them both.

'All right. All right. In that case we're still ahead. And it looks as though we can stay that way. They've already been slowed up by police and Agency rivalry. With a little luck that will get worse. Chew is also going to be finding it difficult to operate in Alabama, unless he hands the case over to the Federal Bureau, which if I know New York's Finest he'll be trying to avoid. There is no love lost between NYPD and FBI. But we have to control the flow of information and we may well need some help.'

Caro nodded and lit herself another Camel. It was a good job they had a suite, she thought. She and John could reduce an ordinary room to smog in hours. 'John's right,' she said.

'If we're on the right track, the time is going to come when we can only break the story open by breaking it to the police here, at home and in Italy. Though in Italy the Dottore may do that for us. But to do that we have to do a whole raft of other things first.'

Alan sat forward, waiting for her to go on. She looked at John, who nodded.

'First,' she began ticking the points off on her fingers, 'we know about the Alabaman banking operation. Through Stefan. I wish you'd told me it was him before, John.' Standing remained impassive within a cloud of cigarette smoke. Alan was beginning to think he might take up wearing a surgical mask. 'But we can't attribute it to him. Someone needs to go down there to check out our information. Second, we need to keep our lines into the police open. Third, and most important, we need to find out what was being shipped between the States and Central America, its source and destination, and the people in charge of the deal. So how do we cut that cake?'

John leaned forward to pour himself another bourbon. This time they nodded when he looked at them. He got up to fetch them glasses.

'The first part's easy,' he said as he returned. 'You talk to the police, Caro. No disrespect to Alan, but Mike's known you a whole lot longer. It also means we can take their eye off the ball. So that Alan can get down to Langley. If the Agency is running scared, the chances are that someone there will leak. And he can stay in DC. Washington's a leaky town, and it'll be like a garden sprinkler before the IMF Conference. Third, I do not like the sound of any of us going down to Mobile, Alabama, without a full consignment of police cover. I know a great deal more about the South than you two do and those guys they play hardball. What we can do is crack it up here. I think I can get us our evidence.'

'How?' Caro was stern. She had to impose some limits.

John smiled. 'By leaning on a few bankers. There are things bankers will tell each other that they would never tell an outsider. I want to get a few telex machines clacking down to Alabama.'

'Is that legal?' Alan asked.

'It can be,' John replied, 'so long as by the end the inter-bank queries are covered by a piece of paper requesting the information from a legitimate client.'

'Such as?' It was Caro's turn.

John smiled again. 'I have my failings, Caro, but I still keep bank accounts in this city. And I am one of the Virginia Standings, which is worth a little credit.'

Caro looked unconvinced. 'I suppose anything's worth a try. But what if Alan doesn't unearth anything? We still don't have a link between Mobile and the Vatican's nominees in Panama.'

John nodded. 'I know. That's why I think all of us need to be in the capital next week. If it's political enough for the Agency to be involved then Washington's the best place for us to shake it out. But there is one thing we could try before next week.'

They sat waiting for him to speak. Caro for one would not prompt or encourage him. She wanted him working for his living. He looked straight at her.

'Last year you covered the Senate Defense Committee hearings into the Pentagon's buying procedures. You've also done three defence industry surveys. Is there anyone you could shake up who might know where at least we should be looking?'

She stared back at him, knowing what he was asking, but too weary to explain it yet to Alan. 'You still think it's guns, don't you?'

He did not move as he whispered, 'I still think it's guns.'

She sat back, thinking a sigh. Her wrist was throbbing gently. She ran through a list of names in her mind. She shuffled her memories of contacts. 'OK. I'll sort the police out here first.' John blinked acknowledgement. 'Then I'd better head out to Seattle.'

CHAPTER THREE

That night, John insisted they all behaved like tourists. He took them up to Mamma Leone's on West Forty-Eighth where they queued for a table in the big barn of a restaurant in the heart of the theatre district. Caro, by now, found it too big, too brash, too noisy, too full of gawping visitors (like them) and the noisy razzle-dazzle of the city. But Alan was enchanted, and she found herself slipping into sympathy with the young man's delight at his first encounters with the world's most gaily anarchic city, and at the size of his lasagna. Afterwards John took them out into the cooler air and walked them back towards Fifth Avenue past small theatres, bankrupt burlesque shows (their hoardings still filled with posters announcing long-vanished hip-grinding stars), discreet gay cinemas and the big porno-palaces which lit up these stretches of Eighth and of Broadway. Caro still found herself delighted by the names, both of the films and of their stars. One drunken evening long ago she and Tom and John and Iain had plotted a never-to-be-accomplished seizure of one issue of the *Examiner*, in which all the journalists' by-lines would be replaced by names like Pussy Purfekt, Eva Reddi and John Meat, while the headlines would be changed to such atrocities as MAGGIE LAYS 'EM ON THE TABLE and TRICKY SLICKS HIS MISSILE. It was the night John had wanted to headline a piece on corporate wars between the US fast-food chains: STAKE-OUT AT THE TAKE-OUT and insisted the most perfect banner headline ever devised for the *Examiner* was: ELVIS RETURNS FROM GRAVE WITH AMAZING UFO DIET. Caro with a passion for fact had insisted Elvis wasn't dead yet. John had simply stared at her in alcoholic incomprehension. It had been a long, long time ago.

He reminded her of that self again as he ignored the WALK DON'T WALK and PED XING signs whenever he spotted a gap in the traffic, greeting the screaming horns of passing drivers with a decorous wave and chorus of 'Fuck you.' As they made their way back toward Fifth he shuffled them towards Forty-Sixth Street, past Scribner's old palace of publishing offices and bookshop. Art Deco out of Rococo. He swept them on towards Park Avenue, where he stood smiling in wonder at the arches of Grand Central Station, the railroad long since bankrupt and the building turned over into offices, saying, 'You know, I had a friend at Harvard, the best scholarship boy of his year, who swore his grandparents – farming people from Jersey – had only once ever come into the big and evil city, on a day trip, and they never got out of the station. It was the biggest, wildest, glitziest place that they had ever seen, and they thought it must be New York.'

He hailed a cab, assuring them their evening could not be complete without a drink at Twenty-One and Caro found herself at once too exhilarated and exhausted to complain. Somehow, barely an hour later, they were in the bar of a restaurant in Little Italy, at a time of night when civilized New Yorkers avoided it, lurking at home awake and forever anxious. John had insisted they served the best cappuccino in the city, and their grappa was a marvel. The liqueur left Caro coughing too much to either agree or disagree. But the waiters were singing opera, and she almost wept to the strains of Nessun Dorma.

Somehow, eventually, he got them home to the Plaza, his pockets clanking with stolen ashtrays, pepper-mills and cutlery.

Up in the suite, some sort of sanity prevailed. Before leaving for the evening they had asked the assistant manager to book a hotel room, any hotel room, for Alan in Washington DC. On their return, as they stood swaying at the desk, the night clerk informed them politely there were no hotel rooms to be had. 'It's the conference, madam,' he explained, addressing Caro as the most sober of the three. 'With the IMF Conference coming up, every hotel room in the city's been booked for weeks in advance. They book from year to year.'

Caro had wanted to swear. Could they get him into wherever the *Examiner* contingent were staying? She doubted it.

The paper's suite would already be filled with spare-beds and couches for the journalists covering the conference and its planning sessions.

John steadied himself, measuring his words out slowly. 'Could you have three large pots of black coffee delivered to our suite? Immediately?' Then he turned to Caro and Alan to say, as if in explanation, 'Don't worry. It isn't a problem.' Caro did not know if he was talking about the hotel room or his condition.

They and the coffee arrived simultaneously at their suite, and the waiter was startled by the sight and sound of a tall American walking intently down the corridor, taking great care over his footing, singing 'The Star-Spangled Banner' and repeating again and again the phrase: 'Twilight's last gleaming . . .' Caro had always believed it wasn't a song for ordinary voices. Only professional singers could handle its range. She wished John wouldn't bother trying. She never got round to asking why he did.

Safely in the suite, John alternated between drinking cup after cup of black coffee and slapping his face with cold water. When he had decided he was sober enough, he picked up a telephone, keyed for an outside line and dialled a ten-digit number.

'Who are you calling?' she asked, nursing a coffee herself. Alan, wisely, was taking a shower.

John put up a hand to silence her, waiting for the call to go through. She could not make out the tired and angry voice which answered. Standing let the voice get through its necessary complaint before saying, 'I know, Robert, and I'm sorry to call you at this hour. But I'm in the same time-zone as you, so I'm not sleeping either.'

This time she could make out the voice on the other end, as it cried in surprise and delight, 'John? Where are you?'

'I'm up in New York . . . Yes, that's right. I'm here on a job . . . Yes, I'm working, for the *Examiner* of London . . . Yes, again. But as a freelance.'

Caro had worked it out. She should have remembered about Robert, John's brother, who lived down in Virginia. John continued talking.

'No, I won't be able to make it down there immediately. I hope to be down in a few days from now. That's what I'm phoning about. I've got a colleague, young man of the name of Alan Clarke. He's English, but he's human. He needs to come down tomorrow and every hotel in town's booked up till the IMF conference. I need the use of Georgetown. There'll be three of us altogether, but he'll be down on his own tomorrow. Can I give him your numbers, so he can call you from the airport? Maybe you could meet him at the house with the keys . . . Dulles? Fine, I'll organize it.'

He nodded to Caro to assure her all was well without interrupting his conversation.

'Yes, I'm fine, big brother. How are Melissa and the kids? . . . Well, give them my love and tell 'em I hope to see you all soon.'

Something was troubling him as his brother spoke. Something he needed to know before the call ended.

'And, Robert, are Evelyn and Eleanor in Georgetown? . . . I see . . . Yes. Yes, thank you. I think I'd better.'

He hung up, looking sadly towards Caro before pouring himself another coffee. Then he reached for his notepad and began writing as they both waited for Alan.

The young man's legs were thinner under the towelling gown than Caro had expected. She rather liked it. But all his attention was on what John was saying. Standing seemed distant. She understood. He could not explain without also saying things he would rather have left forgotten.

'My brother and I used to own a house in Georgetown. The Ambassador's father, my grandfather, bought it during the war, to make sure the family had a base in the city. He willed it to us. Well, over the years, it was about the only asset I had. My share. About eight years ago, my second wife, Evelyn, remarried, and I was broke, as usual, so I put my share of the house in my daughter Eleanor's name. The court accepted that instead of my paying maintenance. Evelyn wanted to sell my half. The house is already two apartments. But she couldn't without my brother's permission. Robert said no. He said I was always to have a place in the city, even if it was only his apartment, and that my half wouldn't be sold until Eleanor was old enough to decide. She was ten. So I suppose I never did pay my daughter's school fees, really, unless she wants to sell it now and pay back her mother. I don't suppose she'll feel like paying her step-father. He ran off with his secretary four years ago. I can't say as I blame him. Anyway, Robert, my brother, says we can use his apartment. He and his family live in Virginia, out among the white folks, but he has an office in the city. Not that there's much going on in the think-tank business while Congress is out of session. He'll be at home tomorrow, so he'd prefer it if you flew into Dulles Airport, outside the city. It's easier for him to pick you up. But he'll come and get you from Washington National if that's the only flight you can get. He'll take you up to the apartment.'

Caro was puzzled. 'I thought Robert was in the Foreign Service.'

'Oh, he was,' John agreed, 'until the Ambassador died. Bob got caught in the fall-out after Vietnam. They never did forgive the officers who said we shouldn't go in. He stuck it out till the Ambassador died. For which I think the Ambassador was always grateful. But then he quit. He got picked up by a couple of the private think tanks straightaway, though officially he's based at Georgetown University, at the Institute for the Study of Foreign Relations.'

He sat back staring into the dregs of his coffee, thinking about the past. 'Anyway,' he said at last, 'I hoped not to have to take his offer of the apartment, but there you are. What I have done, what I was always going to do, was ask him to lock you into the city's networks. I've written out a list of names of people you should ask him to get you into.' He handed a scruffy couple of sheets of paper from his notepad to the young man. 'The one thing I would be grateful for is that, if there's anything you need from the Institute, you don't ask Robert. He has an assistant called Stephanie Vane. If you ask her, and tell her it was my suggestion, she will understand.'

Alan folded the two sheets of paper into his bathrobe pocket and wished them both good night. Caro told him Eastern Airlines ran a shuttle down to Washington, out of La

Guardia Airport, then said she would see them in the morning.

She was very tired, and both her body and mind were throbbing, and the bound-up wrist still troubled her. It had begun itching furiously. As she was heading to her room, she turned to ask John a question. She wondered why she felt the right to ask.

'What happened to the Ambassador's house, John? What happened to the White House?'

John shook his head sadly, remembering the home of his childhood memories. 'We had to sell it, after he died. The one thing I inherited from him was a talent for living beyond my means.'

She left him to the night, to his country and his memories. As she was leaving she saw him reaching for the bourbon.

When they woke the following morning, John had already gone. The bottle of Jack Daniels was empty. His bed had not been slept in. There were no messages, in the suite or at the front desk. She could cheerfully have killed him. She hoped he had merely started on the work he had undertaken, but there was no real way of telling once he had a drink inside him. She should have stopped him. How could she have stopped him? He was forty-two years old and on the slide. Only he could help himself find the long slippery way back. She wondered when he would resurface.

She told a worried Alan Clarke to stop worrying. She could worry enough for both of them. She also told him to call in daily. If she wasn't in New York she was in Seattle, at the Alexis. She didn't want him going off on his own as well. She told him, in emergencies, to leave messages with the *Examiner*'s office in New York, or with the I M F team staying in the capital. She told him to go catch a flight to Washington. Then she telephoned the New York Police Department.

She was more than half tempted to put out a Missing Person Inquiry on Standing, but she knew he would turn up before long. It was true she had given him a float of five hundred dollars in cash, but that would not get him far as a journalist in the city. It might buy him two or three days. If he had left the city, fares alone would have eaten it away. He would have to come back to her soon, if only to raise more money. She knew his talk the previous evening about accounts in New York City was only that. His financial affairs were no great secret from his friends. He had been nearly broke for nearly a decade, and really broke for the past four years. He was not the kind of man who could have left unused money sitting in a bank account across the Atlantic. Besides, the handing over of his share in his grandfather's Georgetown house (a share which might be worth anything up to a quarter of a million dollars now, depending on the size of the house) was not something he would have done if there had been other ways to keep on paying Eleanor's maintenance. Odd, how little he talked about his family, how rarely he mentioned his daughter. Still, there was no doubt that as a Virginia Standing – damn it, as John Standing himself – he would have access to information. The chances were his reputation was less damaged on this side of the Atlantic than it was in London where people had to live with him. She could not blame him for not wanting to reveal his sources or informants yet. Such names were the nearest thing to gold a journalist ever acquired. Only dire necessity would drag them from him. She knew, as well, that he was up to something over the Alabaman aspect of the story. She was also aware that John was honestly trying to protect them, as innocents abroad.

She smiled to herself at the inappropriateness of any word like innocence. Except used of John, perhaps. She also had no doubts that, if he was even remotely right, a field trip would have its dangers. She remembered the warning she had once been given by a woman journalist in Boston, herself a native of South Carolina. 'You have to remember,' she had said, 'there are still those places in the South where rape is an instrument of discipline against prying women outsiders. But at least you're not black. A few years ago the Klan shot an Air Force colonel. He was black, and he won the Congressional Medal of Honor in 'Nam, for conspicuous gallantry, and they figured that was getting uppity.' Even so, John had warned them off that a little bit too glibly. When he resurfaced for a hand-out she would have to kick him into line. Right now, however, her immediate problem was to get hold of Mr Chew in the Fraud Investigation Department.

They could see her for lunch. After fifteen years in the business it still amazed her what people would do for lunch. They arranged for her to pick them up at the little private office the Department kept in Gouveneur Lane, a short block away from Wall Street.

I've missed breakfast, she thought idly, checking her watch, but then remembered she was at the Plaza and she had room service send it up to her anyway. It occurred to her that the most sensible thing to do with the rest of the morning was to get down to Lenox Hill Hospital and have someone check her wrist. The paper would pick up the bill, and she had no desire to be inconvenienced by it later. She might even get the time to do some shopping, though she doubted it. Then she could call into the *Examiner*'s office in the afternoon. But first she had to book a table at a restaurant.

Her taxi-driver to the hospital confirmed her suspicion that New York never changed. Her taxi-driver down to Wall Street merely convinced her that, though it changed, it always stayed the same. The first driver was a figure out of journalistic fairy-tale, the classic émigré Russian Jew.

'Good morning,' he had greeted her mournfully, 'not that it's good for me. Where are you going?'

'Lenox Hill Hospital, East Seventy-Seventh on Park.'

He sighed deeply, and pulled out. 'Me I always go to Beth Israel. I used to go to Mount Sinai, but now that isn't so lucky for me. I need all the luck I can get. All the troubles I had today.'

'Already?' she could not resist asking, smiling to herself. 'It's only ten in the morning.'

He sighed more deeply, assuming a stolidly lugubrious air. 'Nobody knows the troubles I seen. Nobody knows the troubles I had. You want me to try through the Park? You should have seen the trouble I had this morning. All this traffic. Maybe we try the Park? Probably the Park will be closed. All I got today is bad luck. Will you bring me some good luck maybe?'

She smiled again. 'Maybe I will. Let's try the Park. If things don't get better they can't get worse.'

He shook his head at this heresy. 'Oh, I don't know, I don't. You never seen unlucky till you climbed into this cab.' He pulled the cab around the fountain into the corner of the Park.

She brought him luck. The Park was open. He sped her through the cool of the ancient trees left over from an older city out to the Seventy-Ninth Street exit close by the Metropolitan Museum and in one easy move, green traffic lights all the way, down on to Park Avenue and right to the corner of Seventy-Seventh, saying, 'Well, maybe, lady, you brought me some luck after all. Maybe now you get lucky too.'

She rather hoped he was right. The hospital had given her as clean a bill of health as she could expect. It was the cab driver down to Wall Street who reminded her that there were sourer things in this society too. He was another émigré, German this time, who spent the whole journey raving about the influx of Haitians. As far as he was concerned they had everything possible wrong with them. They were black. They spoke funny. And too many of them had become cab-drivers. 'They don't know how to drive. They ain't got no patience. Everything done on the horn. Great sense of rhythm, maybe, but they don't understand machines. Let's send them all to Castro.'

Caro knew better than to interrupt a cab-driver in full flight, but having to put up with it stalled in the city's dense oppressive midday traffic, the humidity at its most intense and not even the comfort of a breeze created by movement, finally broke her temper, and she made him drop her at Canal Street and Bowery. She could walk a mile and a half.

She began to regret it within moments, as she stood on the Lafayette Street corner of Foley Square, the traffic pumping and diving about her. She had forgotten the intensity of the city's heat, both reflected and refracted in asphalt, sidewalks, granite and brutally polished plate glass. It took her an age to cross Park Row at City Hall Park. The kilometre or so down to the corner of Wall Street at Federal Hall took her half an hour and left her melting. She had not realized how much the bomb-blast had taken out of her. Now she knew how frail she was, how vulnerable to exhaustion, and how much she would have to lean on Alan and on John. She would have to tell him there could be no late nights, or none like the previous one. She would have to get him back and working.

She would also be late. At this hour of day the traffic was impenetrable. She would have to continue on foot. She tried to telephone from the call-box on the corner by Federal Hall. The machine swallowed her last quarter. She stood surrounded by banks and brokerages which housed the greatest concentration of telecommunications equipment in history and found herself unable to phone half a mile.

She thought for a moment about walking to the Chase Manhattan Plaza. She knew there were more phones there. But instead she dived into the relative cool of Wall Street's skyscrapered canyon, leaving Washington and the New York Stock Exchange behind her.

Her spirits lifted slightly, entering the heartland of the home of money. She still found herself moved by Wall Street's curious mixture of shabbiness and power. It was narrow, the road surface was terrible and constantly under repair, the exteriors of the great financial palaces thrown up at the turn of the century seemed endlessly grey and dusty. Grit got everywhere. The subway was disgusting, all squalid dirt and graffiti. But inside those buildings, beneath the grime and the linear decoration, lay the legacy of the Robber Barons who had made the street what it was. Here, more than anywhere, the world she delighted in, the world she made a living reporting, put aside the masks it wore elsewhere of style or grace or simple opulence or social responsibility, and revealed its dusty, dirty ageing reality, the relentless face of money.

At Water Street the buildings began to thin out, more widely spaced, and newer, in the less fashionable stretch of Wall Street down to the waterfront and the East River. She turned left down Front Street, tipping an imaginary hat to the anonymous modern offices of Britain's International Westminster Bank, and right again, to the Gouverneur Lane entrance of the building on the corner, the renovated warehouse with its view of the sudden summer flash of the river's grey-blue waters, full of the promise of the smells and savours of the sea. They were waiting for her in the third-floor lobby.

It went well. It occurred to Caro that while bankers were bored and blasé about being treated to the good life, policemen were not. They had lunch at one of her favourite New York restaurants, on the top floor of the old Bankers Trust head office on the corner of Wall Street and Nassau, retracing her steps of earlier in the morning. It was cool and light and airy, lined with blue and white tiles. It felt more like a swimming-pool than expensive floor space in the heart of a financial capital. That may have been because, it was rumoured, the original décor had been put in by the great Pierpont Morgan at the end of the nineteenth century, as a setting for his Wall Street mistress (he would call on her at lunchtimes; he scattered mistresses wherever he was likely to go so that he should never be without one), and had wanted her in a bath-house, to remind him of the dubious pleasures of his youth.

It was also, like all restaurants in the area, quiet, private, and discreet. None of the waiters even glanced at the scruffy raincoat Mike Thomas carried with him everywhere, even in this heat, like a talisman from London. Nor did they raise an eyebrow at what was left of Mr Chew's Brooklyn accent after twelve years dealing with the villains of this quarter. (To her surprise, he appeared no more Chinese than she did.)

They were both relieved to see her. Experience counts for something. So does seniority. She did not tell them anything like all of her suspicions. But she did tell them she would try to keep them informed of anything she might come up with in the work she, John and Alan were doing, of which, she was careful to point out, the Hart case was only a part. She also warned them that she would not hesitate to call on their assistance. They all found it a satisfactory arrangement. But one thing was to trouble her afterwards. One thing Mike Thomas said as they were leaving.

'Look after John,' he said. 'There was a time when I would have followed Standing anywhere. He was that good. But he always had a tendency to try to cover everything. He's almost too ambitious. You have to remember that, for us, this is a murder case. Once we've solved it I'll go home gladly and forget about it. Make sure that John does too. I know there's

154

more to this than we've seen so far, and so do you. But I won't go on for ever. I'll only go after what I need. If I know John, he'll want to take it further, and try to link it up with every bit of funny business anywhere in the world. Tell him Mike Thomas says to be satisfied with local victories. We can't always be chasing from one end of the world to the other. We can't cover the thing from sea to shining sea.'

She might have worried more about John if she had known what he was doing. He had not slept the previous night. Not because of drink, for once. So far he was right about that. He had the tolerance levels of the truly hardened drinker. He got as drunk as anyone else, though it showed rather less, but the catastrophic decline into incoherence, loss of memory, loss of reason, did not come as it did with most other people, gradually. He was beyond that. He existed on an alcoholic plateau. Most times he could drink as much as he wanted there, but eventually, without warning, his body would rebel, and a single drink would drive him over the edge. He spent a great deal of his time these days trying to guess where that one drink might be hiding.

So he had not been wakeful because of drink. He could not sleep because he was thinking. He was wondering if he was finally losing grip on his reason. He knew what he thought was happening, and he knew it made a kind of awful sense. He also knew there was no one he could talk to about it. The chances were they would say he was mad. Even if they did not, just to imagine what John imagined was dangerous. He knew more than most how lethal it might be.

He also knew there was a story there. A publishable story. Something which he and Caro could come to grips with and survive. He found himself believing that he did not want acclaim for himself, not any more. He had had enough of that in years before. But Caro deserved it. She deserved her hour of legend and of glory in the shabby, necessary trade they both pursued. The question remained: how to get it for her?

He knew, as surely as his journalist's nose had ever known anything, that the story of Errol Hart's illicit loans (for that was what they had been, though masked as short-term deposits) to Alabama would unravel of its own accord. Mike Thomas and Chew would see to that. All that Alan and Caro had to do was to stay close to them, to make sure they were the first journalists with the details. He knew as certainly that one error at the Vatican, in making Popolari the guarantor of a few American export credits, gave them the link they needed to tie the Church of Rome into illegal banking operations in the Caribbean. The Dottore could be trusted to supply the rest, Caro could be kept out of it. Caro could be kept safe. More than anything now, after Rome, he wanted to assure her survival. Whatever was happening there – and to speculate was madness; it meant turning again to the one subject he could not tell anyone about – was out of control. Tom's murder had somehow been deliberately calculated to call them into play. But that was supposition again, in the guise of his enemy's name.

Medina, Medina, Medina . . .

He had, at last, to admit it to himself. Even if there was nothing he could do about it.

He had tried hard enough before to impress the old, cynical, derisive master. His own unwitting father's friend. What would the Ambassador have made of them now? He had tried, but he had not succeeded. How could he hope to succeed this time?

Yet there was a story. With or without the old man. Somewhere, he knew, there was a link between Errol Hart's operations and those of the Roman Catholic church. Had they involved Father Tomasso and the Polish Office in the Vatican Secretary of State's Department?

But that was madness.

He could not bring himself to consider it. Then his colleagues would be right about his weakness for conspiracy theories. It was insane. And yet, and yet, as he had said before, just because fear of conspiracy is one of the signs of madness, that does not mean no conspiracies exist.

But his first duty lay in establishing what the Vatican's funds were used for, and what Errol Hart had been – perhaps unknowingly – financing. The answers to those questions lay in two places, dangerous places to ignorant outsiders.

The answers lay, he was convinced, within the jungle-telegraph system of Washington, and in the Caribbean.

He had persuaded Caro and Alan to undertake necessary tasks; but if he was right, he would have to use up his American reserve of favours and he would have to take the risk. A new, young innocent like Alan would be safe in Washington. At least, he would with another Standing to look after him. At least until Medina arrived for his annual IMF party. And Caro would head out to Seattle soon, out to the Pacific, across the Great Republic laid out on the maps from sea to shining sea . . .

So he had to go down to the other waters, the turbulent blue waters in which so much of the sombre history of his country had been written. He had to go to the Caribbean.

And he needed money.

That thought more than any other kept him awake that night. He knew where he could get it. He had always known, but never told anyone, not even Tom and Caro, that there were funds available. But he had always rejected their use before. Some obscure sense of morality had stopped him.

He needed to walk, to think, he needed the sad air of this city in those early hours when even it was peaceful.

As he walked down Fifth Avenue in the fitful hour after dawn, bits of paper, sometimes even a leaf, skittering like metal foil down the sidewalks and the gutters, avoiding bag ladies, the glances of cruising policemen and the early morning drunks returning home from parties or from lust in the razzle-dazzle centre of Manhattan, he could not help but think about Medina.

John had known the old man all his life. Medina was always in and out of Washington. Had any administration ever been free of the taint of that wonderfully necessary man? They had left him alone because he was rich; there was nothing so well respected in these United States as wealth on a colossal scale. And he was useful. His business interests meant he could go where no official would be welcome or where, because of political circumstance, no government officer would wish to be seen. He had been an expedient channel of communication that successive governments had thought was always deniable: he could be dismissed as a private citizen acting without authority.

However, no one dismissed Medina so easily. It was not possible to use him without being asked the occasional favour in return, without having to turn a blind eye to infringement of legality. He had used his unequalled access to place himself beyond conventional morality and law. And not in one country only. What he did for the US government he did for others wherever he had dealings.

He was clever, though, much cleverer than most governments. With all his power, if he had ever posed a radical threat to the relationships between nations they would have turned on him and destroyed him. But he did not work like that. What he loved and what he fed off was crisis, chaos, uncertainty. He played the gaps in government policies, manipulating nations when they did not really know what they wanted.

South Africa had always been the measure of his genius. The West had always been schizophrenic about South Africa. Its moralists declared the apartheid system to be insupportable, and even had an impact on government policy. Yet no Western government wanted South Africa, with its huge natural resources, to fall into chaos and decay. Through a man like Medina, financial assistance, deniable messages of comfort, even weapons could be delivered, without any government involvement. More elegant still was Medina's connection with South Africa and Russia, the two greatest producers of gold and diamonds in the world. It was in their interests to keep the markets in gold and diamonds as stable as possible, just as it was in the interests of the West. But since South Africa could have no direct dealings with Moscow, being sternly, officially, anti-Communist ('Woe to the West if the black Commies ever seize South Africa,' was their constant refrain), it needed someone like Medina, with business interests in Russia, to liaise on its behalf. Once again, without official involvement, Medina allowed two supposedly hostile governments to fix the market in their most valuable exports. No American administration, however right-wing, could then blame Medina's dealings with Moscow, which were so much a part of the safeguards of the West.

But Medina went further than that. He looked at the demography of South Africa, at the relentless migration of all African peoples southwards as the Sahara Desert expanded. He looked at the enclave of white supremacy, outnumbered by its own black citizens and all its hostile neighbours to the north, and knew it would not last. So for twenty years he had financed black liberation movements in South Africa, through chains of intermediaries. When the Blacks finally came to power, they might well seize the holdings he had in their country, but they would unknowingly return them to him in his disguise as the beneficiary of their cause.

The South African authorities suspected what might be going on. Medina was not the only man who played such games. Merely the biggest. But he was careful to ensure that, in his official person, he turned in sufficient numbers of the black revolutionaries he supported to the authorities to make the South African government believe he did what he did only to infiltrate the freedom fighters on its behalf. The South African government wanted desperately to believe him. It wanted to believe its allies, its secret, untrustworthy friends.

What went for South Africa went everywhere. Medina used the unwritten, unadmitted codes by which the world is actually run. Waiting always for the moment of disaster, the crisis, the catastrophe when, by playing all sides at once, he could make a profit in all quarters.

He himself remained invulnerable, isolated in his webs of holding and subsidiary companies. But the tracks of his operations were sometimes visible. It was possible to deduce what had happened, even if there was no way of proving who had made it happen or why. John had examples of that. Still. Material for the series he had been working on four and five years before. He would have to give it to Caro. She was worth that. And it was ideal material for her book. It was time people knew how American governments financed the Soviet Union while publicly attacking it as the bloody heart of communism.

So Medina was no stranger to Washington. And because he was a charming, civilized, gracious man, he and the Ambassador had become friends. Perhaps that was why Medina had let John live, despite his rejection of the old man's final offer.

They had met in London, four years before, in Medina's secure house overlooking the river at Chelsea, John's story and his life lying a shambles about him, and Medina had made the offer. John Standing was the only man ever to have worked out all the ramifications of a major Medina project. It was true he could not prove most of it – not enough to satisfy the newspaper's libel lawyers or a court of law – but he knew. And Medina admired him for it. He had been taken up into the private study, with all the microphones turned off, and Medina had laid before him the kingdoms of the world.

'You understand,' Medina had said. 'You have the necessary vision. You would not have been able to fathom me and my operations if you were not greatly daring. You dared to dream a great dream, Mr Standing. You dreamed my dream almost as well as I. It is what I have waited for all my life.'

The green eyes had shimmered in the gloom of a London afternoon and Medina had looked almost happy, explaining the terrible passion which drove him on.

'The world passes, in a dream, Mr Standing, and all things end. Do you believe, for an instant, that all the power and money the world can bring me is any recompense for that? I think you know me better. I think you are like me. What can we do but play the foolish shadows of the world which the world takes to be real? What can we do but dream greatly, and make the pitiful spectacle of the earth dance attendance on what we imagine? Nothing matters, Mr Standing. Nobody cares. There is only the clear, logical pleasure of the game. And I have waited more years than you can imagine to meet someone who imagines as well as I. Come join me, Mr Standing. Let us play chess with all the world.'

John had been tempted, but he did not give in.

Not that the world could understand that. It had only seen him falling. It did not know that he was paying the price for refusing something he believed was utterly, irredeemably, wrong.

Medina had been gentle with him. And cunning. Two days after their final interview, a bank account had been opened in Standing's name at the New York office of a Swiss investment bank. It was not a large amount, by Medina's standards. Only fifty thousand dollars. There were no strings attached. Except that John could not return the funds. The bank had patiently explained it had no authority to return the money to its source. The one cheque John had ever issued against the account had been one in Medina's name for the whole amount. Medina never banked it. Standing never used it. Yet while the account existed Standing was compromised. There was an account in his name, opened after the dropping of a series of articles on David Medina. The inference was obvious. There was nothing he could do about it.

So for four years Standing had refused to touch the money, though there had often been times when he needed it. It smelt of bribery. It smelt of blood. The money remained in the interest-bearing current account, slowly growing. According to the annual statements he received, his balance stood at nearly seventy-five thousand dollars.

He turned off Fifth Avenue through the silent Rockefeller Centre.

Should he use the money now?

His feet led him up the anonymous affluent canyon of the street. He hardly knew where he was going, drifting back up the route of the previous night's walk as though by memory or instinct, up to the fringes of Times Square, where the last disconsolate hookers of the night were drifting away to breakfast. It felt like a good idea. But he wanted to be away from it, out of it. Away from the places where the city's public roamed as through a vast street theatre. He wanted somewhere quiet, ordinary, gone-to-seed. He wanted some place like himself.

He drifted west through theatreland, through the fringe world of old seedy hotels and the beginnings of the tenements which ran north of here to Harlem and beyond. Up on Ninth Avenue he turned, without any destination in view, past second-hand clothes stores, laundries and hopeful bakeries awaiting the arrival of the middle class in some never-to-be-seen gentrification.

There was a coffee-shop open across the road, across the broad avenue where at this hour only delivery lorries nosed. Right now, by some aberration of the spirit, even he would

161

rather eat than drink. He sat down at the shiny formica counter and ordered their standard breakfast of bacon and eggs (scrambled), wheat toast and coffee. They would serve him hash browns anyway, though years in England had put him off eating potatoes at breakfast. They were already busy, with a mixture of types. Truckers, shop-girls, secretaries, young executives snatching a bite and a coffee before setting off to earn a dollar. '$2.99,' the menu shouted, 'More Bang for your Buck!'

He settled down in front of his coffee, waiting for the first explosion. This was New York after all, at a time of day when no one pretended to be friendly. One of the young executive types sat down beside him and ordered coffee, sausage, hash browns and scrambled eggs – 'I want those really well done. Write it down.' The young waitress whose English sounded Austrian, her blonde hair sweaty from an hour's running already, took the order down and went off clearly wondering who this guy thought he was. She had a point. In this town you scrambled an egg by throwing it out on a griddle and forking it around some. It came the way it came. All glop. What did he think he was saying, asking for it well done?

Sure enough, when it came back he made a fuss. 'Didn't I say well done? Didn't I tell you to take it down? Gimme your pad. Come on, give it to me here.' He snatched it from her hand and John suddenly felt like hitting him, he felt the need for naked aggression.

'What is this?' he felt like saying. 'Leave the kid alone, you mindless fuck. How would you like serving glop to half-assed dorks at this hour in the morning?' But he did not, because it would only be indulging the same thing Brooks Brothers Boy beside him was indulging. There were people who needed a shot of aggression each morning to prove to themselves that they were human, that they were alive. It was a game every New York waiter and waitress understood even if they hated it, as Miss Austria did, taking back the plate.

She would take the plate back to the kitchen. The glop would come off of the plate and on to the griddle. The glop would burn and be returned to the plate inedible. The plate would be returned to Brooks, who would eat it all up anyway, his point already made, and his blood-vessels opened by a little righteous indignation.

Who were these people? Why did they need this crap to live? He forked some egg on to a piece of toast and folded it into his mouth.

He knew. John Standing was the man who knew. That was what they had called him, years ago at Groton. He knew that they were ordinary men and women caught by hope and lack of talent in ordinary half-satisfied lives. People who took what chances they could get to prove they were alive, and had no way to do it, except by pushing around other people.

They were not exceptional. The only thing that made them different from David Medina was wealth, intelligence and opportunity. Maybe John himself was just like them. He had felt like it a few seconds ago. But, no; they were all different from Medina. Some differences in degree were differences in kind as well. It was hardly likely that the harassed and harassing idiot by his side would manipulate the lives and deaths of millions as easily as he had hassled this one waitress.

It took Medina to do that.

Standing paid and went back out into the street. It was brighter now, already hot. It would be an intolerable day.

He still did not know if he could bring himself to use Medina's tainted money, even if he was convinced he would be using it against the man himself. But even on the practical level, Medina would surely know if any of the money was finally touched. Wouldn't he just be alerting the old man? Did it matter if Medina was forewarned that the time had come to settle their unfinished business?

He didn't know. He did not know how to decide. He went walking through the ever more quickly filling streets.

He walked uptown towards the Lincoln Center, along the edges of Hell's Kitchen, aware of the fact that he was a shambling potential victim. He had parked a hire car here once, with a fifth of bourbon on the floor in front of the passenger seat, and had returned to find the windscreen broken, the paint-work scratched, the on-side door ripped clean away from its hinges and dumped on the sidewalk by someone desperate enough to do all that in order to lay hands on the booze. It wasn't that John could not empathize with whoever had done it, he just thought they had over-reacted.

Enough. He headed down towards the Park. He would spend some time beneath the trees with the joggers and the junkies.

He spent too long, half-slumbering beneath a venerable oak. By the time he returned to the Plaza, Caro had left for the day. He took a shower, and decided.

He wanted to see a manager, not some lackey. The first appointment they could give him was noon. He passed the intervening time drinking bourbon and coffee and resting. He was beginning to feel tired. When he got to the bank's offices in Park Avenue he wished at once he had a better suit. Their suite, just up from the new Bankers Trust head office, had that effect, all neatly laid out in prim and proper high-bourgeois Swiss taste. He disapproved, in any case, of banks fashionably moving their offices up to mid-town, especially along Park Avenue. Banks belonged down on Wall Street in the old commercial heart of the city, just as, in London, they belonged in the City itself, not in Hampstead or in Mayfair. He had noticed with pleasure that just as the banks were moving uptown the publishers were moving down, to Twenty-Third Street or beyond. It was as though, always short of money, they were carefully arranging that the Garment District, in the Thirties mainly west of Seventh Avenue, should always lie between them and their bankers, as a kind of fire-break. No creditor or bailiff got through the New York Garment District alive. The men in furs had too much practice dealing with their kind.

The manager was Swiss, efficient, young. John sat in his over-air-conditioned office uneasily explaining what he wanted.

'I assume you know,' he began, 'who my account was opened by.'

The manager neither smiled nor blinked as he replied, 'I could not help noticing your account. It is very easily the smallest we hold. I know that your referee when the account was opened was Mr David Medina. I assume that is why we accepted it. It is not worth our while normally to handle such a small and inactive account.'

John knew too much about the business to be angry. He wondered if Medina owned the bank. 'I do realize that,' he said, 'but you will be pleased to hear I don't intend to leave it dormant. Tell me, who else sees statements of my account but me?'

The manager looked faintly offended. Only faintly. He had been too well trained to antagonize a customer. Any customer. 'No one, except myself, and the accounts clerk in Geneva, who files the master records.'

'I see,' John replied, not knowing if the man could be believed. 'So my . . . referee . . . doesn't see copies of my statements.'

'No. That would be highly irregular. We are a Swiss bank, Mr Standing. I think our reputation for confidentiality is well known.'

John pressed a little harder. 'So there is no way in which Mr Medina could get a statement of my account?'

The young man hesitated. 'That isn't quite the case. The I T I Group, of which Mr Medina is Chairman, is a major shareholder in this bank. Mr Medina is, nominally, a director, though he never attends board-meetings, always sending an alternate. None the less, any of our directors are entitled to see statements of any account, if they should formally request it. I suppose Mr Medina could do that.'

It made sense. Even if they were not managers, directors needed to have access to all a bank's information if they were to fulfil their legal duties and obligations. Even Swiss law and practice would allow that. After all, Swiss bank directors were traditionally even more secretive than their employees. Something nagged in the back of his mind, though. Something about nationality or residence requirements. Was Medina a Swiss citizen as well? It hardly mattered, though it would be interesting to know what the price of citizenship had been.

John turned his attention to the banker. 'And has Mr Medina ever done that?'

'Not to my knowledge. And I would know.'

Yes, John thought, *I expect you would.* 'But you wouldn't tell me even if he had, presumably. I assume confidentiality cuts two ways.'

The banker did not reply. Instead, he asked, 'Can I ask you why you want to know this?'

John nodded. 'I told you I did not intend to leave my account dormant. There are matters I wish to pursue. I trust to our mutual advantage. I am asking two things of you. First that you accept that, despite the smallness of my account, the original reference, from someone so creditworthy as Mr Medina, indicates that I am good for such calls as I may make upon you. Second, the business I have in mind is a project I believe Mr Medina will wish to be part of, but I do not wish him to know the details until I am fully ready. I am therefore asking you not to pass on any information concerning my account to him, until you receive my instructions.'

It would not work, of course. Medina would be told, in one way or another. There were always ways. There were always open files in offices left vacant for a moment. There were always misdirected telexes or mislaid photocopies. That did not matter. What did matter was that he should have a line of credit now.

'My business,' he explained, 'will take me about the United States, and probably abroad. I intend to use the current contents of my account to cover my expenses. I need drawing arrangements against it.'

'Can you give me some idea of where your itinerary will take you?' the banker asked. 'I could then arrange drawing rights with our correspondent banks.'

John shook his head. 'My movements are likely to be erratic. A credit card of some kind would be best.'

'Of course. That is simple enough. Will Mastercard or Visa serve?'

'Admirably. Or better still, give me both. With a credit limit equal to the balance of my account. Shall we say thirty-five thousand dollars on each card?'

The banker reached for two authorization forms. 'I see no difficulty with that, provided I can instruct the credit-card companies to invoice your account with us direct, so that I can arrange payment each month, either of the full amount or some agreed percentage. That would be simplest. If you are travelling. Would that be satisfactory?'

'Perfectly. When can I collect the cards?'

'With a recommendation from this bank, perhaps two hours. You could collect them at the front desk at, say, two-thirty?'

'Admirable. I shall gladly mention your competence to Mr Medina.'

He went out into the brilliant sunshine of the afternoon wondering how much time he had.

That same morning Alan Clarke made what he would come to realize in the end were the two worst mistakes of his life. He failed to go directly to La Guardia airport to take a shuttle to Washington. And he failed to tell Caro of his change of plan and the reason he had made it.

It was understandable enough. He was young. He was ambitious. He was new to the most hypnotic, enticing city in the world. He had begun to break a major story, only to find two old hands seemingly take it away from him. And he thought he had the jump on everyone with one piece of information he could exploit alone and guarantee his position on this reporting team.

He did not, in other words, know any better.

He had not bothered, or thought it yet worthwhile, to tell Caro or John that he had called on an old friend from Cambridge (if any of his friends could be called old: they were both barely twenty-six) now working for a New York investment bank.

He had wanted to see her in any case. She was clever. She was pretty. She was funny. It was an irresistible combination. They had gone to a bar she knew. Then a restaurant. And then another bar. He had met several of her friends, bankers and brokers to a man. And then he had, to their mutual pleasure, gone home with her.

Not so very unusual, the world being the place it is, the young being what they are. What was a little unusual, he might have realized, had he thought about it, was one of her friends showing no surprise at what he had to say about the Errol Hart affair. Suggesting in fact, that Alan might be well advised to stop his prancing round the banking fringes of the matter and look at the most serious aspect of the case.

Alan had risen to the bait, demanding to know what might be more important than international fraud and murder. The friend had smiled and said that everyone on Wall Street knew Errol Hart had been Chief Accountant to the Mob in one of the biggest cocaine operations in the country. If Alan wanted to know more, he had better call on the friend at his office as soon as he was able.

How could Alan resist? From the beginning John Standing had said he believed the operation would involve either guns or drugs. What if he was wrong in choosing guns? He was liable to make mistakes after all. And if it was drugs, and Alan got on to it, his position would be secure, he would have his moment of glory; and, if a major banker was tied into the Mob, perhaps, as some now rumoured, the line of criminally financed corruption spread all the way to the top. He might well yet need John's knowledge of the ways of Washington. He might yet be able to offer Caro the most extraordinary tale of government illegality for her forthcoming book.

But he was not a complete fool. He knew he had to cover his options. John Standing might still be right, and he would still have to follow Caro's instructions. He would have to go to Washington. He would have to try to breach the paper security around the CIA. But what if, as had often been rumoured, the CIA financed and connived with drugs smugglers as cover for its political operations? It seemed at least as much a possibility as anything John had suggested. Nor did he make his appointment with Tom Stoddart (the friend) at once. He took certain elementary precautions. He checked with Mike Thomas and Mr Chew, who told him that, indeed, there were rumours implicating the dead man with the Company, the Organization, Our Thing, The Men in Suits. And he had casually mentioned the name Tom Stoddart, which had provoked no comment and no warning. He had checked with his girlfriend as well, who told him that, although Tom did some drugs, there was nothing else against him.

After that, Alan made the earliest appointment he could, on the morning Caro and John believed he was leaving for Washington. If he had thought a little further he might have realized that dealing with brokers was not necessarily a guarantee of personal hygiene and safety. He might have guessed that if Errol Hart could be implicated in the circles of corruption, then no one was necessarily safe from the sudden vengeance of the families of the underworld. He might have remembered how recently the security systems at one of the grandest brokerages on Wall Street had been penetrated to such a degree that they had accepted cash deliveries of a million dollars at a time, in a suitcase, from an unchecked client, to play the commodities market. And when the FBI had approached the firm about the matter, someone at Hutton had tipped off the cash-rich client, who had withdrawn his presumed drug-profits before the FBI could investigate and freeze the funds. If a firm as grand as Hutton could be compromised (at the very least embarrassed) in such a way, what hope was there for an innocent, unassisted outsider?

But he thought no such thoughts as he called on Mr Stoddart or in the days thereafter. He kept whatever he was thinking entirely to himself. John and Caro never knew about it.

Stoddart had told him he would be working the floor at the new Commodities Exchanges, four exchanges sharing one vast trading floor in the World Trade Center. They were to meet in the Visitors Gallery at 11.15 a.m. Alan left his suitcase with the bell captain at the Plaza.

He was early at the twin towers of the World Trade Center, now the tallest buildings in the city and, to old friends of Manhattan like Caro, a grievous assault on the skyline, tacked on the southern corner of the island, drawing the eye and the balance away from the Empire State and Chrysler buildings in the middle of the town. He went up to the Visitors Gallery anyway, to watch the apparent chaos of the floor. There were parties of delighted schoolchildren watching adults pursuing games even more ferocious than theirs in what seemed like one vast playground. During the short bursts of trading the noise reached levels which would have been illegal in any factory. Main agents stood by banks of visual-display units and telephones relaying instructions to the dealers on the floor, using hand signals because nothing they said or shouted could be heard. Nothing, not even thought, could be heard above the ululating of the traders, desperate to make their deals, balance their books, and come out with a profit in the brief frantic periods of trade. It was a young man's business. Most of the best started at eighteen. Alan would have been an old hand by now had he chosen to go into it. But even in London, and more so here, not all the background and education in the world was any advantage. The dealers came from every sort of background, though the men who ran their firms were often old-fashioned grandees. It did not matter if you came here from Harvard or Peoria High. What mattered was that you had the gift. You had to know how to buy and sell, under unimaginable pressure, dealing with millions as others played with pennies, and come out showing a profit. The child of a second-hand auto merchant or a fruiterer was as likely, more likely, to have the gift than the scion of six generations of Boston Brahmins. On the floor the only background that counted was your trading record. They lived hard, these dealers, and, if they were good, earned big money young. Money they often speculated on this floor on their own account. They would be burnt out by thirty but, if they were lucky, they would come out rich. And if they were unlucky? They were unlucky. It was a world which had no time for losers. There were too many hungry eighteen-year-olds crowding through the doors.

Alan looked down on the whole bright, bawling, electronic spectacle in delighted fascination. It seemed to him the summit of the city's character. But then, he could not see the people who mattered, the people who lasted, men and women in suits back in their offices, tied to this circus by landlines, whose duty, pleasure and profit it was to reckon up the gain, the loss.

Tom Stoddart was thinking of them as he came up to the Visitors Gallery. 'Strange, isn't it?' he said, looking at the eager moonfaced children. 'Kids love the trading floor. Adults love the trading floor. The American Dream. The sudden massive killing. But it doesn't last, you know. They don't last.' He took in the whole trading floor with a wide sweep of his hand. 'They are the infantry, the mercenaries, we send in to do our work for us. It's the generals back at staff headquarters who win the really big medals. And the money they make lasts.'

'So what are you doing down here?' Alan could not resist asking. 'Why aren't you back at your office with the other generals. Where's the red stripe up your trousers?'

Stoddart smiled. He was a sandy man, in his middle thirties, Alan guessed. What Stoddart lacked was the healthful tan most of the American middle class aspire to. But tans had grown uncool. Skin cancer. Hispanics. He had the sort of complexion which would mottle and redden and burn while others were just getting comfortable. With his sandy hair and his militarily cropped moustache and pin-stripe suit, he seemed to pale into insignificance in the colour and vivacity of the floor.

'Most of us started down here,' he explained. 'You have to see some active service, win some decorations for gallantry under fire, if you're to have a career as a staff officer. And we all come down now and again. Half a day a week, a month, whatever, to keep our hands in and keep an eye on the trading operation. Visiting the front, you could call it.'

Alan found himself continuing the military motif. 'And what was your most heroic action?'

Stoddart smiled his thin smile again, a pale hole in his pallid features. 'Oh, they still talk about it round these parts. I'm still living off it. Literally. It made me more money than you can possibly imagine. Didn't do my clients any harm either.'

Alan waited. He knew the man was longing to boast and would go on speaking unprompted.

'Remember a few years back,' Stoddart went on, licking his thin lips but leaving them as dry as before, 'when the Bunker Hunts and a group of Saudis tried to corner the silver market?'

Alan nodded. The Bunker Hunts were one of the richest

families in the Union. With other, equally wealthy, if more shadowy still, figures from Saudi Arabia, the brothers had tried to buy up the whole futures market in silver. It had been a masterly operation and for a few heady weeks the price of silver had rocketed worldwide. The silversmiths of London were flooded by the middle classes trying to cash in on the suddenly rising value of treasured family heirlooms. The Hunts' plan had been to become the controllers of all the world's silver in one short future period. Then every industry which required the metal for its processes would have had to buy from their cartel, no matter what the cost. Yet suddenly, somehow, in one day, the silver market had collapsed, leaving the Hunts with a lot of very expensive silver contracts and a loss which had inconvenienced even them. It was the last time anyone tried to corner a major worldwide market.

'What did happen that morning?' Alan asked, genuinely wanting to know.

Stoddart's eyes were laughing. He was happy with the memory of it. 'Well, it was one of those rare occasions that come along once in a generation when the market-makers themselves had to act to stop the speculation. The whole market was being distorted. Most of the time we're so busy warring with other traders we can't even think about acting together, but every big house in the business has a relationship with the photographic business in one form or another. Have you any idea how much silver gets used up in photographic processes every day? The makers of every kind of photographic film are the biggest users and holders of silver in the world. Bigger than any government. And what the Hunts were doing was killing them. So they squealed.'

He looked thoughtful for an instant. Alan could not tell if he was remembering or examining some misdemeanour on the floor.

'The deal was put together in Chicago, with the Futures Market movers there. We didn't tell anybody. We just went in. We started selling the whole store of futures contracts the photographic suppliers held. It made even the Hunt holdings look puny. It drove the silver price right back through the floor. We blew the Hunts out of the water and they never knew what hit them.'

Alan was puzzled. 'But in a collapsing market like that a lot of smaller people must have got burned. Not to mention a lot of over-exposed trading houses.'

Stoddart still did not turn to face him. 'Who cares about the little people? If they couldn't afford to lose the money they shouldn't have been in the market. As for trading houses, we changed the rules. For one day's trading no one bothered to check if a house was covered or not. If they couldn't get their books in order by the following morning, then we crucified 'em. But we gave everybody who counted on the floor one day's grace just so we could go after the Hunts.'

'How much did you clear on the day? Personally?' Alan could not help asking. Brokers made money whether prices rose or fell.

This time Stoddart did turn to look at him, his pale, almost colourless eyes still smiling. 'Eleven million dollars.'

Alan whistled. 'And that was on the back of personal trades while you were trading for the photographic industry?'

Stoddart looked almost patronizing. 'Oh, no. Chicago handled most of that. Them and our infantrymen.' He waved down at the floor again. 'No, you see, what was really needed to make the whole operation work was to bring in a player as big as the Hunts. Someone whose simple presence in the market would keep the photographic companies selling whatever happened to their holdings. In the last resort there had to be someone who was prepared to go into the market to cover lethal positions.'

Alan thought he understood. 'So you were the dealer for the government in this?'

Stoddart was genuinely shocked. 'Oh, Jesus Christ, no! The government doesn't interfere in these markets. They don't have anyone smart enough for openers. And this is the United States. No, I dealt for the man who led the market. We needed someone bigger than the Hunts. So I brought in David Medina.'

The Englishman hardly knew what to say. He was only just beginning to understand why John was so fascinated, so obsessed, by the shadow of Medina. But Stoddart was thinking of something else.

'You know,' he said happily, 'those sons of bitches had bought up so many futures contracts, and we dropped the price so low, there were whole rafts of them they couldn't sell at any price. They had to take delivery of the silver, when all they wanted to do was control the price. They have whole vaults just filled with useless metal. That's what I did in the war, sonny. But come on. If you and I are going to talk we'd better head for the Powder Room.'

Stoddart counter-signed him for a pass and took him down into the maze of corridors and offices surrounding the trading floor of Four World Trade Center. Alan stopped asking himself why Stoddart had called the men's toilet the Powder Room as soon as he walked through the door. At each of the shining mirrors stood weary-looking traders with small pocket mirrors or pieces of glass and razor blades. They were deftly razoring little piles of crystals on the mirrors into two tracks of fine white powder. Then they used a rolled-up crisp twenty-dollar note to hose the tracks of cocaine up one nostril after another.

'Whatever else you do in here,' Stoddart told him mockingly, 'don't sneeze. Not unless you want to be a guest at your own lynching.'

It was plainly the place where the dealers felt most secure from the prying eyes of outsiders. There was a convention that anything said within these white-tiled walls was private. No wonder Stoddart had brought him here.

'It doesn't take a hill of beans of brains to know Hart's murder was an Organization killing. That prick-in-the-mouth routine is a signature for them. Word on the street is that Panamanian shipping company of his was an attempt to take over the transportation. The men in suits don't like that kind of thing. If you play with guys with names like Luigi, then you're going to end up Jello.'

To Alan, it made more sense than talk of weapons and the Vatican. 'Is there any chance they used a foreign killer?' He had to ask about the Italian connection. If there was one.

Stoddart thought about it. 'It's possible. He was killed in

London. They might have thought it safer not to ship an American out to do the job. And London's cheap. The tariff for killing starts at twenty-five hundred sterling these days, I gather.'

It wasn't what Alan had meant. 'Yes, but might they have brought in an Italian?'

Stoddart shrugged. 'Could be. With the European Community there's no problem in bringing in an Italian. They have a whole team operating out of Brussels. If the word coming out of Falcone's court in Sicily is right, then the men in suits in New York and Italy are working a whole lot more closely together than they used to.'

'OK, but how do I find out more about it?'

Stoddart looked worried, for the first time. It never occurred to Alan to ask what it was that could worry a man who had gone down on to the trading-room floor against the combined wealth of the Bunker Hunts and a group of Saudi princes and, by keeping his head, come out of it eleven million dollars richer.

'There may be a way,' Stoddart said. 'I'm assuming you're clean because you're a friend of Julia. You appreciate I want out of this?'

'I understand.'

Stoddart leaned in to whisper in his ear. 'OK. Well, whatever happened, the dealers on the street are frightened. Even the ones on Wall Street, where they wear expensive aftershave and never go out without clean underpants. There are a lot of suits turning sticky out there. No one knows what is going on or who is doing what to who. That means you might just get someone to talk a little, if you can make them feel important, if it'll help them blow the whistle on someone they want put away. You understand? They might take the view that if any witness is going to be in a position to get blown away they'd rather it was you than them.'

John and Caro would have been experienced enough to query the spate of tough-guy talk out of a pallid banker, but Alan was not. To him, all of this seemed natural. He had not yet developed an ear for the different registers of American speech. To him, all this was as entrancing as a bar-tender flipping a teacloth over his arm and asking the dreamed of, legendary question, 'What'll it be?' on twenty-four-hour TV. He walked right into the trap being laid for him.

'Is there any way I can get to talk to one of these people? I understand the terms.'

Stoddart licked dry lips with a dry tongue again. 'It's possible. I've been asking. I'm trying to get hold of Harry the Prep, who is one of our bigger dealers to the legitimate community. But if I can get him it means he's running, wild and scared. You have to agree to see him whenever and wherever he arranges. Can you do that?'

Alan thought about it. 'How much notice am I likely to get?'

Stoddart walked over to one of the mirrors, talking in a normal voice as people came and went. From here on in, everything he had to say would sound perfectly normal, even to the most coked-up bystander.

'Well, he won't be in any rush. Last time I heard he was in Connecticut, taking a vacation for the good of his health. I could get you half a day. I guess. So long as you undertook not to involve any others.'

Alan decided, without thinking. To be honest he had decided to accept any conditions, even before leaving the hotel. He was that enthusiastic.

'I have to go down to DC,' he said, more importantly than he felt, 'if I'm to cover myself with my colleagues. But I gather there's a regular shuttle.'

Stoddart knew all about it. But then, he would. 'Out of both National and Dulles. You can leave the centre of DC and be in the centre of Manhattan within four hours, maximum. Where can I reach you?'

Alan scribbled down the phone number.

'Fine,' said Stoddart, memorizing the number and tearing the paper into pieces before flushing it down the nearest toilet. 'You have my number at the office. Call in a couple of times each day. And if you have any paper with my name on it, and maybe my number as well . . . burn it.'

This was it, thought Alan. This was the thing itself. He could hardly wait to be ready to write the story.

Stoddart took him back to the public areas, leaving him with one last warning, his pale eyes almost invisible in his undistinguished face. 'Just you, OK? No funny stuff, no fancy footwork. Harry runs too fast for any of that.'

Alan nodded, running out of time. He had to get his suitcase from the Plaza.

Caro spent the afternoon at the *Examiner*'s New York office. Her colleagues were not best pleased to see her. It was always like this, on those occasions when the IMF conference was held in Washington. There was always a certain amount of inevitable tension between the permanent staffers at the New York office and the team sent out to help with work on the IMF or main USA surveys. The last thing they wanted were additional, to them useless, bodies in the shape of Caro, Alan and, most of all, Standing.

Still, they knew her well enough to settle down once they had faced the fact they would have to be her service bureau for the duration of her stay on this side of the Atlantic. Most of the gossip she got that afternoon was personal. They were under pressure filing the annual results of a string of major companies with London, and nothing could be allowed to breach that most basic working obligation.

In the end, however, she snatched some time with the senior personnel. They filled her in with bits and pieces, mainly on the Hart Affair, which seemed to have almost run its course as the scandal of the week. They gave her nothing she could use. Mainly she wanted to establish she was there, and what her movements were likely to be, and those of Alan Clarke and Standing. No journalist was any use without access to communications. This office was her guarantee of them. It paid her to be polite.

It was six by the time she had stopped being polite to everyone, and accepted the sad best wishes of those who had known her longest and remembered the times when she and Tom were happy. She was caught in the rush-hour, trying to flag down a cab, and caught in the slow crawl of the traffic once she had succeeded.

It was seven before she was back at the Plaza. There was a

message waiting for her at the desk, from Alan, confirming his arrival in Washington. It was noted as having come in at 4.15. He took his time, she thought. She would have to watch him. But there was still no sign of or message from Standing, the man she felt she ought to be watching all the time, though that would make him useless to her. There was no sign of him at all.

There was no sign of him because he was celebrating, in a bar off Madison Avenue. He was celebrating a successful day, spent covering his tracks.

He had been sober in the beginning. He had been sensible. He had kept himself down to the best part of a bottle of bourbon while he waited for his credit cards. He had even remembered to go into a drug-store to pick up a spray to freshen his breath before returning to the bank. The formalities had only taken moments, while the manager informed him that fifty per cent of each monthly statement would be paid, unless he notified them of any different instructions, and his credit limits diminished accordingly, after the first month, unless they saw replenishment of his account with the bank. He thought it a curiously intelligent arrangement. As so often before, he found himself admiring, though he could not like, the Swiss.

By that stage he was running out of time. If he had been sensible he would have used the two hours waiting for the cards to set up the initial arrangements, but he had been too relieved to get out of that office where his corrupted money lay. And he needed a drink. Whatever anyone might say. If he could only tank up now he would need less when he was in Caro's presence, which might help to give her peace of mind.

What he had remembered to do was to check out the other banks in that building and the immediate neighbourhood. He started at the Customer Services desk of a branch of Second City.

'Good afternoon, could I have nine and a half thousand dollars' worth of travellers cheques please?'

The girl behind the desk repeated in slow wonder, 'Nine and a half thousand dollars?'

'That's right. Nine thousand five hundred. Eighteen cheques denominated for five hundred dollars each, and ten of fifty.

The girl's mouth moved a couple of times without speaking, as though practising, before asking, 'And how would you like to pay for them, sir?'

He flashed his credit cards at her.

It was an efficient system. It only took a moment to confirm he was good for the money. He had chosen the sum deliberately. For amounts of ten thousand dollars or more the bank would have had to prepare a special notification to the Inland Revenue Service, and the whole point of the exercise was to enable him to disappear, if only for three or four days. He might be over-reacting, he usually was, but he was no longer prepared to trust anyone's integrity, much less the IRS's.

It took him a little time to sign all the travellers cheques, but soon enough he was done.

He repeated the operation at a branch of First Brooklyn. Nineteen thousand dollars of what was effectively cash; but in a form which could take days or even weeks to come back to the clearing system to be settled. A form which was slower than the return and authorization of credit-card coupons. Which would give him an extra few days when no computer would know exactly where he was.

He needed a larger branch of Second City. He had to use a cab.

He walked up to the Customer Service desk. Another face, another smile. He would have to note the address down. He had to be able to retrace his steps, even if no one else was meant to.

'Good afternoon, I'd like to cash twenty thousand dollars on one of these, please.' He handed over his cards.

The girl went for the manager.

'Can I help you sir?' he asked.

'I hope so.' *Use the English elements in the accent*, he thought. *Remember you're an expatriate. It sounds grander anyhow.* 'I'd like to cash twenty thousand dollars on these.'

'We handle them both, sir. Do you have any preferences?'

'The Visa will be fine?'

'Yes, of course, sir. This will only take a moment. Will you require all the money at once, sir? We normally ask for a little notice for withdrawals in excess of five thousand dollars.'

'I won't need any of it. I want to use it to open an account.'

'Well, of course, sir. At once, sir. Please step this way.'

It only took a few moments to get the payment authorized. John hoped he had chosen the right amount. It should be just enough to get him the service he wanted, but still well below the point at which a new account would be specially notified to head office. He planned to come across as comfortable, not rich, so they would not be over-interested. Fortunately, it was impossible for him ever to look rich.

He told the manager some of the truth. He told him he was an expatriate, considering returning to these United States. He said he was considering certain investment opportunities in the South and in the Caribbean. He pointed out that, as a native New Yorker (even John nearly gagged on that particular lie), he felt happier dealing with the financial institutions he had known before leaving the States. He wondered therefore if he could ask the manager to have certain companies checked for him through the inter-bank credit-rating system. The manager was most helpful, greedy for the funds John assured him he would be repatriating as soon as some suitable investment opportunity had been decided on. John handed over the list.

'These are all out-of-state companies, Mr Standing,' the manager said, explaining what John knew already, 'that might take a little time. The system is by no means perfect, as we have all had reason to regret. Now if you could supply us with a banker's reference for these companies we could take it up with the bank direct.

John thought it over. It was tempting to give him the name of the Alabaman bank, but their answers were no use to him without test checks against other banks, to see if it gave suspect companies better than usual ratings.

'No,' he explained, 'it's a little early for that. At this stage

I don't want them to think I'm too interested. I'd just be grateful if you'd make sure to check with every bank in Mobile and in Huntsville.'

Mobile because it was Alabama's major port. Huntsville because it was where NASA's laboratories, parts of Boeing, and a host of defence contractors were located.

'I quite understand, of course,' the manager replied. Business after all was business. 'I see you give your address as the Plaza Hotel . . .'

'That's right, until I'm settled.'

'So when we have the information we can send it to you there?'

John thought again. There was no harm in it. There was certainly none in Caro seeing it. Other things might be dangerous, but this information ought to be harmless, in New York.

'Yes, you could do that. Hard copies for my files. I'll be keeping my suite there, but I'm going to be travelling a fair amount. What I would like is this branch's telephone and telex numbers. I could then contact you for the information.'

The banker nodded. 'I think that would be in order. We would require some security identification, of course, before releasing such material. Some means of identifying that any communication was genuinely from you. Your date of birth perhaps?'

John shook his head. 'Too many people know it. Not secure enough. Take down this number: 103108. Any genuine communication from me will quote that number.

There was little more to say. The paperwork was dealt with in a moment. John could collect his cheques the following day. But it was not the simplicity of it all which made him smile as he was leaving, it was the reference number he had given. It was Medina's date of birth.

He had one final call to make, before the end of the business day. He had to get to a travel agency. He chose one out of Yellow Pages and took a cab. It took a little time before the agent understood exactly what he wanted, but in the end it proved simple enough. He wanted a series of open airline tickets, not confirmed for any specific flight. They were to be merely confirmation of the fact that he had paid the fare and was therefore entitled to a seat. He would have to confirm exactly when he wanted to travel. There were sixteen tickets in all, all of them full-fare returns, on four different airlines. New York – Washington. New York – Nassau. New York – Panama. Washington – Nassau. Washington – Panama. Nassau – Panama. New York – Chicago. New York – St Louis. Washington – St Louis. St Louis – Chicago. St Louis – Seattle. St Louis – Los Angeles. Los Angeles – Seattle. Seattle – New York. Los Angeles – New York. And St Louis – Atlanta, which was the nearest interstate airport for Huntsville, although it was over the state line in Georgia.

He flashed his Mastercard. It ought to work, he thought. Even if the credit-card coupon was traced back to the travel agency, no one would be able to tell from such a selection of open tickets where he intended to travel when, which of the tickets were part of his real itinerary and which were merely covers. And if he turned up at airports as a standby passenger, without confirming a reservation, his name would only appear on the airlines' computer records for the duration of the flight. After that they would be inaccessible on the head office mainframe, which would be purged at the end of thirty days.

He was not looking that far ahead, however. He only needed a few days. And there were some tickets he could not buy within the United States. Possible options which would mean travelling on his British passport. But he did not think this would lead to Nicaragua yet. He suspected his first stop should be Nassau, where Errol Hart had kept the Panamari bank accounts. He would have to think it over.

For now, he was happy. He had money. He had wings. He had access to information. And, if he had got it all even half right, no one would be able to trace him, or predict where he might be going.

All he needed was a drink.

He needed more than a drink. As he always did. It was five bars, three avenues and four and a half hours before he fell into a cab back to the Plaza, put out on the street by a bouncer like so many bags of garbage. It was past ten when he swayed a course back to the suite.

Caro was waiting for him, in a bathrobe. With a towel round her head.

Pretty, he thought vaguely.

She looked as though she had been crying.

She was tired. She was hurt. She hurt all over, in and out. And now he had done this to her. When would he ever learn?

She was too tired to shout.

'Where have you been? Where in God's name have you been?'

'Working,' he chirruped, grinning inanely, and falling into a chair.

'How much, John? How much have you had to drink?'

'Not much,' he lied, even to himself, measuring a couple of inches of air between his right thumb and forefinger. 'So much.'

She turned away from him, trying to stay calm. 'Please tell me, love. How much?'

He shook his head amiably, smiling drunk, trying to remember. 'I suppose, I suppose . . .' he mumbled, throwing back his head. He nearly went to sleep. He had to shake himself out of it. 'Three bottles of bourbon. Maybe less.'

She could not bear to look at him. 'Did you get anything done?'

'Oh, yes. Oh, yes. I've been very busy.' He could not stop nodding his head. 'I did a lot today.'

'What did you do?'

A look of childish cunning crossed his face. 'Not telling,' he whispered, trying to stand up, but falling back into his chair. 'Too dangerous to tell.'

She did not want to cry. Not over him.

'You were doing so well, John. So well. But you're no good to yourself or anyone else like this. I have to go tomorrow, to Seattle, just in case you're right. Your idea. Almost your story now. So why are you throwing it away like this? Why do you do this to us every time we try to help you?'

She could not tell if he was listening or not. He was sitting with his legs together, his arms folded and his head bowed low. She could not see his eyes. She could only see the tangled mop of fine grey hair. Nevertheless she continued:

'I have to leave you here, love. I can't trust you on your travels when you're in this state. I'm going to take most of the money back. You'll have to report to the office every day to pick up your daily advances. I can't leave you with money when you get like this.'

He made no answer. He sat unmoving, silent.

She tried once more, for old times' sake.

'Come back to us, John. Come back to me, from wherever you've been hiding. I need all the help that I can get.'

Quietly, politely, he threw up in his lap, hosing himself with acid, alcoholic waters.

She left him in his slop, retreating hopelessly to bed.

As she went she heard him murmuring, in a small, hurt, childlike voice, 'I'm sorry, Caro, sorry. I'm so, so sorry.'

CHAPTER FOUR

Alan paid for his airline ticket by credit card and marvelled yet again at the simplicity of the system. He had used shuttle flights at home before, but the separate terminal at La Guardia made the whole process simpler than he had imagined possible. He dropped his suitcase on the appropriate ramp, told the desk-clerk which flight he was taking, walked up to the lounge and walked on to the aircraft. The stewardesses came round to check pre-paid tickets and take cash or credit cards from those who were travelling at the last minute. They also handed out little plastic carrier bags filled with biscuits, fruit and a carton of juice. He began to wonder why anyone ever made a fuss about flying.

Still, getting to the terminal had been what a more seasoned traveller would have told him was the usual chaos. There had been the usual traffic jam in the approaches to La Guardia, the usual frantic anxiety about missing the flight (he made it with four minutes to spare). He had told the driver he was heading for Eastern Airlines. It was one of the less useful aspects of American free enterprise that the building of New York's airports had been subsidized by the major airlines, each of which had its own independent terminal. Communications between the terminals were barely adequate, which could make a nightmare of transfers. At JFK the terminals were so far apart you had to take a cab or bus between them. What no one had bothered to tell him was that the Eastern Airlines shuttles left from a separate new terminal on the other side of the airport from the main terminals. There had been uproar when Alan and his driver realized this and had to proceed back against the long arc of traffic. Still, you lived and learned.

It was a short flight, barely an hour, and soon they were drifting down into the long glide into Dulles Airport. He had just about worked out that Dulles was the international airport in northern Virginia, serving the capital, but he remained a bit confused about the difference between Washington National and Baltimore Washington International. He would have to ask John's brother. It occurred to him that he was learning he knew hardly anything about the United States. Like most Englishmen, he thought he knew all about it from films, popular music and television, but it was only now that he realized he had somehow assumed the whole nation was one great suburb of Los Angeles and New York, scattered with a few big National Parks where cowboys and oilmen roamed. But down there was a lush green country, as far as the eye could see, rolling and verdant out to the Blue Ridge Mountains and the Shenandoah, high on the ridges of the Appalachians and Alleghenies beyond. He could tell from passengers about him that the people were slower here, more comfortable of speech, as he caught echoes of the long vowels which sometimes drifted through John Standing's accent.

Dulles Airport proved to be small, clean, new and neat. He walked straight from the aircraft through the boarding finger into the main airy passenger hall. The place was quiet. It looked as though it would always be quiet, whatever excitements might be being organized for the world in the city fifteen miles away. He went down the ramp to the lower level where the baggage reclaim area lay. As his suitcase rolled round on the conveyor belt (it could barely have taken five minutes) a tall, grizzled man with a professional air came over and tapped him on the shoulder.

'Are you by any chance Mr Clarke?' he asked in a slow, courtly voice. 'I'm Robert Standing.'

The family resemblance was unmistakable. Robert did not look much older than John, but Alan guessed he was, by perhaps ten or twelve years. It showed in the way he spoke about the black sheep of the family.

'How's my little brother?' he asked. Seeing Alan raise his eyebrows he added, 'I'm sorry. I keep forgetting John's a grown man. I was already in Groton when he was born, and there's a string of sisters between us.'

Alan was not sure how to answer the original question. He

played for safe politeness. 'He's well, I think.' He hesitated before admitting, 'It's sometimes a little difficult to tell.'

He was relieved to see Robert laugh.

They drove down the long Airport Access Road to connect with the Dolley Madison Highway, at Lewinsville Heights, on its way towards the city. There was a soft haze in the air which gave everything a faint cast of grey, like a soft undershadow. It was hot, in the high eighties, though Robert explained that was quite temperate for this time of year. And there were elms, scores of ancient trees unravaged by the disease which had swept Europe a few years before. Alan almost gasped, as at a sudden recollection.

Robert slipped the big Mercedes into a lower gear as he pulled on to the access ramp to the Highway. 'I didn't hire you a car,' he explained, 'because I didn't know if you'd need one. Public transport isn't great anywhere in the Union, but it passes in the city. We have a metro system now. It kinda works. And parking can be a problem up in Georgetown. Who are you planning on visiting with?'

Alan pulled out the scrappy list John had given him. 'John gave me these names,' he said, 'and told me to ask you to make the introductions. I hope that isn't too presumptuous. I'm mainly here to try to talk to the CIA.' He felt embarrassed saying it. He wondered what would happen if you told a Muscovite you hardly knew you just wanted to talk to the KGB.

It didn't seem to faze Robert at all. 'Fine, I'll check out that list later. But if it's the Agency you came to see, then you came to the right place.'

He slowed down a little to let Alan take in the little town they were passing. It occurred to Alan for the first time that, though he was more obviously an American than his brother, there was something off-centre about Robert driving a European car without an automatic shift. But Robert was explaining something.

'This is McLean. Nearest we get to a nightlife centre in this neck of Virginia. Lot of young folks like you round here. Just back of us is Tyson's Corner. There's a new office park round there. Westgate. Which is maybe why Clyde's opened a new big singles bar back there, if you're ever in need of some action.' The Standings seemed to think of everything. 'Officially,' he continued, 'the Agency's address is Langley, about a mile back to the left, but it's a big spread, and the easiest way in is the side entrance outside McLean. If they let you in.' He saw the frown cross Alan's face and added, 'Don't worry. They've got a Press Office. Would you believe? We can get you into that at least. But I don't suppose that's really what you're after.'

Alan shook his head. 'Not really.'

Robert laughed. 'We need to get you networking. The town's pretty quiet in the middle of July, so it shouldn't be too hard to get a crowd of folks together. Good job you came on a Friday. Might fix up a little party tomorrow evening.'

Alan hesitated. 'I'm going to be based here for a while, but I'm likely to have to get back to New York for just one day. I won't get any notice. I wouldn't want you to go to any trouble and then find I couldn't make it.'

Robert was unconcerned. 'No trouble. We'd just drink it all without you.' He pulled on to the George Washington Memorial Highway, and the city and the river came into view.

On their side of the river they were surrounded by tall new buildings threatening management systems and efficiency. But to their left across the slow sluggish waters of the Potomac was a range of gentle hills covered with old low buildings. It looked surprisingly provincial. Only in the distance was there an expanse of white new constructions. Robert saw him looking at it, and smiled.

'That's the Watergate,' he explained, 'of sainted memory. What you see here is Georgetown. I'll take you straight in there. We can show you your way round the city itself later. Right now we're coming through Rosslyn. That's the Foreign Language Institute,' he waved at an unspectacular high-rise building. 'I was there before I joined the Foreign Service. That's where they send diplomats to learn to speak in tongues. Or did, when they thought those things still mattered. John should've gone there, after Oxford, but instead the Ambassador wanted him to spend some time at Harvard like the rest of us. I guess I'm no different. I sent all my boys up to the Yankees too.'

Another look of puzzlement crossed Alan's face. Robert positively grinned.

'You have to remember this is the South. North of South, maybe, but still a Confederate state. There's a lot still thinks of DC as a Union enclave in God's own country. But that's nothing. You wait till you get down to the Carolinas.'

He turned on to the Francis Scott Key Bridge. Even here, filled by Theodore Roosevelt island, the river was wider than Alan had expected. Part of him still vaguely felt that the Thames ought to be the biggest river in the world, though he knew that was insane. They turned right on what Robert told him was M Street.

'It's the usual American grid pattern,' he explained. 'Numbered streets east–west and lettered ones north–south. What confuses newcomers is the diagonals, the avenues running off the Capitol and the White House. They're all named after states. M Street you need to know, though. It's the main thoroughfare from Georgetown into the city proper. It joins up with Pennsylvania Avenue, which takes you right into the White House and Capitol. The other way, back of us, it turns into Canal Road and runs beside the university, where I am most days, or in the Georgetown U School of Foreign Service between 34th and 35th Streets.'

Alan made a note in his notepad. He was surprised at how small the whole place looked. The streets were broad, but all the buildings here were low and old, like a glorified streetscene from a Western. It was hard to believe this small, sleepy, provincial centre was the most fashionable suburb of the capital of the greatest empire in the world. Robert seemed to know what he was thinking.

'It doesn't look very much, does it? The centre's different, where the federal buildings are. But here . . . when I was a boy this was a black ghetto. Everyone thought the Ambassador's father was crazy when he bought a house here. I thought he was crazy. But nobody counted on the growth of the government. All those people needing a place in town. Georgetown's the one place in the city where the whites drove the blacks out. Most places it's the other way round. Nowadays Washington's four-fifths black. The whites all live in Virginia or Maryland. It's two different cities during the workday and at night.' He did not seem to mind the changes he had witnessed. He was just a detached diplomat giving a visitor an honest report on his posting. He added in a spirit of helpfulness. 'I know it looks peaceful now, but it isn't really safe, at night.'

'Is that why you live in Virginia?' Alan asked.

Robert shook his head in amusement. 'Hell, no. If that were it I'd live further out than the Golden Triangle, in some new place like Vienna or Fairfax. I live where I live because the Standings are a Virginian family, and were before they moved the capital down here and we joined the Foreign Service.' He smiled to himself. 'In his younger days the Ambassador used to put the fear of God into the Service every time he had to fill a form which asked if he or any member of his family had ever been a member of an organization dedicated to the overthrow of the United States. He used to answer Yes, on the grounds his grandfather and great-uncles served in the Confederate Army under Lee.'

They turned left. 'OK, this is Wisconsin Avenue. Runs north–south through Georgetown. It's what you'd call the high street. Runs up to the Naval Observatory.'

They drove slowly up a broad quiet street full of ordinary-looking restaurants and bars, clothes stores and small supermarkets. It ran up an increasingly steep hill and Robert shifted gears again before turning left into a little side road called P Street.

They entered a world cooled by the shade of old trees, full of shuttered houses of brick and clapboard. Alan noticed that even the pavement was made of brick, laid in grid or herringbone patterns. There were a couple of joggers and an encouraging cyclist drifting up the street. Robert cruised to a stop. Here, it seemed, unlike New York, the traffic halted for pedestrians. They pulled away again, jolting along the cobblestones which took over here. Robert pulled up outside a low two-storey clap-board house. There were external steps up to a door on the upper level.

'Well,' said Robert good-naturedly, 'it isn't the Ambassador's old house, but it's the only white house we have left.'

They sat in the long drawing-room, filled with colonial furniture, much of it, Alan suspected, original and sipped their bourbon. Robert explained that he wanted to go up to his office at the university to pick up some papers, but that afterwards he would give Alan a guided tour of the city.

'Then you can use the weekend to learn your way round, though we'll throw that party for you, and I hope you'll eat with us Sunday, so you can get to meet some of these people you're after.' He also explained that John's daughter Eleanor was using the lower apartment during the vacation, but she was hardly ever around.

'I don't suppose you know when John will be coming down? I should've told him that bitch Evelyn is due here later.' He said it without a trace of malice. 'Anyways, there's a lot of other people who would be pleased to see him. It'd be nice to throw a home-coming for my brother.

Alan was embarrased at being drawn into the family's life. 'I really don't know,' he admitted. 'I imagine he'll come down here with Caro once she's got back from Seattle. A few days maybe.'

Robert managed to sound barely interested. 'Caro?'

'Caroline Kilkenny. I suppose she's our boss.'

Robert smiled ruefully. 'Well, I'm glad he's working for someone. He was always a damn sight better behaved when there were ladies present anyhow.' He finished his bourbon with a single gulp and stood up, smoothing down his linen trousers.

'Still, I'd better give you a chance to settle in. I'll be back in about an hour. You might tell Eleanor if you see her. You'd better give me that list, so I can check out the best way of getting you to them.' Alan handed over the two pieces of scruffy paper. Robert read the list through and shook his head, laughing to himself, 'Arlington Hall. John always did say it's worth trying the side entrance.'

Alan admitted his ignorance. 'I don't understand.'

Robert smiled. 'Arlington Hall,' he explained, 'is the Intelligence Service Training School. They always end up knowing more than they're meant to, without understanding what is and isn't important. John's used their ignorance before.'

He turned to go, but as he did so another thought struck him. 'I won't ask what you're looking at,' he said. 'I see John put Stephanie, my research assistant, on your list. I assume that means he doesn't want me to know. But Washington's a strange town. Because John knows it so well I guess he sometimes imagines outsiders can understand it. But it takes a lot of time. It isn't really like other Western capitals. It's a great deal more like a richer someplace in the Third World. Once you get out of Georgetown even the people in the streets make it look like that. This place is almost African. So if there's anything you don't understand, just holler. That's what Virginians are for.'

He went out, leaving Alan thinking what a charming man he was, how much like a cleaner, less damaged, image of his brother.

But Robert Standing, as he walked up the street towards the university, was looking at the list again, and smiling at the names. He wondered why his brother wanted him to waste so much of that charming young man's time.

CHAPTER FIVE

Despite the drink, the dreams came back.

He was walking, up an ill-lit corridor in a third-class European train bound for nowhere. There were peasants crowded into each compartment. Fat women in gaily coloured scarves, breaking black bread and sausage. Sallow, gnarled men, sombre in grey serge caps and jackets. Chickens fluttered hopelessly in wicker baskets in the luggage racks. Children wailed, and screaming babies roused nursing mothers from their fitful sleep.

He did not know why he was walking. He did not know where he was going. There were no seats available. He did not seem to have a ticket. But there were no staff visible, no guards, or ticket inspector. Why did he feel such inchoate anxiety? The train clanked rhythmically through the flatlands of the night, bouncing him from side to side of the corridor. From time to time he walked out into open air and had to cross between carriages, smoke and smuts blowing backwards into his smarting face.

Each time he faced the iron gates grinding over each other above the buffers, the short journey became more fearful. He was frightened he would fall.

At last, one last time, he stood unable to make the passage, while behind him other passengers crowded and pushed, muttering in some dark unknown tongue against the coward who delayed them. But despite those behind him, despite the narcotic rocking of the train, he could not bring his legs to move, lest the darkness and the motion of the plates betray him and cast him to his doom.

Then the locomotive whistle came, building to a hissing fury as the train approached a tunnel, an unnecessary tunnel in these plains, and he had to choose between jumping or being caught in the thunderous darkness which was bound to come. He nerved himself, against the crying of the crowd behind him, against the shuddering impact of the plates, and the train's inexorable whistle, and jumped.

And fell.

He came round before dawn. He felt no pain, none of the usual hammering dehydrated ache of hangover. It was just that he felt utterly exhausted, as though his bones were rubber and his muscles plastic bags filled with water. And he stank.

He tried to move. He rolled his vomit-stained clothes into a ball inside his jacket, turned inside out. He took a shower, scrubbing himself again and again, trying to soap out the self-contempt. He called for the valet service, to take his clothes away, and he ordered two pots of strong black coffee.

He remembered enough to empty his pockets, to hide the credit cards and cash. He looked out his one remaining light-weight suit, a shirt, a tie, some socks. He had to send his only pair of shoes to be polished, if necessary re-stained. He had to send for a housemaid to clear up, to freshen the air. He threw the windows open anyway. Each of the staff who came up at his call seemed to look at him in wonder and disgust.

He would not think about it. It was some other man who did it. He drank down both pots of coffee. Then he ordered more.

He knew the fact he felt no pain must mean he was still drunk, but stable now, just about able to cope, if he could only concentrate.

He would have to face Caro when she awoke. He could not bear it. He wanted to run away, to hide, to vanish till she parted for Seattle. But he knew he could not do that, though he did not know what he could say. There was nothing she could say to him he did not know already. Why did he do this to her, to others, to himself?

She was silent throughout her breakfast, eyeing him with suspicion, and with fear: of what he had become, what he had done, what he might still do, to himself if not to others. And she was tired, and wounded, in spirit and flesh. He knew she was wondering if she should fire him.

He spoke first. 'There's nothing I can say about last night . . .'

'No.' She was curt. 'There isn't.'

'But I had, genuinely, been busy. Second City are checking all the Alabaman corporations. Hard copy of anything they uncover will come here to this suite. And I've made arrangements to be able to get in touch with them wherever we might be for updates or confirmation.'

She shrugged. That was quite good work. He had done what he had promised. But it was no excuse.

'Do you remember,' she asked pitilessly, 'anything of what I said to you last night?'

He shook his head. 'Nothing.'

She put down her coffee cup and sat with her head in her one good hand, eyes closed.

'I'm going to Seattle. I don't know why I should give you that chance but I will. I will see if there's any defence industry talk about what's happening in Central America. But you're staying here, and I'm taking your money back. You'll have to draw a daily float from the office. While I am away, I want you to write down exactly what we know and exactly what you think we're looking for. I'll decide what we do next after I get back. If there's any woolliness left about this story by then, I'm pulling us out of it. I have a book to finish. You have work to do. And I'm going to make you do it if it kills us both.'

He sat, palms upward, unable to look her in the face. 'Caro, I can only say I'm sorry about last night, but I have to ask you to trust me . . .'

'How can I?' she shouted. 'It doesn't do any good to tell me you're sorry. You've done it too many times. I'm sick of "Sorry". All of us are. Fuck you. Why do you do this to us?'

There was nothing he could say. He could only let her anger run its course.

'I mean, what have you to get pissed for? You're bright, you're a looker, you make people laugh, and you're a goddamn Virginia Standing. Wasn't the silver spoon enough, that you have to swallow a tub of bourbon too? It's not as though you had our natural disadvantages.'

He spoke without thinking. 'I can do without the working-class heroine routine.'

She was suddenly cold, school-mistressy. 'Oh, can you? Well, that's fine. That's easy for you to say from your Olympian height. You were given everything, and you threw it all away. I wasn't given any of it. I had to work for it, my parents had to work for it. In the end I gave up my marriage for it, and I'm not letting you throw it away. Go on, mess up your own pathetic life if you have to, but don't you ever fuck up on my work ever again.'

Blind self-preservation made him retaliate. 'I haven't. I don't. I know I'm too drunk too often to hold down a regular job, but I've never let you down on an assignment. Others, yes. But not you. Everything I said I'd do for you I've done. And what did you do in Italy, while we were half-demented on your behalf? When I was out of my mind without a drink grinding through your husband's papers? You disappeared. You vanished. You went off to get fucked by some smiling smooth-tongued lawyer and you left us in the lurch. You left off your high sense of duty the instant he had a hand inside your pants.'

She slapped him, hard.

He did not apologize. He looked away from her, saying, 'Both of us hurt. When you hurt you will do anything to forget. I hurt all the time. I can't tell you why. It's none of the things you said. Not Virginia, not Oxford, not the money, not the Standings. I hurt all over, and I say damn fool things like that.'

She held out her good hand.

'I want your money, John. I'm going to Seattle.'

CHAPTER SIX

She had forgotten she would have to change planes at Chicago. Since deregulation of the airways a few years before, hardly any flights crossed the continent non-stop. She hated O'Hare Airport. She hated the noise, congestion and bustle, She was a small-town girl at heart who, although she enjoyed work in the city, had never got used to living there. She was glad when she was airborne again. She was glad as they made the long haul to Seattle, far away on the Pacific shore.

She liked the city. It was small and peaceable, reminding her of the towns of her childhood. And everywhere you looked, from any of its many hills, there were sudden unexpected glimpses of the sea. But as her flight dipped down over the long chain of the Rockies she was not thinking of Seattle or the vast blue hopefulness of the Pacific. She was thinking of John Standing, and herself.

She did not, in fact, feel resentful any longer about her origins being more humble than those of most of the people she knew. Her father would not have allowed it. He had been a railwayman, and for him education had not been a matter of self-improvement but a means, to greater wealth, to freedom. He had never allowed his children to feel underprivileged or deprived in any way. The world to him was simply the place of opportunities. You made of them what you could. The status of others was an irrelevance. What mattered was what you did for yourself.

So there was no envy in her for John's effortlessly advantaged background. What she hated was that he had used his own talents and opportunities so badly, abusing his body and his chances. Fifteen years earlier he had been spoken of as the one of his contemporaries most likely to fill a national editorial chair. Today, he was lucky to be in work at all. And he had no one to blame except himself.

What she could not understand was why she cared so much. For she did care. It was the only way of making sense of her acceptance of him as a leg-man at all, and her horror at his condition the previous night. But if people wanted to destroy themselves that was ultimately their business. People were tougher than they looked. They could survive most things. And those who could not were almost always beyond any kind of helping. Survivors asked for help when they needed it. Losers rejected it when it was offered. And John always refused it, always walked away. She had never minded so before. She had, in the past, cut herself off from self-destructive friends. There came a time when you had to pull away, in order not to be damaged beyond necessity. Self-destruction burned. It damaged all those close to it with the heat and hurt of guilt. She ought to be able to cut loose now, to back away from Standing. Yet she could not. Was it because she hurt so much herself? Or was it because John was a part of the remnants of those years when she had known herself to be young?

The two flights taken together made a six-hour journey, but the stopover in Chicago more than cancelled the two-hour time difference. It was late afternoon by the time she arrived. She hired a car at Sea-Tac International Airport (she was never exactly sure where Tacoma was) although she knew she would not often use it. The public transport system was more than passable in the centre of the city, but the car might be useful for more outlying parts. They could only give her an Oldsmobile Ciera, rather larger than she wanted, but it would simply have to do. The one advantage of having the car and arriving on the weekend was that the people she most wanted to see would only be able to see her out of office hours and away from the beaten track. Transport and timing gave her freedom. They put her marginally ahead of the game. Except it was the middle of July and who could tell how many would have headed east of the mountains to the sun?

She pulled out on to Interstate 5 past the Southcenter shopping plaza. The drive into town took her past the main reason she was here, the main reason this city still existed, for north of the airport lay the vast private fiefdom of the Boeing

Corporation. Along the highway to the left there stretched the complex of hangers, warehouses and squat functional office buildings of the largest aircraft corporation in the world. On the runways and taxiing-aprons stood the usual muddle of new planes, already painted with their prospective owners' logos and colours. Boeing employed 65,000 people directly, out of the city's half-million inhabitants. Most of the others, and the other one and a half million in the sprawl of suburbs beyond, worked for companies which owed their presence here to the needs of the aircraft builders and their endless appetite for sub-contractors. If Boeing sometimes behaved as though it owned this town, it was because it did.

Over the hill the city skyline came into view, masking Puget Sound in its long roll out to the ocean beyond. It was a city which had no need for high-rise buildings, but it had them anyway: the Kingdome Stadium, a mushroom feasting on the damp climate of the area, the Space Needle left over from the Century 21 World's Fair of 1962, the shabbiest Sixties imagining of what the future would be, with its bright galleries of lights and revolving restaurant, and, over all, the still unfinished Columbia Center, the least necessary building in the world, and the planners' latest folly.

None of it mattered, though. None of it was part of what made her like this provincial West Coast city. What mattered more was her first glimpse of the Winslow Ferry making its slow way across the dark uncomplaining waters of Elliot Bay. She took the Madison Street exit, turning left towards the water, following the hills towards First Avenue.

When she drew up outside the Alexis, the high old buildings of First Avenue, left over from the city's nineteenth-century mercantile past, created such a wind-tunnel effect that she would never have been able to open the big car's door, her wrist still working against her, without the assistance of the tall black doorman. She told him to have the car parked and went into the lobby.

She found it difficult to discover a hotel which came up to her standards. It took a good hotel to give a woman travelling on business a combined sense of safety and a free-and-easy welcome. There were hotels in Europe that got it right, but fewer in North America. Perhaps only the Brown Palace in Denver was perfect, where there was a standing rule for instance that any man who approached an unattended lady except by her express invitation was thrown off the premises immediately, no matter who he might be. But the Alexis was a great deal better than most of the rest, and was becoming one of Caro's favourite hotels. She had stayed here the previous year, working on the Aerospace Survey, and had been surprised to discover that, although in an old building, it was only two years old, a one-off redevelopment project. She had a horrible suspicion it took its name from that character in the soap opera. Still, she could forgive them that, for reflecting the peacefulness of the city the hotel stood in. She liked the muted pinks and greys which seemed to be this season's height of hotel décor. She liked the claret and embroidered furniture, the upturned antique lamps like wine-glasses filling with light.

And she was glad the Assistant Managing Director was on duty when she arrived.

'Welcome back, Ms Kilkenny,' he smiled, holding up a key. 'I've put you in 414 again.'

Why, she wondered, were Americans so good at remembering names? He would have been expecting her from the booking, but how could he match the name to her face after an absence of over a year? It was the kind of detail for which she was glad.

'Will you be needing secretarial services this weekend?' he continued as she signed in.

'I don't think so, thank you. I think I might take this weekend a little easy.'

He smiled again, easily charming. 'That's good to know. My own secretary will be back in on Monday, of course. Feel free to call on her at any time.'

'I will, don't worry.'

She went up to the corner suite on the fourth floor and, feeling better, tipped the bell-hop more heavily than she intended. She would have to watch, she realized, the slight sense of euphoria being on the West Coast gave her. That and being away from the burden of John Standing and his drinking. She thought about telephoning him, but it would be mid-afternoon in New York. She would give him a few more hours.

She was tempted to do what she had done the year before and arrange a session in a total-immersion tank. She still had the number in her address book, but it was up on Aurora Avenue and she was tired, so she ran an ordinary bath. Nothing could approach the total negation of the senses experienced in a blacked-out, sound-proofed flotation tank, but a long soak in a scented bath was pretty damn good in itself. She rearranged the cut flowers in the drawing-room, switched the radio in the walnut wardrobe which concealed the television as well on to a music channel, dropped her files on to the reproduction desk which gave the Executive suites their name, patted the Indian blanket hung up on the back wall, took one sighing look at the darkening half-view down to the water-front, and remembered with a curse that she was in Washington State. The Liquor Laws did not allow hotels to leave alcohol in the guest bedrooms. She rang down for a large gin and tonic with plenty of ice. When it arrived she slipped at long last into the bath.

She was aware how much she needed to rest. She would try to take the weekend as easily as possible. After all, what serious damage could John do except to himself, even in New York, on a Sunday? There were only two things she really had to do to find out if Standing was right about the story. She would have to have dinner with Clara, which would anyway be a pleasure. And she would have to track down Stu Wilcox.

Wilcox would be a bore.

He had always been a bore, but a wondrous necessary man to any journalist covering the aerospace industry, especially its defence aspect. Almost everyone had fired him in his time. Almost everyone re-hired him. He was English, originally, and was in his forties, part of the original Brain Drain to the US in the Sixties. His field was airborne guidance systems, and there was no one better in the business. If it was meant to go up, as well as left and right, Stu Wilcox would make sure it travelled where you wanted. At NASA in the Sixties he designed the automatic terrain-matching system, which tracked the terrain of the moon against a map held in the Apollo landing unit's computer memory and guided it into land with almost uncanny accuracy. In the Seventies he had redesigned the automated landing beacons used at major airports to guide airliners down in the fog or stormy weather and the AWACS airborne radar system. In the Eighties, his triumphs had included refining the land-hugging Cruise missile-guidance system developed from his work on the Apollo project and, as a freelance, improving the heat-seeking systems on the French Dassault company's sea-to-air Exocet missile.

The reason he kept moving job so often, despite his talents, was also the reason he was so useful to correspondents. Like many others at the highest levels of his industry, but more so, Stu Wilcox was halfway crazy.

The West Coast, where he had always worked after his stint at NASA, had fried his brains for ever. It did that to a lot of people. Every cultist, freak and alternative-society-seeker headed westward from the old established centres of population. They always had done, from early pioneers escaping political or religious persecution, to men of the Gold Rush Fever who dreamed of freedom buried in the wrong end of a mine. Once they hit the West Coast, there was no further to go. The sunshine and the endless curve of the Pacific Ocean inhibited them. So on the coast they reinforced each other, creating newer, madder, excesses. Stu Wilcox had tried them all.

It was why you had to be careful with him. It was easy to remember he was a vegetarian. The difficult part lay in not offending whatever cult he was into now, or therapy, or holistic treatment. The previous year he had refused to meet her anywhere except seated along the shore of Green Lake, because he was no longer into chairs. 'You have to maximize your surface contact with Mother Earth at all times,' he had explained, pulling down his pants to grind his buttocks as well as his unshod feet deeper into the health-giving soil. At that time he would only work on ground-floor offices. The word was, the computer company which had employed him then had used the chaos that caused as their excuse to fire him.

It almost certainly had been an excuse. It usually was. The trouble with Stu from his employers' angle was that he was completely schizophrenic about the defence business. He always claimed it wasn't him who built the things which others used to kill people. He saw his work as a series of fascinating games and arduous intellectual puzzles. 'It isn't my fault,' he would exclaim in time-honoured fashion. 'Weapons don't kill people. People kill people.' It was his particular tragedy that only an industry he loathed would pay him to play his games. His reaction to that was not unusual. He leaked like a sieve. He made it his business to know anything which smelled a little suspect in the industry, and there were enough others like him to make that easy. All a journalist needed to do was win his trust by stroking him, then shake him till he rattled. It was rumoured that others had been killed for lesser indiscretions than his. What kept him alive was that no one could do without him. He was too good at what he did to be allowed to die. That, and the fact the hard men found it difficult to take seriously enough the threat posed to security by some bald loony dressed in saffron robes.

But Stu was hard work. Too hard for now. She decided to call Clara instead, and invite her to dinner at the Alexis, an offer she could not refuse. Then she rang New York, and almost lost her temper.

It was raining by the time Clara arrived, raining and dark. It always seemed to rain in Seattle. As a matter of meteorological fact, there was less rainfall here than in Chicago or Atlanta, it just felt like more, because it came down in the form of a fine, apparently perpetual, drizzle. Most mornings a mist hung over the city. It was as though the price you had to pay for views of water everywhere was water in the air.

Caro had known Clara for years, as a friend rather than as a fellow journalist. She was a few years younger than Caro but, if anything, more self-assured. Her business was radio, the unsung little sister of American media and, although she could pass as one of the smooth-talking smiles who were normally chosen to front American channels, she had come up the hard way as a journalist. She had trained with UPI, straight out of college, then kicked around three mid-Western states, reporting agricultural shows between spells deejaying Country & Western tunes, before pulling a job as a news producer with a national channel in Washington DC. That was when Caro had met her, covering the Iranian hostage crisis. It was also the time Clara had come up against the hard truth of American radio: the channels could cope with the idea of women organizing and running the news, but they could not deal with them presenting it. Women were the fluff. They were there to cover sloppy stuff like arts and entertainment, but the voice which told you that your embassy had just been attacked and the President was going crazy had to be the voice of a man. Since Clara was not prepared to do the work and then hide in the cupboard, she had accepted the offer to run the features department of a news channel in Seattle. It wasn't perfect, but she was the boss. What Caro wanted from her was what she had as the first woman to be a network power in the capital: an unimpeachable string of contacts. She also wanted, desperately, to get the chance to talk with at least one other sane woman.

'Hi!' Clara greeted her brightly. 'How're you doing? You look terrible.'

'I'll tell you all about it later. Let's go eat.'

Despite the profusion of fresh produce in the area, including the biggest salmon catches in the world, the Alexis was one of the half-dozen places in Seattle which could satisfy serious eaters, and Clara, though no one would have guessed it from her figure, was nothing if not serious.

'We have to take you to Los Cuatro Esquinas while you're here,' she told Caro gravely. 'Wonderful Latin restaurant. Their Aji de Gallito is simply heaven.'

Caro smiled, for what felt the first time in an age. 'I don't know how you do it,' she told Clara. 'I don't know where it all goes.'

Clara looked suddenly bashful. 'Well, there's a gym across the road. And I've been pumping iron.' She buried her head in the menu as she admitted it.

Caro gasped, mostly with involuntary laughter. 'You've been what?'

Clara looked up, trying not to smile. 'Now come on, Caro, I don't mean Clara loves Conan or any of that stuff. I'm not turning into a meat-head. We're talking three-pound, five-pound weights here. Sometimes no pounds.'

A waiter shimmered over and asked if they were ready to order. Clara returned her attention to the menu, read it quickly and said, without any irony in her voice, 'We'll have it all.'

They did not quite manage that, but with no one watching them and no one to answer to, they managed to put quite a dent in Caro's American Express card. It was the second pudding which saw them off, the strawberry tart which followed the crèmes brulées, the veal en croute, the steamed salmon, the asparagus. They had hesitated at first, protesting that they shouldn't, until the waiter with the trolley had pointed out, 'Ladies, this is a restaurant, not a hospital. You can have whatever you want.'

They had spent most of their time suppressing giggles, and the unlikely sight of two grown women unhinged by good food and conversation in the midst of a select group of serious affluent diners. The hell with it, Caro thought, at once enjoying and deriding the hotel's care over ambience, setting and even tableware (darker, grander, and less feminine at dinner than at lunch or breakfast). Fortunately, they were in the secluded lower level where they could not cause so much offence.

There was one thing in particular which had set Caro wondering. 'How come you're free for dinner at no notice on Saturday night?'

Clara looked aghast. 'Oh, Caro, Caro, have you seen the men here in Seattle?' The look of mock-horror turned into the demure features of a convent schoolgirl. 'And besides, I would have turned any of them down to get to see you.'

Caro rather doubted that. 'Are they really so awful?'

Clara tapped the rim of her wine-glass. 'Worse. If they're not wasted hippies wondering whatever happened to the Sixties, they're married men who look like hamburgers but want

205

to believe they're goulash. Either that or they're the three-date wonders. You know, three dates telling you you're the most wonderful human being they've ever met and how much they'd like to develop a meaningful ongoing relationship with you. So you say, "OK, let's give it a try," and next minute they're out the window.'

Caro was sympathetic. 'I think I know the type. Do you really still have wasted hippies up here?'

Clara nodded vigorously. 'Sure do. This is the hippy hunting ground. You know, it's a nice place; no one bothers you. You can just sit and count your beads and eat tree-bark and do your drugs without any hassle. Everyone who couldn't cope when the Beatles split up drifted here to Seattle. After all, Jimi Hendrix was buried here, right back in his home town. They wanted to name the safari park at the zoo here after him, but some really weird people got together and called it a racial slur. 'Keep Jimi Out of the Jungle.' Can you believe that? Jimi would've loved it. All those tigers and elephants and lions and stuff.' She looked Caro straight in the eyes and said, with a sweet smile, 'And anyway, don't kid me. You know all about the wasted hippies. If you're here at such short notice you must be after Stu Wilcox.'

Caro admitted it with a nod. 'Tell you about it later.'

Clara understood. 'Let's have coffee in your suite. And a large cognac.'

Up in 414 Clara asked sarcastically, 'Do we search the place for bugs? Or is this going to be private enough?'

Caro almost felt apologetic at the elementary precaution she had taken. 'This will be fine.'

Clara smiled. 'That's OK. Anyway, I have a way with American bugs, the official ones. All you have to do is say, very slowly, very clearly, enunciating well,' she demonstrated as she spoke: 'Ronald Reagan is a faggot. Nancy puts out for naval ratings. The CIA is full of child pornographers. The FBI runs the Mafia. Blows out what they're pleased to call their brains.'

Caro opened the door to the waiter with the coffee and brandies saying, 'We'll need the same again in roughly half an hour.' Then, to his bemusement, she asked Clara, 'That's fine, but what about Russian bugs?'

'That's easy,' Clara replied. 'You can scare them out of their listening posts. You tell them communism is just around the corner.' The waiter backed out of the room. Clara became serious. 'OK, my friend, thanks for the dinner. Now, what gives?'

Caro explained. Clara listened. At the end of it she demanded more coffee. When it had arrived, she began.

'The one thing I am certain of is that friend Standing is broadly right.' Caro found herself relieved to hear someone who did not know him say it. 'There is no doubt at all that US military supplies are, despite Congressional limitations, getting into the Nicaraguan Contra, into Salvador and into Guatemala. Technically, those supplies are illegal. Neutrality Act of 1794. But I was in Washington a month ago for the wind-down of the current session and there is a lot of pressure down there to change the law, and almost none to stop the supplies. Your problem is to tie Errol Hart – and isn't that a weird story? – into the supply line, and find out exactly who he was working for.'

Caro nodded, with some hesitation. 'If he was working for anyone. His death might not have had anything to do with this. We could be barking up the wrong tree entirely.'

Clara frowned. 'You could. You really need to know what's being shipped out of Mobile, and who's organizing it all. Which I assume is why you want to see Stu Wilcox.'

Caro admitted that it was. Clara looked thoughtful. 'That might be a little difficult. He's on one of his little holidays at the moment. To the best of my knowledge, he hasn't signed up with a new firm yet, and knowing him he won't until he begins to feel the pinch. I haven't seen him myself in a couple of weeks. He could be anywhere. We have a whole new bunch of crazies in the North-West he might've joined up with.'

Caro nodded.

Clara continued, 'We have a whole lot of Survivalists, neo-Nazis and general Armageddon freaks in eastern Washington and over the borders in Idaho and Oregon. Not that Stu was ever likely to join them. Still, it could take a little time to track him down. Why don't we have brunch tomorrow? I could phone a few people first thing in the morning.'

'That sounds wonderful,' said Caro, stretching in her comfortable chair as a mournful ferry-whistle pierced the cool night air. She was puzzled by Clara's mention of right-wing groups. 'Are the Survivalists a serious worry to you?'

Clara looked sad. 'Honey,' she said, 'we did a feature on neo-Nazi training camps six weeks ago. I'm still receiving the death threats.'

Caro shuddered. She knew Clara had been threatened before. She knew that each time it happened it seemed a little easier to deal with. But she could not help telling Clara the fact she had suppressed. 'Be careful, love. Tom Wellbeck, my ex-husband, was murdered in Italy a month ago. That's how this all got started.'

Clara whistled. 'Oh, shoot. So that's it. I was wondering why you were looking like death. I thought it had to be a bad man or a bad period.'

Caro tried to smile, half-successfully. 'It's both,' she said. Her period had set in in Chicago, with its usual inconsiderate timing. 'But the bad man isn't Tom. I'm pretty much over that now, I think. We'd been divorced three years. And . . . Well, and nothing, I suppose. My problem now is Standing.'

'The lush?'

'The lush.'

Clara shrugged. 'Well, he doesn't sound like anybody's fool. He isn't by any chance related to the Washington Standings, is he? The old Foreign Service family? I knew Robert and his wife in D C.'

'The very same. Robert's his older brother.'

Clara laughed. 'Then what are you doing horsing around here? Just get the guy down to Washington and tell him to lean on his brother. You know what Robert is, don't you?'

'No.'

'Well, he's only, among a lot of other things, the first technical adviser to the Committee on Intelligence Affairs.'

It was Caro's turn to whistle. 'Thanks, Clara. Thanks a lot. And if I could I'd get him down there right now. After bawling him out. But I rang New York just before you arrived. He's checked out of the Plaza and they don't know where he's gone.'

'What garbage he must be,' Clara sympathized.

Caro wasn't sure. 'I suppose so. I suppose I shouldn't worry. He's got no money. He can't get far. But I do worry, Clara . . .'

'Well, don't. You're too nice, that's your trouble. Being nice to men is just being kind to animals.'

Caro laughed.

'I'm serious,' Clara exclaimed. 'You might as well join the SPCA. Especially if you're dealing with a lush. With most men you can at least hope for the sort of pathetic mindless devotion a dog will give you. But drunks are like cats. They're forever taking walks.'

'I suppose you're right,' Caro acknowledged, lighting a cigarette, to Clara's evident distaste. 'Now don't get like that. You eat my food, you breathe my ash. I promise I won't smoke at brunch . . . I suppose he'll be all right. I'll get in touch with our New York office on Monday. I just wish I knew where he was. Either this is the biggest waste of time and money I've ever been involved with or he is on to one hell of a story and he's holding something back. Which is why I want to cover the defence angle myself. I was thinking of talking to Boeing.'

Clara cackled maliciously. 'Boeing! Honey, come on! Outside the staged annual opportunities you've hardly got a chance. You could spend six weeks here and still end up eating clam. No, if you want to know about any potential aerospace angle, if you want to know about Boeing, leave it to me. It's time you stopped believing men are human. It's time to meet the Pretzel Unit.'

She cackled again. She would not explain.

Caro tried not to worry that night. She tried to sleep. But she could not help worrying. She worried about not being able to trace Stu Wilcox and wasting an expensive journey. She should have phoned Clara in advance, but all she had wanted to do was get away from Standing. And now Standing was missing too.

She wished she was back in Rome with Ezzo. She dreamed about him when she drifted to sleep at last. She dreamed of being curled up in his arms while he stroked her back. She dreamed of winey kisses. She dreamed of tumbling with him to the floor. Everything else was too complicated, too difficult to understand. She remembered what he had said about Italy, how though it baffled and enraged outsiders everyone inside it knew how it worked. And they were happy. She would have given a great deal simply to be happy. She wished she could go back to Ezzo. It would feel like going home.

But Tom was dead. Errol Hart was dead. Father Tomasso was dead. And now John Standing was missing. She was an outsider in this puzzle too, still baffled, still enraged.

The following morning dawned unnaturally clear. Her spirits lifted at the sight of the waters of the bay turning with the morning from gun-metal grey to a smoky blue. She went for a walk, to clear her head and think, in the cool air before the onset of the summer heat. First Avenue remained as she remembered it, the part of the downtown area the planners were most ashamed of and yet which seemed most full of life. It was a mix of Victorian buildings shrouded in scaffolds and plastic sheeting as they underwent renovation, bookshops from the second-hand to the sleazy, cheap clothes shops selling nylon work-clothes and one-size-fits-all plastic baseball caps, porno cinemas and a few enclaves of the old Seattle, like Warshals, the sporting goods and camera store, which maintained a reputation along the whole West Coast for old-fashioned service and integrity.

She walked north, stopping at each intersection to glance down to the bay, till she came to Pike Street and the upper corner of the Pike Place Market. There was a dress-shop on this corner, which had just opened last year, which she liked but could not afford. She was glad that it was closed. She gave thanks it was Sunday, till she remembered which country she was in, and that many a store would be open later today.

There was too little traffic on the motorway beyond, cutting it off from the bay, to separate it yet from the clean smell of the sea and the early dazzle of blue cupped into the low grey-green hills beyond. Years before, the Market had marched out on stilts to the Bay. Now it was cut off from its sustenance. Everything got cut off.

She walked up Pine Street, towards First Avenue. She had to be back before Clara called for her.

At ten she telephoned New York. It was seven in the morning there. The Plaza had still not seen or heard from John. She waited another half-hour and telephoned Alan in Washington. She had to check the number through directory inquiries, having failed to note it down. It took some time, as she didn't even have an address, except for the vague notion of Georgetown. Alan, at least, was safe, if less than delighted to be woken at that hour. He had got back late from a party Robert Standing and his wife Melissa had thrown for him in Virginia. He was due back there for lunch today. Next morning Robert had promised to get him to work. 'You'd like him,' he told her. 'He's a lot like John, but slower, if you see what I mean.' She saw. She had always wanted John to slow down. He always moved too fast.

She wondered if she should tell Alan about Robert's advisory role to the Intelligence Affairs Committee. In a sense, cut off in Washington, the less he knew the safer he would be. Safe from what, she wondered? Had Standing made her paranoid? He had done something to her. It was not like her to fail to note down phone numbers. She told Alan anyway.

He was impressed, saying, 'That explains a lot. There were more self-confessed spooks there last night than in the Hammer House of Horrors. I wondered how he knew them all. I'll tell you all about that when I see you. When are you coming?'

She did not really know. Part of her wanted to stay here for ever with all the other lost children of her generation, who had seen most of the hopes and dreams of their contemporaries wither to a need for cottages in France, a bigger wok and a brand-new BMW. *What happened to us?* she wondered. *Where did we go wrong?*

'I'm not sure,' she told him, 'I could be here a few more days.' Then she added, 'Alan, in case I don't get a chance, I want you to make sure to get hold of the New York office in the morning. You're in the same time zone. Standing's gone missing. I've left a message at the Plaza. I want another one left at the office. If and when he re-emerges he's to get down to Washington immediately. When he gets there, put him on a chain if you have to. Better still, hand him over to his brother or his ex-wife. I want him tied down in one place. The old sod's drinking again.'

Yes, she thought, *I could stay here. Get an apartment like Clara up off Broadway. I could take summer holidays down on the Oregon coast and long weekends across the mountains in Leavenworth or Lake Winatchee. I could forget the last fifteen years ever happened. Except I have the bug. I have a smaller infection of John's disease. Somewhere out there, there are bastards trying to do us down. And I want to find them and stop them.*

The telephone rang, Clara had arrived.

She was wearing a grey heavy cotton dress with a big bold red collar and matching lipstick, handbag, belt and shoes. She looked terrific.

'I brought my car,' Clara announced brightly. 'It's easier. I assume you hired some monster.'

'I got an Olds,' Caro admitted.

Clara nodded. 'Yeah. That figures.'

She explained that she had been over to Stu's apartment building that morning and spoken to the superintendent. 'He's seen no sign of him since before the 4th of July. Same as the rest of us. Mind you, Stu quite often takes off around the holiday. He still gets guilt feelings about being English. Like anyone cared. I thought we ought to try all the veggie joints, alternative bookstores, herb-shops, that kind of thing. How about it?'

It sounded sensible to Caro, given the nature of the man.

'Great!' Clara explained. 'That means we get to brunch at Julia's.'

They drove back up to Interstate 5, heading north to the Roanoke-Lakeview exit. Driving high along the hog's-back hills of the city they could see across the land-locked jewel of Lake Union to Queen Anne Hill and the three broadcasting towers which kept the likes of Clara in business. On Lakeview, where the yuppies lived in houses scattered on the hillside under a heavy beard of trees, they slowed down under the underpass as Clara made towards the exit on the left to Lynn.

'It's really East Lynn, you know. Like the play?' Clara explained. She put on her mock-theatrical voice. '"Dead, and never called me Mother!" I love it. Couple of years back somebody came up and stencil-painted crows along these bridge supports. That sums up an awful lot of the dreck here in Seattle. Crows on stilts.'

She pulled on to Eastlake and parked about half a block up. There was a queue outside the restaurant. There was a half-hour wait. (Short, Clara told her, for this time of year.) There was a red-haired waitress from Oregon called Marla who kept up a constant current of back-chat with Clara. There were wonderful cinnamon rolls and granola and omelettes with sour cream. And there was no sign at all of Stu Wilcox.

After brunch they tried the other branch of Julia's, over in Wallingford, near the university, full of a more eclectic techno-wizard crowd. Still no sign. They tried three book-stores on Broadway, near where Clara lived in one of the discreet 1930s apartment buildings. They tried the whole-food store at the end of Broadway, round the corner from the Harvard Exit. They drove back into town and tried the herb-shop in the market, the alternative herb-shop in the market, where Clara tried to buy ground aniseed and was told in a cloud of incense by a blank-faced assistant: 'You know, we only sell, like, whole seeds here.' And no, they had had no sign of Stu Wilcox recently. They tried the fishermen along the wharves whom Stu had been known to come and preach at to change their murderous ways. They had none of them been harassed lately. They tried the bums along the world's original Skid Road because Clara remembered at one stage Wilcox had believed they were the repositories of all wisdom. And they had dinner at the high-tech Mexican restaurant in the market, where he had come to try to convert the waiters, or baffle them with talk about peyote and consciousness-raising, or persuade them to cook their chili without carne. And still there was no sign of him.

Caro had almost surrendered, but Clara, who never seemed to flag, told her not to be defeatist. 'OK, so we had no luck with the counter-culture today. At least they all know we're looking for him now. They'll keep their eyes open, if they can. What we haven't tried is the technicians, the people Stu works with. Why don't we make an early start at the station tomorrow morning? My shift doesn't start till one. If we got in at nine, nine-thirty, we could both hit the phones. And if the worst comes to the worst, there's always the police. OK, so Stu is always wandering off. Our street reporters ought to be able to get the Finest here to take a Missing Person seriously.'

She smiled, suspiciously Caro thought, adding, 'Anyway, if you come in, you get to meet the Pretzel Unit.'

Clara picked her up at nine the next morning. There was still no sign of John Standing in New York. Caro was close to giving up. If nothing positive came up in the next twenty-four hours, she was flying to Alan in DC. If he had been able to find nothing she was firing John and getting back to work on her own ideas for the book. So why did she keep hoping he was right? Why did she keep wondering if he was safe?

On the way in to the big glass and concrete structure on Denny Way, Clara explained about the Pretzel Unit.

'Wim Pretzel,' she said, trying not to laugh. 'Spelt Wim, pronounced Vim. He handles science and medicine for us and I swear this guy just has to be an android. You know those cars they have that talk to you? The ones that tell you, "Hey, Dummy, fasten your seat belt"? Well, he sounds like one of those. He isn't human. Hence the Pretzel Unit. The thing is, because he's a robot, he's the only one of us who can get through to the machine men at Boeing. So somewhere along the way he wrapped up all our aerospace and defence stories too. This man doesn't have orgasms. He has First Strikes. All his dreams are mushrooms.'

Caro was always surprised by the sheer opulence of American broadcasting offices, not only by comparison with the hideous squalor in which British press journalists worked, but also with the low-key look of British broadcasting organizations. Most BBC offices especially looked like slums. Here, though, there was a five-floor atrium, deep-piled carpet, attractive receptionists, elegant open-plan offices with plenty of what was always most at a premium in London, space. And there were banks of equipment beyond London's dreams. Not just operational equipment, but scanning systems which allowed a couple of people to monitor every wire-service and broadcast news programme in the States on a permanent basis. They could plug into it all.

She had no time to whine comparisons, however, before Clara introduced her to the Pretzel Unit.

He looked perfectly normal. Young, quite attractive, in fact. Until he started to speak. But once she had told him what she wanted, what he gave her was gold.

She had to extract it from his verbal dross. His perceptions, his global tactical reorientations, his high-field profile penetration vulnerability, his optimized probabilities and latent potentialities. But what he told her was that Standing was right. That American conservatives had been arming the Nicaraguan Contras and other officially anti-communist groups, in defiance of the law, for over two years. He told her a number of Southern political figures were believed to be directly involved. There was talk that the level of trade was being increased. There was reason to believe the CIA, impatient with politicians and their slow democratic ways, had taken over the operation and much increased its scale. Which was what had the likes of Boeing, all the aircraft manufacturers, worried.

Boeing was clean. He was certain of that. They were too public an organization not to be. Like all US manufacturers whose products had potential military uses they were closely monitored by the administration and Congressional committees. They could not simply sell planes wherever they liked, lest such aircraft be used against America's best interests. All overseas sales had to be to approved purchasers. Which was why their parts and service contracts were so tight. They could not prevent a legitimate purchaser selling a plane on to someone who would use it for unacceptable purposes. But they could refuse to transfer the service contract and deny the new owner spare parts. They aimed to know where every aircraft built by them still in the air was, and who it was owned by. And they tried to keep their record clean.

It wasn't always possible. Some older aircraft in particular slipped out from under their control. McDonnell-Douglas had had that problem for over twenty years with the old DC-3, the Dakota, the great workhorse of the Thirties and Forties. There were dozens of them still scattered round Africa, Latin America and the Far East, flying on home-made spares long after the company had stopped making or servicing them. But in the main, the manufacturers knew where their aeroplanes were and who owned them. What had put the skids under them now was that, in the past ten months, two Boeing cargo jets, one McDonnell-Douglas, and a Gulfstream had gone missing in the Caribbean and Central America. No one knew who owned them now, or what they were being used for, but everyone could guess. The original owners had been struck off the list of acceptable purchasers, of course, but it was a little late for that. Right now the companies were desperate to find the planes and ground them.

'Do we know who the original purchasers were?' Caro asked.

The Pretzel Unit clicked a half-turn towards Clara. 'Is this an off-the-record situation?' he asked. Clara looked at Caro, and nodded.

'For the moment. If you're going to open this one up, Caro, I want to know. I want a piece of the story.'

Caro understood. The Pretzel Unit switched his vocal simulator back to the On position. 'I have a data-base on this. If you give me a few moments for retrieval, you may scan it.'

It didn't take long. Caro was almost disappointed to discover the data-base consisted of a file of neatly typed notes. She had been expecting computer printout at the least. She was as desperate as Clara to find a secluded corner where they both could burst out laughing. But they did not want to laugh once Caro had seen the details of the planes' original purchasers. One was in Nassau. Another in Panama. And the other two were in Alabama.

They hit the phones, with Caro saying, 'Let's start by finding Stu. Let's start by second-sourcing.'

They worked through every name they knew, in computers and in engineering. They put the word out that they wanted

Stu Wilcox. They gave both Caro's and Clara's various phone-numbers as the contact points. By lunchtime and the official start of Clara's shift they had done everything they could, they had talked to everyone they knew. All they could do was wait.

'Do you want me to call Langley?' Clara asked. 'Do you want me to talk to the Agency?'

Caro shook her head. 'It's a little early to spring this on the CIA. They'll only deny everything unless we get a great deal closer to the story.' She punched the desk with her good hand. 'I wish I knew where John Standing was. I wish I could get him on to his brother.'

She wished something else as well, but she could not tell Clara about it. She had avoided telling her anything about the potential Vatican connection. What she needed to talk to someone about was what possible reason Rome could have for supporting the right-wing guerrillas. Was there some aspect of Catholic foreign policy she had simply managed to miss? But whoever she talked to, it had to be someone with enough experience to help her make some sense of it, but close enough to the story not to give it to anyone else. Like it or not, John Standing was the best option she had. If she could find him.

Clara was practical. 'If he doesn't show by the morning, why don't you have your New York office check the hospitals?'

Caro went back to the Alexis for lunch. She sat by her telephone all afternoon, listening to Clara's programme. The main item was on school-board book censorship by religious fundamentalists. She called them that too. Caro smiled. The Born-Again Bible-belters would not like that. To them, fundamentalism meant Iran. They were only following God's Word. She sometimes wondered how long Clara could hope to get away with it.

But it seemed another wasted day. No phone call came all afternoon, as Caro sat yearning for the waters of the bay, wondering why she did not give up hope, why she did not just go out and ride the ferry?

217

The answer came just before eight, with a call from Clara, who sounded hassled, less expansive than usual.

'He just called,' she said, without naming Stu Wilcox. 'He sounded scared. He won't see us anywhere he might be spotted. We agreed the Arboretum, tomorrow morning, at ten. I'll see you at your hotel in an hour or so.'

There was nothing useful either of them could say or do. They could only wait for the morning. They went to the cinema to kill some time. Seattle was a movie town. Films drifted up here from Hollywood for try-out. Thanks to the Film Festival, whole cults began here.

Afterwards, sitting in the B + O, a fashionable café full of amiable gays at night, and named after the long-defunct Baltimore and Ohio railroad, a nostalgic reminder of early industrial America, in the years before the coming of the plane, Caro wondered why Stu had settled on the Arboretum for their meeting.

Clara wiped cappucino froth from her upper lip. 'It's owned by the university. It's close to the university. If he's been holed up in grad-pad land, it'd be an obvious place for him to meet us.'

'Yes, I know that,' Caro protested, 'but why there, instead of at Julia's, say, in Wallingford? Or wherever he's staying. And why wouldn't he leave a number? Why doesn't he want us to know where to reach him? Why does he want to meet us out of doors? Isn't the whole point about the Arboretum that there aren't many people there at ten on a weekday morning out of term?'

Clara frowned. 'I'd thought of that too. I wondered if he was scared of being spotted. He did sound scared. But it's always so difficult to tell with Stu. You never know if some new drug or theory has scrambled his brains to paranoia. They say he spent most of his time at NASA on LSD, doing this really great work while hiding in a cupboard, convinced the Martians were coming to rob him of his ears.'

Neither of them had any answers. They could only wait on Stu. They drifted back down Broadway, towards Clara's building where Caro was parked.

As they parted, Clara told her, 'Hey, don't worry. It's going

218

to be all right. It sounds like you've got a story. And don't worry about Stu. He's another Pretzel Unit. They haven't built the weapon that can stop him.'

Caro promised to come round at nine.

She was a little late. She had been touched that morning to find the hotel had made a special effort. Outside her door lay not only her freshly-polished shoes and copies of the *Wall Street Journal* and the *Financial Times* but also a copy of the *Examiner*. It carried reports of fresh purges in Poland. Trying to catch up with her colleagues' work had slowed her down and she had no time for breakfast. She grabbed a quick coffee at Clara's, then they headed off in the American's car.

'Leave the Olds here,' she was told. 'Help impress the neighbours. But the Toyota is more convenient.'

They turned off I–5 on to State Highway 520 across Portage Bay, taking the Montlake exit to the Arboretum which came on them at the same time as their first glimpse of Union Bay and Lake Washington and the Evergreen Point Floating Bridge. Before she was finished, Caro wanted to cross one of the floating bridges, a strange sensation she enjoyed. It felt like cycling on a water-bed.

The Arboretum lay opposite the university's estate, cut off from it by the Lake Washington Ship Canal. It was at once an outdoor lab for the Life Sciences departments and one of the city's principal parks. According to the guide books its chief attraction was its Japanese Garden, but the previous year Clara had persuaded Caro of the truth of what the local residents knew. The best thing in the Arboretum was hiring a canoe and taking it out in the sheltered backwaters which were part of its grounds, between the overhead ramps of highways and behind the breakwater of Foster Island.

You could vanish here, in waterways amongst high clumps of reeds and water-iris, in channels between a scattering of small islands. Here there were swans, and nesting birds beneath the highways, Canada geese, varieties of ducks, big-billed coots expertly ducking and racing for prey, and the sudden flashing flight of red-winged blackbirds. Lovers came here, and people who thought they were poets, whenever they wanted to be alone. No one would bother you and, on a weekday, no one even needed to see you. Which was presumably why Stu had told them to meet him on the pontoons where the waiting canoes were lined.

He did not come. They waited for an hour and a half, growing steadily more frustrated and angry. Clara checked with the staff at the office. A half-dozen people had arrived before them, taking out canoes. It was impossible to tell if any of them had been Stu. All they could do was wait for his arrival, and the return of the boats already out on hire.

They stood and let the light breeze off Lake Washington chill them despite the bright haze of the sun. And still he did not come.

They did not know why till that lunchtime, when Caro was already packing and Clara was at her office. The police called on them both, wanting to know why they had been looking for Stuart Wilcox.

For he had been found. Twice. The second time by a university zoologist, deep in a reed bed in the Arboretum. The first, by person or persons unknown, who had left him there, garotted.

CHAPTER SEVEN

John had known from the beginning it would not work unless everyone assumed that he was rich. It was why he had needed so much of Medina's money. In the past, when visiting Nassau, he had stayed at the Buena Vista on DeLancy Street. Most people only knew it for the restaurant, the owner Stan Bocus's pride and joy, but Standing, who had never minded being kept awake till the early hours by diners sitting late over their brandy, had an affection for the hotel which stretched back to his days in college. Although he liked the broiled lobster which headed the restaurant's menu, and its glassed-in veranda where a Haitian guitarist picked and played, what he stayed in the old mansion for was its big high-ceilinged colonial rooms, its rag-bag of old honourable furniture and its outmoded pool-sized baths. But this time even the Buena Vista was not grand enough to serve his purposes. He had made sure to eat there on Sunday, but he had booked himself into Graycliff.

He had never stayed anywhere quite as grand as Graycliff since the Ambassador's house was sold. It made him feel uneasy, especially after the past few years. He had been sorely tempted to break his cover and run, to somewhere he felt he belonged, some commercial heartless hotel like the Grand Central, smack in the centre of the city. But he had managed to quell his panic. He had to stay at Graycliff. For the moment he could afford it. He had to act as though he always could.

He had bought himself a couple of decent linen suits in New York, half a dozen shirts, some silk ties, a couple of pairs of white leather rope-soled shoes, and a panama folder. He had even bought himself a decent suitcase to put it all in. He was better dressed than at any time since leaving Evelyn. He looked, for the first time in years, as though he might be, after all, one of the Virginia Standings. All he had to do was live the part.

He had even remembered not to look either surprised or enchanted to be greeted at the airport by old Blind Blake playing guitar and singing his own lewd lyrics while a more conventional trio waited to go on for its set. It was one of the touches about the island a rich traveller would be expected to know, and not to be impressed by. But he was impressed, and he had forgotten, in the six years since his last visit.

He had not chosen to stay at Graycliff as a self-indulgence, for a change. Though he was pleased to have been put in Hibiscus, one of the thirteen rooms in the old house, with a private patio, a bathroom the size of most other hotels' suite bedrooms, and a decent writing-desk. Nor had he chosen it for its location in quiet gardens at the top of Blue Hill Road, looking down the hillside to the noise of Nassau and the vulgar delights of Paradise Island its own residents were too grand for. He had chosen it for its expense.

He had only one weekend to establish himself in the island's tight community as a visitor of substance and a gentleman to be reckoned with. Staying here was as quick a way as any.

He had dined here on the Saturday evening. The bottle of Puligny Montrachet '79 and three 1914 Armagnacs had helped to ease his conscience at not warning Caro what he was doing better than anything else could have done. Then he had gone on to the Pink Pussycat in DeLancy Street to let the regulars know there was a new rich man in town. He had finished off with more brandy at the Buena Vista, remembering his brother and his father to Bocus.

Despite the amount of drink he had taken aboard since Caro's departure from New York, the Bahamian sunshine woke him early on the Sunday morning, early enough for him to play the eccentric and walk downtown, to reacquaint himself with the geography. It came back to him quickly enough. Later he would wander at leisure, but Sunday had been a functional day.

After lunch at the Buena Vista he had had the doorman at Graycliff get him a car to drive him down the coast to Lyford Cay. He was not interested in the beaches or the shopping, though he had done a little of that, picking up some Joy de Patou for Caro at the prompting of another twinge of guilt. He was interested in being seen inquiring about renting a house for the winter in the exclusive 4,000-acre private estate. He was interested in being known as someone rich enough to do it at $10,000 a week (including three servants and three automobiles for the duration, naturally). He left his name with the office and asked them to send him details, at Gray-cliff. They had smiled. He could not remember how long it had been since he had evoked that smile in anyone, the smile born of greed.

On the way back into town in the hardly bearable out-of-season summer heat, he had his driver stop at Cable Beach. He had business at the Nassau Casino in Cable Beach Hotel.

He hated what American democracy had done to gambling. Casinos under American ownership or influence had neither the quiet, priestly calm of those European casinos where serious gamblers gathered like clubmen nor the enthusiastic conviviality of a race-track. Instead, they were designed to let as many people dream their fierce dreams of unearned wealth at once as possible, to the profit of the operator. In this huge hangar of a room, like Las Vegan casinos nearing the size of a football pitch, were hundreds of slot machines lined in rows, craps and blackjack tables and six roulette wheels ceaselessly glittering. They had taken the dreams and fantasies of all men and tied them to a production line designed to milk the millions.

He changed seven thousand dollars' worth of chips and walked over to the quietest of the roulette tables, ordered a drink from a passing cocktail waitress, thought about it, made that two drinks, and sat down to play. He wanted to be seen being able to lose casually.

The busiest hours on the tables were normally eight till eleven in the evening, but Sunday afternoon boredom also brought a particularly heavy crowd, many of them resident Bahamians, the people he needed to be seen by.

He dropped the first two thousand dollars slowly, two hundred and fifty dollars at a time, over his first long bourbon. There was a minor hiccough when the croupier thought he saw another player move his chips, but attention was soon diverted to the serious players once he had been removed politely to a back office. He dropped the next two thousand on two turns of the wheel, picked up his second bourbon and walked nonchalantly over to the baccarat tables. He could feel the eyes on his back as he walked as steadily as he knew how.

At the baccarat tables he grew serious, playing the percentages, the way the Ambassador had taught him. It was the one game which gave him a chance to get and stay ahead. It took a couple of hours, but he won back three thousand of the four he had lost playing at the sucker's game roulette. He did not even think about trying to make back the rest. He had to be the sort of man who could well afford to drop a thousand. He pocketed his chips, ordered another bourbon and waited for the introductions to start.

Which is how he ended up paying for dinner for a group of tax-exile residents who wanted to know all about him at the Café la Ronde at the Nassau Beach Hotel. Which is how he ended up giving Marsha Morgan a lift back to Graycliff in his limo, and parking her in his bed.

He did not remember very much of what happened thereafter, not now, in the bright light of Monday morning. He supposed he had been too drunk to remember. It killed his short-term memory even when it affected nothing else. He supposed it had been all right. She looked contented in her sleep. She would not if he hadn't.

It was tiresome not to know, however. Why was it that alcohol made you feel so much better but then prevented your remembering what feeling better felt like?

What he did know was that from the beginning he had agreed the double-occupancy rate, exactly against such eventualities, and that he had, as always, squared the doorman, desk-clerk and night-porter.

He looked at her again, seeing as if for the first time how young she seemed. When he was twenty he thought he had inherited the world. What made him now think of twenty-year-olds as children? He knew she knew he was a Virginian. He knew they all thought he was over here looking for interesting business ventures of an unspecified nature. He knew she thought he was rich. He remembered she was herself a Morgan of Missouri, one of those proper Confederate families who pronounced the word Missoura. He knew she was the kind of girl who seemed perpetually bored. But he had forgotten what she felt like.

He stroked the long white arm thrown carelessly out of the cover, indulging himself with her soft expensive skin. Then he blew a few wispy drifts of blonde hair away from her fast-closed eyelids. It did not seem to trouble her at all. He envied, for an instant, the dreamless sleep of the young. Then he slowly began pulling back the covers caught under the dead weight of her arm until she lay beside him naked.

He snaked up the bed to crouch over her, one arm on either side of her, his heavy head filling her face with shadow. He kissed her hair and her eyes, the small white shell of her left ear and the long line of her neck faintly fuzzy with hair. She stirred a little, and slept again. He lay beside her, stroking her back in long lines and small circles. As his fingers drifted between her buttocks and up the small of her back, she shivered but did not wake. He began to kiss her again, her throat, her shoulders, her free arm, her breasts, gently sucking her nipples while never ceasing the slow insistent stroking of her back. He rubbed her soft skin with his hair and his growth of beard, bringing a fine pink blush to the surface and causing her to stir as he kissed the dimpled folds beneath her heavy breasts and stroked the taut muscles of her belly.

She rolled slightly, and he rolled with her, easing her shoulders back on to the bed, though her legs remained lightly folded.

He started to stroke her again, in long delicate movements from her neck down to the smooth shallow curve within her hip-bone, hesitating with each stroke to soothe and caress the sides of her breasts and stomach. She unfolded as he crouched over, rubbing her right foot down the length of her left calf. He stretched out above her, supporting himself on one arm, and began to kiss her lightly while continuing his relentless stroking. She gave a little whimper as his fingers ran through her pubic hair, gradually more insistently. Her mouth opened, halfway between a smile and a little girl's irritated pout. As it closed again her lower lip caught on the edge of her front teeth, and the thin line of enamel glistened wetly in the morning sun.

He licked at her lips, then began to push his tongue between them, maintaining the pressure of his hand between her legs. As first she shook him away, but the second time her sleeping teeth parted and her long tongue seemed involuntarily to respond. When he put his knee between her legs they parted without demur.

He lay stretched out above her, taking his weight on his hands and knees, kissing her ever more deeply, his stiff penis jutting at her sex. He moved gently, searching her out, waiting for her to get wet, waiting for her to be ready. She began to stretch out beneath him, palms upward, rubbing her soft arms into the silky sheets and squirming, responsive to the tiny circular movements of his hips. There was one tremendous wave of muscles down her body, and her hips lifted, and he found himself inside her. After that, everything quickened.

He would never be certain exactly when she came fully awake. He was only aware of her small hands pressing flat across his buttocks and her throaty voice murmuring, in an ever faster whisper, 'Yes, yes, yes, yes, yes,' until the sudden violence of her orgasm almost tore at him, forcing him to slow down and move more deeply till he came.

Afterwards, as he lay beside her, his body heavy with sweat, she had looked at him with her clear, genetically unimpeachable, blue eyes and, smiling, said, in an accent much deeper South than his had ever been, 'I suppose that's what you Virginia gentlemen call ringing the alarm cock.'

Sex made him feel temporarily human, but it did not last. He poured them both a drink. She sat up in bed, wrapped in a sheet, shrinking from but swallowing the white rum he had given her while he sat naked at her side taking deep draughts of bourbon.

'I have to get to work,' he told her. 'You going to be here when I get back tonight?'

She wore the look of impenetrable boredom she always

226

had except when making love. 'I don't know. There isn't a pool at Graycliff. Couldn't you take a little time off? We could go back down the coast. I know some folks at Lyford Cay.'

He was almost tempted, more by the mention of Lyford Cay than by her company. He did not imagine it wore too well. But there were things he had to do. Besides, he remembered the only advice his older brother ever gave him: *Tell the pretty ones they're smart, tell the smart ones they're gorgeous, tell the lively ones how shy and deep they are, and ask the shy ones first time out. Otherwise only try never to do anything they ask you.*

So he did what he wanted, and had, to do. 'Can't,' he told her curtly. 'This is business which just won't wait. So are you going to be here when I get back, or are you leaving now?'

She looked at him levelly and said without malice, 'You know, I don't believe you are a gentleman at all.'

'I never claimed I was.'

She shrugged. 'If I am here, do we get to party?'

He finished his bourbon before saying, 'Sweetheart, I get to party, whether you're here or not.'

This morning he wanted to start with the banks. Eight major foreign institutions, including Barclays, Chase Manhattan, Citibank and Second City. If he started with one of those, rather than the smaller local institutions, he could have the whole banking system on the island talking about him over lunch today. The choice was simple. After all, he had only recently opened a Second City account. He was still half-tempted to try one of the smaller offshore houses. The ones whose customers' need for tax and investment advice was not quite up to the standards other banks could accept. But he knew that, although it would be entertaining, it would also be a self-indulgence. If you wanted to be noticed, you had to start at the top. He could, of course, have started at First Manhattan, in the steps of Errol Hart, but he wanted to parallel Hart's path, not to follow it. Simply following Hart invited exposure.

He had the car take him down Blue Hill Road, past the explosive end of Shirley Street's one-way stretch at the Gleneagles Hotel, down towards Bay Street and the heart of Nassau and Second City's main branch.

When he arrived, it took a few moments to organize to see the manager. He remembered to be lordly and demand someone fetch him a drink. What he was here to do was simple enough, and proved easy to arrange. He gave the manager the details of his account in New York. He gave his Swiss bank as a second financial reference. He saw respect grow in the banker's eyes. So he told him he was looking for investment opportunities for a small group of expatriate American investors of which he was the chief. He also admitted interest in a number of companies in the Southern States with interests in this region. Second City in New York, he explained, were running some credit checks for him. Could the manager possibly telex New York, quoting this reference number, to ask if details were yet available? He handed over a list of the companies. He mentioned, casually, in passing, it was possible that, as these companies had interests in this region, the manager might know of them. If he did not, perhaps other bankers in Nassau did. It must be a small community. He wished the banker good day. He would call again before the close of business.

He was feeling in control. He sent the grinning driver off duty, telling him to return to collect him from the bank at three in the afternoon and to wait till he was ready. It was better to walk, he thought, even in this weather. It would help him to earn the thirst he was already feeling. He gave up pretending, and strolled beneath the tin sun-roofs of Parliament Street to the Parliament Terrace Café. He wanted to sit out in the sunshine in a garden restaurant, nursing a long cold drink. He was glad to see Joe Johnson still ran the bar, with Pappy Sam Smith in the kitchen. He made that two long drinks, to celebrate.

They slowed him down. The third one slowed him even further. He knew he should not be drinking so heavily in weather as hot and humid as the tropics in the summer. He knew the British had not been fools to stay off the gin till the sun was over the yard-arm, or the empire would never have

228

got run. He felt the light swaying and thicken. He felt himself falling into darkened tunnel-vision. Despite the weather, he ordered strong black coffee, fast.

He took a cab down to the waterfront, beating its slow way through the lackadaisical traffic of a summer's day, competing with gaudy pedestrians, their brilliant peacock colours flashing against white light, pink buildings, black skins.

He began the long slow walk through the garish chaos of Woodes Rogers Walk beside the Prince George Wharf. Normally he would have taken a tourist's pleasure in the narrow dockside lane, just wide enough for a lorry to pass down and a honking nightmare when two drivers faced each other refusing to back down. It was single-file walking only here, past tiny stalls and stores selling fruit and vegetables and a ragbag of imported goods, to the Straw Market, opposite the pink eighteenth-century government complex, where the city's commerce exploded in everything from woven baskets to papayas in the shadow of docking ships. But he had no eyes for the traders, hawkers, crooks and sharks today, every colour from palest cream to indigo after centuries of piracy, whoring, slavery, oppression and simple fornication. He was after bigger crooks.

He had to call on every import–export agent on the waterfront, and every shipping master, to explain his business and leave his name and make the point that his address on the island was Graycliff.

It was after lunch by the time he had finished. It was time to return to the bank. He took another polite but labouring taxi, impeded by the city's careless attitudes to time. It did not matter. The manager was waiting for him respectfully. He opened his office door. 'Good afternoon, Mr Standing,' he began, almost bowing, 'would you care to step this way?'

It was as he had expected. His presence was beginning to cause a stir. There was no news for him yet, either locally or from New York, but it was clear that there soon would be. He made the point he was always available at Graycliff round about breakfast time. The banker promised to be in touch, and asked if Mr Standing could give him any indication of the precise nature of his interests, and those of his consortium. John answered with an enigmatic smile, and left the banker guessing.

The hotel limo was waiting for him. He needed to shower and change before he made his last official call of the day.

His old shirts had been returned by the hotel laundry, still hideously frayed, but a good deal less dejected. He put one of them on. He took the second linen suit, crumpled it into a ball, put it on the floor, took one of the pillows off the bed and laid it across the suit, then jumped up and down on the pillow. By the time he had finished it looked affluent but shabby. He put it on, then slipped on a pair of shoes without socks.

Examining himself in the full-length mirror in the bathroom he decided he looked rich enough, but still respectably so. He needed to look a great deal more like he usually did: disreputable. He knew the answer to that. He would pour himself a couple of stiff bourbons. And he would walk. Nothing could better remove the gleam from his fascinated attentive eyes.

It worked. He was feeling distinctly seedy by the time he began the short sweaty walk south out of the city into the Over The Hill district.

It was here, directly behind the city's oldest Millionaires' Row, that the most poor and corrupted citizens swarmed. Over The Hill was the quarter which never slept, a warren of tenements, shanties, bars, bordellos, gaming halls and illicit shops and markets. It was true you might see white faces here, cruising the danger and excitement, squeaking at the heavy pall of ganja it imagined everywhere, safe in taxis or in groups, or visiting the dilapidated cultural and recreation centre, but rarely in the crowded insanitary back alleys and runways of Nassau's most populous and least policeable quarter. Exactly where John was headed, in fact.

He cut off Blue Hill Road and vanished into the restless heart of Over The Hill.

Here, more than anywhere on New Providence Island, he needed to do nothing to be noticed. He was white. He wore a jacket and trousers which matched. Small children with distended bellies and the first signs of rickets shrank behind their mothers' skirts as he passed. The women's heads nodded sleepily closer together as they asked themselves and each other who the white man was.

It was cooler in the side streets and alleys of Over The Hill than in the broad avenues of the wealthy official parts of town. Here, buildings and shanties grouped together, offering a few hours' shade at each end of the day from the otherwise flat and merciless sun. There was a smell of cooking everywhere, mainly of peas'n'rice, the staple of the poor, the nutty peas which grew everywhere on dwarfish green-brown bushes boiled up with rice and tomato-paste and chili. But he could smell something sharper too, as he passed an open-fronted store where old toothless men sat grinning and drinking rum; something beneath the sudden tang of spiced fried chicken. It smelt like blood and burnt skin. Then, thinking of the chicken, he understood. Someone was scorching rooster comb, before grinding it as a treatment for boils and chickenpox. He was in that world where bay geranium was used against colds, and papaya to treat slipped discs. These were Obeah people, many of them not even pretending to a veneer of Christianity, still governed by the dark faith of their West African ancestors. Here, spirits roamed, and monsters flew.

He went further into the heart of the area, not knowing exactly what he was looking for, but knowing that it would find him. He moved by taking each second right turn, alternating with each first left.

He found himself at last in a slightly more open space, where a number of alleys gathered. There was a pump in the middle of it. There was one shop, partly-shuttered, selling fly-blown staples, the big island cockroaches scurrying freely over the sacks. And there was a bar, where a few men sat, drinking home-brewed liquors.

He sat down, at a rickety table, on an ancient wooden chair which swayed unconvincingly under his weight. The other men looked away. It did not matter. He was in no hurry.

He waited twenty minutes, ignoring the insistent reggae thud from the ghetto-blaster in the back room, the unabashed stares of children and the anxious mothers who scurried them past him. He just sat, watching people come to the pump for the island system's good, but precious, fresh water. He smoked two cigarettes while he was waiting, remembering not to look tense, not to smoke them right down to the filter.

At last one of the men lounging inside came out to him. A Rastafarian.

'You want somethin'?' the Rasta asked sullenly.

'Rum.'

The man brought out a dusty bottle of Bacardi and an unwashed glass. John was patient with him.

'I said rum.' He looked up at the white expressionless eyes in the unresponding face, and added, 'Not water.' The face broke into a smile. The man came back with a bottle of yellow oily liquid even John treated with respect. The other men gathered round him.

He said nothing, for some time. He just drank. Steadily, with professional determination. He might well pay for it later, but it was a matter of respect. When he had finished half the bottle he looked about him again.

'What you want, man?' the barkeep asked.

John did not reply.

'We got women. We got grass. We got coke. We got boys.' The barkeep said the last with evident distaste.

John's silence made the man go on.

'We got gamblin'. We got cock-fights. We got guns and we got transportation.'

John hoped his eyes remained as dull and listless as he wanted. He poured himself another glass and drank it down in one. As he intended, it prevented him answering too quickly. When he was good and ready he said simply, 'I want to see the Man.'

No one answered. No one moved. He poured another drink.

The silence did not matter. It did not worry him. It meant they took him seriously. It was too late for them to ask in mock-innocence, 'What Man?' They knew who he was after. Even if John did not.

The barkeep looked him in the eyes. 'Why? When? Where?'

John drank what was left in the glass before replying. 'My business. Any time. Anywhere.' The barkeep still looked suspicious. John licked his lips. 'If I was police,' the very word made all of them stiffen, 'all I'd have on him was that you said he was the Man. That's hearsay, not a crime. Like I told you, it's my business. I'll tell him to his face.'

The other man hesitated, then asked, 'How you going know each other?'

John smiled. 'He'll know me.' He took the two banknotes he had brought with him out of his pocket. American currency passed as easily here as the brightly-coloured Bahamian notes. He tore the hundred-dollar bill in half, handing one piece to the barkeep. 'And I'll know him when he gives me this. He can get messages to me at Graycliff. But tell him to get the messenger to take a bath. I have a reputation to maintain.'

The barman smiled. John punched the cork back into the bottle and put the bottle in his jacket pocket. As he got up to go he put the other bill, the fifty-dollar, on the table.

'Keep the change,' he said.

It was a tricky walk back to the hotel. The stuff in the bottle had been stronger than he had known, and the out-of-season heat made any walking difficult. It made him miserable.

He did not want to be in this city. He did not want to be doing this. He had had to make himself look bored, and he was perilously close to becoming it in fact. He could understand how someone like Marsha, despite her youth, could end up permanently bored. There was something limiting about islands, however much money and sun you had. You could not get away from them. You got desperate for something new.

He wished he was up in the country, high in the hills, under the palms and casuarinas, amongst the bougainvillaea and frangipani and the flowering yellow elder. Away from crowds he could think and drink in peace. There were places where the long trails of roadside scrub gave out and opened into pineapple plantations and groves of the big bitter local oranges. There were places where the air was filled with the scent of limes and lemon-flowers, and where the dark shine of sandbox trees and Jerusalem thorns was brightened by sudden bursts of white-crowned pigeon or the yellow and brown Bahamas woodstars flickering in and out amongst lignum vitae. He had come hunting in these islands in his boyhood. Simpler, cleaner hunting than he was doing now, for ring-necked pheasant, night herons, guinea fowl, jacksnipe, coot and mourning doves, instead of for murderous and corrupt men. He wished he was where the breadfruit grew, and the egrets ducked and dived, while herons from the north and pink flamingoes and spoonbills from the south cruised in as stately as royal barges. He wished he was in the Biminis, fishing for marlin and Allison tuna in the waters off South Cat Cay.

He knew it was the drink and the day-long heat which was depressing his spirits, but that came as no consolation. He found himself quite pointlessly enraged to find she was not there when he returned.

He tried to calm himself. He tried to think over what he had been doing. He poured himself another drink.

Everyone would know now, everyone who mattered on New Providence Island, that he was here. He was not interested in respectable bankers at major institutions. He was not interested in Second City, though he hoped like hell they came up with some answers from New York soon. What mattered was that on the grapevine the word would have gone out to the smaller institutions and, especially, to the ones which operated on the fringes of legality. They would also know by now that he had been checking out small fast cargo vessels from the islands. Boats mainly, but he had remembered to ask about light planes. That combination of easily gambled cash, interest in the Southern States, and need for transportation, would add up in their minds, as he had intended, to one thing and one alone. They would have guessed that Mr Standing was in the freelance smuggling business, the business Errol Hart had tried to join with such lamentable consequences. All he had to wait for now was for people already in the business to make their approaches, wanting to know more about him, probably wanting to warn him off. But he needed to know about them. He needed information. Which was why he had gone Over The Hill today.

New Providence was one of those places where the underworld split into groups. It was true wherever American influence extended. The local people maintained their traditional business, but they had no foothold in the big money, international trade the Americans brought with them. An uneasy peace reigned throughout the Caribbean between the local organizations and the power of the men in suits. It only worked because the Americans sub-contracted their pin-money business to the locals. Which was why he had to see the Man, whoever the Man was now in Over The Hill. It was his business to know what the men in suits were up to, and what openings for his people those operations might afford. He also had to keep an eye on potential new business opportunities. It was the only bait John had to dangle before him.

If he was right, John knew he should be able to tie it up here. The banking operations in the States and Panama were only the financial mechanics. Somewhere, somehow, the goods themselves had to be transported. And whether it was guns or cocaine, it was unlikely to happen through areas of direct American influence. Which ought to rule Panama out. The Bahamas would be perfect. A former British colony made up of a string of islands, any one of the smaller ones of which could be used as bases for smuggling, combined with a banking centre in Nassau which, because of its tax laws, attracted enough dubious customers to put the financial aspects of the deal together. His nose told him the answer was here, and he had nothing else left to rely on.

All he could do was wait.

She came into the room without warning. He must have left it unlocked; but she had probably picked up the duplicate key anyway. He had stretched out exhausted on the bed, too tired even to shower. He opened his eyes when he heard her footfall, light and easy in her summer clothes. She was wearing a crisp white cotton blouse and a pleated linen skirt. She must have been home to change some time. He wondered where home was. She sat down on the bed beside him, her broad hips stretching the linen of her skirt. Her perfume smelt of something vaguely citric. He liked it.

'You look as beat as I feel,' she said. He nodded. 'Have a

good day on business?' He nodded again. 'Are you going to ask me what I've been doing?'

He lifted himself on his elbow. 'I think you're going to tell me anyway.' She put the square white cards she was holding into his hand. They were targets. Each of them had a big ragged hole torn out of it at or near the centre.

'Nice grouping,' he told her, genuinely impressed.

'Do you know anything about shooting?' she asked, with her usual bored disbelief.

'A little. I am a Virginian.' She almost smiled at that. 'I used to hunt when I was younger.'

'Shotgun or rifle?'

'Rifle. And a little side-arms stuff for fun. Where do you shoot?'

She shook the blonde hair out of her face and pouted. 'At Lyford. There's a range. I told you I knew people out there. You should have come. You could've helped me change.'

He pulled her down to him to kiss her. Her mouth smelt of cloves and apples. 'I like you just the way you are.'

She pushed him away, saying, 'Oh, you boys!' When he protested that he was old enough to be her father she told him age ought to have taught him wisdom. 'Anyway, it's something to do.'

'Is that what I am?' he asked, adopting a grave expression. 'Something to do?'

'Oh, yes,' she confirmed. 'A little swimming, a little shooting, a little flying, a lot of sex. What else is there to do on the island?'

'You fly as well?'

She was proud of it. 'Got my private pilot's wings on my nine-teenth birthday. Joined the Mile-High Club that afternoon.'

He laughed. 'If you hate it so much what are you doing on New Providence?'

She mocked him again. 'Why, Mr Standing, I'm just a poor Southern girl born outside her time. I had to come live somewhere where I could have a whole heap of moon-faced darkies running about on my orders.' He could not tell exactly how serious or sarcastic she was being. 'I work at the Embassy. That's the excuse I gave my family, to get me out of

Missoura. Not that anyone works there much in the summer; it gets too hot to work. I just call in once in a while. Besides, ain't it a shame what the Union government done? That ugly, ugly new building in that pretty, pretty street?'

He could only agree with her. No recent building seemed to take account of the island's colonial tradition or have any respect for the beauty of its sightlines. He tried to pull her down to him again, but she stiffened and resisted. Her young body was firm beneath his hands.

She was matter-of-fact. 'I bought some clothes, so I don't have to keep going back to Lyford. Now I'm going to need to shower, if we're going out to party.'

He smiled as she vanished into the bathroom, her clothes a crumpled pile on the floor where she had dropped them, and he called after her, 'I think I need a shower too.'

He heard the hiss of water on heavy English porcelain. Then he heard her throaty voice, filled with laughter, saying, 'Come on in, the water's lovely.'

She was wearing a pink silk shift. She was an expensive lady. Only he would know she was wearing only silk stockings beneath it. It almost made him want to cancel the car, but she wanted to party, and he needed to be seen on the town, and a beautiful young woman was part of the uniform for people in his supposed business. The only thing which worried him was her job at the embassy. He wondered how many people knew about it. Almost everyone in the Island Establishment he suspected. Would she compromise him with the people he needed to get in touch with? Perhaps not. Not if the Agency really was involved. They probably all thought of her not as an embassy staffer, but as a young woman who liked to get laid a lot.

Thank Heaven, he thought to himself, *for little girls.*

They walked down the main stairs into the hallway. The desk clerk smiled at them. The Maître D bowed. They made a handsome couple. John realized he would have to watch himself. He had always had a weakness for being one half of a handsome couple. It had cost him two brief marriages, two daughters' worth of guilt, and half a house in Georgetown.

The doorman had the grey Mercedes waiting for them. John handed Marsha in and took his place himself. As the door slammed shut behind him he realized there was something wrong. The big black man in the driver's seat was not the man who had ferried him round before. That man had worn no dreadlocks. Where had his river gone? And what was this man doing here?

The big black driver turned. He wore a T-shirt, not a uniform. And he was grinning.

He was also holding out half a hundred-dollar bill.

'Hi,' he said, 'I'm Babylon.'

CHAPTER EIGHT

Of the three of them working on the story, only Alan Clarke was not exhausted. He was too young to be tired out by the past. What he felt was more confused exhilaration than any other emotion. He sometimes felt as though he had not touched the ground since taking off from London Heathrow Airport.

Robert Standing had organized him over the weekend. On the Friday night he had the tourist view of Washington, of official marble Washington, from the Lincoln Memorial and Foggy Bottom to the Supreme Court, from Lafayette Square and the White House to the Department of Transport building. He could work the Metro system now, though he still panicked slightly at machines that could swallow up your banknotes and return you change invariably in nickel pieces. (It said something about the speed with which he adapted that he already thought of them as nickels instead of five-cent coins.) He could talk knowledgeably about the Federal Triangle, locating each of the departments of state. He knew what the Rayburn Building was (a Congressional office building beside the Capitol on Independence Avenue). He knew that Union Station, though it smelt of derelicts' urine, was grander as a building than the Government Printing Office beside it. But he still kept being taken by surprise.

He was surprised that so much of the heart of Washington was grass, the long lawns of the Mall linking Lincoln and the Capitol, in which the bleak black wall of the Vietnam Veterans' Memorial with its thousands of dead names, and the blank white obelisk of the Washington Memorial stood. He found himself surprised at his embarrassment at a lifetime assuming any half-way decent neo-classical building would be on his side of the Atlantic. He had thought of all American official classicism as a fake, an attempt to ape the Europeans, but many of the buildings and memorials were older and finer than their equivalents in London. He was surprised at how open the government and its records were. Robert took him to the Archives Building and showed him how any member of the public could, say, consult the medical leave-of-absence records for the Revolutionary War, or officers' commissions on either side in the War Between the States. But he had also shown him how to access the Congressional Record, the minutes of committees and the records of Cabinet and Departmental deliberations also indexed in the Archives. He found himself wishing he could be here in session to attend a committee in person, instead of seeing extracts hours later on television news broadcasts in Britain. Suddenly, decisively, although by nature deeply conservative, he found himself no longer believing the British arguments in favour of Official Secrecy. He had finally become a journalist.

But what surprised him most of all was how black a city Washington was. Robert had tried to tell him, but it had not sunk in. He noticed one absolute class distinction between the races. The passengers in buses were almost exclusively black. Outside the safe zone of the Federal Triangle which housed the government offices and agencies, he might often just as well have been in Africa. And the climate suggested that he was. It was as though the white marble, green-lawned capital of a pink-and-white-fleshed empire had somehow been dropped into the heart of a great African metropolis, to remind it what its wealth had first been founded on. This, he realized, was a foreign city, and the makings of a time-bomb. For the first time in his life he found himself being careful where he walked, after a middle-class black told him there were whole areas of the city where he was afraid to go.

On the Saturday he spent the morning walking and taking the Metro, to make sure his feet knew where they were going for the future. And he had played the tourist, visiting the Smithsonian Museums, buying freeze-dried astronauts' ice cream in the Aerospace Museum for his nephews. He had noted how small the White House was for a Presidential Palace. And he called on his *Examiner* colleagues gathering at the Hyatt Regency in New Jersey Avenue for the International Monetary Fund Conference preparatory talks. They had not had much time for him, but they did arrange for him to be accredited to the talks. He found it a relief. It gave him some kind of acceptable role. They also introduced him to some colleagues on the *Washington Post* and took him drinking in the Cosmos Club on Embassy Row, because they could not find a member of the grander Metropolitan.

He did not remember very much about the party at Robert's that evening. He had been grateful when, the following day over lunch, the ex-diplomat supplied him with a typed guest-list, giving each guest's occupation and office telephone number. 'I'm very bad with names myself,' he explained, 'and it's such a chore having to remember all those details.' What Alan did remember was that the party seemed to divide along native and visitor lines. The outsiders, the people moved to Washington by their part in government business, drank Perrier water and talked about jogging and pumping iron, about Assenmaker fry-pans and their holidays in France. The natives were a different matter, and entirely relaxed. They drank hard and heavy and seemed to have no discretion in talking about their work in government departments mainly, it seemed, to do with intelligence matters and foreign affairs. It was not until the next morning, in the middle of a hangover, that Alan realized that they were only displaying the high-handed assumption of people bred to power anywhere in the world: Robert Standing was one of their own, so anyone he invited would be safe. There was no need for them to remain silent. Nor did they have the need newcomers had to make their jobs sound more important than they were by being ostentatiously secretive.

Lunch on Sunday had come as a pleasant change and a sober relief, though Alan was constantly anxious lest the telephone ring at Georgetown in his absence. It was not Caro he was worried about, nor John, but Tom Stoddart, and any message which might come from Harry the Prep. It was only a small consolation that the apartment had an answering machine.

He found himself entirely charmed by Robert and his wife Melissa, who shyly deprecated herself as being 'a mere

Yankee from Maine'. He found himself telling them the main substance of the story he and his colleagues were working on, though suitably amended. Robert had looked at him with new respect and told him to come to the university in the morning. That evening he attended the first discussion session, the keynote speeches by Michel Camdessus, new head of the IMF, and by his opposite number at the World Bank, Barber Conable.

The evening ended in the paper's suite at the Hyatt Regency. Alan found himself being drunkenly annoyed that the sofa in the bedroom did not match the rest of the pink and lacquered black furniture. It was blue. One of his colleagues explained a mistake had been made in designing the rooms. The original pink sofas intended for the bedrooms had been too large to make it through the doors. The only ones which would were these. You had to choose between furniture which looked wrong or no furniture at all. It wouldn't, Alan thought, do at all. And still no word from Stoddart.

He called New York on Monday morning. Stoddart told him to be patient. The Prep was not an easy man to find if he had reason not to be discovered. All would be well. He should await the call.

But he could not wait. He had a whole new city and world to discover. He could only be sure to come back twice a day to check for any messages.

He spent the bulk of Monday in the institutional pale-green offices, woodwork picked out in cream, of the Rayburn building, talking to a member of the Ways and Means Committee who had fled back for a long weekend to Washington, away from the dreary claims of his constituents. His view was simple. No budget had been drawn up for involvement in covert operations in Latin America besides the CIA blockade of Nicaraguan waters. If such operations were under way, the money was being taken from some other budget. He insisted on taking Alan through the grind of figures made available to the committee, saying it was hard to see where such expenses could be hidden.

Alan did not believe that. He suspected Robert did not either, though the older man would not discuss it as they sat eating lunch outside La Colline in the bright sunshine below the Capitol and Union Station, the tables around them filled by journalists and congressional researchers. They finished the day with the Clerk of the Foreign Affairs Committee, who explained that his committee had been trying for a year to obtain a precise account of US commitments and involvement in the Central American arena from the White House, and so far all it had done was fail.

By the time they got back to the Georgetown house, Alan was feeling in need of a shower, a drink, and something to relax his mind. He took the shower himself. Robert fixed him a drink. And by the time Alan rejoined him there was a very pretty, very young, dark-haired girl sitting in the drawing-room.

'Hi,' she said, getting up, politely, 'I'm Eleanor Standing.'

Robert introduced them formally, apologizing as he did so. 'I hope you don't mind, Mr Clarke. I heard Eleanor parking her car while you were in the shower, so I invited her up for a drink.'

'Not at all. It is your apartment,' he remembered to use the American word, 'and I am charmed.'

Eleanor did not react. Instead she waited for Alan to sit down and for her uncle to hand him his bourbon before remarking, 'Uncle Bob tells me you're working with my father.'

'Yes. I am.'

She looked wistful. 'In that case, you must know him rather better than I do.'

'I wouldn't say that. We haven't known each other very long.'

Eleanor smiled ironically. 'I haven't known him at all. How is he?'

Alan took a drink. 'All right. Pretty much. The last time I saw him. To be honest, I gather no one's very sure where he is right now.'

She nodded. 'That doesn't surprise me. He's always been elusive. Tell me, does he still drink as much as he used to?'

Robert looked wounded. He interrupted his niece. 'I think that's enough on that subject, Eleanor. I think you're embarrassing poor Mr Clarke.'

She was; and by the look of it she enjoyed it, Alan thought. She was enormously assured for her age. If he had been only a few years younger he would have found it rather attractive, but he was just sufficiently older than her to find it a fraction disconcerting. He tried to change the subject. 'What are you doing in D C?'

She shrugged again. 'Not so very much. Waiting to go up to Vassar. I, properly, inherited the apartment downstairs last birthday. I thought I ought to use it, and Uncle Bob was prepared to use me as a research assistant, to stop me running off to Lebanon or Kampuchea. But I've extracted a heavy price. He's paying to send me to Mexico and Peru later in the summer.'

Robert looked rueful. 'Eleanor has inherited the family gift for negotiation,' he explained. She smiled, looking like a happy little girl for that one instant.

'What will you be reading?' Alan asked her.

She shook her head. 'It isn't like that. Not in America. But I'll be majoring in Japanese and taking a Spanish minor. I think they are likely to be the most important languages for our diplomats by the end of the century.'

'You sound very ambitious.'

'I am. I know what I want and I know I can get it.' As she was speaking, the phone rang. Robert answered it while Eleanor continued regardless. 'And, unlike either of my parents, I intend to hold on to the things I want, once I have acquired them.'

Robert cupped his hand over the telephone receiver and interrupted her. 'Mr Clarke, it's for you. He didn't give his name.'

It was Stoddart. His voice sounded strained, excited. 'Say nothing,' he ordered. 'Write nothing down. This Wednesday. At seven in the evening. Inside the Southern bend of Harlem Mere. North Central Park. Wear a yellow-rose as a boutonnière. He will approach you.' The line went dead.

As Alan put the phone down, Robert apologized again. 'I'm sorry, Mr Clarke. I keep expecting the phone to be for me.'

Eleanor rose to go. 'Please, Mr Clarke, as we are to be

neighbours, don't hesitate to call on me.' She sounded like a little girl trying very hard to be grand. Robert watched her with avuncular pride as she departed.

'She's a lot more like her father than she knows,' he explained. 'The rest of us are simple diplomats. John's the absolutist of the family. There's always been a strain of that in us. I guess John just got it neat. I think it was what made my great-grandfather and his brothers quit the Foreign Service of the Union they believed in to fight for the State they were born in and a policy they despised. I don't know what that kind of attitude does to you, Mr Clarke, but it scares the shit out of me. Do you have any idea where he might be? Or when he's likely to get here?'

Alan could not help. 'None, I'm afraid. That call, by the way, was for me to go back to New York on Wednesday. I expect I'll be back before the weekend.'

Robert Standing looked distracted. 'Fine, fine. If you could leave the keys with me or Eleanor, if John or Miss Kilkenny hasn't arrived by then.' He looked away, out of the window, into the quiet door-yard with its single leafy elm. 'It's why he drinks, you know,' he said, as though of some passing acquaintance of them both. 'It's the only way he can rid himself of his own, damaged, stiff-necked sense of virtue. It's the only way he knows how to forgive himself.'

Alan was too embarrassed to say anything. He asked about Eleanor instead. 'Mr Standing, if you don't want Eleanor in Lebanon or Kampuchea, why are you letting her go down to Peru? Our Foreign Desk gives it not more than six months before it falls apart.'

The old man smiled. 'In one sense, she's right, Mr Clarke. If she's going to work in the Foreign Service she shouldn't run away from the dangerous places. And, besides, there's a lot our people can't control, even in Peru. But it is on our back-doorstep. If anything does go up, I have a fighting chance of getting her out of there.'

He left Alan alone, wondering what he meant, what unlikely action a mild-mannered university professor might take. He could not puzzle it out, so he got dressed and went back to the Hyatt Regency to dine and drink with colleagues in

Hugo's Restaurant on the eleventh floor. He got back after two, just missing the call from Caro. It was not till the morning, just before Robert Standing called for him, that he played back the tape and got her message to meet her off the TWA flight from Seattle arriving at Washington National that afternoon.

CHAPTER NINE

John admired Miss Morgan's composure. She did not react at all to the black man's strange introduction. It really was as though she was an ante-bellum plantation owner's daughter, who made a policy of never noticing the whims and vagaries of slaves.

Babylon just kept on smiling, and asked, 'Where we heading?'

John blinked, once, and said, 'Depends on whether the Man wants to eat and talk or drink and talk.'

Babylon shook his head. 'Don't use your kind of drink.'

'Then take us to Nettie Symonette's.'

The black man put the car in gear.

They bounced out of Nassau in the honking summer traffic, the richer Bahamians cruising and showing off their wagons, flashing teeth like bank-books at the talent walking in slow, hip-grinding pairs up and down Bay and Shirley Streets. They were headed west, back towards Cable Beach, the way Marsha had first come. As they got further from the hot, unpoliced enclosure of his home Over The Hill the black man's smile diminished.

'I hope Nettie's cooking's still all it's always cracked up for,' he said, grimly.

John smiled. He felt that he could handle it. He waved a formal hand at the driver and said to Marsha, 'Miss Morgan, meet Babylon. Babylon . . .?'

'Smith,' the black man finished, flashing a grin in the rear view mirror.

'Smith,' John accepted, disbelieving. 'Not one of your customary circle on the island, but a wondrous necessary man. Unless I have been misled – and if I have, there are friends of mine who will be very angry about it – Mr Smith is the manager of all of Over The Hill.'

Marsha turned to him and gave him the full dazzling value of her clear blue eyes, tilting her snub nose up towards him. 'Why, Mr Standing,' she cried, her low Missoura voice all innocence, 'if what you say is true, how did you arrange to meet the man the whole Royal Bahamian Police Force is always looking for?'

All of them smiled as he replied, 'Why, Miss Morgan, I did what I always do. I simply went and asked. I never overlook the obvious.'

No, he thought, *I never do. So why didn't I notice that she's smarter than she pretends?*

They were headed out to the western end of Cable Beach, to Nettie Symonette's Round House Lounge at Casuarinas Apartment Hotel, but everyone just named it after the woman who ran one of the best Bahamian restaurants in the islands. Tonight they would not eat imported Beef Wellington or Nova Scotia salmon; they would not feed on cakes put together from flour flown in from France and dairy cream brought over daily from Florida. They would eat fish or fowl, grouper or chicken, cooked in mild pepper sauce, and just-dry-enough peas'n'rice and conch or crawfish chowder, the pink strips of the conch flesh marinated in thyme and the juice of local limes and bitter oranges. They would give the Man a spread.

It worked. After they had eaten, John laid out his proposal and the information he needed. He knew he could deal with Marsha later. He told the black man that his principals were aware a new arms trade had been established through the islands into coastal Central America. He also explained they knew the inflated prices being paid. His own consortium believed that competition was essential to all healthy business. That, after all, was the American way. John had the goods. He had the price. All he needed now was the market and distribution.

Babylon licked the chicken fat off his lips and nodded. 'Sure,' he sympathized, 'but why you come to me?'

John smiled back, enigmatic. 'Unless I am very much mistaken,' he explained, 'the operation here is being run by the men in suits. A very profitable operation your own people get very little part of. I assume you would welcome more. That might be arranged, if you came up with the kind of help we need, and the right level of information.'

The black man thought about it. 'Maybe. Might work. But sounds like one-way traffic . . .'

John interrupted him politely. 'Not necessarily. We wouldn't want our transport to go home empty. Who knows what it could carry?' He rolled a twenty-dollar bill into a tube and set one end of it on the table. He was aware he was sweating. This much was guesswork. He was assuming there was a return cargo. He was assuming it was cocaine.

Babylon nodded. 'I heard you was down in Harbourfront checking our transportation. And I hear you got funds. Maybe we do some business. Maybe not. I need to think it over. I was thinking you must be crazy, hitting the island so hard all in one day . . .'

'I don't have time to waste,' John interrupted. 'My time is very expensive. When do we meet again?'

Babylon fingered his dreadlocks, his gold rings shining in the matted darkness. 'I get to you,' he said, 'when I ready.'

'How will you find me? I move around a lot.'

Babylon smiled a crooked smile, full of ragged teeth. John saw Marsha's eyebrows lift, but she came from a country where dentistry was power. 'No place on New Providence,' the black man told them, 'you can go without my knowing. I seen everything you done since you crossed the ridge of Over The Hill. I know every drink you drunk today. I know you like to do it in the shower. I find you when I ready.'

As he got up from the table John told him, 'I think you owe me a driver.'

Babylon nodded. 'He's waiting in the car outside. He follows us all the way from Nassau. You ought to know you need eyes in this island. Eyes every place.'

Marsha pursed her lips. 'He has. The blue 78 Mustang, right?'

Babylon looked her over, more impressed than he had been by the mere fact of her superstructure. There were more pretty white women on the island than anyone knew what to do with, though they looked a little too like unfried chicken for his taste. He turned back to Standing. 'Smart woman. You ever want to bring her Over The Hill, you just show anyone the other half of this.' He flashed his half of the hundred-dollar bill. 'And it's Babylon's party.'

But Marsha was not finished with him. 'Forgive me, Mr Smith,' she asked in her over-bred voice, 'but if you are the Man you say you are, isn't it a little unusual for you to show yourself alone? You have no idea what we might be packing.'

Babylon turned his full attention to her. 'I told you,' he said simply, 'no place on New Providence my eyes don't reach.'

He looked around him. Two big black men at opposite sides of the room got up and looked to him, awaiting his instructions.

'See?' he grinned, and vanished through the crowd of diners, his uglies drifting behind him under tow.

Once he had gone she turned to Standing and asked, 'Are you really in the import–export business?'

He smiled, and asked, 'Are you really just a clerk in the US Embassy?'

'Let's party,' she replied.

They went on to the Casino to drop more money publicly, most of which John won back laboriously at the blackjack table, despite the increasing clamour in his head. They went on to Cinnamon's, where she danced and he drank. And they ended up at the Drumbeats Club on Bay Street back in town, despite a depressingly family audience, because John had got it into his head he had to hear Peanuts Taylor play the drums.

They were exhausted by the time their driver got them back to Graycliff, and John was drunk. Too drunk to want to work out the puzzle of Marsha Morgan. He would do it in the morning, if the morning ever came. As they wheeled into the bedroom she turned and took him in her arms and kissed him. Then she fell away from him across the bed. She looked happy, he thought. He liked people being happy.

'Come to bed,' he heard her low voice saying.

He raised a finger, wagging it like a disappointed parent. 'In a moment,' he said. He desperately needed a leak.

The light in the bathroom hurt his eyes. He turned if off, leaving the door open so he could see by the soft fall of the lamp-light in the bedroom. He was very tired. He could not stand. He sat down on the toilet. He did not want to think about it, but he knew tomorrow was the day. He had to preserve the momentum. He had to see it through. But his mind was fuddled and would not work. He just wanted to relax. He heard her low voice calling, full of erotic laughter, 'Oh, John . . .'

But she called in vain. When she went through to the bathroom a few disgruntled minutes later, she found him sat on the toilet with his trousers down about his knees, his jacket thrown carelessly into the bath, and his head resting against the cool porcelain side of the wash-basin, imperturbably asleep.

When he awoke the following morning he was curled up on the bathroom floor, his eyes full of sleep, his head full of fog, and his angry bones all complaining. All of him ached as he tried to stand.

The bedroom was empty. He wondered where she could be. He assumed he had lost her, another victim of his appetite for bottles. Then he remembered her composure the previous night, and began to wonder. But she returned, wearing the clothes she had worn last night, looking limp and sweaty. She peeled herself naked without saying a word and almost fell into the bath. He sat down on the edge beside her, watching her work the soap to a lather on her clear white skin.

He wanted to apologize, but something told him she was not the kind to listen to apologies, so instead he asked her where she had been. She looked up at him with mocking unconcern.

'Well, Mr Standing,' she said slowly, 'you weren't no good to woman or beast last night, and I wanted to get laid. I went up Over The Hill and picked myself a slave. You have to keep 'em working.'

He looked down at her in disbelief. 'You went Over The Hill? On your own? And you didn't get robbed? And raped?'

She smiled to herself, remembering. 'Why, surely. Your protection worked. I am impressed. You'll find your half of a hundred-dollar bill in my clutch-bag. When I waved that, everyone was nice as pie. Nicer. All night long.'

She stretched out in the soapy water, running her hands between her breasts, between her legs.

He had been very stupid. It had been too good to be true. 'You're Agency, aren't you?' he asked her calmly.

She shook her head. 'No. But I am at the Embassy, and, fascinated though I am by you, and much though I like rolling in the dirt now and again, I need to know what you're up to, before either of us is stupid.'

He understood and he knew the only power over her he had was the strange American respect for the supposed might of the press. He swept his jacket off the floor and showed her his various press cards. She nodded her head. 'I didn't think you were a villain. A soundrel, perhaps, but not one of the Luigis. I wondered when someone would get on to it. It's the Perez murder, right?'

He stopped himself asking what she was talking about. Distant bells were ringing in his head. Something he had seen tucked into the front-page News Briefing of the *Examiner* what seemed a long, long time ago. But it would not come. So he told her, 'No. The Hart murder. In London.'

She looked surprised. 'You think there's a connection?'

'Tell me about Perez,' he said.

She stood up in the bath, water cascading off the smooth surfaces of her body and dwindling to a slow tropical trickle. She held out her arms like a little child. He reached for a towel and began to rub her down. She kept pushing her weight towards him as she spoke.

'Enrico Perez. Colonel. Nicaraguan. Big man under Somoza. Murdered in Panama City on Midsummer's Eve. Very nasty. Drowned in the toilet. Word is, he was one of the . . . Gently, lover.' He shifted the towel, wrapping his hand in the dryest part, and slipped it between her thighs. She bent at the knees, eyes closed, rubbing herself down against it. She threw back her head and went on speaking. 'Chief armourer for the Contras. He was here in Nassau a lot. A lot of folks here are sympathetic to the cause. Mainly Americans. I'm pretty sure he was shipping stuff from here.'

He leant forward to kiss her nipples, and to ease her from the bath. 'Is that what they're saying in the Embassy?'

She took the towel from him and began to dry her feet. He envied her the ease with which she bent down, the long athletic curve of her back. He envied her her youth. 'They don't say anything,' she said. She stood up, holding the towel between her breasts and pressed herself against him, holding the towel between them by the pressure of her belly and hips. 'There's a message at the desk,' she told him. 'A man from Second City is joining us for breakfast. But we have time.'

He felt no response to her presence at all. He felt dead below the waist. 'I can't,' he told her, sadly.

What he found most seductive was her simple presence. He had been lonely far too long. There was, despite everything, despite the drinking and gambling and haphazard fornication, a terrible urge towards domesticity within him. Twice before it had seduced him into marriage. Twice before his need for new sensation had broken his marriages apart. He was almost grateful for the temporary, unpredictable impotence his drinking visited on him. It seemed to stop him getting too involved. He invited her to breakfast anyway.

What the banker had to tell him was simple. The first credit checks were drifting in from New York. More important, he had been talking to his contacts on New Providence, as John had known he would.

'The fact is, Mr Standing,' he explained, 'though I would deny it if you ever quoted me, I wouldn't authorize an investment in any of these companies. And I'm not so sure I'd want to do business with someone who did. It isn't very clear to anyone exactly what they do, besides being in import–export. And they obviously have connections. At least one of them has trade licences both in Latin America and Eastern Europe, and you don't get those without political clout. But this is the Caribbean and I wouldn't finance anything unless I knew exactly what it was. I advise you to do the same. I can put you in touch with a number of reputable local companies looking for new investors, but I can't help you with these.'

He paused, wondering if he had gone too far, eager to hold on to John's personal business, whatever became of the speculative investments. Diplomatically, he let fall the fact that he was not sitting in judgement. 'There are other institutions on New Providence which might take a more flexible approach to such investments. I have no doubt they will be in touch with you. But that is all I can do. I'll have the telexes sent over to you, Mr Standing, as they come in from New York.'

John sat in silence after the banker left, ignoring Miss Morgan's inquiring gaze. He had been right. There had to be political connections. He wondered how much the girl knew. He was inclined to trust her. If she had been Agency she would not have reminded him about the Perez murder. If that was the tie-in, if it was arms for the Nicaraguan Contras, one problem, one irony, remained. Why would the Vatican finance arms for right-wing guerrillas? Did they hate Liberation Theology as much as that? It didn't make any sense. But he could think about that later. What mattered now was proof. Evidence of physical shipment. Part of that he might get by doing the paperwork with agents. For the rest he had to rely on Babylon and his people. It made him feel uneasy. All of it made him feel uneasy. Even, especially, the girl. But there was nothing more he could do.

He turned to her, the amiable Virginian once again, and said, 'I think I need to buy a camera.'

He took the car down to John Bull in Old Bay Street and dropped her at the Embassy. She had said she ought to call in for an hour. All the cameras in John Bull were too complicated for his unmechanical mind. He ended up buying a bottom-of-range Olympus at the Nassau Shop. He remembered to specify a zoom lens. They met up together again in the Parliament Terrace Café. It was hot. He needed a drink.

For an hour, he did not speak. For an hour, he did not move. She gave up trying to talk about the boredom of the Embassy. She did not bother to try to match him drink for drink.

He was thinking. He was wondering if, in fact, he should deal direct with the transportation agents in the offices above

Woodes Rogers Walk and all down Bay Street. Or if he should leave it to Babylon and his people.

He never did have to decide. A man came to their table, holding half a hundred-dollar bill and told them:

'The Man, he want to see you.'

They rose and got into the waiting battered blue 78 Mustang.

A half-hour later they were deep in the heart of Over The Hill in the first-floor bedsit Babylon called his office. There were the carcasses of stepped-on cockroaches all over the floor, and the deathstains of mosquitoes on the table. An out-of-date Penthouse calendar was pinned on the wall, open at a picture of a girl sprawled in gynaecological frankness. There were dirty glasses in the sink, dirty sheets on the bed, and dirty wooden chairs on the floor. None of that troubled John. He was not here for the hygiene. And Miss Morgan seemed to be enjoying the burst of local colour, though it was hard to be certain beneath her perpetual sullen mask. The only clean thing in the room was the flash of Babylon's teeth, and John had no intention of getting close enough to check out the big man's breath, or put himself in range of the coiled muscles of his arms and shoulders. He was explaining why he had sent for them.

'I can show you what you came to see, and I will talk about alternatives, after you've seen the competition.'

John nodded. 'Where is it?'

The black man looked coy. He knew the information was valuable. 'What you come to see costs. There's finders' fees, and transportation.'

John nodded once again. 'How much?'

Babylon stopped smiling. 'Ten thousand U S dollars. Cash. Plus transportation costs. It's about a hundred and eighty miles from here. Fast boat would do it from Nassau. Sea-plane would be better.'

Marsha looked at Standing. Even she showed some reaction at the price. She showed stupefaction. John's face gave nothing away at all.

'I need about half an hour to get the money,' he said. 'We'll take a plane.'

Marsha turned to John and asked, 'Are you looking for a pilot? I told you, I can fly.'

He showed no emotion, none of the fear he felt, none of his suspicion of them both, but something deep inside him sank. Something like his heart.

CHAPTER TEN

Alan Clarke went directly from the morning session of the IMF talks, and lunch at the Monocle, to meet Caro's flight at Washington National Airport. His colleagues on the *Examiner* team had told him to make the morning session, so he fobbed Robert Standing off. They had been right to do so. It was not the official platform they were interested in, it was the sub-committee working sessions. There were rumours dynamite was scheduled for this Tuesday. They proved correct. In separate sub-committee sessions, the Brazilians had once again threatened to repudiate their national debt, the Governor of the Banca d'Italia had suggested he might ban Italian citizens and corporations holding accounts with the IOR, the Vatican Bank, unless the Church proved more co-operative in tracing fraud, and the Chairman of the Moscow State Export Bank had repudiated suggestions that the Soviet Union should in any way be responsible for the external debts of other Warsaw Pact nations.

It was the last statement which proved the loudest talking point amongst the bankers and journalists gathered over lunch. The Russian banker was present only as an observer, which was why his remarks had been made in subsidiary session, but all of them knew the import of what he said, and the threat to the banking system his remarks constituted. The threat was Poland.

Poland had borrowed more heavily from the Western banks than any other communist country. The very fact that lending to governments behind the Iron Curtain was unusual had made such projects attractive to many bankers, who are as subject to the effects of vanity and curiosity as anyone else. In the easy-money years following the oil-price rises Poland had found it easy to become one of the biggest borrowers of dollars on the Euromarkets. All the while, the covert assumption among bankers as the country's political and economic situation steadily deteriorated had been that, if the worst came to the worst, the Russians would step in to guarantee the Polish Debt, if only for political considerations: to prevent the civil unrest a complete collapse of the Polish economy would lead to, and to deny suggestions by outsiders that the Communist system was anything but a great engine of wealth creation, and well able to settle its debts.

Political considerations had always been paramount over Poland. There were those who rumoured that American banks had only become so heavily involved in lending to the Poles because of pressure from American governments, who saw it as a way to lever an already shaky Russian ally out of the grasp of Moscow. There were others who claimed the only reason the banks did not foreclose on Poland now was that they were under equal government pressure not to reveal just how much business good American capitalists actually did with the Communist menace. It was already embarrassing enough that government after government in the United States had helped to feed the Filthy Reds by subsidizing exports of US wheat to Russia as a means of securing the agricultural vote.

This morning, the Russian had been brutal. The Soviet Union had already issued several quiet warnings about the Polish debt, but today they had actually disclaimed responsibility. And the Russian had added something more, to the printed version of his comments which had been circulated to chosen journalists in advance. He had pointed out what some Western commentators had already suggested: the Russians would shed no tears if Poland defaulted on its debts and brought about the collapse of the banking system. Such an event would only prove that Marx had been right after all, and that the capitalist system was inherently unstable, and was bound to self-destruct. Alan's colleague had already burned up the phone lines to London, rewriting the front page lead for next day's paper, and nearly giving Iain MacKinnon heart failure. Not to mention the senior leader writer, who had to be called back from a cocktail party at the House of Lords to put together a considered editorial comment in under twenty minutes.

So Alan was a little preoccupied as he took the Metro on the Blue and Yellow lines out to the airport. He was preoccupied with wondering what meetings might even now be taking place in the Administration and Old Treasury buildings on either side of the White House, preparing the American response to the Russian banker's statement.

When he got to Washington National, the full humidity of the afternoon hit him, rolling off the slow Potomac, the grey air denying the clearness of the blue Virginia sky. He was glad he had not driven. The circular access road within the airport complex was clogged with a motionless traffic jam pumping blue fumes into the overpowered air. He took the free Metro Bus round to the small TWA terminal on the far edge of the complex.

Caro's flight was late in from St Louis. He used the time to check the shuttles to New York the following day and, at last, to hire a car. He wondered if he should tell her about his planned meeting with Preppy Harry, but he decided against it. He still wanted it to be a surprise.

He had warned John's brother of Caro's impending arrival, and received no real reaction at all. He guessed the old man was only waiting now for the arrival of young John, as he incongruously called him. Alan wondered idly where John might be. He had allowed the old lush to slip out of his mind in the excitement of the past few days, but he knew that, somewhere, John was up to something. Caro would be going frantic. She would want to know what it was. But Alan was not overly concerned. He had caught the city's sense of excitement, its feeling of power at play, and had grown confident. It was true, he thought, that Standing had got the story going when everything seemed stalled. But he and Caro could handle it now. Real journalists, accredited to the *Examiner*. Not has-beens. And not drunks.

When Caro finally bustled through Arrivals, she looked distracted. She did not speak or greet him. She merely kissed him automatically on the cheek and handed him one of her bags. He walked her out to the hire-car pick-up point, asking the usual questions about her flight and her visit to Seattle.

She did not answer. When they were in the car, and he

had pulled out into the crawl to join the Washington Memorial Parkway, she said, without any relevance to anything he had asked, 'You know, I don't understand this country. They emptied the plane at St Louis. Problems with a fuel pump. They wanted all the electrics down while they replaced it. And I swear there were two consecutive messages on the tannoy. The first said (this was an official in the middle of a busy airport): "ET, phone home." And the second said: "Will Mr Williams please come and collect his party? In the police station." I thought, *What the hell is going on*? Maybe John's right. Maybe I'm the wrong kind of person to cover urban America. That's why he always used to say he was the right man for this place. Crazy town. Crazy guy.'

She turned to Alan, her soft eyes looking tired, and the early creases in her face hardened by exhaustion. 'Is there any sign of him?'

Alan shook his head. 'Nothing. Did you find out anything in Seattle?'

She sat back in the passenger's seat, closing her eyes and saying nothing, as though she had not heard him, until, as they passed under the twin bridges across the river behind the dead impersonal façades of the Pentagon, she said, 'Wait till we get home.'

He took them across the Arlington Memorial Bridge and skirted the Lincoln Memorial to pick up 23rd Street to Washington Circle, past the plain exterior of the State Department at Foggy Bottom, exiled in the damp air by the river away from power and the White House, and the few run-down houses left between State and George Washington University. He turned on to M Street, over Rock Creek Park, and bore them into Georgetown. She had opened her eyes and was watching him, fascinated by his rapidly acquired knowledge of the city's layout, but he had to concentrate too much to notice. It was a different city from behind the wheel of a car, quite different from the one he had got to know on foot.

The black crowds were no longer the natural inhabitants, tolerating their white masters. They were the unavoidable eyesore of a servant class. From inside a car, Washington became a capital city. Its broad streets were no longer hazards

260

and delays, but the sweeping avenues besides which were displayed the offices of the greatest power in the world. From the road, white marble and green lawns dominated the city, and the poor, who did not belong to that world of power were mere excrescences. From a car he no longer noticed the derelicts, the bums, the mentally retarded and deranged who shambled the streets of the city in filthy rags clutching their possessions in carrier bags. They had been thrown on the streets by this government's cut-backs in Medicare and Social Services, but from the quiet air-conditioned world of offices and cars they did not matter. They were invisible in the world of power, irrelevant to its capital city.

A few minutes later, they were at the house. Eleanor arrived just before them. She was letting herself in to the ground-floor apartment, one of her uncle's shabby Chevys pulled up in the drive behind her. Caro wondered who the little girl was, with brown hair trimmed short with executive severeness, and an even trimmer body beneath the silk blouse and designer jeans. Alan introduced them, and invited Eleanor to join them upstairs for a drink.

The first thing Caro needed was to shower and change. By the time she came back through to the drawing-room, Eleanor was curled up in a chair nursing what she called a spritzer. In Caro's younger days they had only been drunk by older men with liver problems, who called them hock and selzters. She was getting out of touch with the switching fashions of a day.

But there was no doubting the girl was pretty. She had her father's eyes and certainty of gesture. Perhaps his hair colour, too. Caro could not remember a time when John's hair had not been grey, but it must once have been as dark as or darker than the girl's. The rest, though, must come from the mother. Eleanor had the soft skin and slightly heavy figure of a woman who would be perfect through her late teens and early twenties, but only hard work would preserve her after that, giving her the worked-on, strained, tight look of so many American women. If her mother had looked like that when young, no wonder a drunk young Standing had married her. But she was not built to last.

Caro wondered if Alan was interested in the girl, or merely politely attentive. She was surprised to feel a slight twinge of envy as the young girl watched his long legs unfolding across the Bokhara carpet. However, he turned his attention to Caro.

'What news from the West Coast?' he asked.

She slid into a colonial willow rocking-chair filled with needlepoint cushions and took a sip of her gin and tonic. She thanked God for the American obsession with ice. 'John's right,' she said, 'it looks like weapons. And on a commercial scale, too. Not little bits of gun-running. More like an airlift.'

'Is there any word from my father?' Eleanor interrupted.

Poor kid, thought Caro, unexpectedly. She hadn't done too well with her parents. 'None, I'm sorry. I wish there was.' She took another mouthful of gin and sat back, gently rocking. 'If he was here, he might be able to tell me why my best source in the defence industry was murdered yesterday morning in Seattle. I think the police might be quite grateful too. I spent seven hours in a police station last night convincing them I had nothing to do with it.'

'Oh, shit,' Alan said, in what sounded like sympathy.

Caro shook her head, newly aware of her own exhaustion. 'Doesn't matter. I'm out of it. He was a strange man, tied up with some very funny people. The police are treating it as a possible cult or ritual killing. They may be right. I don't know. I just wish people would stop dying all around me. I'm beginning to feel I'm carrying plague or something.'

Eleanor did not smile, though Alan did. Dear Alan. Caro turned to the girl, trying to be the confident older woman she looked like. 'Don't worry. I'm sure your father will show up. He usually does in the end, and I don't believe he'd cross the Atlantic without getting to see his daughter.'

'I don't know why,' Eleanor replied. 'He's done it often enough before.'

When the girl had gone, Caro briefed Alan on her trip to the West Coast. He did not tell her about his talk with Tom Stoddart. What he told her was that Mike Thomas and Mr

Chew wanted him to fly up to New York in the morning, but had not told him why. He expected to be back in the evening, or by Thursday lunchtime at the latest. She agreed to it readily enough. She trusted him, and he was not officially on her team. He could act as a free agent on the Errol Hart affair. All she asked was that he give her the list of names John had first supplied him with, to add to her own contact book. There were people she would need to talk to. She wished even more that John was here, to split the underside of DC open for her. Official Washington she could deal with herself.

Alan told her about the events of the morning at the International Monetary Fund talks. She was most intrigued by the Banca d'Italia statement. Did it mean the Dottore was already on the move? She knew, however, the important statement was the Russian one on Poland and, surprisingly, it made her laugh. It meant tonight at least MacKinnon would be working for his living.

She was too tired to join Alan for dinner with their colleagues and an assemblage of bankers at 209½ on Pennsylvania Avenue after the Chase Manhattan party.

She was already in bed by the time he returned, sleeping a shallow, anxious sleep. She was woken by him sitting down on the side of her bed, looking as weary as she felt.

'You look exhausted,' he said, then laughed. 'I'm sorry, that was fatuous. People do when you disturb their sleep.'

She put out her bound left hand. He held it lightly in his. 'Don't worry,' she told him, not really knowing what he might have to worry about.

'I'm not. It's just that I was thinking John and I have led you quite a dance of late, without really getting anywhere. But it's going to be all right. We'll all of us be famous.'

She smiled to herself. 'You've taken quite a shine to his daughter, haven't you?'

She thought she saw him blush, though it was hard to tell in the lamplight. Anyway, he denied it. 'Oh, no. She's a pretty girl. But she is a girl. A bit too young for me.'

Caro laughed. He sounded impossibly old and serious. He was barely out of boyhood himself, she thought, until she

263

remembered that Tom Wellbeck at Alan's age had been married over a year. While Alan was with her she could believe nothing had changed. She felt no different from the young woman she had once been. No wiser, not transformed. Merely more tired. She did not want to be tired. She wanted to be what she thought herself to be: young, assured, and desired. She wanted the intervening years cancelled, with all the troubles they had brought. She stroked his hand, watching the way the lamplight speckled his curly hair with flecks of silver and gold.

'Alan,' she said softly, 'why don't you come to bed?'

CHAPTER ELEVEN

Marsha eased herself into the seaplane where John and Babylon were already waiting for her. 'OK,' she said briskly, 'we're fuelled for a four-hundred-mile round trip. I've logged a flight plan out to Little Abaco. Where are we really headed?'

Babylon would not answer till they were airborne. He simply heaved a thumb upward at the sky. Marsha looked at John and shrugged.

'It's your party, Virginian,' she said, and made a final check of the instrument panel.

Once they were airborne, Babylon told her to head southeast, making for Long Island.

She frowned. 'It's further out than Abacos,' she explained. 'We've got the range for it and beyond. And this is a pretty poky aircraft. So long as we keep low, we aren't going to embarrass the flight controllers' radar, and we don't have to check in on any beacons, but if we haven't returned by nightfall they will put out a search alarm.'

Babylon shrugged. 'Don't matter. Be looking in the wrong place.'

Marsha sighed. That had not been her point. She shut up and flew on towards Long Island. Once they were under way Babylon began to explain.

'Stuff comes in by fast boat from Miami and Mobile. All above-board and legal, bound for Nassau. Except it never gets to Nassau. Heads on straight beyond to pick up airborne transport into Costa Rica, Honduras, you name it.'

'Airborne?' John wondered aloud.

Babylon flashed a grin. 'Big operation you're competing. Got their own airforce. Don't care who know about it in Costa Rica. Costa Rica got no army. Honduras might as well not either. Only scared at the US end. Return traffic. Is why they use the boats. Small, fast. Outrun customs vessels and hide in any of the cays scattered around the bigger islands. Small boat can get lost out here.'

John looked down into the clear intense blue of the Bahamian waters, clear right down to drifting sands and shelves of flowering coral. Below them to starboard he could see a lozenge of darker blue beneath the surface, parts of it picked out by little dazzles of light. It would be a school of Allison tuna, cruising just below the surface. The dazzle would be the big back of some of its members breaking out of the water. They should see dolphin, too, and later, towards sunset, the phosphorescent skip of flying fish. Babylon gave Marsha new bearings.

'That'll take us south-west of Long Island,' she protested. 'There's nothing that way but cays and water two hundred miles to Cuba.'

Babylon smiled again. 'There's Ragged Island.'

'Oh, shit,' she said.

'Problem?' John asked. She nodded.

'Maybe. It's a group, not just one island. Jumento Cays to Great Ragged. Maybe forty, fifty people live on the big island. Place called Duncan Town. Fishing, farming. Used to work the salt flats, but there's no business left there now.'

'What's the problem?'

She glanced at him, almost smiling, till she remembered it affected her as well. More. She was the pilot. 'Winds,' she said curtly, 'Off the Jumento Cays. About the most beautiful place God ever made and the worst winds in these waters. Good yachtsmen love it. Bad ones die there. No commercial shipping goes through there. So if he's right, your people could do whatever they wanted unnoticed.'

Standing was about to swear, under the thunder of the engine, when Babylon tapped him on the shoulder and pointed down to the water. What looked like a converted torpedo boat was skipping south-west below them, flanked on either side by a couple of racing speedboats.

'Look like it your lucky day,' Babylon told him. 'Look like they making to deliver.'

Marsha eased the throttle up and left the boats below behind them.

They had been airborne for two hours before Marsha signalled for his attention, pointing to the pinprick islands darkening the surface of the water beyond. 'I'll take us in as low as I can,' she said, 'and make a circuit of the cays. If there's anything there I'll try to get to the other side of the cay it's on. Make it look like we haven't noticed.'

Babylon tried to reassure them. 'Nothing to worry about. Till those boats come in sight, they all going to be sleeping in the sunshine. We be in and out before them.'

John hoped that he was right.

They found what they were looking for on the third of the small islands which made up the Jumento Cays. There, on the fringe of the biggest of these high volcanic islands, lay one of the salt-flats which had once been the mainstay of the economy. A flat, shining, merciless surface about a half-mile long. There was a small jet standing on it. John pulled out his camera and prayed.

'Well, I'll be a nigger,' Marsha said, without rancour, to no one in particular, 'salt-flat runway, just like the space shuttle, and they can bring the small boats right up to it.'

She headed on past the island, and the two small cays beyond it, looking for somewhere to turn. 'I'm going to cut between the next two cays,' she announced, cutting back the power. She looked earnest. 'Hang on,' she warned them. 'It looks gorgeous, but God knows what the winds are doing in that channel or beyond it.'

John looked at her, surprised. 'Can't you tell which way it's blowing from the way the airplane handles?'

'Honey,' she told him, 'down there, the winds come out of nowhere.'

As she veered to port John asked Babylon if his people ran the boats out to the island.

Babylon looked sullen. 'That the problem, man. The suits don't want to let us have it. That's our natural business. But all we got is office work, down on Prince George Wharf. Unloading permits, custom receipts, making the whole thing look legitimate.'

John suddenly realized why he did not trust the Man. For

all his dreadlocks and his flashing eyes, he knew as much about the paperwork side of business as any college graduate: John trusted people who pretended to be fools as little as he liked people who really were fools. He felt the fear rise in him again. He wished he had a drink.

He stopped wishing anything the next instant, as the little seaplane plummeted, making him feel as though he had left the contents of his stomach three feet above his head.

Marsha pulled back on the controls and put them into a sharp port-side bank. For an instant it seemed as though he had only to lift his hand above his head to touch the rocks flashing above (or was it beside?) him. Then the horizon came back into view and she was working the plane against the wind, bringing it down to the sea.

When they were down, she turned to him, sweating lightly, saying 'Are you serious about going ashore?'

He nodded.

'Can you swim?' He nodded again. She turned back to Babylon, 'Can you?'

'Sure,' he replied.

'Why?' John asked.

She pointed back in the direction they had just come. 'That little somersault back there? You know, when the wind came down like a great big hand and shook your ass up to your teeth? Well, I think that's standard. I think that's what drove the salt flat up against the other side of the island and blew the water out. I've got no way of knowing which way it's going to blow this side next, or what the currents are going to be like. If I take her in and moor her up against the rocks, chances are, when we get back, we'll find her matchwood. We've got a sea-anchor. Let's leave her out here and swim. Better still, let's go home now. I don't like it here, Virginian.'

John thought it over before replying. 'Neither do I, Miss Morgan, but I've got to get more snapshots.' He put the first roll of film into a plastic bag.

She put his camera in her waterproof pilot's case and pushed it before her as they swam ashore.

They were nearly there when the mortar blew their sea-plane out of the water.

They were ashore when seven men in uniforms stood out of the rocks, pointing machine-guns at them.

The man in charge walked out on to the beach and handed Babylon a machine-pistol. 'Shall I kill them now?' the black man asked.

The white man shook his head. 'Nope,' he said, 'we'll take them up in the plane and ditch them out at sea. Or give them to the Contras. They could use a little practice.'

John recognized the accent. The man was Alabaman.

'Pity,' Babylon said unemotionally, 'I'd have liked to kill the guy.'

They were led over the rough paths of the cliff and down to the salt flat beyond. It was a low-key operation with a small complement of staff. Just the seven men guarding them, Babylon, and the pilot. And however many there were crewing the boats they awaited. Not that any of that mattered to Standing. He was not made for heroics. What he was made for was drink.

They were sheltered under the wing of the plane. Marsha looked about her with professional interest. 'How do you get this darling airborne in only half a mile?' she asked the pilot.

He was a tow-haired Alabaman burnt raw by the sun he shielded his eyes against under mirror-shades. 'Underload it,' he said flatly. 'Still a bigger payload than frigging around with seaplanes. Pray. Be a darn good pilot.' He looked at her thoughtfully. 'Must be pretty good yourself, slipping through that channel. I thought we was going to lose you there and then. The winds round there are crazier than a preacherman in hell.' He looked at her again, registering the fact that she was a woman, and a pretty one. 'I learnt my flying dusting crops and zappping Charlie. Where you learn yours?'

'My father taught me,' she answered. 'Fifty-two bombing missions over Italy in the Second World War.'

The pilot looked pleased. 'Yeah,' he said, 'thought that weren't no art-school flyer.'

The man in charge came over to shut them up. All his men looked frazzled, bored, hostile. He looked pretty hostile himself.

As they sheltered by the port-side undercarriage, Marsha asked John, 'Well, Virginian, can you see any way out of this?'

He tried to joke about it. 'We could always drink ourselves to death.' Except he wasn't joking.

Neither was she. 'We don't have any drink.'

'Then I haven't any idea.'

'Neither have I,' she said.

It was an hour later before she thought of anything. She thought it could not be long before the boats arrived. Then everything would be tumult till the loads were switched. If she got through till then she probably would not get raped. Just killed.

She sat on her haunches in front of Standing, wiping the salt out of her eyes. 'I should've thought of it sooner,' she told him. 'They must use the powerboats to bring the stuff inshore. The torpedo boat would never make it.'

'So?' he asked listlessly.

'So we only have the powerboat crews and the people here to worry about. In a powerboat we could outrun the big boat.'

He looked at her ironically. 'That only leaves about a dozen people to deal with, before we get the boat. And the plane could still outstrip us.'

They were interrupted by Babylon's shadow leaning over them. He had come to play. 'You think you pretty cute, don't you, Mr Standing? I should've killed you back in Nassau, but a fuss gets made when white folks go missing out of Graycliff. 'Cept everyone understands when one of them just skips off without settling his bills. Powerful lot of white folks in Nassau got sweet money as turns sour on them. So I suppose I can leave it to them crazy people to kill you their own way. Slower than mine, Mr Standing, and more painful. Pity about the lady though. There's at least one boy over the hill as'll be whining like a widow woman when he hears all that pink meat's gone.'

Standing looked up at him, thinking how like his housemaster the black man was, and said, 'Babylon, go fry in hell.'

Babylon walked away laughing, saying, 'Mr Standing, I probably will.'

Marsha sat back to think about perhaps a dozen men with guns.

It was another hour before they heard the distant saw-like buzzing of the boats, another fifteen minutes after that before they saw the fringes of spray on the water approaching like false eyelashes drifting down a face. The man in charge, the one the others all called Colonel, came over to them, waving them upright with the ugly barrel of his machine-gun, saying, 'Into the plane, you two.'

She had to force herself not to cry Hallelujah. They would be perfectly safe inside.

The Colonel walked behind them through the emptied belly of the plane, over its spars and skeleton. The only thing it was carrying was a single gunny-sack. John could not help stopping to look at it in wonder. The Colonel nodded. 'Yup. Cocaine. About three million dollars of it. All that money in a little bag.'

John looked at him in surprise. 'I thought you people always said you were the good guys. What are you doing shipping this stuff back to the States?'

The Colonel almost spat out his answer. 'Son, if they're the kind of scum as use this stuff they don't deserve to live. I don't care if all those blacks and liberals spoon it up their noses with a shovel. Might just stop their frigging whining.'

John could think of nothing in reply.

They crowded on to the flight deck with the pilot, watching the two powerboats making their first approaches from the mother-vessel. Marsha stood behind the pilot, with the Colonel beside her. The powerboats were turning back. They had not taken aboard enough cargo for their first run.

'Assholes,' the Colonel said, meditatively. He looked as though he ought to be chewing a piece of gum.

'Colonel,' she said brightly, in her most refined Missoura accent, 'would you mind taking that machine-gun out of my ear?'

He began to shift it uncertainly. As he did so, she seized it by the barrel, twisted it once, jabbed the butt into his groin and threw herself backward as his reflex action fired it, burning her hands and smashing the cockpit windscreen. She bent her right arm and smashed back, punching his throat with her elbow. As the gun dropped from his hands she grabbed it and fired enough rounds in a second to take the pilot's head off at the shoulders and blow his body out of the already shattered window. Then she swept down to the Colonel's limp body, took his pistol from its holder and put one round through his skull.

She handed the pistol to John, who stood open-mouthed in a confined space that, a few seconds before, had been an aircraft flight deck but now looked like Armageddon. She had no time for shock. The other men were running in from the shore. 'You said you could use one of these things,' she said. 'Well, got to the loading door and hold those bastards off.'

He stumbled out through the bulkhead, heading for the door.

It burst open as he got to it. An armed man swung round it. John fired once, punching his teeth through the back of his skull in a gobbet of blood and bone. His body crumpled and John went down too, squirming along the floor of the plane towards the sunlit opening. Then his heart sank. He could hear her trying to fire the engines.

'Are you crazy?' he shouted as he blinked at the door in the sudden brightness of the day.

'No,' she shouted back, but he did not hear it, deafened by the echo of his pistol as he fired at a soldier running towards him.

It was a wild shot and took the man in the hip. His pants turned scarlet as the bullet bloomed. John aimed again, and hit him in the stomach, jack-knifing him back across the sand six feet till he sat touching his toes in a gritty pool of blood and entrails.

John threw up.

She was shouting something. She was saying, 'They'll never open fire on the plane, it's too valuable. They have to get us out of here. We're safe if I can get this bitch out to one of those boats.'

He did not have time to wonder what she meant for, just as he saw the other men with guns racing from cover, the engines roared into angry life. He felt the judder as she ground the undercarriage over the chocks and felt the strain as she began to turn it on the salt-flat runway. He slammed the door shut and prayed.

Why, he thought crazily, suddenly noticing, *why is she sitting on the floor of the control deck at the Colonel's feet?* She glanced down the plane at him and he saw that she was smiling. *This woman's mad*, he thought. Then, as he heard the silence after the guns, he understood. She was keeping herself out of their sights.

'Here goes!' she cried, stretching her arms above her, handling two sets of controls at once.

The jet finished its back-breaking stationary right-angle turn. There was a seeming lull, then the engines whined up to screaming pitch, and they were gone, plunging forwards across the white crystalline shore to the sounding blue waters before them.

The whole plane seemed to lift, nose first, as they hit the water and spray and surf broke in through the shattered windscreen, racing in rivulets all down the aircraft. Then a sudden settling came upon them, like a vast sigh, and he realized they were, at least partially, afloat. He saw the crazy woman was heading down the plane towards him, bent double, a machine-gun in her hand. She began opening the Emergency Exit over the port wing of the aircraft.

'Don't just sit there,' she called down in exasperation. He stumbled towards her, the pistol still in his hand. As she opened the door, the first powerboat was almost upon them, trying to pull up to the wing.

Two men, he thought. One each. But before he could lift his gun she had fired. One of the men blossomed redly and fell forward on to the wing. The other just seemed to disappear, backward, into the water. She dragged him out on to the wing, firing bursts into it as they began to walk out on the slowly sinking plane.

There were boxes in the boat, crates. He shot them open. Guns. Grenades. There were men running down to the shore, guns raised. She reached down into one of the crates, yelling 'Yee-hah!', picking up a grenade, pulling its pin and throwing it, all in one movement, with a cry of: 'Missoura For Ever!' The explosion threw the four men apart with the neatness of a choreographer.

A burst of machine-gun fire spat along the wing. Standing went down, turning and firing as he fell, one round, two.

The two men who had climbed over the plane from the other boat fell, blood pouring out of their nostrils, mouths and chests. John felt a great deal better.

She did not have time to congratulate him. He was already running back across the wing into the plane. She wanted to scream. The man was insane. There was chaos out on the torpedo boat, but they would open fire any second. Then he stepped back on the wing, clutching something to his chest, and ran back towards her.

She gunned the powerboat's engine as he dived aboard.

Something burst out of the water beside them, cascading droplets like diamonds into the boat, and a shadow fell between them. Something struck the back of her head, and she fell against the controls. When she turned, head spinning, she saw something squirming in the boat, something which made no sense, something fighting with itself.

Why couldn't she see?

She was on her hands and knees, trying to shake sense back into her head. What was that thing in the stern?

Then she saw.

She saw Babylon forcing John back across the side of the boat, one powerful black arm forcing his neck backward, back till his spine was nearly breaking.

She could not stand up. She could not even shout, to distract the black man's attention. She could not . . .

She fumbled blindly for the controls, searching, hoping, and pulled. The boat's engine roared. She saw John falling overboard, on to the wing. She saw Babylon thrown to the stern. She fired the controls again, and the sudden movement flung him out of the boat.

Then she reversed, and the engine keened, and there was the shrill whining of naked propellers, as blood, bone, flesh and water filled the air, falling back into the cloudy crimson sea.

She helped Standing back on board, said, 'What the hell,' picked up another grenade, unpinned it and threw it on to the stricken aircraft's wing.

As they roared away, they were masked from the mother vessel by bright plumes of fire and clouds of thick black smoke as the grenade ignited the fuel leaking from the aircraft's wing-tanks. They rounded the long cay just as a last explosion broke the aircraft's back in half.

They raced for open water, half-airborne, thudding up and down across the ocean swell. He was incapable of thinking, and too astonished to thank her. He could only ask her, 'Why didn't you just fly us out of there? Wouldn't that have been easier?'

She looked at him as though he had made an improper suggestion. Which he had. 'Why, Mr Standing,' she explained, 'I couldn't have done that. I'm not checked out on commercial jets.'

An hour later, he stood beside her, Nassau still far away, scanning the horizon. She knew what he was thinking. 'I wouldn't worry,' she said, 'I don't think they'll try to follow us. Not after that little party.'

'Doesn't matter,' he said. 'They don't have to. They can always radio ahead.'

She looked disbelieving, astounded by his innocence. 'Don't you know anything? No smuggler's going to break radio silence while still at sea. They still have most of their cargo on board, remember? They hardly want to announce their presence in these waters.'

'No,' John agreed, 'no, they don't. But I do. Can the radio on this thing pick up the nearest coastguard?'

She looked uncertain. 'I think so . . .'

'Then let's try raise them. I want to tell them John Standing of Examiner House, Queen Victoria Street, London, is claiming salvage rights under international law on the wrecked Boeing off the Ragged Island cays. I want them to notify Lloyd's of London.'

*

She managed part of it. She got through to the harbourmaster at Deadman's Cay on Long Island. They could only hope the message was referred, or picked up on the open frequencies by ocean-going vessels, any one of which would relay a message to Lloyd's.

If the message did get through, it would not work. He knew that. He would never be allowed the salvage rights, not even under the ancient rule of finders-keepers. But if a message did get through to Lloyd's no one could tamper with the wreckage without running the risk of discovery. At the very least, the great London insurance market would institute inquiries to establish whom the plane belonged to and if, in fact, it was insured by any of the market's members.

At the most it would buy time, but time was what he needed. He took the wheel, as the hours lengthened, and luminescence began to shine in the water breaking at their bows. Before long the flying fish would rise, cutting the air and sea beside them in escort, as they beat the long way home.

He wanted to thank her, but did not know how. How did you thank someone for saving your life, over and over again, because they were paid, by someone that you hated? He wondered how to tell her that he knew. But she was preoccupied with practical details.

'We have a problem in Nassau,' she told him. 'We have problems all over New Providence. Babylon's people will know he went with us. If we just show up without him, they're going to come after us. They're going to wonder where he is. We're the people who were supposed to disappear.'

She was right. She was better at these things than he was. Where had she learnt so much so young? 'What do you suggest?' he asked with due respect.

She was trying to puzzle it out. 'Your money and papers are all at Graycliff?'

He nodded.

'You're safe there. You're safe anywhere the moneyed people go. We'll be arriving at night. I can take us into Lyford. That's private. Fences. Armed guards. If we move just before dawn I could drive you to Graycliff and the airport safely. I've got a pass. I can get you on to the apron. If we can book you on to a flight. You won't be able to clear any luggage. Hand baggage only.'

'Flights aren't a problem,' he told her. 'I pre-booked tickets. I only need to phone to confirm. Might not even need to do that if you can get me the right side of airport security.'

She looked impressed. 'Where are you booked to? Back to DC?'

'There. And New York. And Panama City.'

'Then we can get you out.'

'What about you?'

'I'm tougher than I look. Or hadn't you noticed? I can always get out by plane, or by boat from Lyford. And will.'

He felt sad she was on the other side. It hurt him that he would never, finally, be able to trust her, despite what she had done. 'You work for Medina, don't you?' he asked, as the thin rind of the moon came up like a sail-boat's hull high on the horizon above the pale pink clouds.

She answered with a question. 'How did you know? I thought I made a pretty convincing mindless hussy.'

He laughed. 'Why, missie, you did.' She almost hit him. He flinched. He suspected she could kill him with her bare hands, the small hands on those soft white arms. So he was serious. 'It occurred to me I only knew one man rich enough to live at Lyford who hired women who can kill.' She showed no reaction, not even when he said, 'So tell me, who did kill Enrico Perez?' He probed the silence once more. 'If it was you, and I guess it was, I guess all of this is Medina's doing, why did you draw my attention to it? Why did you remind me? Why did you – why does he – want me to know?'

She did not even look at him. He tried again.

'What puzzles me,' he said, 'is that I thought what went on back there was a Medina operation too. I was certain of that. I was convinced that, whoever fronted it, from the CIA down, the old man was really in charge. So why did you protect me? Why did you blow it all apart?'

She gave nothing away. 'I don't know about that. And I'm not interested. My instructions were not to get in your way and to keep you alive. I think I did both those things.'

'You did. You did a lot more.'

She crinkled up her nose. 'Yeah. I did. That was kind of fun. You're pretty cute for a man your age. If you drank a little less so you could guarantee the ball-game, I might consider a season-ticket.'

He smiled and squeezed her arm. 'I didn't mean that, Miss Morgan.'

'I know you didn't,' she said.

He watched her in the gathering gloom, her paleness like another phosphorescence against the evening air, and told her, 'But if you see your boss before I do, which I doubt, tell the old man John Standing's coming to see him, to ask him why he wants me to know so much, to ask him why he doesn't want me dead.'

Part Three:

THE OTHER SIDE

CHAPTER ONE

He came through the Arrivals gate at Dulles airport that lunch-time like a lost soul fleeing hell. Marsha had kept her promises and done her obscure duty and John Standing was mad and home.

Soon he would go out to Georgetown and explain to his brother and Caro and Alan. And, if she was there, to his daughter. But there were things he had to put in motion first. There were things he had to check. He wanted to know, above all else, how deep David Medina's cover ran, how much protection he was afforded. He took a cab to the Archives Building, to the researchers' entrance on Pennsylvania Avenue. All he had with him were the clothes he stood up in and the papers he carried. But those included the papers he had carried from the plane. He wondered exactly how vulner-able he was. If the Agency was involved in this operation they would have no mercy on him now. Could even Medina protect him on American soil? Could Robert, for that matter? Only time would tell. His best bet, after this, was to make a noise, to get himself noticed. In Washington, a public enemy was safer than a private nuisance. Look how long Dick Nixon lasted.

At the Archives, he presented his passport and asked for a researcher's pass. The process took little longer than it took to complete the form. He signed in at the reception desk. Then he took the corridor to the left of the lift shaft, avoiding the huddle of people waiting to take the big dark wood lifts inlaid with chased brass up to the General Search Room and the Genealogy Center. He knew who his ancestors were. He was looking for someone else's. He walked down the depres-sing corridor with its dingy cream walls trimmed with brown marble, its dark green marble floors, its green-stained metal doors gleaming dully under the strip lighting. Why did the

Archives have to be decorated in the colours of vomit? He came to Diplomatic Stacks 5(E) and let himself in.

He knew, it was a matter of public record, that David Medina had been born in Bratislava on the 31st of October 1908. His birth would have had to be registered at the American consulate in either Vienna or Prague. So his birth certificate would not be in one of the distributed nationwide centres where local births were entered. It would have to be here, in Washington, where the consulate archives were lodged. And the diplomatic stacks index would tell him where. He explained his problem to the young black archivist (a rarity in herself: the clerical staff tended to be white, the menials, black; it was even true at the door, where white pass-issuers faced black security guards). She led him to the microfilmed index of births registered overseas. It had still not been re-classified alphabetically by date. Instead, he had to take the microfilms for both Prague and Vienna from 1901 to 1919. He found Medina in Prague. The birth had been registered on the 14th of November. He noted the index number and went back to the archivist, explaining he wanted sight of the original of this registration. She looked at the number and shook her head. She took his inquiry away looking anxious.

'I thought so,' she said on her return. 'I'm sorry but we can't help you. This suffix on the number means all documents referring to this individual are classified. If you want access to them you'll have to seek the permission of the Archivist of the United States, and, in this case, the Secretary of State.'

It was as he had expected.

No. It was worse than he had expected. Medina had never made a secret of the details of his birth. And access to birth records was the most basic function of the Archives. To prove which citizens had been born citizens, and which had not. No one, for instance, could run for the Presidency unless their birth certificate, their American birth certificate, was demonstrably authentic. Yet no one could check that simple fact about David Medina without the full authority of the state. So now John knew where Medina stood, what his position with successive governments was.

It was inviolate.

He braved the heat and walked the mile or so to the main city post office beside Union Station. On the way there, he swore to himself he would never do anything so foolish again. He was old enough for taxis. He was young enough for the Metro.

At the Post Office he went directly to Window 14 at the long open counter on the left-hand side. This building, at least, remained unchanged from his childhood. Long lines of brass-fronted Post Office Boxes still filled the walls furthest from the door or stood in free-standing blocks across the room on either side of the kiosk selling confectionery, tobacco and newspapers. It reminded him of what Grand Central in New York had been like, high-vaulted marble halls filled with rich materials grown grubby, or let down by cheap counters, chairs and shelving. He asked the woman behind the counter for a Post Office Box. She was politer than he remembered the US Mail Service as being. Some things at least were getting better.

They established that he wanted a medium-sized mail-box, suitable for letter-post and small parcels, for the minimum allowable period at this office, six months. It cost him fifty-one dollars. The woman reminded him to be careful with the key, and told him that oversize mail would be held for him at the window diagonally across the room, where an additional charge might be levied. If he did not renew the box at the end of six months, its contents would be cleared. Non-return of the key was an offence.

He thanked the woman and went back into the stifling humid heat of the city. He needed a telephone.

It depressed him to discover that most of the palatial white marble hall of Union Station had been closed to the public, awaiting some new use to be discovered for it. It had often occurred to him that it would make a great State Department Office. Infinitely more impressive than the modern horror down at Foggy Bottom, and ideal for ambassadorial receptions. Moving State up here, so close to the Capitol, instead of under the mists of the Potomac, would also put the fear of God into the National Security Council, the Pentagon and the President. Which, as far as he was concerned, was as it should be.

The only part of the station still operational was a small cubby-hole entrance to the platforms under the western arcade, facing the Metro elevators. But it had phones.

He called Second City in New York, quoting the reference number he had given them, scowling at the memory of his visit to the Archives, and asked them to hold the credit-rating information he still awaited. He did not want it going anywhere he could not control it.

He had one thing left to do. But he had time. Even in D C, even in the summer, with the Senate and House of Representatives in recess, the men who mattered would not be at their watering-holes much before five. He had time to get back to Georgetown to change.

He took a cab, and let himself into the upper apartment with his own set of keys. His clothes were still hanging, neatly wrapped, in the wardrobe in the spare bedroom, where Robert always kept them. He showered and changed into a dress shirt, a dark-blue pinstripe light-weight suit and black leather tasselled loafers. He had to think about the tie. He chose the kind of paisley the Ambassador used to wear in the days he played the dandy.

Going back into the drawing-room he was taken by surprise. His instinctive reaction was fear. He hardly recognized the young girl who stood before him and said, 'Daddy.'

He stood in the centre of the room, not knowing what to say or do. He wanted to take her in his arms, but part of him knew that would be false, embracing the daughter he had never taken care of. He could only look at her sadly, unable to find the words which might make everything up to her, which might explain. All he could say was her name.

She was as diffident as he was. Much younger, as uncertain, and no wiser. 'I thought it was you,' she said. 'I saw you get out of the taxi when I was walking back from campus.'

He avoided looking at his watch, managing not to appear the stereotyped too-busy separated father. But he told her, 'Eleanor, I have to go. I'll be back this evening. Perhaps we could talk then.'

284

He scribbled a note for Caro, asking her to meet him here at nine or nine-thirty, and fled.

The cab dropped him on H Street, on the corner with 17th, in front of the red-brick, bow-fronted, stone-porticoed building of the Metropolitan Club, in the shadow of the White House and the Old Executive Offices, the one place in the world where, at his father's request, he always remembered not to get too drunk. He went through the swing doors to the wood-panelled foyer and the big marble lobby beyond. The log-fire was blessedly unlit today, leaving the men standing around the big wooden table in the centre of the room, where the periodicals lay, untarnished by the fine sheen of sweat which was the mark of Washington's disadvantaged. These men had stepped from air-conditioned offices to air-conditioned limousines to air-conditioned club. He had not been so fortunate, but he knew that was not the reason why they stared, or why the two men on the stairs were turning to send whispers up to the floors above.

He recognized some of them: Wilson of the Federal Reserve, McAlan Brown of State, Bill Wainwright of the START negotiating team talking to Jackson of the National Security Council, and Stephen Taft the corporate lawyer. If they were here, the Senator would be here too. He stepped into the lobby. The Ambassador's boy was back.

'Been a long time,' Wainwright noted, in his sleepy South Carolina drawl.

John knew what they were thinking. They were wondering if the stories they had heard about him, or which they remembered witnessing in person, were still true. He looked respectable enough today. Was this the man who fell down drunk at the West Point Passing Out Ball? Was this the man who danced naked across the first green at Chevy Chase? Was this the man who in fifteen hours played the whole of the New York Stock Exchange Blackjack Association out of its collective wallet? He looked too human for that.

'Long time,' John finally agreed. 'The Senator at home?'

They all knew who he meant. Everyone who mattered in Washington would know who he meant. The Metropolitan was the city's oldest, grandest club. Founded in 1863. Its members drawn from the senior ranks of government and legislature, from the city's great corporate law firms, firms which bred many of the nation's politicians (even Honest Abe Lincoln had been a well-heeled railroad lawyer), and from the families of the cave-dwellers, the local magnates who had created Washington D C. By nature and inclination, John might have been happier as a member of the Cosmos, among the intellectuals in their French Renaissance mansion on Embassy Row, but almost since the beginning the Standing men had been members here, where the power-brokers and the fixers dwelt. The Ambassador had had him elected on his twenty-first birthday, just like his big brother before him, while his sisters were members of the Sulgrave, the Metropolitan's sister institution on Dupont Circle at 1801 Massachusetts Avenue. The ladies might take tea, play bridge, and wear white gloves, but principally the Sulgrave was the most private, most exclusive dance-hall in the Union.

Now he was asking after one of the fixers, one of the small group of older men who made it their business to know the business of the capital. They were old money and old houses. Their forefathers had backed fellow members of this club for the lesser office of the Presidency, in the Union's hours of boredom and frustration. The campaigns for Ulysses S. Grant, Theodore Roosevelt, for Taft, Harding, Hoover and F D R, had been mounted from these panelled rooms. And while the old families admitted they could not necessarily prevent the people's choice getting himself elected, they could make it virtually impossible for him to rule if ever he was. As Jimmy Carter of Georgia discovered. The Southerners among them in particular had not taken kindly to the liberal sell-outs of one of their own.

The former Senator was the dean of these. Still referred to by his honorific title. Grown fat now on the donations of a thousand lobbyists who only asked him to have a quiet word with his friends, he sat in the bar drinking whisky sours and waiting for the world to come to him.

'He's here,' Wainwright acknowledged. 'Usual place.'

John nodded and went up to the bar. The Senator was

286

sitting at his corner table, entering a note in his diary with the solid gold propelling-pencil the former Iranian ambassador had given him, along with twenty pounds of caviare, an expenses-paid winter holiday in Gstaad and a stretch at the Lincoln Continental for certain minor services rendered in the days when the Shah bought weapons from the United States. It was the nearest you were allowed to get to visibly working on the premises of the Metropolitan. Producing work-papers in here was grounds for instant expulsion.

John sat down at the table and beckoned a barman over to order two whisky sours. The Senator's jowls tensed and his fat dark-suited body seemed to stiffen. 'I wasn't aware,' he said slowly, not lifting his eyes to look at John, 'that I'd invited you to join me.'

Standing was aware that other members were drifting into the bar wondering what business the Ambassador's scapegrace boy, the black sheep of the family, might have with one of the secret, silent powers of the city. They were expecting some kind of show, and he did not disappoint them.

'I didn't ask for an invitation, Senator. I came here with an instruction for you.'

The jowls turned purple. The fat man rose from his chair. 'You are impertinent, sir. I am glad your father . . .'

John interrupted him, smiling cynically, 'Don't cite my father at me, Senator. The Ambassador always said you were the greatest knave in Washington, which probably meant you were the greatest knave alive.'

The old man was trying to pass by in silent outrage, but John did not move his long legs, blocking the fat man's exit from the corner. 'You incommode me, sir,' he blustered.

John smiled again, more broadly this time. 'Indeed I do,' he said. The barman was hovering a few feet from them, pretending not to hear what passed between them but as fascinated as the gathering members. John snapped his fingers and pointed at the sours he was carrying. The barman put the glasses on the table and backed away.

'Sit down, Senator,' John said, lifting the drink to his lips, 'I didn't tell you you could go.'

But the fat man could not back down now, embarrassed in

front of his fellow members. 'I insist, sir,' he palpitated, 'I demand . . . I shall report you to the committee . . .'

John finished his drink in a single gulp and slapped the empty glass down on the table, its clot of ice already melting, despite the air-conditioning. Then he stood up, towering over even the great bulk of the Senator.

'Tell anyone you please,' he said. 'It was scum like you and your committee who blackballed my great grandfather after the War Between the States. Do you think I care what you say about me? All I care about, Senator, is the message you're going to carry to your paymaster. You go to the Madison, Senator, and you tell David Medina that John Standing wants to see him. He will be as delighted to get that message as I am to send it. So don't you delay, or I swear I will eat whatever is left of your hide once he has finished with it.'

Then he turned, and strode out down the stairs.

In the lobby, MacAlan Brown of the State Department caught up with him and took him by the arm to make him stop. The big administrator looked almost sad behind his tortoiseshell glasses. 'Nice show,' he admitted, 'but you just killed yourself in this town.'

John shrugged. 'Hell, Brown, I don't know what you sons of bitches think you've been doing, but I'm not sure I want to stay alive in Gomorrah any more.'

He sauntered though the lobby, but at the door he turned to say, 'Oh, and Brown, tell the committee John Standing just quit.'

He went next door to the Everett Hotel. He badly needed a drink. Back in the Metropolitan, MacAlan Brown shook his head in wonder. He knew already that the committee would ignore John Standing's resignation. He was a Standing, after all. And besides, too many of the members had for half a lifetime longed to treat the fat old fraud the way the Virginian just had.

Standing took a drink at the Everett. Then he crossed behind the White House on the south side of Lafayette Square past the hideous layercake Treasury Department building to the Washington Hotel to have another. He tried to stand, but could not, and realized at last how badly the events of the past day had shaken him. It was a kind of drunkenness. Everything was very clear, very sharp, very still. He had reached a point of rest. One more drink now and he would be finished. He willed himself to his feet. He fed a quarter into a callbox.

'Hello, Madison? Could you put me through to Mr Medina's suite, please.' There was a pause, a couple of clicks, and he was through.

'Yes?' an anonymous voice asked. Ismail, he guessed, the old man's secretary.

'It's Standing. Is he ready?'

'I just need some confirmation,' the voice replied, 'of your identity. Can you tell me the number of either of the credit cards you took out in New York last week?'

He wanted to swear, but he complied. Medina had missed nothing.

'That's fine,' the voice responded. 'He's hosting a reception for the Saudi princes in the Mount Vernon Room. You are expected. And he asks you to join him for a drink before supper in the Board Room.'

Yes, thought John. *He would.*

Caro did not learn of John's arrival till after seven in the evening. Alan had left for New York before she rose that morning. She spent the day in the Pentagon trying to ferret out what any of her contacts might know about the missing aircraft, but they were all sullen, if not overtly hostile. The whole thing was slipping away from her, and she knew it. She hoped that John, wherever he was, had found the missing pieces.

It was Eleanor who told her he was back, when she dropped into the apartment to change before attending the Medina reception. Robert Standing had swung her an invitation, after she admitted a fascination with his brother's old adversary. She had never realized the Standings had known Medina so long. Perhaps that was it, she thought; perhaps you always turn most violently against one of your own.

Eleanor came up as she was changing. The poor child

looked miserable. It did not take her long to tell Caro why. It was only then that Caro noticed the note on the telephone.

Her instinctive reaction was fury, at John's high-handedness, with her, and with his daughter. But the near-African heat of the capital was sapping her energy. As she talked to the girl she realized that both of them could forgive him almost anything if only he would explain. But he never did explain.

Robert and Melissa Standing drove her to the Madison Hotel, for they were regulars at the city's grandest parties. Medina's party for the IMF was always one of the smallest. It was also one of the most famous. She was aware it said a great deal about Robert that he managed to get her invited at all. Unless Medina knew of her work. She dismissed the thought as ridiculous. Medina would not take note of mere journalists. He was the kind of man who had his private staff scouring the world's press before dawn, to hand him a manageable folder of cuttings he ought to take note of or might be interested in. He did not have the time to follow growing reputations.

The Mercedes sighed up to the M Street entrance of the hotel, diagonally opposite the new *Washington Post* building. Robert handed the keys to the doorman and hesitated on the sidewalk. Caro noticed that Melissa too looked anxious, as though Robert had briefed her about what he had to say, which almost sounded like a plea for help.

'Miss Kilkenny,' he began, formally, though he and Melissa had already taken to calling her by her first name, 'you know John's back. Well, he made damn certain this afternoon that everyone who matters in this town knows it.'

Caro wondered how, but did not get the chance to interrupt. In any case, she knew how efficient grapevines could be, especially in a city at once so powerful and provincial as DC.

'You know him well, I gather. I also gather you've managed to keep him working,' he continued, 'which is more than most have ever managed. I think he may be losing control. And I think he's likely to try and get in here tonight. Can I ask you to keep an eye on him if he does? I would rather he was not allowed to embarrass himself again.'

She realized that the older, gentler brother meant it. He

was not, as most men would be, worried about his own reputation, or even his family's name. He was secure enough not to worry about those. But he was concerned for his little brother, the brother he hardly ever saw, the brother he had insisted should always have a base in the city. She wondered what had drawn two men of such significantly different ages so close together, and she found herself wondering what manner of man the Ambassador had been.

'I'll do the best I can,' she said. 'There's a lot I want to talk to him about.'

They stepped into the lobby of the Madison, and back a hundred years. It was, in fact, quite a new hotel, founded by Marshall B. Coyne in the early sixties, but it felt a hundred years older, filled with its proprietor's immense antique collection. It looked more like a product of the sudden spate of wealth after the Civil War than of anything out of John F. Kennedy's tawdry vision of Camelot. Even the hideous things, like the ormolu clock in the lobby, were hideous in character, and Caro always found herself strangely reassured by the profusion of English oil-paintings and French furniture. It was not the world she had come from, but it was the one she would, in her private dreams, most have liked to inhabit.

It was bigger than it looked, with over four hundred rooms, which was why people who preferred privacy and quiet tended to stay at its little sister on the opposite corner of 15th and M, the Dolley Madison, with only forty-two rooms, each perhaps more exquisite than anything in the main hotel except the Presidential Suite on the fifteenth floor, and the biggest suites on the second and third. The hotel had the highest security reputation of any in the city, because of certain features of both buildings. Not just the restricted and heavily watched entrances, and the inaccessibility of the roofs, but the fact that the floors which housed suites had been designed with flexibility in mind. All the rooms interconnected, and by locking or opening particular doors the management could create a suite of almost any size and configuration. Whole floors, or parts of them, could be isolated, with their own entrances and exits. It was the State Department's favourite hotel for housing visiting dignitaries who posed a security problem. The President of El Salvador and Rajiv Gandhi of India's entourage had been housed here, within weeks of each other, during the height of terrorist attacks on El Salvador's capital and India's people and property. Security chiefs could never sleep easy in such circumstances, but putting people up at the Madison was sometimes the only thing that allowed them to sleep at all.

Almost since the hotels' joint foundation, David Medina had stayed at the Dolley when in Washington and entertained at the larger Madison. It reminded him of his houses across the Atlantic. He had long since given up running houses in the United States. He was here too little, and the high-technology of death was too readily available for him to feel entirely safe in any house in his own country. He stayed at the Pierre in New York and the Madison here (visiting Washington only when the IMF Conference was held there, or for Presidential inaugurations – he had attended twelve – or for those rare pieces of lobbying so secret, so obscure yet so necessary he could not delegate them to his staff). He conducted the rest of his American business meetings in the relative safety of his private jet.

They stepped across the lobby up the open marble spiral staircase which turned around a crystal chandelier and a Chinese Imperial altar table, lacquered black and trimmed in gold, a porcelain Famille Rose plaque inset in its surface, to the Upper Lobby where the hotel's entertaining facilities lay.

Some Third World country was spending the bulk of this year's Gross National Product on a party in the full ballroom. Security staff in frock coats were on hand to divide Medina's guests from these less important people. Robert, Melissa and Caro were escorted through to the Mount Vernon Room in the far corner of the lobby.

It was the purest, lightest room in the building, decorated in the palest pastels, like the presentation rooms of a European palace. Medina was holding court. This year's excuse for the party was a reception for the Saudi princes attending the Conference planning sessions as observers. It was the kind of thing Medina did supremely well, in apparently unreflecting service of his country. He had already, that afternoon, taken them hawking in Fairfax County, indulging the Desert Arabs' favourite sport and presenting them with the eagle and falcons he had had broken for them. This evening he was presenting them to the small world of American power-brokers.

Caro felt out of place at once. But she watched him with fascination. She had never seen him before. Few enough people ever did. There were hardly any photographs of him in the public domain, available for use by the media. And she had no idea what his voice might sound like.

He was shorter than she expected, a little below average height, but even under elegant evening clothes it was obvious he was powerfully built. She had heard something of his prowess as a hunter during her stints for the *Examiner* behind the Iron Curtain. Now, despite the perfect calm and sophistication of his person and the setting he created for himself, she could imagine something feral about him. She could see him as a thing of blood, tearing its prey apart without the aid of any weapons, dark, relentless, malevolent.

But watching him again, standing at the far end of the room while his private staff circulated the people he wished to speak to before him and the princes, she told herself to stop imagining things. She must have listened to John too often, for the head and hands were not those of a killer. The hands were big, and doubtless powerful, but as Medina gestured lightly in conversation it was clear the power was delicate, like that of a surgeon or violinist. And the aged head was almost shockingly beautiful still. He looked more like the graven image of a Roman Emperor than any man she had ever seen. The white hair had receded with the years, away from the high forehead, but he wore it long at the back, like some superstar pianist of the late nineteenth century. The straight, broad nose and the full mouth dividing his square face neatly spoke of a confidence which verged on the complacent, but she had never seen such eyes.

They were the palest green, startling in the pale brown complexion inherited from his father, mottled a little, as were his hands, by liverspots and age. They looked immortal. They did not, as most other people's do, glance carelessly around a large room, taking note of anything of actual or potential interest. They were completely still, unblinking, attending to the person he was speaking to and no other. And yet they were impenetrable eyes. They gave nothing away at all. They made her think of Standing.

As she thought of him, he walked into the room.

She could tell that he had been drinking. He was the only man out of the seventy or so there not wearing a dinner jacket or their national formal wear. He looked tired, and impoverished, and out of place. Yet for an instant Medina's eyes lifted to look at him with their level green stare, as though he had been telepathically aware of the big man's entrance at the other side of the room, and there might as well have been nobody else present. For an instant the two men looked at each other, for no longer than the blink of an eye, but Caro understood at last that they were bound by some complicity too deep for her to understand. Then both of them looked away, and it was as though normal life had been clicked back on at a switch. John did not even acknowledge her presence. He walked over to his brother, said something brief, and left the room. She followed after him, aware that Medina's staff were watching every move.

He walked out of the Mount Vernon Room with the exaggerated steadiness of the drunk back towards the staircase and round the corner to the Board Room. He sat down there. She sat down with him.

He started talking at once. 'I told Robert I was seeing Medina here after the reception. I asked him to wait downstairs with you till I was finished. It won't take long. Then you can take me home and I'll explain.'

She was too tired and too puzzled to be angry with him, but she was tired of being kept waiting. 'Explain it now. What has Medina got to do with anything?'

'I wish I knew,' he said. 'I wish I knew that more than anything in the world.'

'Then why are you here? And where have you been? Don't you have any consideration? If not for me at least for your daughter?'

He blinked once, otherwise unmoving. She realized he had

got to the stage of drunkenness where he was completely calm, but needed a single focus for his attention. If he was diverted he would fall. She had to tell him anyway.

'It's weapons, John. It's big. Big enough to need illegally operated airliners.'

'I know,' he said, blinking one more time, 'I was there when one of them was blown up.'

She blinked this time. 'You were what?'

Then he began to laugh, trying hopelessly to rein it in, and failing, rocking back in his chair in quiet mirth. He calmed down at last, and began to tell her quickly, quietly, what he meant.

'It all fits. The Nicaraguan Contras are being supplied with US arms. The deal was originally financed by what were effectively short-term loans arranged by Errol Hart. The Contras pay through bank accounts in Panama and Nassau. They pay heavily over the odds. The dealers are Alabaman corporations masquerading as general import–export houses. The paperwork is drawn up for legal goods delivered to Nassau, Freetown, Costa Rica. But what's actually shipped out, in fast boats, is arms. They're transferred to aircraft on the Ragged Island cays in the Bahamas. The planes fly them into Honduras, Guatemala, you name it. The boats return packed to the gunwales with cocaine.'

He closed his eyes and sat back in his chair. He appeared to be asleep. She looked at him for a long time. Either he had finally gone mad, or he had hit the jackpot. 'Can you prove any of this?' she asked.

He jerked wide awake again. 'All of it. There's a ruined Boeing on the Ragged Island cays which would take a hell of a lot of explaining or spiriting away. I have documentation taken from the plane. I have circumstantial evidence from the Nassau banking and shipping communities. And I have photographs.'

'But why?' she wondered, more to herself than to him. 'Why is the Vatican paying for the Contras?'

He was about to speak, but stopped himself, and changed tack. 'Can't tell for certain. Could just be that under this Pope the anti-communists have won the power-struggle in the Vatican. I think it's more than that, and I aim to sort it out, with your help. But the first thing to do is to break this story. The one we have. Because I think if we do we're going to shake out CIA involvement in the traffic. I think it's a covert operation. I think the United States is effectively at war in Central America without its citizens being told.'

'How did you do all this? Where did you get the money?'

He pointed towards the Board Room door, back in the direction they had come. 'Him. His money. Long story. Something he was trying to prove. But that's what worries me. He also saved my life yesterday. Or had it done. I want to know why. I don't know what he has to gain by publishing the story. I may be paranoid, but he scares me stiff.'

She shook her head. 'I still don't see it. He clearly hasn't anything to gain. If he was involved he'd want the story spiked. If he's not, there's no point in any involvement.'

John sat forward, holding his face in his hands. 'Caro,' he whispered, 'you don't know Medina's Law: Crisis is the mother of fortunes. For all I know, the old man may be looking for a war.' He stretched back, lifting his hands high above his head and yawning. 'In any case, for now, I want you out of here. What he and I have to say to each other is still a private matter.'

She knew he meant it, and she rose to go, but one thing remained to worry her. 'You say he saved your life. Who is it tried to kill you? Why aren't you taking precautions?'

He looked at her in puzzlement. 'But don't you understand?' he asked. 'No one kills you if Medina wants you alive.'

The light at the door thickened. Ismail was standing there. For an instant, Caro thought he was smiling. All he said was: 'Mr Medina will see you shortly, Mr Standing. Alone.'

They waited for him in the lobby till after ten. The last of Medina's guests had departed over an hour before, after the Saudi princes had been led away by the Saudi Ambassador, himself a Royal prince. They kept themselves going on black coffee ferried to them from La Provence, the coffee shop up the corridor. When he came down he was silent. He was silent all the way home.

When they got to Georgetown he turned to his brother in the car and croaked, 'Big brother, I need . . .'

Robert understood, but gave them no explanation. All he said to John was: 'I know.' Then he turned to the two women and said, 'Melissa, Miss Kilkenny, will you go in? There's something John and I need to talk about. I don't think we should be too long, but will you tell Eleanor to go to bed? It's probably best that she waits till the morning to talk to her father.'

Both Melissa and Caro knew when they were being dismissed. They watched the car jerk slowly up the hill towards the university. Melissa turned to Caro, smiling wryly. 'You know,' she said, 'there are times I wish I hadn't married an honest man.'

They were not going far. Just a few blocks up to the little grey pebbledash townhouse on 36th Street North-West which housed the Institute for the Study of Foreign Relations. Robert let them in using his passkeys and led the way up to his little office on the third floor, bare save for a desk, a couple of chairs, a couple of dozen books, and a computer terminal.

Robert snapped on the strip-light and turned to face his young brother. 'Well, little brother,' he said calmly, 'you sure as hell made certain everyone in town knew you were home.'

The two men looked at each other for what seemed endless time, then both of them grinned and nearly hugged each other to death. Robert took John by the shoulders, shaking him in his big countryman's hands. 'My,' he said wonderingly, 'but you look terrible, boy.'

John could not stop smiling, though his words were sombre: 'I told you before. I wasn't built to last.' He looked around the bare office. 'This isn't much for a lifetime in the service.'

Robert shrugged. 'It's all I need, so long as I got that whizz-bang in the corner.'

John nodded. 'How much do you already know?'

Robert shook his head as he lowered his vast frame into a chair, reaching into the desk drawer for a bottle of bourbon and two dusty glasses. John waved the offer aside.

'No,' Robert recognized thoughtfully, 'you done enough already. But I still need one. And if you're asking, can I tell you if the Agency is running drugs into the USA and exporting arms out, the answer is No. I don't know that. I suspect plenty. The Committee suspects plenty. But I haven't got an ounce of freeze-dried shit to go on. If it is them, my suspicion is all they're doing is helping with the money. I think somebody else is doing it as a favour. Hands-off operation, so the Agency looks clean. Guess you know who I think set it up.'

John poured himself a bourbon anyway. Robert took another. 'Yes, big brother, I think I know. I thought he was looking old tonight.'

'We all look old,' Robert protested sourly.

John's smile as he sipped the bourbon was that of a newly proclaimed saint in heaven. 'This stuff is so good it can't be legal.'

'It ain't. Last year's Christmas present from the FBI, after they broke up a whole stack of stills in 'Ouisiana.'

John took another, more respectful, sip and said, 'Thank the Lord for the Louisiana Purchase, despite the Constitution.' Then his mood changed abruptly and he asked, 'How much of it do you know?'

Robert cocked his left eyebrow. 'How much is there?'

'Caro fill you in?' Robert nodded. 'There's more I don't understand. Some at least of the money is coming from the Vatican. Do your people have any knowledge of what they might be up to?'

'News to me,' Robert said. 'But nothing would surprise me about the Gentlemen in Black. Remember Nicaragua after the Sandinistas took over? Calvi's Ambrosiano was the only foreign bank allowed to stay in operation, but everybody knew that he'd been financing the Somoza regime. Never did understand that. Figured it had to be the Vatican, till the Church fell out of bed with the Sandinistas.'

'That's happened?'

'Oh, sure. Poland operation. The Church as the unofficial opposition to a Communist regime.'

'Maybe that's it. Maybe they really are backing the Contras.'

298

Robert shook his head. 'I'd believe it if you told me it was our Catholics. Chicago, say. They're as redneck as anyone comes. I'd believe it if you told me it was Opus Dei. But I don't believe it of the Vatican. This Pope isn't Julius II. I don't think he'd pay for armies.'

John disagreed. 'The outfit washing the money is run by Opus Dei. And the boss of the Vatican Bank is a Chicagoan. Marcinkus.'

Robert laughed. 'Hell, little brother, Marcinkus doesn't have the brains for this. If you're looking for a connection you have to go a tier down, to the real administration in the Curia. The way I see it, that Polish clown they hired as Chief Operating Officer's played right into their hands. Great public-relations front-man, deep conservative who hands them nice little weapons like the Inquisition to play with, and he's so busy running round the world jumping out of aeroplanes and eating dirt he doesn't have the damnedest clue what his administrators are up to.'

John remained unconvinced. 'I agree about the Pope. But are we sure about Marcinkus? OK, he's just a Chicagoan heavy, and it looks like he got taken to the cleaners by Calvi, but there were people in Nixon's White House who believed Sam Ervin of the Senate Committee when he said he was just an old-time down-home country lawyer. And he was the best man Harvard Law School ever had. They're still wondering how the country boy got them all in prison. Hell, there are still people who think you're just a Virginian cave-dweller. You can see it in the thinks-bubbles over their heads: Robert Standing, the Neanderthal Man of State.'

Robert smiled and nodded. 'I know, I know. But I swear to you I'm right about Marcinkus. Frankly, unless it's green and got eighteen holes in it, he isn't interested.'

John slapped one hand down on the desk. 'OK. Suppose I buy that. I still have a hunch left to play. But what I'm getting nowhere about is how the old man might tie in. I told him tonight I'm convinced he does, and he just smiled and smiled and smiled. I keep feeling he knows everything I'm doing, yet he not only doesn't interfere, on one occasion at least he's also stepped in to save my skin. I do not understand it.'

Robert eased back in his chair, sprawling his long legs in front of him, and swinging his left leg up on to the desk. 'Little brother,' he began, after another pull at the bourbon, 'you and I have always believed Medina is a dangerous man. So did the Ambassador, however much he liked him personally. I spent a decade trying to keep him out of policy. But you stack up our fears against what the politicians can point at and what have you got? You got a wondrous necessary man. He can go where the rest of us can't. We owe him for getting the Iranian hostages out, when no one else could deal. A year ago he pulled the fat out of the fire for us in Egypt. For twenty years he was the only channel we had into China. When all else fails you can turn to Medina and he will usually deliver. It wouldn't be surprising if the clowns they have running foreign policy these days turned to him and asked him to get arms into Central America. And it wouldn't surprise me, or you, if he did it, hoping the whole thing would unravel. What the politicians will never understand about Medina is the fact that he isn't like them. He doesn't have policy-objectives, he doesn't have a world-view. He is the last of the opportunists, always looking to find or create a crisis so that he can exploit it.'

John signed. He lit up a cigarette and used the waste-bin as an ashtray. 'All accepted,' he said, exhaling a long column of smoke. 'But I don't see what he'd have to gain by embarrassing this government of all governments.'

Robert smiled. 'Did it never occur to you that with you, uniquely of all journalists, it might be double bluff? The most perfect way of silencing you would be to persuade you that publishing is somehow in his interests.'

John had to disagree. 'There's a better way. He could kill me.'

'Why would he do that?' Robert asked reasonably, 'He still wants you to work for him. He's right too. If you hadn't been a Standing, if you hadn't had me for a brother and the Ambassador for a father, you would have been a Medina. You have the talents. The only one you're short of is the absolute carelessness. But you do care, don't you? Which is why you still can't face Eleanor. Which is why we're here rather than in the comfort of the apartment.'

John rubbed his cigarette out in the waste-bin. 'I'm not so sure of that. There are times when I wonder if I care at all. Sometimes I think that that's what I'm ashamed of.'

'Bullshit, John. But you ought to talk to her in any case. All she really wants to know is if it's true what that mad bitch Evelyn kept telling her and her daddy has two horns, a tail and cloven feet.'

'Well, have I?'

'No. Just the most heavily decorated kidneys since World War One and a liver that's crying to be sent back home to momma. Have another drink.'

They had another drink. Musing over it in the hot Georgetown night under the flat acid glare of fluorescent light Robert said, 'My guess is that it's all about black money.'

John nodded. 'That occurred to me too. You know Calvi kept talking about it at the end. No one knew if he meant ordinary black money, the stuff that's never declared to the authorities, or if he meant money from the Men in Black. At the end it looked as though he was hoping desperately to be bailed out by anybody, and pinned his hopes on the Vatican.'

Robert snorted. 'Lots of people do that. It's what keeps the place in business. Anyhow, in Italy Church money is black money in the usual sense. It doesn't have to be fully declared to the Italian authorities. What if Medina just spotted that, after Calvi . . .'

'I know,' John interrupted, 'what if he said: "This isn't my money. It can't be traced to me. Its owners are desperate to get it out of Italy. If I do that for them, they can't stop me using it on the way." That's the thing about black money. Nobody can complain about the uses it's put to because it isn't supposed to exist. So while it's going wherever it's intended to, he can use it to spawn off his own purposes . . .'

'It wouldn't take much either,' Robert continued the thought. 'A few million dollars of seed capital. What if he came to the Contras and said, "Look, I can raise you the money to buy arms so long as you do me some favours when the time comes." They say, "Go for it." So he comes to our people and says, "I just discovered the Contras are serious people with real money to spend, not the usual pack of whingers looking for free aid. If I set it up and keep you out of it, you turn a blind eye, OK?"'

John had pulled out his notepad and was trying to sketch out the way the money might go. 'That's right,' he said enthusiastically, 'and in the process he says to the Contras, "You need more money than I can bring you. Let's use what I've got to run in cocaine to the US to get you the money to buy more arms." And the whole operation gets the original black money into the United States. Which is presumably where the Vatican wants it. Do you still think Marcinkus is a clown?'

Robert shook his head. 'Assumptions, asshole. I warned you about those before. What makes you so certain this is the destination? Do we have any idea where the money's intended for?'

John slammed his pad and pencil down against the desk. 'No. We don't. Just guesswork. Wouldn't you want to put your investment dollars here?'

'Oh, sure, but I'm not the Vatican. How much advance notice are you giving me?'

For an instant John looked suspicious, but it was his brother he was dealing with, after all. 'The American section of the story is the only part I'm certain of. I can go with that at once. And think I have to while there's a jagged Boeing sitting in the Bahamas inviting the attention of other reporters. But I can't run the Vatican part of the story till I know the final destination of the money.'

'Not my problem. You can piss all over Rome whenever and however you want. My job is to try to keep my people clean in anything you put together about the US.' He saw the look on John's face. 'Oh, screw it, John. I'm not asking you to pull your story. I know you wouldn't, and if you did I'd only have to deal with another journalist later. All I want to know is how much time I've got to get my house in order. It doesn't matter, in the end, if the Agency, the President and the National Security Council all come out of this smelling like shit, though I imagine it's been Medina's job to provide them with impenetrable cover, so long as the Legislature Committees come out of it clean. The system works, the

302

system maintains international respect so long as its parts police each other. We proved that when the Senate and the Supreme Court hung Nixon out to dry. People were saying that was the end of the system. Well, it's still here.'

John looked suitably apologetic. 'I'm sorry. I've been paranoid these past few weeks. The answer to your question is, I can either draft a telex now, to follow up a telephoned story, in which case it hits the *Examiner* in London in time for Friday morning's paper, or I can go to the networks here now and blow it for the breakfast television news, or I can pull the *Examiner*'s main news editor over from London and he and Caro and I can cover the whole deal properly, in which case we'll be out with the whole US story in Monday morning's paper. Which one do you want?'

Robert smiled as he reached for one of his brother's cigarettes saying. 'Filthy habit . . .'

'You have to die of something,' John responded.

There was silence as Robert lit the Chesterfield. 'You know I want the last. I don't believe you'd go to the networks. I suspect you owe that to Miss Kilkenny.' John acknowledged it with a nod. 'Nice lady.'

'Too nice for me.'

'I agree, but I still think you'd want to give her and the *Examiner* priority. So I've really got a choice between Friday and Monday. I want Monday. What's the price?'

John swallowed. 'I still think Medina's at the heart of it. But I can't prove it. I'd hoped publishing the Central American stuff might allow us to shake the papers free under the Freedom of Information Act. I discovered today it won't be easy to get any documents on Medina . . .'

'Could've spared you the effort,' Robert told him flatly. 'All documents relating to Medina have been classified for nearly forty years. And there are standing orders in State and the Agency to shred them all in any case. Nothing hits the files.'

'OK. So my best bet to nail him is to establish the final destination of the black money. If I can't pin it to him in transit I ought to be able to do it wherever he makes delivery. All I know so far are the names of the companies who supply the arms. I want the use of your security classification to find out where their money's been going. I want to know who their business partners are, and their investments. I want you to give me the money route.'

Robert looked tired all of a sudden. He looked the older brother for a change. 'I wish you wouldn't, John,' he said glumly. 'I know you want him, and I understand why. But I don't believe he's takeable. I think he'll see us all off in the end.'

John looked equally saddened. 'Maybe you're right. But I have to try. And I have to lean on you to do it.'

Robert nodded and turned to the computer terminal. He switched it on, and started to key in his security codes and clearances. John looked aghast. 'You run it from here?' he asked.

'Sure. Safest place. No one ever thinks college professors could do anybody any harm.'

'Can you access the Department of Trade records on this?'

'Little brother, with my classification I could get you the most secret information in DC today.'

'What's that?'

'The name and phone number of the First Lady's plastic surgeon. The only thing I can't get you are Scale Nine papers.'

'What are they?'

It was Robert's turn to look appalled. 'Didn't the Ambassador teach you anything?' he asked. 'Scale Nine papers are archival documents too secret to be shown to presidents. Don't look so surprised, John. They're politicians. They leak. Especially when they leave office. Do you really think we'd let them see the searches we do on them and their opponents? Do you think we ought to show a President the plans for what to do if he goes mad and tries to pull the nuclear trigger?'

An hour later they had the answers John needed. Answers which meant nothing to Robert but confirmed his younger brother's hunch. It was Poland. It had always had to be Poland. It explained Father Tomasso's death. It explained why Father Zbigniew had been murdered on the same night as Wellbeck, Perez and Hart. They were the four points on the circle. They were where the money passed. The import of goods from Poland was how the money was passed to its destination. But in Poland black money would have to run underground again, to avoid the eyes of the authorities. He had to find out exactly where it went. He had to find out what advantage David Medina might possibly gain from its transmission.

And there was one more thing which worried him. Robert identified it too. 'You know, John,' he said, 'the bit I don't like, in this whole story, is the cocaine. It doesn't sound like Medina. It's big enough but it's tacky. And for all his faults, he is almost one of us.'

'Maybe,' John said. 'Or maybe it's just that there's a moral version of Gresham's Law. Bad money drives out good. Perhaps that's true of everything.'

He was too tired to work it out now. There was only one thing he had left to do before he slept. He asked to borrow Robert's car, after dropping him at the apartment. Robert looked doubtful. 'I know,' he had had to admit, 'that the police in most civilized nations and I have an informal agreement: I don't drive, they don't arrest me. But I do need it, if only for an hour.' So Robert agreed and, after dropping him at the house, John drove down silent provincial M Street, into Pennsylvania Avenue and down 23rd Street to the West End of The Mall, parking just past the corner with Constitution Avenue. There were bollards to be negotiated, everywhere in front of official buildings, since the suicide attack on the Beirut Embassy and Marine Barracks, and he knew he was a great deal drunker than he felt.

He also knew he was not safe, a rich-looking white man with a Mercedes walking in unpatrolled Washington long after midnight, when even the guard in the spotlit Lincoln Memorial had long gone off duty, but he always came here, once at least, whenever he came home.

He climbed the shallow marble steps two at a time to the classical temple which housed the monumental statue of Abraham Lincoln, the saviour, reinventor and martyr of the

Republic from which one humble disgraceful citizen had been so long and so often absent. Here he could remember that not all things were for the worst. Though all things ended, not all things failed. It had been his father's favourite maxim. Years before, when John was five years old, the Ambassador had brought him here and read an uncomprehending boy the Gettysburg Address, carved in stone on the south side of the temple. His voice had stumbled when he came to the passage which read, 'The world will little note or long remember what we say here . . .'

He had shaken his head and said, 'Not true. Not true. Only deliberate lie he ever told the people. He didn't always tell the whole truth. He was too good a politician. But that's a lie. What we remember is what he said. Men without words are really dead.' His voice had choked at that, and long afterwards John knew it was the moment which decided him against his family's occupation. It was the words of diplomats, not poets, which were writ in water. In any sense that mattered, the Ambassador had been silent all his life.

Now, thirty-seven years later, a worn-out old hack, drunk most of the time, sat down on the floor with his back to the plinth on which the statue stood, Lincoln towering over him like a guardian angel whose speech was tongued with fire. John Standing had been born in the final throes of one war, which had allowed his country to inherit an empire. He had lived to see it flex its imperial powers in Korea and in the slow long agony of Vietnam. He had seen it grow to enormous wealth, fulfilling for most of its free citizens the ancient promise of a more abundant life. He had seen the Founding Fathers' dream of a tolerant society revert to religious fundamentalism. He had seen churches encroach on the authority of state. He had seen arrogance, childish optimism and stupidity drag his country into the worst kind of boastful adventurism. He had lived to see most of the freedoms guaranteed in the Constitution mocked as the idle dreams of liberals and communists. He had seen the brilliant colours of the Republic's dawning fade. In his youth he had fled from the spectacle of a great power manacled by ignorance and pride. Now, older, too often defeated, he wondered if it mattered.

He wanted to know, of Lincoln, and the Capitol shining whitely in the distance, and the ripe Virginia moon, if it mattered a damn, at the end of things, if one nation founded in tolerance and hope should hand its power to knaves and fools and the likes of David Medina. He looked down the long green manicured lawns of The Mall, with its reflecting pool, its Washington monument, its cherry trees which had lost their bloom, and wondered why, or even if, he cared. Why men like his brother still gave a lifetime of service to a nation designed by and for grotesque industrial magnates and five-star generals. He had spent an hour with one of the victors of this society, a man whose cool green stare had once again offered him the luxurious dreams of his fellow citizens. Why had he turned them down? What was it which made him want to tear down everything that man and his kind would always stand for?

Was it vanity, what was left of his tattered self-esteem that drove him? Was it folly or stubbornness or fear, fear of the great majority with its simple unwashed hopes and expectations? Was it only the aristocrat's contempt? Was that why in his own country he would not let Caro, a woman, a foreigner, and low-born, accompany him in his endeavour to establish the truth of this corruption?

But he could not – would not – believe it. Not here, in one of the high places of his country. Not with Lincoln behind him and far across the Mall, over the Tidal Basin, the obdurate eternally thoughtful presence of Jefferson of Virginia. Not while the Potomac rolled on steaming down into the opulent waters of Chesapeake Bay. Not while the all-night truckers hammered their rigs down the great arterial highways of the nation. Not while the all-night deejays played their shallow tunes and whispered little words of consolation to those lost and grieving in the night. Not while parents lay awake over the frightening futures of their children, and older children worked their way through college, dreaming that anything might be accomplished. It was shabby, foolish, confusing and depraved, but it was everything he had.

So he stood up, and swaying in the warm night air, a drunk pathetic and unsteady on his feet, he spoke from the steps of the Memorial the reason he was here, the reason he could never rest until he or Medina lay silent in a prison or a grave. It was an old reason, in old words, and David Medina would not have understood it, but it had driven the railroad lawyer from Illinois behind him to his destiny and his doom.

'Four score and seven years ago,' he recited, to the silent moon and thoughtless air, 'our fathers brought forth on this continent a new nation conceived in liberty and dedicated to the proposition that all men are created equal . . .'

His voice broke on the word, and vanished to a whisper, and he knew himself to be an old drunk beyond redemption, out-marshalled and out-manoeuvred by the forces of darkness and night, but he croaked it anyway, he spoke the words as though using his last weapon in a battle he was bound to lose.

He said, simply, quietly, as he walked down the steps back towards the car, 'Now we are engaged in a great civil war testing whether that nation or any nation so conceived and so dedicated can long endure.'

When he got back to the house in Georgetown he found the lights in the upper apartment blazing. Caro was nearly in hysterics. Melissa was trying vainly to comfort her. Robert remained calm, sipping bourbon and waiting for his brother's return.

It seemed that Mike Thomas had telephoned from New York. He had got the number from the *Examiner* party staying at the Hyatt. He had bad news.

Alan Clarke had been found by Harlem Mere in Central Park, along with a banker called Stoddart. Both of them were dead. Both of them had had their lower spines ripped out with meat-hooks.

CHAPTER TWO

Ever afterwards, even MacKinnon would admit those next few days were Standing's finest hour. He did the two things no one else could have managed. He pulled the story together. And he kept Caro Kilkenny sane.

There was a price for it, of course. He kept himself going on what he called his high-octane mix: good bourbon, black coffee, and mean cigarettes.

He made Caro go to New York, for the formal identification of Alan Clarke's corpse. He told her that unless she acted, moved, she would fall apart. Clarke's death was not her fault. She could not be for ever responsible. She had not been negligent or careless. Alan had had no clear instructions to answer to her. His death was no more her doing than Tom Wellbeck's had been.

He called MacKinnon across the Atlantic and insisted that nothing less than the personal presence of the City Editor would allow them to write the story they had broken. He would not tell MacKinnon what the story was, over the phone. The Scotsman came anyway, anxious about Caro, and wanting to know why his journalists were dying.

They worked together in New York throughout Friday night, Saturday and Sunday morning. MacKinnon pulled in every journalist and stringer he had in the continental United States. They parked themselves outside the houses and office-doors of bankers, politicians, government agencies, import–exporters, arms manufacturers, and yahoo conservative activists. Though MacKinnon begged him to back off, John Standing kept Caro walking and awake throughout that period, insisting that she and she alone should write the major feature pieces on the present government's steadily deepening involvement in Central America, on the years of political manoeuvre, on smuggling in the Caribbean, on the narcotics industry, on the rules governing bank loans to weapons-system producers, on the Glass-Steagull limitations on interstate banking, and on the narcotics industry. Whenever MacKinnon protested he was working her too hard, John told him patiently that Caro had long been snapping in for a section. Unless she saw through this story now she would pack up and turn into the kind of has-been John himself had become. MacKinnon let him have his way.

Standing wrote the main news piece on how the Errol Hart murder had led them to unravel the arms and drugs connection in and out of New York, Alabama, Nassau and Central America. There were some things he could only surmise. They had few of Alan Clarke's notes. They had to assume his death had been a consequence of uncovering the New York cocaine connection. On Saturday morning they got the green light from Mike Thomas to make the connection, if only in the hope the story would kick up more evidence, would start a scare in the narcotics community.

The hardest job of all in many ways, however, was the Scotsman's. He spent a day and a half burning up the transatlantic telephone cables. He remade the Monday paper, he silenced the lawyers and, in a four-hour conversation, he made the Home Office believe that if they did not remove all obstacles in the way of coverage of the Hart Affair he would publish the story and be damned. They surrendered at lunchtime on Sunday, Eastern Daylight Time. On top of that, MacKinnon had to run the administration. The senior members of the *Examiner*'s New York office were turned into copy-takers and copy-tasters as material came in from the stringers. But he had to edit the five-page news and feature section they finally found themselves delivering. He had to cut, check, yell for evidence, demand constant second-sourcing of everything. He could not have managed it all if Caro and John had not, late on Saturday night, turned themselves into sub-editors, accomplishing much of the most grinding detail of his role. The whole process was made no simpler by John's insistence, working on the safe assumption that by now their suite in the Plaza would be bugged, that all the copy should be telephoned through to London from public call-boxes. Only queries after setting raised by London were to be discussed on the hotel's open, too-easily-traceable lines. Even so, they might have got through the weekend without one of MacKinnon's classic rages had not John insisted that new copy be telephoned from a different call-box every time, preferably not in this area. Caro would always remember afterwards the scene as MacKinnon had disappeared down the corridor in search of a taxi to take him up to Harlem, incensed at John's insistence on the detour.

As he stomped away from the suite, cigar butt clamped between his teeth, the Scotsman had hissed, 'I'm never going to hire a fucking Yank again.'

Somehow, over the clank of his typewriter and through the fug of tobacco smoke, Standing had heard him and leapt up from his chair, racing to the door to shout after the dwindling form of the editor, 'Listen, needle-dick, we saved your ass in two world wars and we beat the shit out of you in York Town. You got any arguments, bring 'em here.'

Caro had had to drag him back to his desk and pour him another bourbon.

The worst moment for them all came in the early hours of Sunday morning. They had couriered John's roll of film to London on the Friday night. No chances were taken with over hasty development. The prints got back to the *Examiner* on the Sunday night, where the Picture Editor had thrown up his hands in horror. Like any other seeming tourist, John had bought a colour film. A number of shots were good, or good enough, but the ten or fifteen per cent loss in quality which would take place in producing monochrome copies would leave the black-and-whites unusable, at least for the heavy impact of the presses on newsprint. In the end, all they could do was arrange for the best of the black-and-whites to be retouched to a just acceptable level and publish it alongside a line-drawing with a key. The colour photographs could be syndicated to magazines, news agencies and television channels round the world. The income would help offset the cost of the investigation, for John was already considering an expenses claim. He had a feeling Caro and MacKinnon would find a way to authorize it.

It was eleven o'clock on Sunday evening in London, six in the evening on the Eastern Seaboard of the United States, when the first edition of Monday morning's issue rolled off the presses. The print-run of the Frankfurt edition had been quadrupled, to ensure there were enough copies for the expected demand in the US. The American copies were loaded at Frankfurt airport by 2 a.m. They would land in New York by 6 a.m. local time. MacKinnon had a staffer standing by at the airport to rush copies to the Plaza. All they could do was wait, and watch television.

In London, the editorial team took no chances. Copies of the first edition were with the other British media, and the foreign agencies, bureaux and networks represented in the capital, by midnight, with covering letters politely reminding fellow journalists of the laws governing copyright and syndication. Associated Press were the first to get the story on the wires, beating Reuters by thirty-five seconds. UPI and NBC notified their parent offices in Washington and New York at once. CBS, ABC and CNN were not far behind them. By nine, they had tracked the British team down at the Plaza. The telephones started ringing. Then the camera crews arrived.

John simply disappeared. Neither Caro nor MacKinnon saw him slip away, and before too long they were too busy to be bothered. Everyone wanted statements. Everyone wanted clarification. By the time the ten and eleven o'clock news broadcasts were being put on the air, they and the paper were on the way to being media sensations. But all the while MacKinnon remembered his business, noting each interview they gave, each telephone call they answered, so that the paper's syndication department could follow them up with an invoice.

Standing re-emerged the following morning before breakfast. The whole *Examiner* team had congregated at the Plaza by then, in front of four televisions, to watch the first news broadcasts featuring not only the two reporters but also shots of the paper's first edition. They were all almost too busy and elated to notice him. It was Caro who finally took him aside to ask him where he had been, why he had not been on hand to help them.

He would not tell her exactly. He would only say he had been out drifting, drinking, shooting a little craps. Then he shook his head sadly and whispered, 'It wasn't my story, Caro. Not really. Yours, MacKinnon's, Alan Clarke's. But not mine. I was just the leg-man. You can't put me up front.'

She had felt appalled, and embarrassed, and a little ashamed, but there was no arguing with him. It was only then, with the paper in front of her, that she realized he had, in the sub-editing process, removed his by-line at every stage. The whole thing had gone out under her and MacKinnon's name. She wondered why he had no use for the brief causal glancing fame or notoriety which was the only glory their trade could bring them. And she wondered about his brother.

John had too. The time-differences had been his one miscalculation. He had promised Robert till Monday morning. He had forgotten the American networks would have the story by Sunday night. He had telephoned Robert, who had understood. His plans were well advanced in any case.

The three journalists stayed in the States for three more days. They watched the great machines of the American media which had been sniffing on the edges of the story wheel into action, and they prepared daily updates for their own paper's mainly European readers. But they knew that having broken the story they would be pushed aside by the local press. It had the personnel, the money, and the national interest. What fascinated John most in those days was watching with an ironic smile what he recognized to be the traces of his brother.

Rumours flew everywhere in those days, of direct CIA involvement. Everyone knew the Agency had been mining Nicaragua's harbours. Everyone had long suspected it was arming and advising the Contras' three main groupings: the FDN in the North, across the Honduras border, the Misura Indians on the Caribbean coast, and Eden Pastora's group in the south. But no one had been able to prove the Agency was involved in illegal activities within the States. The operation the *Examiner* uncovered was certainly illegal. The hard part was proving Agency involvement. A couple of the corpses recovered from the Ragged Island cays proved to be those of former Agency employees, but that in itself was not enough. It only encouraged speculation. There was talk in Washington of agonized phone-calls from the President to each member of the Senate and House Committees pleading with them, in the national interest, not to order another public investigation into the CIA's possible involvement. There was equal talk of sudden drastic house-cleaning on the estate between McLean and Langley. Senior figures fired without notice, and truck-loads of documents shredded. But, try as they might, no journalist could prove a connection. No excuse could be found to demand a Senate Investigation, an investigation which, in unravelling the truth, might have damaged other of the Agency's, perhaps legitimate, covert operations. The kind of operations which Robert Standing had always seen it as his duty, to his country and to brave men and women, to protect, secure, and defend.

He knew what Robert wanted now. He knew it was why he had accessed the secure files for him in Georgetown those few nights ago. He wanted the world press's attention diverted from this episode in the Intelligence Community's slow agony at the hands of an open society. It only seemed fair to do what he wanted, especially as, if it had been a Medina operation, the Agency for once might be genuinely clean. But that meant closing the circle. It meant following the money home. It meant they had to deal with Poland.

He asked Caro and Mackinnon to meet him for dinner at Twenty-one.

Caro looked unhappy, and tired. 'It's turned into a circus,' she complained. 'What I most want to know is who killed Alan. The whole thing's turned into an elephant, and the things that matter are getting crushed.'

John tried to be sympathetic. 'The things that matter to us, Caro, because Alan was one of our own. But to them it doesn't really matter; it isn't very much, that one Englishman should be murdered in Central Park while out looking for cocaine. It isn't unusual here, and it doesn't matter while they're trying to find out if their country's at war. My country. I understand. And they have jobs to do. Every Mac-

Kinnon in the United States is asking his people, "How did these limey bastards get on to this story before you?"' MacKinnon managed to blush with shame for the editorial profession. 'So the whole thing balloons as everyone tries to match our original coverage, all scrabbling for any new fact which might possibly be significant. The same thing happened over Watergate. This could run for years. I don't see there's anything we can do about it. I, for one, don't want to hang around waiting to be subpoenaed, or watching a bunch of criminals all suddenly finding religion. Besides, Mike Thomas has already said they may never find the individuals who murdered Alan and Errol Hart. The people they've arrested in Alabama don't seem to know anything about the killings. All we can do is hope to stay ahead of the whole of the story. What we've done so far is uncover the central part of it. If we want to know who's responsible for the killings, we've got to follow the story through. We have to follow the black money.'

MacKinnon looked uncertain, and unlikely, toying with something as delicate as asparagus, the kind of thing he was liable to dismiss in a burst of Gaelic temperament as fancy food for fairies. 'What else is there you haven't told me yet?' he asked.

John looked to Caro, who nodded. He started with a question. 'You're still proposing to serialize Caro's book?'

The Scotsman was definite. 'More than ever. We're looking a bit tired after breaking this story. I'd like to advance the serialization but do it over a longer period, so we can start now with the stuff that's already written. I meant to raise it with you, Caro, as soon as we were done.'

John smiled. 'In that case, she may have a bigger finish for you than you expected. We know, Iain, that part of the money the Contras use to buy arms comes to them from the Vatican. I know that the arms dealers who sold those weapons, at inflated prices, passed the money into Poland.'

Caro looked as surprised as Iain. It was the first time John had spoken about what he took to be the money's destination. Both of them started to ask questions, but John held up his hands to silence them.

'Look, I know. I'm sorry. I might have told you this before, but I wasn't certain until last week, and I can't prove it. Yet. What I did know was that we had the Central American story sewn up tight, and I wanted to get it away. Especially after Alan was killed. It was the only way I could guarantee Caro's safety, for a start. No one's going to take a crack at her when it's bound to be linked to the current investigation. It was working alone and in the dark that cost Alan his life. The other thing is that, if I'm wrong, or if we can't get the evidence, at least we've already got away the mother of a story. I think there's more. I think there's bigger. But I thought we ought to go with what we had.'

MacKinnon growled. 'I think you ought to have left that decision to me, laddie. We're not paying you to edit. I'll not have you keeping secrets from me.'

'Well, tough shit, Iain,' John said quietly, flaring into sullen anger. 'You weren't around when I had to make my decisions.'

Caro stepped in to calm them both. 'It doesn't matter now,' she said. 'We got a good story. What you'd better tell us is why you think you've got a better one.'

John pushed his plate aside and lit up a cigarette. Caro reached for a Camel. It looked like being a heavy session.

'I think all of this,' John began, 'has been a black money washing operation. I think it's been a classic of its kind. I never guessed even the Vatican could be so cynical, even after two thousand years in business, and I think we got on to it by accident.'

They were both watching him now, unblinking, attentive.

'I think it began with the election of a Polish Pope. I think someone, very high up in the Vatican, decided funds needed to be pumped into Poland.'

'To Solidarity?' Caro interrupted.

'That has to be my working assumption. But it is obvious that any direct transference of funds would have been seen as gross interference by the Communist authorities. And not just in Poland. The Catholic Church could not afford that. They had to find a way of laundering the money. I think it was Calvi who gave them the idea. If only in the aftermath of the Ambrosiano affair. They were already spiriting funds out of Italy into Liechtenstein. They'd helped Calvi out at one stage by giving him letters of comfort, admitting they owned those weird Caribbean companies through which he borrowed the missing millions from Ambrosiano to buy the bank's own shares. Companies like Manic and Bellatrix and Belrosa. They didn't come up with any money when Calvi fell apart, but they learnt how to use the Caribbean tax havens.'

'But why?' MacKinnon asked. 'I've never trusted the left-footers myself, but why should they back the Contras?'

John smiled in quiet triumph. 'Because everyone would ask that question. Because it doesn't seem to make any sense. I think it was the most cynical of double-bluffs. They wanted to cover their tracks completely. So they washed the money through Liechtenstein. Then they washed it again through Panama and Nassau. Then once again by handing it to the Contras. Yet again through American arms suppliers and again through their trading partners, till it finally shows up in Poland. All of those links make sense except one. All but one of them can be taken at face value. After all, what could be more reasonable than a bunch of American right-wing arms dealers funding Solidarity? No need to consider Vatican involvement. Especially as the money seems to come from trading to a group the Vatican is believed to have no time for. Except the Vatican doesn't have much time for the Sandinistas' Marxists either, except it's worried by its own left-wing liberation theology priests in South America, and except somebody got careless and left a single link in the Popolari guarantee to the Alabaman bankers. A Vatican-controlled company helped fund the whole Contras arms deal. We are the only people who know that. And we only know it because Caro started us off in Italy instead of America.'

Caro stopped him. 'So you think that if we can uncover the money's destination in Poland we've closed the black money circle?'

'Exactly.'

'In that case, maybe we're all wrong about the CIA. Maybe this was just a Vatican operation.'

'It's possible. I don't know. I think they may have been

dragged into it. A cocaine operation certainly was. But that's the thing about black money. It attracts dirty hands. I don't think the Agency was essential to the operation. Just a bonus. Another smoke-screen round the essential fact of money being shipped out of Italy into Poland.'

MacKinnon stuck a thick finger into his mouth to clean out a piece of asparagus caught between his teeth, before saying, 'There is a problem.'

'Which is?' John asked.

'It's almost a moral one,' the Scotsman replied, strange words indeed from him. 'If the money really is for Solidarity, do we want to be the ones to announce it? Can you imagine how the Russians might react, when they've just denied any responsibility for the country's debts? They're not in a happy mood. What are they going to do if they find Rome's been stabbing them in the back?'

John looked abashed. 'I've thought of that too. But I think it's something we have to deal with once we know the whole story. And that's my problem. I have no past dealings in Poland to fall back on. I have no links with Solidarity.'

'No,' Caro acknowledged, 'you don't. But I do. We can start by talking to Tomasz Sobieski.'

CHAPTER THREE

There was someone John wanted to see before he saw Sobieski. Not *wanted* to see, exactly, that was the wrong word. He was too nervous for that. Someone he knew he ought to see. MacKinnon had booked them on to an evening flight to London, which gave him the best part of the day. He took the shuttle down to Washington, and met Eleanor for lunch in Georgetown.

'I'm honoured,' she said, with open sarcasm, over a whisky sour. He was glad to see she wasn't one of those girls who only drank Perrier. He could have smiled at that. He was on mineral water himself. It occurred to him for the first time that she was really very pretty. He knew she was bright. It seemed that he and Evelyn had got one thing right. Not that they had deserved it.

He looked down at the untouched salad on his plate, unable to look her in the eyes as he spoke. 'I can't blame you for hating me . . .'

'You flatter yourself, Daddy. It's nothing so violent. You're hardly worth the energy.'

'No,' and now he did look at her. She had Evelyn's eyes. 'I'm not. I'm a lot of things, Eleanor, but I'm not particularly dishonest, and I know I don't have any virtues as a husband or father. Which is why I wanted to see you.'

She was brightly bitter. 'I suppose you're going to tell me that although you never bothered with me, never wanted to see me, you do love me after all. What am I supposed to do, Daddy? Fall to my knees in gratitude? Hug you, sobbing, saying: "There, there, that's all right I knew it all along?" Cue music, cue credits? Is that how it's supposed to be?'

Christ, how he wanted a drink. 'No,' he said finally, his voice breaking, 'not that. No late Shakespeare recognition scenes.'

'Good,' she interrupted, 'because when did you ever do any of that stuff for me?'

'I never did.' Again, more gently: 'I never did. I didn't come to see you to ask your forgiveness. I've done nothing to deserve it. I came to see you because there is only one useful piece of advice I have to give you, and you'd better have it now.'

She wiped some vinaigrette away from the corner of her mouth with the heavy linen napkin before saying, 'Considering the shape you're in, I'm not sure how valuable any advice of yours could be.'

'That's true about most things, but not about this. This is the one thing I really do know about.'

'What is it?'

He sat back, toying with his fork, suddenly tired. 'You're a Standing,' he said softly, 'and that's good. It may not seem it sometimes, but it is. It means that, if you've never had me, if you've never really had Evelyn, at least you've had Robert and my sisters. Families have their virtues.'

She looked at him sadly. 'Sometimes I think you love Uncle Robert more than you ever loved me.'

He shook his head, his eyes closed. 'No. No. It's just that he reminds me, all the time, of the Ambassador. And that's what I wanted to talk to you about.' He looked at her again. Her skin was golden in the light of early autumn. 'All the Standings,' he continued, 'have one great weakness. Maybe all strong families do. We tend to make ourselves, to create ourselves, in response to our parents. Whatever I am, whatever Robert is, we are as ways of dealing with the fact that we are the Ambassador's children.' He paused, aware of an unexpected tightness in the muscles round his eyes, round his mouth, in his throat. He had to press his fingers against his forehead to ease the strain before he could go on. 'The Ambassador was a good man. A good father. I'm not. But that doesn't really matter. Any parents can have that effect on their children, if only they're good – or bad – enough. I'm bad enough.'

He was blinking rapidly now, his eyes unfocused. 'I'm bad enough. All I wanted to warn you against is wasting too much time and effort and energy trying to cope with that. You don't have to deal with it. It was my fault, not yours. All I'm asking is that you don't waste time on coming to terms with me. What matters now is you. You are a grown woman, with your own fate and future before you. What matters is what you want, is your decisions, not what I was or wasn't. What matters is being yourself.'

She had softened as he spoke. Now she said, 'What I never could understand ... what hurt most – still does – is why you turned round and virtually said that a sick little girl who was hardly aware of your existence was more important to you than Mummy and I, who knew who you were, and loved you, in spite of everything.'

He tried to take a sip of mineral water, but his hand was shaking too much. He set down the glass. 'I don't know that I can explain that to you. I don't know that I understand it myself.'

Her voice was kindly, but firm. 'I've thought about it a lot, Daddy, and the best I can come up with is to say I think some people are just born damaged, are just born with a piece of them missing, and they spend their whole lives looking for a way to suffer, for something outside them to explain the pain they feel. Because, you see, if it isn't that, then it's something horrible. It's just some crazy self-indulgence. It's just exhibiting your agony to make the rest of us feel what a good, poor, broken, feeling man you are. It's showing off.'

He looked at her again and said, 'My money's on the showing off,' and they both laughed, but soon Eleanor was serious again.

'I sometimes think that's why you like England so much,' she said, 'why you stayed. All that past, all those ingrained social customs, they make things so easy. People never have to be themselves or work out what they are, what they want to be. I can understand that. Hate it, but understand it. It's kind of lonely being free, being solely and entirely responsible for what you are.'

She had surprised him. 'So much wisdom in one so young?'

'Not really,' she demurred. 'England, Emily, alcohol – what

were they all but attempts for a single explanation, a single excuse for what you are? "One balm for many fevers found",' she quoted.

John smiled. 'I didn't know kids read poetry any more. Not if it rhymes.'

'Some of us do.'

He took her left hand in both his, and spread the fingers, and told them, not daring to look in her face, 'It seems to me you've gone most of the distance by yourself. Just keep on going. And try not to think of me.' He looked at her now. 'I'm proud of you, Eleanor, and I'm wise enough to know I never deserved you.'

It was her turn to be serious. 'Why are you telling me all this? Now? Why aren't you playing the ace-shit father? You are the Headline King right now.'

He denied it. 'Not me. Not my story.'

'You did the work. Uncle Robert told me. Some.'

'Just a hack. I can take some money for it, but no credit.'

'So why are you telling me this?'

'I don't really know.' He coughed, and added, 'Well, I know some of it.'

'What?'

'That poem you quoted . . .'

'Yes?'

'Finish it.'

She looked at him, a puzzled look in her eyes, not understanding, not knowing what he meant, as she quoted: 'Whole of an ancient evil, I sleep sound.'

CHAPTER FOUR

Tomasz Sobieski told them they were wrong.

Like most exiled Polish leaders he had gravitated towards Paris, where Caro had first met him. When she got in touch this time he arranged to meet them in the gardens of the Rodin Museum, round the corner from the Invalides.

Paris was half-deserted, by Parisians at least. Half the citizens fled in July, the other half in August, fleeing the hot dusty weather and the unwelcome attentions of tourists. Only the poor, or disaffected, or foreign remained to mope and cough in the stifling atmosphere of summer. The gardens of the grand house where Rodin had once lived were one of the few cool sanctuaries in the city. They walked round from the Metro station under the lowering bulk of the Army Museum and the great domed church where the remains of Napoleon lay into the quiet, aromatic residential quarter, reserved for the rich, in which the Museum stood.

The old man was waiting for them, sitting looking at the near life-size statuary group of the Burghers of Calais, lost souls in chains walking in an endless circle of damnation, captured in bronze in an eternal instant of despair. He looked more like one of the bronzes than a living human being. His white hair had grown long and ragged, strained at its tips by the nicotine from the endless cigarettes he smoked, as stained as his stubby fingers.

He tried to laugh when they told him what they suspected, but it came out as the dry wheeze of the candidate for lung-cancer. His explanations poured out in a bitter, accented French.

'I wish it were true,' he told them. 'I wish the Church was funding us, now we are illegal. We need all the help and friends we can get. But they aren't. They helped to make us illegal. They have a compact with the General. They are frightened of us. They are frightened of our power with the people. They are happier dealing with the Party. The Church and the Party are two of a kind. We threaten the authority of both of them.'

They did not understand. They knew that priests had preached for Solidarity. They knew that priests had sheltered its members. They knew that Father Zbigniew of Gdansk had died for it. They knew that both Church and Solidarity were opponents of the government. They thought my enemy's enemy must be my friend.

The old man disabused them, his leather-brown labourer's face, sunburnt and windburnt by years in the shipyards, crinkling like a walnut in an expression of disgust. 'Zbigniew was a good man,' he conceded, 'a true Pole. There are others. But the Church is not a few priests. It is an institution, full of grey men with no balls who only drink on Sundays and never have a woman. The grey men in black talk to the red men in grey and they crush the life out of the Poles between them.'

He looked about them furtively, eyeing each of the few visitors strolling in the garden before continuing. 'There is money coming into the country. Church money, that much we have heard. But the Church keeps the Church's money. It doesn't come to us. I do not know what it is used for. Not for the things we need: food, medicines, schoolbooks. There are priests who think that this is wrong. Zbigniew was one of them. Maybe one of them will tell us one day where the money goes. Then, perhaps, we can detour a little bit of it.'

Caro took the old man by the shoulder. He looked into her eyes with something like gratitude, glad of the presence of a pretty woman on a fine summer day. 'Is there no one, Tomasz,' she asked, 'we could talk to? Someone in the Church? We need to know what they are doing.'

The old man shrugged deep and raised his palms to the open sky. 'They tell us nothing,' he complained. 'Ask anyone. Anyone in Poland. Ask Walesa, if you can get close to him, now he is a famous man.'

Caro took him by both arms, lowering them from his pose of cosmic protest, and brought him back to her point. 'All I need is a name, Tomasz. One name. I need an honest priest to talk to.'

He looked sad, and poor, and far from home, but he was proud and Polish and he could not deny a pretty woman. 'There are a few such left. Not many. And they are not safe. But you could talk to Father Jerzy Matejko of St Stanislas in Praga. He might be able to help.' He leaned towards her, suddenly secretive, shielding himself from John. 'But if he does,' he explained, 'you must tell our people. We no longer know what they are doing.'

He let her go, and shuffled away from them, dissociating himself. He looked more like an old tramp, she thought, in his rough blue workman's clothes, than one of the leaders of a revolution. Perhaps they always did. Perhaps that was why revolutions always came as such a surprise. 'Is there anything you want brought back?' she asked. 'Is there anything you miss?'

He laughed, a big high laugh, and slapped his thigh with the cap held rolled in his left hand, and almost shouted, 'A girl! A nice Polish girl. About seventeen, with big breasts and a happy disposition!' His face creased in delight at the thought, the broken veins glowing redly beneath the nut-brown skin. Then he added softly, 'But what I miss mostly is good black bread.'

They left him to his lonely thoughts among the memorials of a richer, if not more contented, world.

Back in London, they found MacKinnon facing problems. The paper had not been in good odour with the Polish authorities since publishing details of the attempted coup at the beginning of July. The Foreign Desk's sources for that story had simply vanished, to prison or firing-squads, most assumed. And they had damaged their official links by taking up the story. What saved them having to go down on their knees was a long-awaited event within Poland. The day they returned from Paris, one of the Secret Police officers arrested in the aftermath of the attempted coup was formally charged with the murder of Father Zbigniew in Gdansk.

The press had been waiting for it, ever since similar occurrences three years earlier, when other security men were charged with a similar murder. It was a dangerous path for the

Polish leader to tread, but it had worked for him so far. It was meant to show the people he was not the monster they feared, much less the monster they would undoubtedly get if they provoked the Russians to intervene. It bought him time and some respect in the outside world. And it served as a warning to his own hard-liners, and to others in the Kremlin, that he was not to be taken for granted.

As soon as the news came on the wires, MacKinnon was on the phone to the Polish Embassy in London, explaining what an ideal opportunity the trial would be for the paper to make sure it had a clear, unbiased image of the country, to stop it making the unfortunate errors of the recent past, and how much he would like to present a free and fair trial to the world and his readers, who might have been misled by what they had read before.

It worked. He was granted all the accreditations he wanted. He put one reporter permanently on the trial. He got Caro and John passed to follow a wider brief, making preparatory investigations for the next Polish Survey. They flew British Airways, because they could not face the alternative.

They found themselves booked by the authorities into the Victoria Intercontinental in Krolewska Street, one of the two Intercontinentals in the Communist capital. In some ways it was something of a relief to find themselves in sanitized Western comfort with a hard-currency shop in the lobby selling luxury items from Kent cigarettes and Dove soap to authenticated icons, but there were the usual disadvantages as well, which Caro was used to but John was not: nothing quite worked as it was meant to, everything had been allowed to run quietly to seed and room-service was as big a joke as it was in Cairo or Tamanrasset. This time there was also an unusual disadvantage. They found themselves surrounded by the international media circus. The authorities had, intelligently, confined them to this expensive high-rise ghetto.

It was not so bad for Caro, who found herself something of a star. She was deferred to and asked for advice. The woman from *Newsweek* asked her what she thought of what Armand de Borchgrave, a former Foreign News Chief of her magazine, was doing as editor of the Moonie-owned *Wash-*

ington Times. The Canadian Broadcasting Corporation's National News team asked for a five-minute interview on political conditions in Poland today, billing Caro to her amusement as 'The *Examiner* of London's leading commentator on international affairs'. She wondered what the Senior Editorial Writer would have made of that. And three separate German publications offered her large contracts to spill the beans on CIA use of sexual blackmail. They would not listen when she protested she knew nothing about it.

John, however, was not so lucky. No one knew about him, no one cared. He was just another hack, a little old and battered for the rough-and-tumble of the circus, but fair game for the scrum of journalists trying to get closer to officials and translators during official statements, and a suitable kick-starting block for the television crews here to cover the first day of the trial and in the meantime apparently running up and down corridors, stairs and lobbies simply for the joy of it. As soon as he could, he took himself out of the hotel, and set about searching for a drink.

For once, Caro would not have been able to complain. They had agreed to play 'Good Guy/Bad Guy'. Caro's behaviour would be impeccable. John would do everything he could to break free to get to the people they really needed to talk to. In theory, even if he failed, as he expected to, Caro ought to be able to ask the authorities to arrange some interviews for her, simply as a means of putting an end to her colleague's unruly behaviour.

Language, he realized, was bound to be the problem. He spoke good, if unidiomatic, French, the language of the Polish intelligentsia's dreams for centuries, and he spoke a little German, one of the two languages, with Russian, most Poles had found it useful to have a smattering of through their long, much-invaded history; but Polish might have been Mandarin Chinese, for all that he could make of it. He did not need any to guess what the policeman who escorted him back to the Victoria was saying, but in his brief excursion he noticed what would be his strongest impression of life behind the Iron Curtain. Everything was grey.

Grey prefabricated tower-block housing for the workers,

grey concrete buildings for the government and party, grey coarse clothes for the people, grey faces haggard with malnourishment, grey hoardings filled with party slogans, grey furniture, grey shop-windows, black official limousines grey with dust and age. He found himself longing for Benetton, punks, advertising, custom cars and Habitat. Anything, anything at all, with some life in it, with some colour.

Defeated in his first venture, he retired to the hard-currency shop (they accepted his sterling, but what they were really after was explicit in its unofficial name: Dollar Shop) to buy an overpriced bottle of vodka and retire to his room. He would miss out tonight on the barely-warm gourmet food, the toasts to international friendship, the gossipy reminiscences of the trade and its loud and public drunkenness. He was going to get drunk quietly, alone. He found himself sympathizing with Tomasz Sobieski. Where were the seventeen-year-old Polish girls? His daydreams were filled with fantasies of apple-cheeked maidens bursting enthusiastically out of peasant costumes vivid with purple, magenta, crimson, peagreen, lilac, viridian and gold. But then, he was not yet properly drunk.

The following morning the circus was taken in a fleet of Ladas to the Palace of Justice for the start of the trial, the route specially organized to include a trip round the sights of the Old City, largely reconstructed after wartime destruction. Caro and John had been assigned a car, a driver, and translator of their own. For half an hour John's head buzzed with Royal Castle, Staszic Palace, Tin-Roofed Palace, Church and Convent of the Blessed Sacrament Sisters, Krasinski Mansion, St John's Cathedral, Belvedere and the Seym ('Is our democratic parliament of the people's institutions,' they were told), when all he really wanted to do was sleep, curled up around another bottle of vodka and a complaisant village maiden. The translator/guide/guard simply would not do. The only thing he took in was Bialy Domek, where the fat man who became Louis XVIII of France and lost his toes in his socks had lived in exile. The name meant White House. It reminded him of Virginia, of the Ambassador, and of home.

He had to concentrate in order not to think of Eleanor. It took enormous effort not to think of all the things he had not done.

At the Palace of Justice, chaos reigned. A restored eighteenth-century court had been chosen at first by the authorities, to show off Polish culture. This was the first time a Polish institution had been opened up to foreign cameras, and they wanted to present only the best. Which was one reason no direct broadcasts were being allowed. All video and audio tape would have to be presented to the censors. What they had not counted on was the sheer bulk and demands of the equipment shipped in by competing crews from the West. The location was moved to a larger, concrete, modern courtroom. It was grey. Then finally television crews were banned. A cheer went up from all the assembled print journalists when the soldiers came in (dressed in grey masquerading as green) to frogmarch out the cameras.

John passed the bulk of the day very publicly asleep while Caro attended to the simultaneous translator. Both of them knew perfectly well the translators would be editing as they went, as much as the transcripts they would receive that evening. Almost everyone would actually work from the transcripts. The only additional precaution they had taken was to bribe a waiter at the hotel to have his mother attend to the radio broadcasts of selected evidence in the trial and supply them with edited, translated highlights. It was not much, as journalism went, but it had got them into Poland.

Most of the journalists flown in for the occasion surrendered that evening. There was nothing for the circus here. The following morning it broke camp, leaving Poland to the regular foreign correspondents and the few with other reasons to remain.

It took three more days of drunkenness to attend the Sunday evening mass at St Stanislas in Praga, across the River Vistula. It had only taken him an hour the day after they arrived to find a member of the hotel staff who worshipped in the parish who would take a message to Father Jerzy telling him a journalist craved an interview in the privacy of the confessional.

Caro attended a diplomatic reception that evening and found herself explaining John's behaviour to an outraged British Head of Chancery. She dared not intimate that the madness had some method. She could only promise to try to keep him under control. It was not a promise which caused her any worries. Their official schedule over the next few days was too hectic for any of his antics, real or feigned. She only hoped he got to see the priest. They could not know how much time they had, before other journalists picked up on the route the money had taken. She did not have John's certainty that most of their colleagues were too idle ever to investigate something as arduous as the trail they had stumbled over. More importantly, she remembered the bargain John had made, what seemed an age ago, as she lay unconscious in a Roman hospital. They needed to establish the destination of the money if they were to have the Dottore break open the Liechtenstein route. It all depended on John Standing now, and this time she could not stop him drinking.

John had already established that Praga was the right bank of the city, on the other side of the Vistula. Once it had been a separate city, but in 1791 it was formally swallowed up by Warsaw. But its traditional function as the dwelling place of the workers was still evident in its very appearance. Crossing two-level Gdanski Bridge (in rather better shape, but not as much fun, as Queensboro in New York, he thought), he could see Warsaw spread out behind him in the pale straw light of the soon-to-be-sinking sun. Even if largely restored after bombing and devastation, the old city was magnificent in the late light on the long bend in the river. Here Eastern and Western Europe met, in a skyline of onion-domes and architraves, the splendours of classical France all mixing with distant echoes and memories of Byzance. It was a meeting which had made the city, but time and again had ruined the fortunes of the great farming country it controlled.

But in Praga, where a third of the city's inhabitants lived, everything was, if possible, greyer than in new Warsaw. None of this was intended to enlighten or enliven tourists. It was the grey reality of full employment in the comprehensive state. Perhaps, he thought, the acres of car factories, power generators and cement plants were no more depressing than Newark, or Detroit, or Cincinnati, but they felt it. Not because breezeblock ruled. It ruled in other places. After so many years in Europe, he found a curiously fragile aspect to most North American cities, strung out newly around their necessary roads, as though a single strong wind might roll them away like tumbleweed. There was none of that fragility here. This city would not blow away, but it was already in a state of perpetual, diminishing decay.

It was not even the endless grey towerblocks and utility housing which surrounded them as his keeper drove him into the Brodno district. He had seen the same or worse in developments in the poorer parts of London, Birmingham, Paris or New York City.

It was the fact the greyness was unrelieved. West of here, in the world of Coca-Cola and General Motors, however limited ordinary people's choices might be, they were enough to allow them to express some small measure of themselves. There was nothing to indicate that here.

Where were the lunatic slogans spray-painted in bright day-glo colours? Where were the kids in home-dyed T-shirts? Where were the trucks and vans proclaiming their occupants were serious heads whose destiny was to boldly split infinitives none had split before? Where were the hookers in acid colours, with legs up to their ears?

Where was the crazy vanity of human life?

Even the church they pulled up outside was grey, a high building consisting entirely of a sloping steeply pitched roof, with no walls in evidence at all. The thirty-foot cross before it was made of welded girders, painted dull brown to rust-proof them. It was the nearest to a patch of colour here. Even the soil in front of the church was dun, baked out by the urban sun, whipped by polluted winds, and washed by sulphurous rains till no blade of grass remained.

As John got out, the keeper remained stolidly in the car, winding down the window to tell him she and the driver would wait outside. He was to present himself to them as soon as he was finished. He wondered why they would not come in. What were they afraid of? The moment he stepped through the plywood and hardboard doors, he knew. He knew what kept the instruments of authority scared, what kept them waiting in the dull greyness beyond the doors.

It was life.

He knew little about churches and religion, and cared less. He suspected they were engines of paranoia, division, contempt and hatred. He had no doubt at all that they grew into great and powerful institutions as cynical and manipulative as any others. But he also realized that here they were a way of saying No to the pervasive dullness of the world. The older men and women, it was true, wore sombre serge and worsted in black and dark blue, but even they were lightened by touches of pride and self-respect: a big-knotted painted tie here, a pocket handkerchief there, a treasured shawl or scarf. But the young came here to be themselves. There were young men in open-necked cheesecloth or lumberjack shirts and blue jeans. There were girls in brightly coloured peasant costumes, their blouses opulent and their skirts a display. They were singing in deep throaty voices a slow hymn which seemed to John to fill with determination, courage and endurance. They were a people who would not easily be moved. And within its grey concrete and breezeblock, the church itself came alive with colour. The crude stained glass and the larger than life-size murals would have won no prizes or Arts Council grants, but gaudy and garish as they were, they were filled with colour, and the hope of better days. Even the very ceremonial of the Mass spoke directly to human beings' ingrained love of theatre and display. He knew the fine cottons of the choir's vestments and the intricate encrusted embroidery of the priest's robes must represent a fortune in rationed materials and willing helpers' time, but there could be no resentment as Father Jerzy, gorgeous in the emblematic costume of his role, raised the glittering chalice turned from a single block of carbon-steel by local workers in the dead hours after their shifts had ended. For here, now, in conversation with his God, high and dramatic amidst the drifting clouds of incense, he represented these people's hopes of better mornings and brighter days.

John stood at the back till the ceremony was done, half wishing the Latin Rite had not been replaced by Polish, so that he could follow it more closely. Once the priest had asked his God to let His servant and His people go in peace, John joined the queue of people waiting to have a quiet word with the priest.

His tasks accomplished, Communion achieved, the priest became a focus for social work and gossip. John had been expecting a young man, from what Tomasz Sobieski had said, a radical firebrand. It surprised him to see an old, worn man in his sixties, very mortal and frail once removed from the context of the rite, reassuring old ladies and trying to calm the fractious tempers and enthusiasms of the young.

John waited till last, when the priest's proper flock had set off home, or were congregated in the entrance of the church, like any congregation, plotting fêtes and flower-arrangements and parish committees.

'Monsieur Standing?' the old man asked.

John felt surprised, though he had already established the priest spoke no English but did speak French. He nodded in reply. The priest gestured towards the confessional.

It was dark inside the box, dark and cool. John wondered if death were like this, lying in a cool box in the ground, far from the tumult of the day.

'They are outside?' the priest asked.

John nodded, then realized the priest could not see him through the grille. He had never done this before. 'Yes. They're waiting for me. I don't have much time.'

'No. You had better tell them you are Catholic. But they will suspect you whatever you say.'

'And you?'

'They always suspect me. I was told you wanted information. We all do. It is the rarest commodity in Poland today. Rarer than fresh meat. You are of the *Examiner* in London. We had to listen to the World Service of the BBC to get your reports about what happened in the south a month ago. We had no other way of knowing.'

John began to lie. 'I'm here because of that, Father. There are things we need to know, to understand, if we are to tell the truth about Poland.'

'What is it you want to know?'

John swallowed. All he could do was ask. 'Father, I know that in the last ten months, at least twelve million American dollars have come into Poland from the United States. I also know that the money came from Rome, from the Vatican bank. I don't know what the money was used for when it got here. I need to know.'

The priest was silent. John wondered how to encourage him, but could think of nothing. The confessional made him feel small, and guilty. At last the priest spoke, not addressing the question directly. 'They are good people, my people. They are proud, and brave, and full of wit. And they are faithful children of Mother Church. But they do not understand. And they are mortal, which makes them impatient.'

John waited. He understood. Here, in the darkness, in a foreign tongue, to a man he did not know and would probably never see again, the old priest was confessing.

'But the Church,' the old man continued, 'is not mortal. It must be patient. It must endure. It is the last best hope the people have. They want immediate change, and for the better. I cannot blame them. I am a Pole. But I know what we face. I know what even the General faces. We have to move slowly, to compromise. Some things can be achieved better in secret and silence than by all the protest and publicity in the world. I do not have to deal with it myself. It is a matter for more senior servants of the Church. But I understand, as my people do not, that sometimes Mother Church must buy time.'

He used the word *acheter*. To buy. John asked him. 'Do you mean bribes, Father? Do you mean the Church is buying politicians?'

The priest said nothing for what seemed a long while. Then he said, 'It is not your friends you have to encourage. It is your enemies. That is what our people would not understand. There are times when you have to buy your enemies' silence and inaction. I do not mean the government. We deal with them as equals. I mean the apparatus of state.'

He meant the secret police. The rest came out of him steadily, patiently, as though he was glad to be rid of it.

'Sometimes I think we make mistakes. We are human,

though the Church is not. Sometimes I think we play into other people's hands. Some of it is bound to come out in this trial. It is the small talk of the services here that money is always available in Warsaw, and in Gdansk, from the International Transfer office. I do not know what this company may be. But I fear it may be us. I know my own bishop has turned to it in the past for money to release good men from jail.'

John could not see what the current judicial games had to do with the Church. It didn't seem to make any sense. 'But what,' he asked, 'do Church funds have to do with the murder of Father Zbigniew?'

'Nothing,' the old man hissed. 'I am certain of it. We are not murderers. We do not kill our own. I think the trial may be contrived, to damage us with the people. It may be happening only to tell them the Church pays off the policemen they justly hate.'

'Can they prove that?' John asked. 'Can they prove International Transfer is the Church?'

'I do not know,' the old man almost wailed, his voice echoing in the confined space of the confessional. 'I will not ask. You do it. Ask Cardinal Glemp. Ask Rome. Ask anyone you like, but do not ask me. I do not know these things. I only suspect. And if I suspect them, so will many others. There will be others of your kind who ask these questions. I do not know if it is possible to keep a secret for ever, if there is a secret to keep. The only secrets which are absolute are the secrets of the confessional, Monsieur Standing. Leave an old man in peace. I am old and very tired. Tell Tomasz Sobieski how much his half-brother misses him.'

When John got back to the hotel, silent under the suspicious stares of his officials, Caro was waiting for him in his room. He held up his hand in warning as he came through the door, before she could blurt out what she had to say. She was puzzled for an instant, then nodded. They went down to the lobby and told the desk-clerk firmly they were going for a walk.

It was almost dark outside. Warsaw lay under a pall of

grey with no gleam of the gold of the earlier evening left in it. They both knew they were being followed. It did not matter, so long as they kept the proper distance. They stopped to light up cigarettes. In the dim glow and acrid tang, John spoke.

'The trial, Caro. Has there been any mention so far of an outfit called International Transfer?'

She nodded. 'Yes, sleepyhead. In the accused's evidence on Friday afternoon. You were asleep again. The prosecutor was after it like a shot. My guess is he's going to try to prove CIA funding. Foreign powers seducing Poland.'

John inhaled deeply. 'It's possible. I think they're our outlet. If they are it's true the funds are American. No, I don't understand it either. What was it you were going to tell me?'

She took him by the hand, relighting her cigarette off his. 'I want you to behave yourself on our tourist trips over the next two days. It seems that we have company. I was informed while you were out. Not that I needed much informing. There was chaos when he arrived. His own security guards and equipment. Dogs, telecommunications, you name it. He's taken over the entire top floor. They've even cut out one of the lifts so only that floor can use it, and put an armed guard in it all the time. The hotel staff are seriously pissed off about it. They say it happens every time he arrives. Anyway, it seems he's joining us. Or rather you, on tomorrow's trip to Oswiecim. I've done it before. I'll pass. See what I can dig up about International Transfer.'

He stared at her, kindly. He had been as over-excited in the past. 'Would you mind,' he asked gently, 'telling me who the hell it is you're talking about?'

She blinked, once, her eyes bright in the darkness and the glow of their cigarettes, then explained, 'Why, David Medina, of course. He arrived about three hours ago.'

CHAPTER FIVE

The next morning, John woke into his dreams. They were taken from the gaunt, grey, concrete Warsaw Central Station by first-class train to Oswiecim on the Krakow line. It was a journey of about a hundred and sixty miles and one which the Polish authorities believed, rightly, most visitors thought they had to take. It had become something of a tourist centre, this gaunt memorial to the millions of Poles and other nationalities who had died here, their ashes flushed away in ponds. There was hardly any mention of the fact that a majority of them were Jews. The world knew it better by its German name. To foreigners, Oswiecim would always be what it had been known as for a handful of terrible years. It would always be Auschwitz.

In the train, isolated for three hours, watching the shifting plains of Poland unrolling out towards the Carpathian Mountains in the south, he recognized the landscape of his dreams.

He knew at last where the flat plains of nightmare lay. He knew the indecipherable tongue. He recognized the brown sullen faces of the peasants toiling in the fields. He could imagine them in their travels, kitted out against the cold and carrying baskets filled with sausage and black bread. He was grateful they were not travelling at night. He was grateful the locomotive was a diesel. He could not have borne to see the great plain stretch away in darkness, the villages glowing in the distant fields. He could not have borne the constant wailing whistle of the night train. He could not have borne the soot and smuts which were the price of being hauled by steam.

It was enough he had spent a lifetime enduring these nocturnal anxieties. He did not want to be faced by them in life. He wondered where they had come from, these visions, unprompted by his conscious mind, of travelling fearful along iron tracks which forty years and more ago had carried men and women and children in their millions to an inexorable death. He wondered why for him, asleep and troubled, trains had always been the engines and emblems of his own inevitable end.

Although they were both the guests of the state, the only guests that morning, they were kept separated until the train pulled to the end of the branch line which led away from the town and into the camp at Oswiecim, and shunted into a siding. They met before the gates bearing the legend *Jedem Dasein*, To Each His Own, the trivial reassuring slogan of what new arrivals were assured was a comfortable labour camp. As they met, for the first time since John's arrival in Poland, the guards, translators and officials vanished. They hung back in the train. Medina took him by the arm and led him through the gates.

'Forgive me, John,' the old man said, 'for the dramatic meeting. I am sorry Miss Kilkenny chose not to join us. I had thought something might be gained if she finally saw us together. She might, at least, understand that you are not insane, nor obsessional, about me.'

John looked about them, at the low barracks and showers and receiving stations, at the crematorium before them. It seemed too clean, too sanitized to believe it was a place of murder. But that was the point, of course. The very orderliness was the crime. The machinery of destruction.

'Is this some kind of ghastly warning, David?' he asked.

The old man looked amused, and started to walk him through the prison blocs which had been turned into a museum. None of it seemed to affect him. Not the piles of human hair. Not the photographs of lost hungry souls in striped pyjamas. Not the terrible eyes which stared from them, nor their last haunting reminders, the piles of spectacles which would stand robbed of sight for ever. He took none of it in at all. He devoted his attention to his fellow American.

'I must admit,' he said, 'I had not expected you to try to see me in Washington. Which is why I was unforthcoming. I had expected us to meet here, in Poland, where the story

338

ends. I enjoyed your arrival in DC, by the way. It was charmingly dramatic. The Senator is inconsolable.'

He picked a speck of imaginary fluff from the arm of his jacket. *They are magnificent hands*, John thought. *They look so right when he is handling porcelain, or mounted butterflies, or silver. They look so wrong when you know him for what he is.* The old man was ignorant of the reason for John's silence. It did not bother Medina in the least. The weak were usually silent in his presence.

'I don't think you understand it all yet,' he said, 'but I think you will, soon. And when you do you will see that I win, whatever happens, whatever you decide. I always do. You ought to know that by now. I cannot tell you how much pleasure it has given me to watch you work again. Even when you were too drunk to see, you were marvellously sure-footed. Others could have done it; others would have done it. Working in groups, or independently, small parts of it coming out in different media and slowly being put together. That was what I expected. That was what happened on similar occasions in the past. But whatever credit may be due to Miss Kilkenny and Mr Clarke, the truth of the matter is you did it alone. All they could do was speed your path.'

John pulled himself away from the old man's dominating presence, from the strange consolation of his level stare. 'You flatter me, as usual. Caro got us here, into Poland. Caro did all the initial work in Italy. Alan uncovered the drugs connection on his own. And Caro confirmed the sheer scale of the operation. No one works alone. No one is indispensable.'

They had come through to Bloc 11. They had come to one of the places of death. Prisoners had been sentenced here. Prisoners had been tortured and the instruments were here on display. And there was a wall eloquently pitted by gunfire, where the firing squads had worked. Medina smiled ironically at the sight.

'Perhaps,' he said. 'Perhaps the world would be much the same whatever you might do. I had counted on that. The whole thing would have been impossible if I had to rely on you alone, on your remaining sober. But there are people who make a difference. Not admirable or attractive people, necessarily, but they change the world. Himmler made a difference. If you need a memorial, look around you. Adolf Hitler made a difference.'

A sudden surge of contempt cleared John's head. 'Are you comparing yourself to them?'

'Oh, no,' Medina replied evenly, 'I am unique. I survive. But if you believe what you say, why do you mind what happened here? A million dead are still just a million individuals. None of them indispensable. So why should it have mattered? Why do you fret so about the future of your country and other people's? Why does it matter so much to you? If you could only teach yourself not to care, you could be me. You could be my successor. You have the imagination. So you know the one real tragedy in the world is personal extinction. The only thing which horrifies me is the knowledge that I must die. That seems to me nothing short of monstrous. While I live, I want the world to dance attendance on me. And when I die, I want to see it fall.'

John looked him in his pale green eyes, impassive as his brown face, and asked, 'But what would that leave for me? What would I have to inherit?'

Medina laughed, a low, dark, gravelly laugh. 'If you were with me I would not need to sow the seeds of destruction. I was born the way I am, but you were born an honest man. There is nothing I could do which would be as terrible as what you would imagine if you ever fell from grace. There are no sins so terrible as those of a good man gone. Imagine what the world would be if you did to it what you have been doing to yourself. I could leave it all to you, certain in the knowledge you would surpass me.'

'You've always hated us, haven't you?' John asked flatly. 'Ever since the Ambassador took my mother from you. We know, David. She told us not to trust you.'

Medina looked amused, an expression those who knew him dreaded. 'Sarah was a very beautiful, very stupid woman. She married a man like herself. That did not trouble me. She was dispensable. But you, you troubled me, over the years. You were the son I should have had.'

John towered above Medina, but looked slighter than him,

as he said, 'But I'm not. I am the son of Thaddeus and Sarah Standing; I am the brother of Robert, Julia, Margaret and Deborah Standing; I am the father of Eleanor Standing. Whatever else I may be, I am a Standing. Which makes me more than you will ever be.'

Medina laughed. 'Yes, it is the other weakness you inherited from your father. My dear John, you are a snob.' He took Standing by the arm again. 'There is something you should see.'

He led John on a short walk through the woods, a mile or so away from the camp, till they came to another enclosure. There was another train here, and a platform. To the right were wooden barracks. To the left, they were made of brick. About them stood other ruined structures and an ugly monument.

'Wooden barracks for the men, brick for the women,' Medina explained, shaking his head. 'I never did understand that. It seemed so ... sentimental. They were sorted on the platform. This is Birkenau, John. This is what most people mean when what they say is Auschwitz. This is where the Final Solution was put into operation.'

He almost dragged John towards the ruins, waving his hand towards the vacant, shattered buildings. 'Crematoria, undressing halls, gas-chambers,' he snapped. 'I helped to build them. I brought in high-grade iron ore from Italy through Switzerland. I sold them chemicals. I sold them cloth and wood and bricks. So did the others. So did Krupps and I. G. Farben. Down the road the Poles still use the factory slave labour built for Farben. This is ruins now, but we remain. I remain. You weep, the world weeps, it swears it must never happen again when it is happening every day, but I endure.'

He said it with pride and relish and arrogance, as though he had never said it to anyone before. 'I endure. I remain. When all else fails, as all men, all the men who matter, know, there is always David Medina. Come join me, John, and put aside your dreams.'

John shook his head and leaned down to the old man. 'No, David. Not while you're afraid of me. Perhaps you're right. Perhaps I am indispensable. Perhaps I'm the only person who knows you well enough to have linked you with this endless circle of money. I don't know how to do it yet. I can't link you in for certain yet. But I will. And when I do, I will break you. Then you will see. You've stood outside any law or decency for so long now, you don't know why the rest of us have to have them. We have them because all of us are a little bit like you, and we need to be protected, from ourselves. But you stand outside protection. When you fall, you will find the world has no pity or mercy for you.'

Medina shook his head. 'I doubt that. I am too useful to them. Do you know why I am in Poland, officially, besides the pleasure of your company? I was really in Washington, John, because I knew the Russians were about to disclaim the Polish debt. I was in Washington waiting for the call. It came. I have been asked by the Central Banks, through the Bank for International Settlements, to try to negotiate an orderly rescheduling of the Polish external debt. They come to me because they need me. They always have and always will. And they will never question any actions I may take to give them what they want or any benefit which may accrue to me along the way. Grow up and join the world the rest of your family have always lived in. Do you really think there is any other? Do you think the Church whose services you found so moving yesterday acts any differently from the empire which is, this afternoon, on manoeuvres on the Polish border? We understand each other, you and I, and I understand the world. All you have to do is to learn not to care.'

John felt very tired and very old and very ill. He was beginning to understand, but he still could not admit defeat, not in David Medina's eyes.

'You're wrong,' he said. 'I don't care. I really don't. You know what broke me up when the syndicated loans stories got spiked? It wasn't you. It wasn't caring about unmasking you. It was the realization that I didn't care. I'd been faking it for years. It was the only way I could keep myself going. It isn't possible to spend weeks and months tracking through every avenue of a story like the ones I worked on unless it really matters to you, or you can pretend it does. But it didn't. I'd been covering it up with alcohol for years. I knew I ought to. I never really had. Not for my wives, or my work, or even my daughter. My brother did, my father did. I could see that. But I didn't. It's all I've ever really wanted, and I can't make myself believe in anything I do.'

The old man's eyes looked sad. 'So what happened to you in Washington?' he asked.

John wanted to sit down, but there was nowhere he could sit. He wanted to lie down for ever. 'Some places,' he said, 'I can pretend, even to myself, for a little while. Home is one of them. But it wasn't that which kept me going.' He looked up, suspicion in his eyes. 'How long did you have me followed?'

Medina denied it. 'I didn't. I didn't have to. You or anyone else. I knew what was going on. All I had to do was watch whoever drifted towards the operation. You kept on coming into view.'

John chewed his lower lip. It made a kind of sense. Economy of effort. He could not help admiring the monster who stood before him looking the very picture of the billionaire connoisseur.

'It was you,' he said. 'That's what kept me going. David Medina, I've lived for you for years. Not because I care much, in the end, what you do to other people, but because you keep me from boredom. What keeps me going is the prospect of taking you. I don't want to be you; that would be no fun. You are the only opponent I've ever wanted, the only man whose plotting and designs are intricate enough to keep me happy. I have been doing what you asked me to, years ago, playing chess with all the world, against you. One day I will defeat you. Then I can die in peace.'

The old man fastened the double-breasted jacket of his silk sharkskin suit. 'Come on. Let's go back. I wanted you to have the chance. I always will. You know better than most how to find me. But you ought to know that, if you ever come close to taking me, I will kill you, as I would kill any servants you might use.'

'I know, David. And I understand how difficult you can make it. The genius of it was in using other people's money.'

'You understand, then?'

Standing smiled sleepily. 'Now. At last. The hard part will be proving the link.'

'It is, I assure you, impossible.'

'You said that to me once before. And, David, there is something you should have remembered, before you brought me here, to demonstrate your epic carelessness. They killed people like my daughter here.'

They set out back through the woods, leaving the empire of death behind them, and entering the shabby, confused and uncertain world of living men on trains.

CHAPTER SIX

At the end, he thought, as he stretched out in the bath, it was monumentally simple.

Medina would kill him. John knew that. But only if he moved too slowly. He had to be rid of his encumbrances. He could finish it and get the story out too quickly for Medina to kill him. And then the old man's former allies would turn on him and deny him.

But first he had to be rid of Caro. He had to make her safe. He whispered lines learnt in school to himself, and stretched out in the bath: 'Down to Gehenna and up to the throne, He travels the fastest who travels alone.'

He wondered if he could tell her any of it yet, to give her some kind of warning. But no, it was too dangerous. The only man who understood what he might have to face was Oliver Ireton. He would have to enlist the old Italy-hand's help. That ought to be easy. Caro had told him it had come out that International Transfer was a Swiss import–export outfit. Ireton ought to be able to hold her down in Switzerland for an adequate number of days.

Again, he found himself thinking the sheer simplicity of it was what made it beautiful. Medina undoubtedly had a kind of genius. A genius of the damned.

He was on the point of giving a number of his major clients exactly what they wanted.

The Vatican wanted a power in Poland it could deal with. It had never understood the freedom and variety of Solidarity, and the General's compromises made it nervous. The right-wing Southern and Central American regimes and factions wanted the Americans back as active and open supporters. The C I A wanted to be there. And the Western banks wanted Poland's financial problems sorted.

Medina was nearly there.

All along, the press had got the Vatican wrong. It had assumed its sympathies lay with the oppressed, with the poor of Poland and Nicaragua, the poor of all the world. That was wrong, criminally wrong. Medina had been right. The Vatican was a power like any other, with interests of its own. It had used its money to support, not Solidarity, except as a kind of charity work, but the hard-line men it could reach a compromise with. That was the truth Father Jerzy was afraid of, and Father Zbigniew had been about to reveal. Rome might hate the Russians, but it knew they were two of a kind.

But Rome also knew its believers. Some things had had to be done in secret. So they did what great powers did. They turned to David Medina.

He had washed the money for them, again and again, and used it for his own purposes. He had satisfied the Contras and the Agency. But he had grander plans than that, from the very inception of the money-run. There were things his clients wanted which they could never admit, but which he could supply.

The Americans wanted to secure their Polish loans.

The Russians wanted to secure Poland.

And the Vatican wanted someone in Poland it could talk to.

All those added up to one ideal solution: invasion.

The Russians would need an excuse. Church infiltration of the security services would provide it.

Gallant resistance to the invaders, on the surface, while dealing directly in secret, would secure the Vatican's reputation in Poland.

And once they were in charge, the Russians would have no option but to guarantee the external debt.

Except that the Americans could not stand by and let the Russians walk into Poland. Unless they were busy, as they had been before. In Iran, when the Russians went into Afghanistan. In student anti-war turmoil and with a potential revolution in France, when the Russians went into Czechoslovakia. And sorting out the Franco-British mess at Suez, when the Russians went into Hungary.

All they needed to be was busy, and they would get exactly what they wanted.

And thanks to John and Caro they were busy now, trying to sort out their relations in Central America.

The time was now. Medina had said the Russians were manoeuvring on the border. All they needed was an excuse. All they needed was for someone to expose the money-run from Rome.

Black money could give the powers what they wanted.

All that was needed was for the story to unravel.

Medina had set them up. Oh, not them in person. John's presence was an added bonus. Any team or teams of journalists would have done. He had had Tom Wellbeck, Enrico Perez, Errol Hart and Father Zbigniew murdered on Midsummer's Eve to signpost the underlying story.

It just happened that, for personal reasons, John and Caro got to it first. All Medina was waiting for now was for them to run the story.

And if they did not? If they let their consciences prevent them?

Medina still won. That was the genius of it. He could turn to all his clients and tell them he had tried. There would be other times and other occasions. Perhaps that was even what Medina wanted. It was possible to track his actions, but his motives remained a mystery. He had done everything his clients could have asked, yet John could not help wondering if what Medina wanted was for it to stop right here. Did he have his own reasons for wanting the American administration embarrassed? Did he have his own reasons for wanting the Vatican disgraced in Eastern Europe and Latin America? He had industrial holdings there to which the radical individuals who filled the lower tiers of the Church might constitute a menace. Was he even playing straight for once with the Bank for International Settlements, the Central Bankers' Bank in Basel? Was he using the threat of invasion to bring the Poles to some settlement with the bankers? Was that his sop to the USA for leaving them exposed in their own land-mass?

It was impossible to tell. John suspected that Medina had planned for both eventualities, and several others. The main point was, he had done as he had been asked and could hope to take advantage of the ensuing chaos.

347

His only weakness remained what it had been throughout. His only weak spot was Italy.

Everywhere else he operated, the authorities were his allies. The duty of men like John's brother was to clear up the mess, no matter what lunacy Medina might involve them in. The same was true of the hard-liners in Poland. John would not even have been surprised to discover that Medina was backing every side in Latin America. He did it successfully elsewhere. And there was Calvi's example in Nicaragua to follow, backing the Sandinistas and Somoza. But in Italy, the Vatican was not the state. It was a foreign power, and one which half the country's politicians loathed and feared. It was the one place he might be taken, if there were brave men enough to chase him into court. Men like the Dottore. Men like Tom Wellbeck.

Which must be why he had chosen the muscle he was using this time. There were things he could sub-contract, as he had sub-contracted the Alabaman arms operation. But there were some things which would lead directly to him, where he had to have control of the violence. Four murders, for instance. Like the execution of a priest in the Vatican's Polish desk whose conscience threatened the whole operation. Like the removal of Zara Francchetti. He needed a force violent and powerful enough in Italy to cover his back.

So he had selected the Camorra.

John had been hiding from the truth of it for weeks. It now made too much sense to be avoided. He had provided the money and equipment which allowed Raffaele Cutullo's family to win the internal war which had riven the Neapolitan organization two years before. Medina must have been thinking about it for years.

He had had to pay a price for Cutullo's support, a price which made sense of the one thing which had puzzled both Robert and John Standing. He had used the weapons operation to buy the Camorra into the lucrative American cocaine trade. The price of their support had been a crack at a slice of the Colombians' and the Mafia's action. It was dangerous, but it was deniable. It was just another worldwide Italian gangster feud.

In Italy, David Medina was no better than a common criminal. And it was there he had the greatest concentration of force. The one thing John had to be certain to do was to keep Caro out of Italy. He could not tell how Medina or his minions might react. None of them was going to Italy till Medina was safely in prison. Even then, it might be safer to travel no further than the southern slopes of the Alps. He had not forgotten how Oliver Ireton had been driven out of the home he had slowly grown to love.

What John needed now was space and time, which meant finding some way of throwing Caro off the scent. Perhaps he should throw her his papers on the Kamu River Project. He would certainly have to think of something.

It seemed that he had allies. She burst into the bathroom and threw a towel at him.

'Get dressed,' she said sharply. 'Something's happening. They're throwing all foreign journalists out.'

CHAPTER SEVEN

They took the first flight out, to East Berlin, then crossed into the West, where they took their leave of colleagues flying back to London, Paris and New York. John insisted they head on to Basel. On the flight he explained his reasons, or those few he was prepared to admit to.

'Screw Poland now,' he told her. 'What we have isn't a news story. There are other people covering the daily news out of the country for the *Examiner*. If there's civil war, or rioting, or even a bloody invasion, it isn't our business to cover it. Our job is to finish this feature, and come up with a finish for your book. Haven't you understood that?'

She sat back and took a sip of gin-and-tonic. 'I'll be glad when this is over,' she said. 'I haven't been in control of it from the beginning. I haven't been in control, full stop. You have. You've run around wherever you wanted, telling me half-truths, telling me lies, leaving me exposed and ignorant. Well, I'm sick of it, John, really sick. Would you like to tell me what the hell is going on? Because as soon as this is over, I'm going back to Italy. I think I deserve the break.'

'Caro,' he said sorrowfully, 'haven't you worked it out yet? If we ever close this up, you may never be able to go back to Italy again. Have you any idea what the reaction of the Catholic establishment will be if they find themselves and their currency swindles exposed for international entertainment? Can you imagine the violence of their reaction if the Dottore gets his way?'

'Oh, balls,' she said bitterly. 'It won't last. It never does in Italy. Once it's all died down, it'll go on in its own sweet way. It always has and always will. Why do you always over-react about Italy? Why can't you let them go about things their own way? Who does it harm? It's a hell of a lot more fun than anything you showed me in America. Face it, John, your whole bloody country is full of machine-men who wouldn't know a good time if it came up and gave them a Nevada handshake.'

It made him so angry he needed another drink. 'You are so fucking naïve,' he told her. 'Hasn't it occurred to you that just because they go around in Guccis and Ferraris, combing their coal-black hair and looking like the fantasy of every Wigan housewife, it doesn't mean they aren't killers, pimps, pushers and general all-purpose shits? Oh, sure, the men in suits are gentlemen, but what difference does it make if you're lying dead with your face in a plate of soup that they said grace before they shot you? All I'm asking you to understand is that people can smile and smile and still be villains. You aren't safe until I say so.'

She had had enough. It showed on her face. He was frightened of what she might do unthinking, exhausted. All he needed was a way to keep her busy for a very few days. A week at most. He prayed he was right about Basel.

Oliver Ireton met them at the airport, looking more excited than either of them had seen him in an age. It took years off him. He almost skipped as he walked them out to his car. 'What news then?' he asked, 'MacKinnon's been going crazy on the phone for the past few hours telling me to head you back to London.'

'You probably know more than we do,' Caro told him, truthfully, 'Everything looked clean as a whistle. John being taken out on tour, me spending a day at the trial. Then whammo, everybody out. No questions even acknowledged. There were the usual rumours about Russians on the borders, but there always are. Have you had anything on the wires?'

He shook his head and let them into the BMW which was his pride and joy. 'Bugger all. Total shutdown. Telecommunications, airports, harbours, border posts, the lot. Same as last time. Could it be the same as last time?'

John did not think so. 'I was in the south twelve hours ago, not thirty-five miles from Krakow, without a whisper of trouble. We went by train, and the train lines would be the first thing to be cut I'd have thought.'

Ireton was working it out as he pulled out for the short

351

ride home. 'Thirty-five miles? Tourism? They took you to Oswiecim by train?'

'Sure. What's wrong with that?'

Ireton rolled up his eyes. 'You were honoured, my boy. For fairly obvious reasons they don't much care to lay on passenger trains to Oswiecim. Too many unfortunate allusions. They must have thought you were pretty special not to throw you into the regulation Lada.'

'It wasn't me. It was Medina.'

'Medina was in Warsaw?' John nodded. Ireton whistled. 'Did he get out?'

John shrugged. He did not know. He gestured to Caro.

'Now you mention it,' she said, 'I'm not at all sure he did. He had a pretty sizeable entourage with him, and there was no sign of movement from his suite when we left.'

Ireton seemed to deflate. 'Then it can't be very serious. There is no way in the world that man would get caught without an escape route. If he stayed it means he knows whatever's happening is under control.'

Perhaps, John thought. Or perhaps he was cleverer than even they gave him credit for. If he was caught in Warsaw by a Russian invasion, who could accuse him of having helped organize that attack? Criminals vanished from the scene of their crimes. What the hell was going on?

It was the question MacKinnon wanted answered when they called him from Ireton's apartment. Caro took charge and bawled the Scotsman out.

'For Christ's sake, Iain,' she yelled as though trying to make herself heard in Examiner House without the benefit of electronics, 'my sabbatical isn't even half-way over, I've landed you the biggest goddam story of the decade, and here you are treating me like some cub reporter straight off the *Surrey Mirror*. Screw you, Iain. I don't know what is going on in Poland. You have people who are supposed to. One of them should be back with you from Warsaw by now. Ask them.' She slammed down the receiver to a round of applause from Ireton and Standing.

'If you keep that up,' Ireton grinned, 'they'll kick you upstairs to editor. Now what do you two scoundrels want?'

John explained. He gave Oliver an abridged account of the black money circle from Italy to Poland. 'The point is, Oliver, we can't be certain of the point of dissemination in Poland. We think it may be through a Swiss import–export house called International Transfer. What we need to do is try and track it down. We need to know who runs it, and we need to establish if it has any connections with the operations in the United States. Without that link we do not have a story. So where do we look?'

Oliver smiled and got up to pour them all a drink. 'You're in luck,' he told them. 'This is Switzerland. We phone the registrar of companies in the morning. And we check with directory inquiries and the Post Office for an address and phone number. You couldn't make it easier if you tried.'

But they could.

Almost anything would have been easier. They found an address and telephone number easily enough. Further investigation proved it to be an uninhabited private house in the suburbs of Basel itself. The neighbours had seen no life or movement in the house for at least a year. As for the register of companies, it had no trace of any International Transfer, or anything which might remotely be the company they were seeking. They collapsed exhausted back at Oliver's apartment in the evening. Caro was tired enough to taunt Standing.

'Well, come on, leg-man. You're supposed to be the wizard at tracing hidden companies. What do we do next? Where do we go from here? What happens when you draw a complete blank?'

He stretched out on the floor, staring at the ceiling. His back, which had behaved for months, was trying to tear its way out of him. He thought of Alan Clarke. Right now, he almost envied him.

'We haven't drawn a complete blank,' he said patiently. 'It's a pity we can't get into Poland to try to find out more about it, but we've still to look at the registers of unlimited partnerships. We haven't checked the deeds and rental records of the house. We haven't approached the other people in this business. All it takes is time.'

Caro groaned. 'John, you old bugger, you're a dear, dear man but don't you understand that time is what I've had too much of? In the last few weeks I've seen my ex-husband, a colleague and a Catholic priest murdered, not to mention Tom's mistress. I've been blown up and held as a suspect in another murder. Not that I'm sure Stu Wilcox was ever alive. I've been told to break the biggest story of a lifetime by a leg-man who was almost always drunk and who vanished every time I needed him. I've travelled fifteen thousand miles and been promised an even bigger story. I've been thrown out of an Iron Curtain country and I even finally got to lay my eyes on David Medina, and I've still really got no idea what's been going on. Would someone like to enlighten me, before too much more time is over?'

She faced both of them with a look of patient amusement. She had hurt for a long time, but she had grown up now. She knew what she was responsible for, and what was someone else's problem. She knew how much to care. 'I'm not a fool, John,' she said. 'I know what you're doing. I know why we're here. I know we have only a single piece of evidence linking the Vatican into this whole circle, through Popolari in Nassau. I know you want another. I know you want to second-source something as big as this. All right, so we can tie International Transfer into Alabama, but we don't know who owns or controls it. You're hoping for another Vatican connection. I can understand that, but, John, the whole thing is on the verge of blowing. Poland's closed. It could go any moment now. We have a choice between writing news and writing history. Thanks to you, thanks to the American part of the story, we could get MacKinnon to carry the whole thing as it stands, and other people to take it seriously. It isn't perfect. It isn't ideally what we'd want, but why don't we do it? Now. While it still matters.'

John winched himself off the floor and reached for Oliver's bottle of whisky. He poured himself a stiff drink and lit a cigarette. Deep down, he had expected this. He had expected her to face him down. She was right. She was nobody's fool.

He was glad it had happened here. In the calm bourgeois anonymity of Basel, away from the pressures of the news-

354

room, or of a country falling apart, where her self-esteem, anyone's self-esteem, might cloud the issue. And here at least he had Ireton as an ally. Ireton would understand. He drank off the last of his whisky and poured himself another. It took his attention off his back.

'We have a decision to make,' he said at last. 'I knew we would have to. It's one of the reasons I wanted to be here, because I wanted us to talk to Olly. He had to make a similar decision once. I thought we might benefit from his experience. Before I tell you what it is, I'd like Olly to ring MacKinnon to get the current position in Poland.'

Ireton made the call. There was no change. Total news black-out. A silent face to the outside world. In London, they anticipated invasion. John sat, with his long legs tucked up and his head in his hands, and began to explain.

'Iain asked you once to consider what the effects on Poland might be on releasing this story. It's a tale of Vatican involvement in Polish affairs. Of interference. The Russians have recently made it plain how sick they are with Poland. There are manoeuvres on the border. They could walk in at any second. Do you know what the West would do? Nothing. Just like Afghanistan, Czecho, Hungary, 1956, 1968, 1978. It happens about once a decade, but there's nothing to stop them marching a little early. The West wouldn't move because it's preoccupied with the mess America's making in its door-yard. And because the Russians would guarantee the Polish debt. It lets everyone off the hook.'

Caro shook her head in frustration. 'John, we can't change history. We can only cover it. And I don't believe that anything that happens will have been caused by our stories. It isn't our fault.'

John was definite. 'But it would be. You told me to behave myself with Medina. I didn't have to. After all, who would believe anything I said? He was in a good enough mood to talk. We did well, Caro. We did really well. But we were set up. The chain of events is not an accident. It may be an accident that we broke it, but I don't altogether think so. I think he played to our strengths and weaknesses. And I think the best team won. But I think a number of the murders were designed to keep us going, to keep us convinced we were right about the story. I think that's why Father Tomasso and Stu Wilcox were killed when they were killed. Let's face it, their deaths persuaded us we were right to keep on looking. And I think Alan Clarke was murdered to make us angry. Angry enough to say, "The hell with the consequences, let's go with the story." Medina is waiting to see which way we jump. It hangs on us. If we publish, the Russians move in.'

Caro didn't want to believe it. 'And if we don't? If he's set it up so carefully, how does he end the crisis?'

'I think he's ready for us. He's been ahead of us all the way. He told me he was officially in Poland for the Bank for International Settlements to renegotiate the Polish debt. I don't know what the mechanics are, though I can guess, but if we don't publish I wager there'll be a hard-line government before it's over in Warsaw and Medina will come out with the renegotiations successfully begun. That would be more than enough for the Americans, and for the Russians. All they're looking for is a solution. Medina's offering them a range of options. All of which he controls. That's how he exerts his power. His speciality is crisis. I suspect the real beginning of this was the secret police's attempted coup last month. That set the international momentum going, thanks to the *Examiner*'s coverage. I think he may have been behind those temporary contacts. Just as I'm certain the coup was financed with the Vatican's black money.'

Caro found it making horrible sense. One thing still remained to puzzle her. 'I don't see what the Vatican has to gain by this.'

Oliver Ireton had the answer. 'I do,' he told her. 'If the Russians invade, Holy Mother Church will be able to do no wrong as far as ordinary Poles are concerned, and Rome will have the leverage it needs with any new government. As it would if you don't publish. It would be entirely characteristic of Rome to want a tougher, harder regime in Warsaw. It would fit in with two thousand years of foreign policy. They love their enemies and they burn their friends.'

Caro almost wanted to cry, but found she was laughing to herself instead. 'The trouble is, John, we only have your word for it. Your word that it's Medina, when our clear journalistic duty is to run the story as it stands. We ought to publish and be damned.'

Olly came to John's rescue again. 'That isn't quite true, Caro. John has given us one new fact. Or what he claims is one. He says Medina is officially working for the Bank for International Settlements: B I S is in Basel. Why don't we just ask them if that's true?'

'Oh, sure,' Caro snorted, 'as though we could. It's the kind of fact I'd make up in John's position. How the hell do you check with the Central Bankers' Bank? The most secretive of them all.'

Oliver laughed. 'Not the most secret. The Paris Club is that. After all, the Paris Club doesn't even formally exist. But I'll tell you how you ask them. What you use is threats.'

He lifted the phone receiver and tapped out a number. It must have been a direct line, for he did not have to go through a switchboard.

'Hallo, Pauli,' he began, all jovial reassurance, 'I'm sorry to trouble you at this hour. Oliver Ireton here, of the *Examiner*. Pauli, I have some information for you, off the record. I've been speaking to two colleagues of mine from London. They are planning a feature on David Medina, and it seems they want to run the old chestnut about Medina organizing the Swiss breach of the blockade of Germany and Italy during the Second World War. The only thing stopping them is the work Medina's supposed to be doing for your people in Poland. But they can't get any confirmation about his working for B I S. They're sentimentalists, Pauli. I think if they got the confirmation, they might pull the feature. So I need to know, on the record, is it true?'

There was a long silence. There were a few phrases. The line was put on hold. There were a few more phrases. Oliver hung up.

'I'll give you his number, Caro,' he said, 'so you can phone him yourself if you want confirmation. I thought it best not to say you were with me now. But John's right. On the record, but with the request for an embargo on publication for at least seventy-two hours and prior clearance from B I S. It seems they and the Paris Club called him in for hands-off negotiations.'

'Shit.' Caro did not know whether to be relieved or desolate. 'This doesn't happen. Journalists don't affect the news. We're not important enough.'

John found himself agreeing. 'No, we're not. Not finally. In the long view of history, does it matter how Poland gets its hard-line government or how the Vatican gets its accord with Warsaw or Washington firms up its Latin American commitments? It would happen one way or another in the end. What we can affect is which way it happens. That's the price we pay for whatever power or influence the media have. And they do have it. We know that. Otherwise we wouldn't bother. We can't help Solidarity. We can't help the ordinary people of Poland. But we can influence whether or not they face Polish or Russian tyrants.'

Oliver Ireton looked sombre. He was an old man scarred from a whole generation of journalistic wars, with all the compromises his temporary victories had inevitably demanded. He knew some things were necessary even if they left you ashamed.

'There's something else,' he said quietly, 'something else you ought to take account of, Caro. As a journalist, I take my hat off to you. You and John appear to have done an astonishing job. But as a friend, I want to know no more about it. I hope I never read a word of this story or of your background files. I know there are people who think I'm a coward, that I ran away from the field of honour after eleven years in Italy. But I wanted to live. What neither of you has taken into account is how much of your story depends on Italy and the Dottore. I'm not sure even he could survive the aftermath of blowing the whistle on the Vatican and the whole of the Catholic establishment. I'm not sure he cares. What you may not know, what you may not have taken account of, is that the Dottore's wife died two months ago. He may not care much any longer about going on living. But you should. Hasn't there been enough death already? Sometimes we have to admit we lose. Let it go, Caro. Give it up. Medina wins. But then he always does.'

John curled up over his glass, his long locks hanging down. He looked as grey as Poland, bleached out by weeks of trying, of running himself close to the grave. When he looked up and spoke his voice was breaking. 'I don't see what else we can do. This time I thought we had him. I wanted him so badly I could taste it. But I don't see how we can.'

They were right, she thought. Six weeks ago she would never have believed what they had uncovered. She would have hestitated to believe the opulence of Medina's skills and malice, but she had lost too much and too many to deny it now.

'All right,' she said, surrendering. 'If we don't publish, what happens? Am I to believe Medina is sitting in Warsaw waiting for each morning's Frankfurt edition before deciding on his policy? What happens now?'

Oliver answered. 'I think we can assume that the thing has its own momentum. He set it up so that it could play in the widest possible variety of ways, all of them beneficial to him. He'll make his own decisions, under the pressure of events. As will everyone else involved. As you have.'

John looked around for more whisky and saw the bottle was empty. Oliver got up to fetch another. When he had returned and given the big man another shot, John admitted, 'There is a way we can cover ourselves. There is a way of getting messages to Medina, wherever he is. I can tell him we surrender.'

Ireton was impressed. 'How do you do it?' According to legend, he doesn't allow telephones in the presence.'

'That's true. He doesn't. You can't get hold of him. But he runs the same system as the White House and the big American banks. His personal secretariat's number is a New York switchboard. All his houses are extensions of that main line. And he carries radio extensions with him on his travels. Doesn't matter where he is, Monaco or Maiduguri, you get hold of him by calling the secretariat on the New York number.'

Caro felt too deflated to be impressed. They had left too much undone. And she had another, more pressing problem.

'You bastard, John,' she said unemotionally. 'What have

you done to me? I've only got a few weeks left to finish this bloody book, and I no longer have a main story to finish it. And I don't have time to undertake the stuff I hired you to look at and get the writing done.'

John laughed, and she felt better. It seemed such a long time since she had seen him laugh, laugh properly. 'I've been saving something up for you,' he said, 'in case this story blew up, or you had to fire me. I wanted to have an apology and an alternative on hand and available if ever this should happen. Ten years ago, I could only guess at it. Five years ago I couldn't publish it. But it isn't news now, it's history. It's stuff for books, not for front-page splashes. You want governments interfering with commercial decisions? You want short-term political considerations outweighing long-term economic and strategic advantage? You want strange bedfellows? I got 'em. I can give you all my papers on the Kamu River Project.'

Simultaneously, Caro and Ireton turned to look at him, and said in unison, 'Christ!'

CHAPTER EIGHT

It was true that what John gave Caro was history not news, but it was news that the truth about the Kamu River Project was even known. It was precisely the kind of story she needed, with an added bonus. She had expected her main example to deal with the use of economic coercion and corruption between the First World of the West and the Third World of the poor. She had not dared to hope that she might be able to show the same game being played between the superpowers.

It had happened a decade before, in the first frantic flush of the Euromarkets, primed with Arab petrodollars. The banks were still learning how to gather together in large syndicates to spread the risk of the biggest (and not always just the biggest) loans. And the US administration had just begun learning what a potent political weapon international lending could be. There would always be rumours that some loans were made more for strategic than commercial reasons. Bankers would always deny it, pointing out that they had stockholders, management boards and Central Bankers to report to, who all frightened them a great deal more than any politician. But there were some loans which did not seem to make sense, except within strategic considerations. There was the added advantage, of course, that any slightly suspicious loan could always be sweetened by charging higher rates of interest ('fattening the spread', they called it, increasing the difference between what they charged the borrower and what they would have charged each other for the same amount of money).

The Kamu River Project had long been rumoured to be a classic of political considerations. It had been during the high period of East–West détente. For obvious reasons, the Soviet Union hardly ever borrowed, at least openly, on the Western *capital* markets. The very word was anathema. It was also true, however, that Russian technology lagged up to a decade behind the West. Détente allowed one perfect opportunity to address both problems.

The Kamu River Project was to be the Soviet Union's largest ever automobile production facility. It needed Western technology, and it needed Western funds. The USSR went openly into the market, the sexiest borrower of the year.

They did it well. They had to. They had to show the capitalists that they could play the game as well as or better than the West. If they did not normally do so, it was because they chose to march in step with history not with profit. They put the loan together well. The terms were right. The interest-spreads were right. It was a fashionable deal. The lead banks charged with putting it together, mainly American, sent out the telexes inviting other banks to participate in the syndicate. Then they sat back and waited.

What happened next was silence, at the lead banks' end. Not for very long, but minutes can make fortunes in the world of banking, and this was a delay of days. At the end of it, the lead banks announced the total size of the loan was being increased, because of the enthusiasm of the banking community's reception of the deal. It had to be bigger to let more banks take part at an attractive level. That in itself was not unusual. What was unusual was that, without warning, the lead American banks announced they were increasing the level of their own participation, doubling the amount they were prepared to lend in some cases. It could not be faulted on purely banking grounds. The interest spreads *were* attractive. The Soviet Union was a cast-iron, copper-bottom Triple-A borrower. But that one participation tore a hole through most of the banks' concerned prudential lending limits, their country lending limits, their single-project limits, and their industrial limits. The rumours began at once. The reason for the delay, everyone assumed, had been the time it had taken for the US administration to make it clear to its greatest financial institutions that this deal, during the period of détente, was too important to let much credit pass to other banks and other nations. The US banks were asked to buy in, at higher levels than they intended, as part of US foreign policy.

362

No one had ever proved it. It had been the classic stuff of rumour. These things were not achieved on paper. No memoranda were issued, no orders signed. It was done when small groups of men met after tennis games in Georgetown, at cocktail parties in New York, and chalet suppers at Aspen. But John had proved it. John had notes of every conversation he had had in the aftermath of those decisions. All of them unusable, all of them off the record. All of them kept in a safe deposit box in London.

And as he said to her, history was her friend. What he had been told (she wondered how much Robert had had to do with it), he had been told off the record, because it had been done by men with careers in government to pursue. But that had been ten years ago. Administrations changed, and the men who ran them dropped out of the limelight. They grew bored without the fame they had once, so passionately yet so briefly, enjoyed. Now that the tumult and shouting had died, they were bored, they wanted to be turned to and quoted as elder statesmen. They would do almost anything to get their name, their photograph, their career triumphs, into a newspaper or, better still, a book. All Caro had to do was pick up the telephone and ask them to corroborate or expand on their remarks of a decade before.

John had asked to stay behind in Switzerland for a few days. He had the call to Medina to make, and when it was done he would want to hide away a while to nurse his wounds. Caro believed him. It was the performance of his life.

Ireton suspected, but he wanted nothing to do with it. John could not blame him. He had survived too much to squander his safety now. And what John needed to do he could do on his own. As so often in the past, the answer to the whole thing had to lie in the papers. He had to do the paperwork. It was the lesson Alan Clarke had never learned, which cost him his life. The paperwork was essential.

The only way to publish the story was to present it all as Medina's personal plan and responsibility. To give his clients the opportunity to disclaim him and to bring him down. But that meant proving Medina's involvement. John did not have the kind of proof he could publish.

Medina had been so certain at Oswiecim. He had said the link was impossible to make. But it couldn't be. There were two points at which Medina would have had to be directly involved: the initial collection, and final dissemination of the money. Which meant Liechtenstein and Poland. Or rather, Liechtenstein and Switzerland. Liechtenstein he knew to be impenetrable, so he had to crack it here. But there was no International Transfer registered. Whatever John had told Caro and Oliver he knew he had to be looking for a limited company. It was Medina's way. It allowed the greatest measure of anonymity (they actually called them that in France: *société anonyme*). It allowed refinements of control.

So where in God's name was it? It had to be registered somewhere. Somewhere which made masking it as a Swiss company credible. He could not believe it would be Liechtenstein, not for a trading company. It had to be here. The papers had to be here, close by. He had to have the paperwork. He had to think.

It came to him after he had drunk nine stiff cognacs in a row. He remembered the tax evaders' solution. It was extremely difficult to set up a presence in Switzerland, without giving the authorities a great deal more information than most people wanted. Opening an office or company here could be a protracted nightmare. That was not true in Germany. If your operation was small enough, in administrative terms (the sums of money did not matter; money could be moved in millions by a few taps on a computer keyboard), you could base it in Switzerland as a residential address and telephone number without ever drawing the attention of the authorities. Provided all your business was conducted outside Switzerland. If it was, they had nothing to go on. For legal purposes, to cover your own back, you could register in Germany, giving a German address on all paperwork. Only someone who knew what he was looking for would ever make the link. There was no paper chain between the legal and the postal entities. But the only way to prove it was to check every corporate register in Germany.

It took him three days, flat out, hopping in and out of aeroplanes and overnight trains. He had to go to Berlin, Stuttgart, Munich, Hamburg, Frankfurt and Dusseldorf. By the end he was no longer sure where he was or what he was doing. The news he had been waiting for came through on the second night, while he was in Frankfurt.

He had called in on the newspaper's office there to watch the overseas edition being pulled together. It had come over on the wires. Poland had reopened its communications with the Western world. The General survived, but most of the Politburo had gone, replaced by harder men. Another round of austerity measures had been prescribed. Martial law was to be intensified. Rioting in the capital and in Gdansk had been put down by force with the assistance of the comradely Russian allies, who had had two divisions in Poland on Warsaw Pact manoeuvres. That *was* news, and a manifest lie. But Cardinal Glemp had asked the Polish people to face the new situation with calmness and reason, while he tried to work out compromises with the new régime. And Russia was increasing its economic assistance, while Poland met with Western banks to clarify its external debt position.

He's done it, thought John, almost in admiration. *The old bastard's done it*. The brilliant thing had been to leave the General at the top. In international affairs such small things mattered. Everything looked the same, but everything had changed. What it did do was give him time, and a little breathing-space. Medina was only human. Even he would need time to rest and regroup his forces, before deciding what to turn to next.

John needed less time than he had feared. He telephoned Caro that night. She had heard the news and did not know yet what she felt about it. She asked him if he could be in England the following evening, Friday, and come to Examiner House. MacKinnon had a surprise for him. John wondered what it could be, and told her he would try. He told her to take care.

He found nothing in the Frankfurt register the following morning. He took a flight to Dusseldorf. It was his final hope, and it came good. He found what he was looking for. He found International Transfer, about the smallest imaginable limited liability company, with a capital of a thousand marks, divided between Popolari of Nassau and Genassets Liechtenstein 499:501. He felt triumphant. He had tracked the spoor of David Medina. He ordered photocopies of the records.

He flew back into London on a drizzly summer night after three weeks' absence which had felt the best part of a lifetime. Or the worst. But he felt alive, extravagant and in control. And he was already roaring drunk.

He did not know exactly how he would do it yet, but he knew he could take David Medina. He had a little time. He had the weekend to write it, to put it all together. He would put it to Caro and MacKinnon on Sunday night or Monday morning. There was no doubt about it. He was back.

He took a taxi all the way to the *Examiner*. As he walked through the door into the newsroom, the first champagne cork exploded.

'You bastards!' he shouted.

They all laughed.

He had forgotten, as Caro had before him. It seemed so long ago. They had lost good men. They had lost what was left of their innocence. They had lost most of their hopes and some of their integrity. But they had come through. They had, from the United States, with MacKinnon's undeniable and invaluable help, given the paper the devil of a story. There was a chance, a good chance, Caro would take the Granada Television Journalist of the Year Award. The paper had wanted to party the moment the issue was put to bed, but MacKinnon had insisted: no party till the whole team came home. Till the three of them were together.

Caro led the cheering, raising a plastic beaker filled with Krug. (In honour of newspapers' traditional class divisions, the team and the editors drank Krug that night, the menials drank anything they could get their hands on.) Then they were all singing 'Hail to the Chief' in terrible phoney American accents and somebody was putting a glass of champagne into his hand.

MacKinnon must have arranged it, he thought. MacKinnon must have timed it. The Saturday morning paper was one of the larger, but one of the simpler, ones to organize. Much of it was a résumé of the previous week. If the *Examiner* could not manage a party on Friday night it could not party at all. He was never to remember very much of it. He had arrived drunk and rapidly got legless. He remembered Caro leaving early, looking tired but happy, her eyes shining and her skin alive. He remembered feeling pleased for her. He remembered she kissed him on the cheek, to the noisy guffaws, grunts and cat-calls of every other journalist present. He remembered she gave him something.

He remembered swaying in front of a MacKinnon glowing red beneath his short blond hair as the Scotsman pumped his hand and told him he had done the Old Hacks proud. He had taught the young pups how the thing should be done. He remembered asking if that meant MacKinnon was going to offer him a job. He remembered seeing the Scotsman's eyes go dead. And he remembered the girl he found himself twined around before a couple of hours were done. He did not know her name, or what she did or where she came from, but he knew she had terrific tits and peroxide hair. He did not know how they got home. He did not remember what they did.

He did not know where he was when he woke up. It was dark. There was a noise. He was swaying. He turned, and nearly fell. His arm made no contact, and he felt his body lurch out into darkness. Something in his head was spinning. Somehow he kept himself from falling, but he wanted to be sick. Lights flashed past outside the windows in the darkness. Someone had forgotten to draw the blinds. He recognized the smell coming through the ventilation window. His brain made sense of the sounds his ears were hearing. He was on a train. This must be a sleeper. He did not know where he was going. He wanted to get up and check, but he did not know the language. He did not dare to try to put a foot down on the floor. There would not be a floor, he knew it. He would try to stand, but he would fall, and if he fell it would be forever. He lay there in the darkness, sweating and afraid.

It isn't true, he told himself. *It isn't real. This is a dream. You aren't awake. Nothing here is real.*

He wanted the dream to end. He wanted his nightmares to stop. They could do anything to him they wanted, the men in uniforms and leather greatcoats. He could abide whatever loneliness or torment they might devise for him, if only they could put an end to these bad dreams.

Then there was a crash of metal upon metal, the sudden squealing of brakes, sparks flying outside the window up into the still night. He had not been prepared for it, and he fell.

He fell awake. He still did not know where he was. Slowly it came back to him. It had been quite a thrash. This must be her place, whoever she was. She was sleeping too heavily, snoring, to stir. He got up to look for some coffee and a drink.

As he put himself together, parts of it came back to him. He checked his jacket anxiously. The photocopies were safe. He drank some coffee. He drank more vodka. His head hurt, his back hurt, and his kidneys were begging to go home, but he would have to pull himself together. He had a story to write. He wondered if he should call in Caro. Two typewriters were better than one. It was tempting. Whatever happened, they would share the by-line. But it really was his story. He wanted to see something to completion on his own. He wanted to be what he had been before. He wanted to win back his pride.

He took another vodka. It made him think of that morning, weeks ago, when Caro had first called on him and he had nearly lost the job she thought he should never have been offered. He hoped she had changed her mind. He thought she had. It was going to be all right.

She had looked happy last night, at peace with herself. She had not known much peace of late. She deserved what she could get. Should he call her now, he wondered? To see if she was well? He checked his watch. It said three o'clock. When he drew the curtain a fraction there was something strange about the light. Something was not right.

His heart sank. He understood. It was three o'clock in the afternoon. He had lost the best part of a day. He should have known better than to keep on drinking. He would certainly need any help she might give him now. He tried to telephone her. Unobtainable. Something wrong with the phone. Then he remembered she had given him something the night before. It ought to be in his jacket. It was. It was a letter.

Caro was humming to herself as she walked down to the boarding gate that Saturday morning. She did not know if what she was doing was wise. She suspected that Olly and John would have said it was not. But she knew that it was necessary. She had been lied to for too long.

So now she was going to a place where she had been happy. She was going back to where she had been loved.

He had lied to her, of course. She had known that all along. Not out of malice or thoughtlessness or contempt, but because he was John Standing, and in his own obscure way he thought he was protecting her. But she was not a child. She was a grown woman, with her own life and her own skills and her own responsibilities. And the news from Poland had set her free.

She knew that John and Oliver would be outraged and fearful, but there was something patronizing in their concern. She had told John that much in her letter. All this had begun with her, with her guilt at Tom Wellbeck's murder. A great deal had happened since then, and most of what they had achieved had been achieved by the obdurate infuriating diligence of John Standing, but now they were free. Free to leave the story they had launched to their American colleagues. Free not to fret about Poland. They weren't very good at being moral about big issues. Big issues were hardly moral at all. They kept shifting in each of their aspects till you never knew where you stood. What was right, what was wrong.

For them, ordinary people, caught up in a difficult, vulnerable, limited, treacherous trade, the most you could hope to do was to try to do the right thing in those small decisions where you made a difference. You had to do the best you could, in the areas where what you chose to do mattered.

She did not know that anyone could ever sort out the hornet's nest of Italy, where everything was prohibited and everything was possible. Perhaps John and Olly were right. Perhaps underneath the vigour and vivacity it was a nightmare, its dark underside lined with corruption and violence. Perhaps even men like the Dottore would never be able to change it. They had tried before and failed. But there was something small she could do. Something certain and something definite. She could act against one stain on the place where she had last been happy.

If John was right, and she believed he was, if Medina had planned it all, then he must have planned the murders which began it. Tom's murder must have been premeditated. And what did that make Zara Francchetti's apparent suicide? She did not suppose that Medina could be brought to book, but perhaps his tools might be. She owed it to herself to try, and she owed it to Tom. She could not pursue it. She could not investigate it. But she could acknowledge and report what she suspected. Then she would be able to live again. Then she would be free.

She stepped into the plane, thinking all she had to do was tell the magistrate. All she had to do was talk to Ezzo.

Standing tore open the envelope. Caro's handwriting was both firm and delicate. She was an admirable woman. Who had chosen to do the admirable thing. He could have wept for the pity of it. He had counted on her exhaustion, and now he feared he was too late.

Revulsion rose in him. He had done enough. He had worked and he had fought. He had no reserves of energy or spirit left. He wanted Medina. It had been the work of half his life. And now she risked everything through ignorance and folly.

He owed her nothing. He had brought her more than she could ever have accomplished without him. She acknowledged that. Why could she not leave well enough alone?

What he wanted was to stay, here. To finish the work he had begun so long ago. He did not want to go after her. He did not have the time or strength. If he went after her, Medina would find a way to take him, and everything would have been lost. And he did not want to die. Not when he had only just begun to live again. And he would die, he knew it. Medina had been too patient with him.

He had one hope left. The magistrate. He might smile and

smile and still be an honest man. He checked his battered address book and called the number in Rome. There was no reply.

He reached for the bottle of vodka. He would drink the problem away. Except he could not. Nothing would rid him of the problem. He had deliberately, time and again, concealed things from her. If she had known them she would not have gone. Not even honest women chose to tangle with the Camorra. But he had not told her, for the best of motives, and now she put herself at hazard.

Were they the best of motives, he asked himself once more? Or was it pride and emptiness which drove him on? Had he forgotten everything in the pleasure of the game? He didn't want to think about it. He didn't want the blame. He had blamed himself too long for everything already.

But most of all, he did not want to die.

He did not want it to end, as it began, with a squalid death in Italy. He did not want to be the completion of the circle, but he knew the story which Medina had so meditatively started was finally coming home. He wished that he could fly.

It was too difficult, too painful, and he was too afraid. He wanted someone else to take the decision for him. He wished that Robert or the Ambassador were here. He wanted it out of his hands.

As he sat drinking vodka, he decided. He decided how to deal with a world where so much was left to chance. He reached into his jacket for a one-pound coin. He held it in his right palm, feeling the weight of it, everything its shining surface change colour in the dim light of the room. *Everything ends in chance*, he thought. *Everyone loses control.*

He tossed the coin high into the air, sitting back in the chair to watch it spinning, thinking: *Heads I go, tails I stay. Heads I go . . .*

It came down tails.

He sat looking at it, gleaming in the soft light, stable on the back of his hand.

Tails I stay. Tails I live. Tails all the rest of the world I leave to make and take its chances.

Then he tossed the coin again.

*

She wanted to surprise him. It didn't matter if he wasn't in. She could always book into the Raffaele. But it was a lovely summer Saturday morning in Rome with the plane trees unfurling their leaves like little plates which filled with sun. The only thing which could make the day more perfect would be to see him straight away, but nothing could hurt her, nothing could spoil her mood. She was in Italy and everything would be well.

The cab dropped her outside his apartment building. The main door was open. It was Saturday and sunny. The occupants were coming and going as they pleased. Nothing mattered enough for locks. She began the climb up to his apartment.

She had to ring the bell three times, and wait. He came to the door in a towelling robe, his hair still wet from the shower. He looked angry to be disturbed. His mouth did not smile when he saw her, but his eyes did. They looked like amber fires. Then he swept forward and caught her in his arms, calling her name, and bore her back across the card table, and they were reaching desperately for each other's mouths, hands roving, till he lifted her skirt and swept down the silk which still restrained him as she pushed back at his robe and he was inside her, crushsing her without hurting as though their lives depended on each slow shuddering thrust, on his leaving his seed deep within her.

Afterwards, in his arms, on the couch in the drawing-room, she told him why she had come. He listened gravely, earnest, accepting her intelligence and independence and her good sense as easily as half an hour before he had taken her as a woman. She would be safe, she would be happy, as long as he was with her.

He told her he could not stay, not for the moment. He had to go now, to the police, to the coroner's office, to keep the case alive and reopen the active investigation. It would not take him long. A couple of hours at most. He wanted her to wait for him here. He wanted to arrange for her protection. He would care for her himself. Why did she not stay here and relax? Why did she not make herself yet more beautiful

372

for him, so that they could take time and pleasure in each other when he returned?

He left her, and she took a bath, and put on his robe, smelling him on it as she smelt him on her fingers. She dozed. She examined his bookshelves (not too much law, she was glad to note). She thought about cooking lunch for them both, and opened a bottle of wine.

When he returned he had two men with him. Officers, he said. One very tall and broad, almost a giant. The other almost dwarfish. They would have to go to the station, he explained, to make a formal statement. She pleaded with him prettily, asking if it could not wait till Monday, if he could not take her statement down, but he insisted. It was for the best, he said.

It was too late, in the car, when she turned and saw him looking guiltily away, that she realized wherever they were going, it was nowhere within Rome.

When Standing got to the *Examiner*, MacKinnon hustled him into the editorial office, near crazy with worry. 'Where the fuck have you been? And where's Caro?' had been his first greeting, the red veins throbbing on the pink scalp beneath his translucent hair. John calmed him down and asked him what had been going on. 'Are you out of your mind?' MacKinnon asked in what was a reasonable tone for him. 'Where have you been? We've had the police crawling all over us. Both your flats have been turned over. We've been looking everywhere for you.'

Standing felt very, very sick. What he needed most was a drink, but he did not have the time. He was urgent with Mac-Kinnon.

'Iain, don't ask any questions. Just do exactly what I tell you. Caro's gone to Rome. She's in danger. So am I. But you've gathered that already. I want the police kept away from me for twenty-four hours. You can tell them where she is. She probably went to the magistrate, Ezzo Spaccamonti. He'll be on her or Alan's files. Oh, sod it, I've got the details here.' He scribbled them down for the editor. 'Get them to get in touch with the Italian police. Tell them to pick her up. Get hold of Mike Thomas at the City Police and tell him you think the people after us may be the same people as got Errol Hart. Tell him to get behind it. She may not even be safe in police custody.'

MacKinnon was truculent. 'And what are you going to be doing?'

Standing was taking no stick. 'That's my business. But there are some things you have to do for me, if Caro's to have a chance. Trust me, you Scottish bastard, I'm the last best hope she's got.'

He stood over the Scotsman. He was drunk, he was untrustworthy and he looked like death, but what else could MacKinnon do? Some things you had to take on trust, whatever they might cost you.

'What do you need?' MacKinnon asked.

'I need to get to Lugano in time to get to Chiasso before eleven. That means a private plane. Book it. I'll need Italian cash. I can indemnify you if that's the only way, but I must have lire.'

Iain nodded. 'We can fix that at the airport. What else?'

'As soon as I'm on my way, get hold of Oliver Ireton. Tell him to book me a first-class sleeper compartment, two people, return from Basel to Rome, travelling out on tonight's Loreley express. He'll have to move. It leaves at eight minutes to six. Tell him to go down to any of the big hotels in town and pick up the first expensive-looking girl who's got a clean passport handy. Tell him to pay her for twenty-four hours and put her on that train, in the compartment with the tickets. He can tell her I'll meet her at Lugano. All she's required to do is make the return trip to Rome.'

MacKinnon was looking at him as though he was demented. John threw up his hands to prevent the Scotsman protesting.

'One day I will explain. It does make sense, I promise. And finally, take this key.' He pulled it from his pocket, grabbed the first envelope on the desk, put the key inside it and scribbled out an address: to David Medina at the I T I offices in New York.

'When Caro gets back,' John explained, 'as soon as she gets back, courier this to New York. Get it off the premises as fast as you can. If she doesn't come back, if I don't come back, take it to my brother in D C. He'll know what it is and how to use it. Take what you find to Oliver Ireton. If we don't make it back, it's up to you two to decide what you do. But you must promise me, if Caro gets back, you'll courier it off, unless I'm here to tell you different. You must promise me that.'

MacKinnon was understandably suspicious. 'What's it the key to, John?'

Standing wanted to tell him. He wanted to be certain someone would know how much he had done, how much he had achieved, but he could not risk it. It was the last bargaining point he had, so all he could tell MacKinnon was, 'I promise you, Iain, it's better for you not to know.'

MacKinnon shook his head, absolving himself of responsibility. 'Fuck you, John. We'd better get you moving.' He put his head round the door of the office into the newsroom and bawled, 'I need some *men* and I need them now!'

John Standing took a deep breath, as though it might be his last. *I must have known*, he thought. *But no, I'm not that clever. Just training. Always leave yourself one safe dead-letter-box.* He had the German documents in his pocket, already sealed into an envelope, and addressed to his Post Office Box in Washington D C, the box to which MacKinnon had the key.

He would express the documents from the airport.

A brass-fronted box in Washington was the last safe place that he had left.

CHAPTER NINE

They took her north, on the coastal road, through Pisa and Genoa, where they cut across the Apennines towards Milan, before turning north through Lombardy to the Alps. It was eight in the evening before they approached Lake Maggiore, though the dwarf, who drove, had not dawdled at all.

They had given her no explanation. They would not even talk to her. Ezzo sat guiltily at her side, staring out of the window watching Italy unfold. It was some time before she would admit to herself what the raw metallic emotion in her stomach and her throat was. It was fear. She had been taken when she had been happy. She could not be certain of anything now.

They drove along the eastern edge of the long lake, past Stresa, before their path came off the main road into minor roads through fragrant woods. She could take no pleasure in the trees. Tonight they seemed intent on curling over her and cutting off the sky and all her hopes. She tried to remember all the twists and turnings of the road, but she was quickly lost. They came at last to a clearing, fronted by barbed-wire fences twelve feet high and a security gate. It was not until they had been checked through, by guards leading hungry-looking Dobermans, that she realized they were at the edge of an estate. There was a drive of over a mile through rolling country before she realized it surrounded one of the most spectacular houses she had ever seen. It was built into and on to the cliff's edge, in two wide tiers, looking down over the lake. She had some idea how much a house, location and grounds like this might cost. Her heart sank as she realized how few people she knew rich enough to own it all, and only one of them might have any cause to spirit her from Rome. Escape across the lake, at the foot of the cliff, seemed hopeless. There was no way back through the guards across the rolling hills or through the woods. Medina chose his secret places well. No one knew she was here. Only John Standing knew she was in Italy, and he might be anywhere now, almost certainly drunk.

The old man was waiting for them in the study. Even afraid, she was impressed, by antique Chinese carpets, simple Indian rattan furniture, and what she suspected was a Raphael *Christ Amongst the Sinners* on the wall. He saw her looking at it, and shook his head.

'No,' he said softly. His voice was almost kind. 'Not a Raphael, I'm afraid. A Giulio Romano. I can't say I'm wildly fond of the High Renaissance, as a collector at least. I own Raphaels because I must, and leave them in New York. Please sit down, my dear.' He did not extend the invitation to Ezzo. She was glad. She did not know Medina was deliberately drawing the distinction between a guest and one of his servants. 'Can we offer you a drink?' he asked.

'Gin and tonic.' There must be some sort of microphone and speaker system, she thought, for neither man moved or said a word, but the doors of the study opened and a butler came in, bearing a bottle of Gordon's, tonic, ice, slices of lemon and lime, and one already perfectly poured gin and tonic. He left the tray beside her and disappeared without bothering to ask if either of the gentlemen had changed their minds.

She was wondering if simple protest over her abduction might be best, but before she could decide Medina spoke again. He was apologizing.

'I am sorry about the dramatic character of your invitation here, but your arrival in Italy was so fortuitous I could not miss the chance of seeing you again and talking to you at last. And you might have refused a more formal invitation.'

Caro could not be bothered with his unctuous talk. 'Why am I here?' was what she wanted to know.

Medina stood with his back to the fire. The study was air-conditioned, so that even on summer evenings Medina could have an open fire if he chose to. He had thought, tonight, it might make her feel more at home. Evidently he was wrong.

He did not bother to tell her lies. 'I imagine John Standing told you everything?'

She snorted. 'I rather think he didn't. But he told me enough. And now you force me to believe him.'

The old man forced a thin smile. 'Oh, you must always believe John when he talks about me. The more fantastic he seems, the more truthful he is likely to be.'

'You must be feeling pretty pleased with yourself. Why reduce yourself to kidnapping a single woman, after overseeing the downfall of nations? And how long has he,' she jerked her head back towards the still-standing silent Spaccamonti, 'been in your employ?'

Medina shrugged. The movement was barely perceptible. He adapted himself to his surroundings. Here, in his study, with a lady, his manner was so physically discreet as to be virtually immobile. 'How should I know?' he asked. 'I do not personally follow the career paths of my minor executive officers. I did not even hire this one myself. But as to your question, yes, I am proud.' He smiled another wintry smile and quoted, '"I must be proud to see, Men not afraid of God afraid of me."'

Caro knew perfectly well she was not here to talk about the satires of Alexander Pope, but she still did not know what she was here for. 'You still haven't answered my question.'

And he still did not. 'Where are the German documents, Miss Kilkenny?'

She was genuinely puzzled. 'What German documents?'

He did not believe her. 'Oh, really, Miss Kilkenny, your loyalty to Mr Standing does you credit, but your thespian skills are woefully inadequate to the occasion. Where are the German documents?' He closed his eyes, slowly, cutting off the green light which seemed to be the focus of any room he stood in. The study felt suddenly desolate and cold. 'As you wish,' he whispered. 'I rather fancy Mr Standing will be with us shortly. I am sure he can supply the answer. But I hope for your sake he does not take too long, Miss Kilkenny, because if he is overly delayed I shall be forced to use other methods to get the information I need from you.'

Spaccamonti responded at last, to the threat, stepping forward and saying, 'No!'

Medina's eyes snapped open, the green fires alive again.

Spaccamonti went on talking. 'I never agreed to her being hurt . . .' he was saying.

Caro noticed the doors of the study opening. Ismail, Medina's secretary, was standing in the doorway flanked by two, very beautiful, young women, awaiting the old man's instructions.

Bodyguards, Caro thought. *He uses female bodyguards.* They must have been standing by, waiting, lest anything untoward should happen.

Either Spaccamonti ignored them or he had failed to hear their entry. All his attention was on Medina, who smiled, and jeered. 'I was not aware,' he said steadily, 'that you concerned yourself with the physical security of women.'

The magistrate blanched. 'Francchetti . . . Francchetti was different,' he stammered. 'She was one of our own . . .'

Medina's eyes flicked to his guards, a single, scarcely perceptible, basilisk, movement. One of the women stepped forward, towards the magistrate. Spaccamonti did notice her this time, and her approach made words tumble from him, 'No, I won't, I . . .' as he closed in on Medina.

That moment was enough. The woman was behind him, and hit him, hard, in the kidneys. As he staggered she raised her arm, half-turned, and struck him on the ear with the heel of her hand, felling him, to his knees, and shattering his eardrum.

Medina spoke quietly to the humiliated figure at his feet. 'There are people,' he explained, his courtesy imperturbable, as though nothing had happened, 'whom I pay for their advice. You are not one of them. They are welcome, indeed encouraged, to disagree with me. My servants are not.'

Spaccamonti kneeled before the old man in what looked almost like a pose of supplication. It did no good, for with one swift movement Medina reached down, jerking back Spaccamonti's head by pulling at his hair, and thrust his right thumb deep into the Italian's eye. One horrible scream filled the room, going on and on till it was joined by something else, by the sound of Caro screaming, too, as the old man pushed out the eye and pulled hard, severing the optic nerve. Ezzo fell back on the carpet, twitching, in shock, his voice a sustained sob, and blood surrounding the gaping hole in his face.

Medina looked towards Caro. She was crying. There was no gentleness in his voice as he said, 'I gather you have been some comfort to this man, Miss Kilkenny. Perhaps it would soothe him to share your bed tonight.'

Ismail led her from the room. The women carried Spaccamonti. As they went through the door Medina said again, 'I want those German papers, Miss Kilkenny.'

Then there was a hissing and foul burning as he threw the eye on to the fire.

John had couriered the envelope to Washington from the airport. Now he had to get to Italy without Medina tracking him. That was the object of the exercise. He hoped to hell Olly had done his stuff.

He knew Medina, and he was getting some sense of how close the old man had wormed to the country's corrupted centres of power. He had to assume all scheduled flights, ferries and trains into the country were being watched. As well as all the border posts. They would expect him to fly direct from London, but he could not take any chances. The only things he had going for him were that they did not know when to expect him, and the people doing the checking were Italians.

The Lear jet touched down at Lugano airfield. He was fortunate Switzerland catered for the rich. For the next twenty-four hours he had the balance of the credit against the account Medina had opened for him in New York to play with. The pilot had radioed ahead to have a car waiting to rush him to the station. He could only pray he was in time. He knew the Loreley passed through Chiasso just after ten thirty. It could not pass through Lugano very much earlier. He made it to the station, he later realized, with seven minutes to spare.

The stationmaster was wary of the strange American, trying to travel without a ticket. John explained again, in halting Swiss–Italian, that his travelling companion would be on the train with his ticket. When the express pulled in, he had to race down all the first-class carriages, waking people indiscriminately, the babbling stationmaster behind him, till he almost overshot a door with the name Standing scribbled on the card on its identification place.

'Here,' he cried, swinging open the door. The girl behind the door looked up.

'Mr Standing?' she asked.

He could have leapt for joy. 'You're American?'

She nodded, and handed him his ticket. He passed it to the stationmaster who checked it and retired defeated. John slumped into the compartment.

'That man Ireton is a fucking genius,' he said with passion. She raised her eyebrows. She was pretty. She could have been any college co-ed. She could have been his secretary. Or his daughter. He did not know whether or not to thank Ireton after all.

'Mr Ireton's the gentleman who hired me?' she asked.

'Never mind,' he told her, remembering his discretion. 'Did he tell you what I wanted?'

She giggled in confusion. He found it rather fetching. 'He said I was to take the return trip to Rome. I don't have a reservation for the return part. Will you organize that when we get to Rome?'

He shook his head. 'You'll have to do that yourself, I'm afraid. I'm not going as far as Rome.'

The train began to pull out of the station.

'Listen,' he told her, 'we don't have much time.' She adopted an earnest, almost studious, expression.

'This train crosses the border just beyond Chiasso,' he explained. 'It picks up the immigration and customs officials there. We're due to pass through Chiasso at ten thirty-seven.'

'You've got this pretty well organized, haven't you?' she said; kindly, he thought.

He had to disabuse her. 'Not really. Spur-of-the-moment decision.'

'You seem to know the train schedule pretty well.'

He laughed openly. 'I do. Let's just say it's for old times' sake. When I was very much younger, I used to fuck a lot on Alpine trains. Anyway, the point is, I have to be inside you from the time we hit Chiasso to the time they've finished the official checks.'

She was severe, and surprised. 'Can you keep it up that long?'

'I hope it won't be long. To be honest, I'm not sure I can get it up at all.'

She rolled her eyes up. 'Don't worry; working business hotels in Switzerland, raising the dead is my business.'

I like this kid, he thought, wildly. 'Why didn't I meet you half my life ago?'

'I probably wasn't born. What is this, vaudeville?'

He laughed again. He thought he must be getting hysterical. He had never laughed through fear before. 'Anyway, the reason you weren't told in Basel was that the man who hired you didn't know. So if there's an extra charge . . .'

She shook her head. 'You're covered. Twenty-four hours, straight sex. No specials. You're a smuggler, aren't you, or a runaway banker? Common criminals don't have friends like your old man in Basel.'

He had no intention of telling her. The less she knew, the less she could get hurt. 'You don't want to know. I promise you. It's not very terrible, but the less you know the better. I'm not going as far as Rome. We're taking that nameplate down now. You're going to forget you ever knew my name. If anyone comes to talk to you, you never saw me or heard of me. Understood?'

She nodded again. She was a sage child. He ripped his name out of the little frame on the carriage door. He knew he should have thought of it: should have had Olly use a false name. But it hardly mattered. That could have meant false papers, and he had none.

'This is just to get you past the officials, right?'

'Right.'

'Do you have any papers at all?'

He flashed his American passport and asked for hers. She gave it to him, smiling. He was not so indiscreet as to open it. He did not want to know her name.

'Well,' she said, grinning, 'get out of those clothes. Let's see if we can't run up Old Glory and see if anybody cheers.'

She was expert and gentle and attentive, and none of it seemed to work. She told him it would be best for his purposes if they did it standing, with his back to the door. She hooked her legs round his and crossed her hands behind his neck, grinding and bobbing and weaving across his naked flesh, to no avail.

'Pretty desperate case we got here, mister,' she admitted, as the train clanked into Chiasso. 'Drinker?'

He nodded.

She shook her head and sighed. 'Look what it's doing to you.' She thought for a moment. 'It's your face you don't want them to take too close a look at, right? Presumably they don't have any women guards who could identify the rest of you.' She thought some more.

'Lie down,' she ordered. He lay down on the lower bunk. They had not dropped the upper one yet. She made him turn so his head faced the door of the compartment. 'I know it puts you closer to them, but they're going to be so busy looking up my ass they won't even notice you're there.'

She straddled across him and took his penis in her mouth. It remained limp and flaccid, but they were not to know that from the door.

'OK,' she said cheerily, sitting up and almost smothering him as she dropped their passports on the floor, 'when they open the door, you start eating me out like fury. Leave the sound effects to me. You just hand them the passports. They won't notice a goddamn thing inside them.'

The train was moving again. They could hear the sounds of officials moving up the corridor. They did not have to wait long. When she heard them speaking to the occupants of the adjacent compartment she ground her pelvis into his face and took up his sorry penis once again. She did not so much moan as shout, 'Oh, yeah, baby, harder, do it again, yeah . . .'

John found it difficult not to laugh, so completely did she fulfil the grossest kind of masculine fantasy, but if he had laughed, he would have died, of suffocation,

As the door slid open, her cries and actions rose to a pitch of rococo sexual desperation, as she crashed into him like a power press. He reached for the passports, but out of the corner of his eye he could see the officials' stupefaction as her rump rose and swayed and plummeted while she, forgetting the lessons of her childhood, cried, mouth full, 'Oh, baby, baby, yeeeeah!'

They waved the passports aside, wishing him good luck, and took one last awed look at the performance, before reverently closing the door on the overwhelming power of such sexuality.

They had to fight to suppress their giggles till the guards had passed on to the next carriage, giving them quick résumés of the original gala performance to speed them on their way.

When they were gone, she dressed quickly, her business done. 'I hope you realize,' she said sweetly, 'I charge extra for specials.'

He paid her with pleasure. He was glad that because of her profession she had not expected to come, or both of them would have been disappointed. He felt as though he himself would never come again.

The train pulled into Milan a quarter of an hour before midnight. She already lay slumbering on the lower bunk, evidently exhausted by the dramatic intensity of her performance. Or was it just youth, he wondered, which could forget so much so easily because it had so much more life to live? He kissed her as he left.

He hired a car at the station, paying in cash, to the deep suspicion of the clerk. He had to hand over his passport as identification. After that he took off like a demon possessed, before Medina could trace the booking. For the moment he wanted simply to get away, away from anywhere Medina's agents might be looking, because at some stage he would have to announce himself, and he wanted to be safely out of the way. He suspected there were only two places the old man could be. He imagined Caro would be there too. Either they would be in Rome, as the centre of Italian communications. Or they would be in the Lakes. Medina had had houses on both sides of Maggiore for years, it was said, so that he could skip back and forth across the Swiss border

384

using the lake as his highway. John guessed he was there, but it *was* guesswork. For the moment, he drove away from both places, away from the routes Medina and his people would expect him to follow. He was heading for Ferrara, a hundred and fifty miles to the east in the Po valley, on the grounds that nobody ever did.

He drove carefully, keeping within all speed restrictions, observing all traffic signals. The last thing he wanted was to be picked up on some driving technicality. He found he enjoyed driving. It took as much and yet as little concentration as drinking. Perhaps that was why he could not do them both.

He pulled into Ferrara a little after three. It was a sleepy town, one of many in Italy which had brief moments of glory when governed by and for the Papacy, or by the Este dukes, or in the time of Savonarola, with Tasso its most famous native son, but which mainly had been what it was now, an insignificant market centre for the rich farming country about it. One thing about it always made him feel at home, however, or rather gave it a homely feeling; it was built almost entirely of brick, rather than the plastered walls and stone and marble to which other Italian cities aspired. He parked his car in the square below the monumental oppressive castle and started looking for a hotel. He found two within ten minutes, and settled on the Astra. It looked more used to dealing with the international business traveller, if anything in this town could be. That was how he had to pass himself off. In a way, it was exactly what he was. He did have business to settle.

The night porter was chary of him, but he managed to explain he was an English businessman whose car was giving him some trouble, so he had pulled in here rather than continue through the night to Livorno. If they would believe that, he thought, they would believe anything.

They would believe anything. When the porter showed him to his room he asked for an outside line to be connected to the phone. It took some organization, but finally it was done.

There was another struggle with the international operator, the night porter chipping in periodically while listening to the call. John sincerely wished him joy of it. There were things he was better off not knowing or hearing, even if he did not understand a word.

It was four o'clock in the morning, ten the previous evening New York time, before he got through to Medina's secretariat, for his second little chat in less than a week. He told them to get hold of Medina, on an extension of this number, or to have a number where the old man could be reached waiting for him, when he called again, at eight a.m. Italian time.

It was all that he could do, for now. He had to believe Caro would be safe at least until his second call. All he could do was think and prepare. As last desperate hopes, he telephoned Spaccamonti's home number again, to no response, and the Hotel Raffaele, where Caro had not been seen at all since her last departure. He took a shower and lay down for a few miserable sleepless hours. But the lack of sleep was some consolation. He could no longer bear his dreams.

It was morning. It was time for him to try. He did not see how he could hope to do it, but he had to try. The only power he had was information. The only weapon he had was what he carried in his head.

He put his second call through to the secretariat. This time he did not have to bother about keeping the call below three minutes. It did not matter if they traced him now. At this distance, they could not know what route he might take, or how he might approach them.

The call was short in any case. Medina was expecting him.

'I have Kilkenny, Standing,' he said, without any introduction.

'I know,' John answered, 'and I have the German papers. They are as safely out of the country as I am in it. You couldn't stop me finding them. You failed. I want her back.'

'I want the papers.'

'Something can be arranged. Where are you?'

Medina gave him the details. 'When should I expect you?' the old man asked.

'When I come,' John Standing replied.

*

386

He took the most direct route. The high road, through Bologna, Modena, Parma, Piacenza, past Milan to the southern tip of the lake. All the way there something told him he had already lost. Somehow, long ago, before he was really conscious of what he was, he had made himself unfit for this last venture. All he could do was try.

He skirted the eastern shore of the lake, following the telephone directions. A couple of miles out from where the fringes of Medina's estate should be he pulled off the road and hid the car. He set off through the woods. He wanted to take a look. He did not want to drive blithely on, only to find Medina had set an ambush for him.

What worried him most was the thought that Medina might simply lose patience. What if he decided to kill Caro and John in any case, without recovering the papers? But that did not feel right for Medina. Medina was a methodical man. He would suspect that John had made arrangements for the papers to be recovered in the event of accidents. The papers might not mean very much at first, but they would do, given time. It was a risk Medina was unlikely to take. They gambled the same way.

At the edge of the woods John almost walked straight into the high barbed-wire fence. He had to pull himself back into the trees. The wires hummed, giving off an acrid ozone odour. Electrified. That might help. But Medina was bound to have his own generator and a power-loss override. Was there anything to be gained by a noisy entrance? John thought so. He had instructed the old man to phone to warn his goons of his impending arrival, not that you could ever be sure with Camorra, which is what he assumed they were. But at least a proper entrance would teach Medina not to take him for granted. Anything, anything at all, might help.

He headed back towards the car, skirting the main road from the estate, noting the long downhill slope to the gates, secured by two armed guards. It was exactly what he needed. Could he kill people, if he had to? The question almost amused him. It had seemed so simple and so casual on the Ragged Island cays. That had been thoughtless, unreflected reaction, however. Could he do it now? He could only find out by trying.

He drove the car to the estate, stopping just below the crest of the hill whose long slope rolled towards the gates. He opened both the front doors. Then he started the car and put it in gear and set it off along the road to the estate, lying on the floor, his head hanging out behind the door, holding the accelerator down by hand.

He heard them shouting to the car to stop as it approached. He heard them yelling when they noticed it had no driver. Then the shots began, punching out the windscreen and puncturing the on-side tyre. The car began to pull to the left. He waited till the last moment, what he judged to be the last moment, through the shouting and the gunfire, and reached up to pull right on the steering-wheel hard. The car began to spin. He jumped out as it breached the gates and the electrified fence side-on, shorting the circuts in showers of sparks and sending the guards flying. He leapt through the gate to the first guard, crushed beneath the car, and tore his holster open, lifting the hand-gun and snapping off the safety catch in a single movement to pick out the second guard. He pulled, and watched as the man's head exploded. Somewhere in the distance he could hear alarms begin to sound, and dogs begin to bark.

John picked up the telephone in the guardhouse and told the startled switchboard operator, 'Tell Medina Standing's here.' Then he set off to the nearest clump of trees.

He moved from grove to grove as all the guards made their way towards the wreckage at the gate. In fifteen minutes he was in sight of the house. What worried him were the dogs. He heard Ismail's voice on the tannoy instructing the goons to hold their fire.

Where he wanted to be was on the other side of the wall along the clifftop. It would mask him from the house and from the grounds, and it ran all the way long the front of the house. The wall could give him access. He ran for it, and got over it in a scramble.

It was low drystone, with barely a foot of crumbling soil between it and the empty air. He had dreamed of places like it before. It took what seemed an age before he could control the panic and the sweat. He would fall. He was afraid to fall.

He could not look. He could only squirm his way blindly forward, as soil slipped away beneath his hands, his knees, his feet. The wall was the only security he had. He pressed himself against it. He forced himself to go onward.

The voices seemed further away. They were not expecting him here. If he could only force himself onwards he would arrive before the house. He could not judge how far he had come. He did not dare look to take his bearings. He could only guess.

It must be here. He had come far enough. It felt like hours bicycling in empty air. He could not stand the sliding topsoil very much longer. He launched himself upward, over the wall, the ground giving way below his feet as he did so, so that he had to hand himself over on to the patio, and into the jaws of the Doberman.

What he felt was pain, pain overwhelming fear, suddenly absolute pain grinding his gun arm. Then the thing was on him, big, snuffling, rank and animal, tearing at him with its claws, drowning him in its stench and mindless violence, trying to rip the rest of him open with its feet, while the jaws on his arm blanked out any hope or thought of opposition.

There was something like an explosion, as if the animal exploded flying from him, its unkillable jaws dragging the flesh from his arm, remaining locked, wedded to his bone, while the rest of it lay strung out in fur and blood and entrails.

The woman holding the .357 Magnum at the shattered animal shifted it so its stubbly solid barrel poked at him.

'Come on in, Virginian,' Marsha Morgan said.

CHAPTER TEN

'No, Iain,' Mike Thomas explained again, 'There is damn all I can do.'

The voice on the grey telephone exploded, 'Oh, come on, you damn Goth, hasn't he done enough for you? These people aren't screwing around. Two of my people's places have been gutted, and Caro's gone missing. All John asked for is a little help. Just notify the Italian police, for God's sake.'

Mike Thomas felt tired of explaining. He also felt ashamed. 'I can't Iain. Report what? A grown woman's gone to Italy. Believed to be spending the weekend with a responsible adult. Male. Who's away from home at the moment. If we asked police forces to go chasing after that, there wouldn't be a safe adulterer anywhere in Europe. She isn't a missing person, Iain. She's a grown woman gone to Italy for a fuck.'

MacKinnon's voice was quieter, but no calmer. 'You bastard, Mike. You know, don't you? You know what's going on. You know it's the same mob as killed Hart, and Alan, and you're just letting Caro and John walk into it, straight into it. Who warned you off? Whose filthy bloody business is this?'

Thomas was silent for a while, wondering what he could say. At last he whispered, 'Stay out of it, Iain. It's no longer our affair. From my point of view it's a narcotics investigation in New York. Nothing more. If we all stay out of it, if John keeps his head, they might just get out of it alive. But it's out of my hands, and yours. If you don't believe me, contact the Italian police yourself and see how far you get.'

'Don't worry. I will.'

The line went dead.

Mike Thomas telephoned the Foreign Office.

Later, in final desperation, MacKinnon called Robert Standing. He wanted to know what the key was for. Robert's heart sank as he listened to the Scotsman. He could guess. He had taught his brother the trick himself. But there was nothing he could say.

Could he notify his own people in Italy? There was no hope of it. The Agency was compromised too deeply in this affair already. He had inflicted too many wounds on it of late to ask it to come to the aid of the man who had forced him into action. He could only trust to whatever might be left of John's good sense.

'All, I can tell you,' he said, 'is that John's thrown away the rule-book. If he's gone in alone and wild, there's no one can help him. But, Mr MacKinnon, I know my brother. There's always been some method in his madness. If he's flying solo, without support or back-up, it must mean he doesn't believe that anyone can help. I don't know what the key is for,' he lied, 'I can only tell you to do exactly what John asked of you. In the end, it's his responsibility.'

That was the word. Responsibility. The word which had always divided them. They had both wanted so much the same things. What they had always disagreed on was the means, the responsible course of action.

To act alone, or in concert.

Robert knew his own way was safer. He wondered if it was better. He wondered if it mattered.

Oh, yes, he thought. It mattered.

It mattered to the dead.

Caro wondered if she was going mad. She had lain awake all night, watching Ezzo shake and moan. He had had all his dignity stripped from him, all his manhood. She could not bear it. She could not bear to witness his collapse, could not bear to consider his betrayal, to think that each time he had lain with her, held her, he had been ready to throw her away, to cast her into Medina's murderous clutches.

Morning had spared her. They had returned her to the monastic, sound-proofed drawing-room where, two hours earlier, Medina had joined her. He had ignored her all that time, smiling to himself as he read, something in a Middle Eastern script, a book of poems it looked like. He looked up quiz-zically as the intercom came to life. It was a woman's voice. American.

'Mr Standing is here to see you, sir,' it said, and for an instant Caro's stomach turned over in hope. And then she realized he must be here because of her, and that there was no hope left, if he had had to come.

Medina smiled, his green eyes calm in the clear light. 'Send him in.'

There was a pause before the woman spoke again. 'Very good, sir. Will you need . . .'

Medina cut her off. 'No. Thank you. He is quite harm-less.'

The door slid open soundlessly. As John stepped in, his clothes crumpled and grubby and grey as his face, Medina murmured, '"Closing your mouth this side, open it there . . ."'

As he looked back down at the book, John completed the verse: '"Your shout of triumph will ring in the unbounded air." Jalal al-Din. I'd thought I might merit Hafiz.' He looked over at Caro, and for an instant she wanted to rise and go to him and weep in his arms, the arms of someone she could finally trust, but something in his eyes, some warning, some final exhaustion, held her back.

Medina seemed marginally impressed. 'I didn't know you had a taste for Arab and Persian poetry.'

John shrugged. 'A little. In translation.' He looked at Medina directly now. 'I know it's a poem about death. And I know that Caro doesn't know a thing.'

It was Medina's turn to shrug. 'I'd expect you to say that. It goes with being a gentleman. It goes with being here at all.'

Standing shook his head, his long grey hair falling into his eyes. 'No. Not any more. My being here's the proof she doesn't know. If she knew, I'd have had to publish. I'd have had to assume you'd get it out of her, and get to the docu-ments, and kill her. So there wouldn't be any point in not publishing. As it is, she doesn't know. Only I do. Which means we still have some room for negotiation.'

Medina put down his book. 'Unless I kill you both now,' he said gently.

Standing smiled. 'I have taken certain precautions. There's only one left to put in place.' He nodded to Caro. 'She mustn't know. Get her out of here.'

Caro felt sick, almost abandoned, but she checked herself. John sounded calm. He sounded as though he knew what he was doing. And he was the only person she had left to trust.

Medina nodded, and the door slid open once again. There must be hidden cameras, she thought. She looked at John. He nodded too, and she stepped out into the antechamber where Medina's guards and secretaries sat.

'Disconnect the mikes,' Standing snapped.

'Disconnect,' Medina whispered.

The two men sat down and considered each other in silence.

'Cigarette?' Medina asked at last. John waved the offer aside. 'Drink?' John grinned but said nothing.

Make the old man wait, he thought. *Make the old man sweat.*

But Medina was almost abstracted as he spoke. 'I want the German documents.'

'I know.'

The old man closed his eyes. The action made the whole room seem several degrees warmer. 'Where are they?'

'Safe.'

Medina drew in his breath and said, without any great force, 'You aren't.'

Standing could only acknowledge the truth of it by bowing his head. It was his turn. 'Let us go and you'll get them back.'

Medina shook his head. 'Even if I believe you, even if she doesn't know, you do. While you're alive, it doesn't matter what I get back. I know that you only took one copy in Dusseldorf, but I don't know how many more you've taken since then. And even if there is only one set, if I let you go you can always get another. I can't let you go.'

The silence came down again as they both looked out over the grounds and, in the distance, the glinting waters of the lake. There was something about Medina's mood Standing could not quite fathom. Then he realized what it was. The old man was sad. He wanted a way out of this. He didn't want John Standing to die. He didn't want to be alone. A strange, foolish hope began to rise in the big American. It had to be worth a try.

'You know, of course, I've made arrangements for the documents if Caro doesn't survive?'

Medina nodded; he had assumed that.

'It was good, David. It was genius. Only one direct link into the money circle, and that across a border. Brilliant. But it's falling apart, isn't it? Cocaine, David? Thugs in London? Kidnapping women? That isn't you. It's falling apart. Because you had to use the Neapolitans. And now all you want is for it to be over, because you've done everything your clients asked, you've had the intellectual satisfaction of proving it could be done and, in me, the pleasure of an audience. But now you just want it finished. Let's do it, David. Let's close it down.'

'I was closing it down. Then you closed in.'

'It's not important. We can deal. The documents for Caro.'

The old man sighed, impatient, disbelieving. 'And what about you?'

'The documents for me and Caro.'

Medina shook his head. 'The trouble is your wretched integrity. Don't you think that if she believed you'd sold that for her, she'd do her damnedest to track down your last moves, to try to buy you back?'

Standing cut in on him. 'There is a way. There is a way to capitalize on her fear. She's scared half to death as it is. What did you do to her?' He tried to keep his voice level as he asked it.

The old man seemed almost embarrassed. 'I ... I hurt someone.'

'The Italian?' Medina nodded. 'You should have killed him.'

This time the old man smiled. 'I will,' he said.

'There is a way,' John repeated, 'with Miss Morgan's help.'

*

Outside, Medina's aides leapt to attention as the intercom crackled back into life, but Caro was locked too deep inside herself to hear Medina's quiet voice saying, 'Miss Morgan, please bring Miss Kilkenny in here.' She was too damaged to pay much attention as the blonde took her by the arm and ushered her back into the drawing-room. But, tensing at the sight of their enemy again, she was not too absent to notice the sudden look of bewilderment on John Standing's face at the sight of the woman who had brought her in, and the way he began to say something but then thought better of it.

And she was perfectly conscious as she heard Medina say, 'Miss Kilkenny, I do hope, for all our sakes, that you can make Mr Standing here see reason.'

The blonde and two other guards led them away. Not back to the room Caro had been brought from, where Ezzo Spaccamonti still lay bleeding, but down below the heart of the house, into its cellars, down long grey institutional corridors, till they came to an airless, windowless room, lit by strip-lights and fronted by a grey steel door. As they were let into the cell, Caro saw the blonde looking at John and wondering if she only dreamed, or in fact saw, him barely noticeably shake his head.

But as the door clanged shut, all such thinking fell from her, leaving her a victim to pain and to despair. She began to cry, soundlessly. John folded her into his arms saying, over and over again, 'Oh, my dear, oh, my dear.'

Two hours later, the blonde came back alone. John spoke as soon as she stepped into the narrow room. 'Are we miked in here?'

The woman shook her head. Caro lay on the cot in the corner of the cell, blinking, bewildered.

John half turned to her, casually, saying, 'Caro, this is Marsha Morgan. We met in the Caribbean. She saved my life.'

Marsha shook her head, her blonde hair rising, exasperated. 'Honey,' she said, 'why in hell d'you come here?'

John made no apology. 'I didn't think I had a choice.'

395

Marsha sat down on the bed next to Caro. 'You have something he wants. Badly.' John started to speak but she ignored him. 'No, sugar, I don't want to know what it is. Seems to me the less I know the safer I am.'

Standing buried his hands into his ruined jacket pockets, looking down on her shining head. 'It's big enough to keep us safe, all of us safe, if we can get out of here. Getting out's the problem.'

Marsha laughed. 'Sure is, after the mess you made on the way in.' John shrugged. She looked him in the eyes steadily, weighing his resolve, evaluating his honour. At last she said, 'I'd have to come too. I wouldn't want to die.'

John nodded, once. She looked back down, at her fingernails, refusing to look at John and Caro, as though even speaking to them was a betrayal. 'It has to be the Lake,' she whispered at last. 'We have to get out of Italy, and it's the only way we'd have a chance.'

Standing rubbed his eyes, scratching the stubble on his cheeks. 'There is someone who could help us, on the other side,' he said, 'if you can get hold of him. If you can get to a phone.'

She looked at him again. 'I'll see what I can do,' she said.

Iain MacKinnon was half-asleep at his desk when the call came through from Oliver Ireton, was woken by one of his subs calling across the newsroom, 'Iain! Olly, Basel.'

The Scotsman dived across his desk to his own phone shouting, 'Put him through.' He gave Ireton no chance to speak before asking, 'Anything, Olly? Anything?'

The old Italy hand paused, and when he spoke he sounded many more miles distant than was possible. 'I don't know, Iain. I don't know.' He paused and MacKinnon waited, recognizing the silence for what it was. It was fear. 'I've had a call, Iain. Woman. American. Said she was speaking for John. Said to get a motor launch, and to get it to the borderline on Lake Maggiore at midnight tonight. She said she'd be bringing them out.'

MacKinnon licked his lips. For the first time in years he could feel his own pulse, could hear the beating of his heart.

'Do it, Olly. Please do it. No one else will help us. Them. Please do it.'

Another silence, longer this time, then, 'Iain, it's Italy. Across that border I'm a dead man. How do I . . . It could be grand slam . . .'

MacKinnon closed his eyes, cradling his head in his spare hand, pleading. 'I can't make you do it, Olly. And I can't get there in time myself. I don't know what's going on any more. I only know there's been a complete close-down by the authorities. If you don't help them, I don't know who will. But I can't make you do it because, because you're right. It could be . . . Oh, Christ, Olly.'

Connected only by wire and a small electric pulse, two ageing men sat at opposite ends of Europe and silently shared fear and loathing and despair. It was Ireton who broke the silence. 'If I come out of this alive, you Glaswegian bastard, I never want to see you in a pair of Guccis.' MacKinnon hung from the phone, half smiling, half wanting to cry, but Ireton was suddenly practical. 'And don't you dare query the expense,' he said.

Robert Standing sat in his rocker in the Georgetown apartment, aching for a bourbon. Not yet, he told himself.

He had to think. He had to work out what to do. What was John doing? Did John know what he was doing? A key. Dead-letter-box. Where? Why? What was it best to do? If John had laid his plans properly, doing anything was the worst thing to do. Never shift a lifeline a man's put down himself. But Italy? And Medina?

Could you let your brother walk into the inferno without trying somehow to help? What was the right thing to do?

He hardly noticed Eleanor come in, but his niece had noticed him. 'What is it?' she asked. 'I've never seen you like this.'

No, he thought, *you haven't.* No operation ever made him feel like this. Not even the ones he had not known about. The ones the Agency screwed up and he had to sort out afterwards. The last time he'd felt like this Eleanor had not even been born. The end of 1963, after Jack Kennedy had been blown away, and he realized how deeply, and how dumbly the Agency had been involved. The afternoon the man who had had the job he now held had called him in and asked his help in dealing with it. Jesus, with such friends . . .

Eleanor had fixed him a bourbon, brought it to him, looked him squarely in the face, and asked, 'Is it Daddy?' When he did not reply she rolled her eyes up, looked up, at the ceiling, as though she was trying not to cry. 'It is Daddy.' She shook her head. 'What's he done this time?'

Robert Standing sat back in his rocker, sipped his booze, and answered, 'I wish to God I knew.'

Far away in Italy, Caro Kilkenny lay sleeping in John Standing's arms. When she woke he was stroking her hair and whispering to her, something she could not understand. His voice was soothing in the darkness, and the cell seemed darker. Somehow she guessed it must be night. She drifted to sleep again, feeling almost safe. He went on with his whispering, reciting, something remembered from his childhood.

She could not tell what time it was when Marsha came for them. Caro never really would understand what happened. But she would remember she shied when Marsha came in bearing guns.

'MAC Ten,' she said, handing one of the squat, boxy machine pistols to John. 'Best I could do. You know how to use it?'

'Yes.'

'Her?' pointing one of the pistols at Caro, who backed deeper away, as though she were trying to bury herself in the wall. John shook his head. Marsha looked displeased, but let it pass. She had more important matters to deal with. 'The boats are kept in an artificial cave cut into the cliff face,' she explained. 'There are two ways down. There are stairs cut in the cliff, but they're no use to us, because the house and grounds are crawling with Neapolitans and even I couldn't get you past them. But there's also a lift down. If we get to that we've only got the two guards in the cave to deal with. You'll let me out of the lift first, and keep the door open. I'll be able to deal with the first one, but you'll probably have to

398

take the second one yourself. If you can do it without shooting, so much the better. OK?'

John nodded. Caro did not. 'What about Ezzo?' she whispered. Even now, even in her current state, she could not quite bear the thought of leaving the man she had let touch her so deeply to Medina's revenge.

'Oh, darling,' Marsha said, shaking her head, as though explaining to an injured child, 'he's been a long time dead.'

Their footsteps seemed to echo down the long grey corridors for ever, loud enough to stir both the living and the dead. But no one came for them, no one pursued. They were alone, except for Caro, who travelled hereafter in the company of her own anxiety. At last the lift doors hushed behind them, and they began the long descent to the surface of the Lake. Marsha returned her pistol to the holster strapped into her armpit.

Then they waited, as they dropped into the darkness and their futures. The opening of the doors, when it came, took Caro by surprise. She had almost hoped their journey would last for ever, that they would be entombed in the relative safety of this small metal world.

Marsha stepped out into the brightly lit docking-bay cut out of the cliff-face. John pressed the Doors Open button and stood back against the side of the lift, trying to hold himself and Caro out of sight. They could hear Marsha enter into conversation with the two men guarding the boats, speaking a soft, sibillant, lightly accented Italian. Then they heard a grunt, a shout of surprise and dismay, and a heavy falling sound, as Marsha punched the first guard in the kidneys. John swung out of the lift, raised the machine pistol, drew a sight on the second guard, and ignored Marsha's startled shout of 'No!' and squeezed the trigger.

The powered rounds roared like explosions in the confined space of the cavern. The guard's body lifted on impact, half turning in mid air, and sprayed blood like confetti.

The automatic alarms went off, klaxons wailing into the night. John took Caro by the hand and almost threw her out of the lift. Then he stepped back into it, firing a burst into the control panel, which split open in a sudden shower of sparks. He raised the pistol above his head and fired again, burst after burst, spraying them, ripping out the roof, and smashing the mechanism above beyond recovery.

As he stepped back into the cavern, he saw Marsha standing mute and stunned while Caro stood clutching her ears and wailing at the hellish noise. The second guard was still on the landing jetty where Marsha had felled him. Standing walked over to him, with steady deliberation, put the muzzle of the pistol against the prone man's head and fired again. The skull exploded, showering bone fragments and pink and white gobbets of brain against his clothes.

There were two boats moored at the jetty, the foremost a long sleek cigarette boat, the other a launch. John moved to the bows of the cigarette boat and began to cast off. Marsha and Caro stood motionless.

'Get in,' he snapped.

They broke into movement like puppets coming to life.

'Start her up,' he told Marsha, and continued on down the jetty to the launch. He stepped aboard and raised the pistol again, shooting out the controls, in a crash of broken glass, torn steel, tangled cables. Then he moved aft, making out the fuel tanks, and fired again and again and again till at last sparks and vapour met and a first spit of flame licked across the deck.

He stepped out of the launch without any sense of hurry and walked back to the cigarette boat. Marsha was already gunning its engines. He stepped in.

They roared out of the cave, into the still dark waters of the Lake, just as the first tanks on the launch exploded, filling the dock with a flower of smoke and flame, as particoloured as a bruise.

'What the hell was that about?' Marsha asked. John did not reply. 'Did you have to kill them?' she added, as they raced into the clean night air, leaving the carnage and klaxons behind them.

John blinked, and his throat was dry as he spoke. 'They owed us two,' he said. 'For Tom. And Alan.'

*

Oliver Ireton went cold when he heard the dull spit of gunfire on the far shore of Lake Maggiore. If he strained, he thought he could hear the thin fly's buzzing of engines. He hoped that he was right. Some ten yards away, by his best estimation, the invisible border lay across the water, marking entry to a country where the time of year was always open season for Ireton, and a language which, for him, had no future tense.

He hoped they were coming. He hoped they would come soon. He was too close to Italy, and to death, not to be afraid.

The buzzing drew closer, turning to a roar. His lamps were low, but they must see him, surely, in the darkness. He fired the engine, preparing, not knowing what he might be waiting for, expecting only to have to run. To run forever if necessary.

The cigarette boat slowed down as it approached, its pale wash luminescent, hissing in the night. Three figures. He recognized Caro, and the tall stooping figure of John Standing, like some ghastly revenant from the far side of death, but he did not recognize the third, the woman. The American who had called? He had no way of knowing. Ignorance made him afraid.

The unknown woman steadied the cigarette boat alongside Oliver's launch. The only sounds were the turning of the engines and the unhappy lapping of the wild waters of the lake. They had not been pursued.

John handed Caro across into the launch. Ireton waited for him to follow, but he did not stir. He spoke instead. 'Get her back, Olly. As soon as you're somewhere safe on the other side, phone MacKinnon. He knows what to do. In a few hours you'll be safe.'

Ireton suddenly felt old. 'What about you?' he asked, hopelessly.

Standing shook his head. 'For you two, it's finished, but not for me, not yet. Get her back home, Olly, and tell them all to forget it. The old man had it all stitched up and there's nothing she can do.'

'What about you?' Ireton's voice was expressionless, but

both men knew what the question meant. It meant: *Forget it. Come home.*

John shook his head. 'It isn't over for me, Olly. It can't be. I have to finish this. So does the old man.'

Ireton bowed his head. He looked as though he was praying. 'What about your friend?'

Standing grinned, his mouth a sudden flash in the darkness. 'Sometimes even I get lucky,' he said.

Ireton tried to think of something to say, something simple, something direct, something undamaged by whatever madness John Standing might be planning now, but all he could manage to call across the darkness was, 'Take care.'

The words hung futile on the air. Then they both gunned their engines and slewed the boats back to the opposing shores from which they had come.

As the cigarette boat passed back into Italian waters, out of sight and earshot, Marsha Morgan raised her machine pistol to John Standing's temple and said gently, 'I think I'll have that gun back now, honey, if you please.'

CHAPTER ELEVEN

Medina was waiting for them when they returned to the burnt-out wreckage of the docking-bay. The old man was surrounded by his own people. The Neapolitans had retreated, with the corpses of their soldiers.

The old man looked about him as the cigarette boat drew in and he asked, 'Was all this really necessary?' John did not bother to reply. As he stepped out of the boat, Medina placed a strong hand on his shoulder saying, 'If you try to cheat me, I will unleash Cutullo's people. And they will destroy everything. As it is, they would take great delight in killing you slowly.'

John shook himself free. 'I don't have anything left to cheat you with, David,' he said. 'You win. As usual.'

Medina smiled. 'We shall need your fingerprints, of course. And photographs.'

John looked down into the old man's green impassive eyes. They were as clear as conquest. 'Yes,' he said. 'Of course.'

Seventeen hours later they met again. And then again, four hours after that, just the three of them, for the last time, in the cool of the evening air, on the long lawn down from the house to the cliff face. What John had wanted most, in those intervening hours, once the formalities were done, was sleep, but it was the one thing he could not have. The whole estate had been in uproar, as the machinery of Medina's administration had been ripped out for transfer to his house on the other side of the Lake, in Switzerland; the other half of the twin bases from which he had run his empire for half a century. He had meant it, John thought. He was closing it all down, his commission accomplished.

And now the old man was in a good mood. 'Very simple, John. Very intelligent. To put the documents into transit.

Even I could not arrange to sift every parcel in the post or with a courier.'

'Your people have been to D C, then?'

'Yes. After you explained what the key was for. The documents were waiting for them. Welcome to I T I, John. We both waited far too long.'

Standing shrugged, noncommittal. His grey face lined and unresponsive as stone in the long evening light. 'What happens now?' he asked.

Medina was practical. He had some experience of disposing of the dead. 'I had thought,' he said, 'since the magistrate's build was so similar to your own, that we might simply char the body, and return it with your fingerprints and photographs. You will have died in a car crash. We still have the wreckage of the vehicle you arrived in.' The old man smiled, urbane as ever. 'However, what with dental records and new deep-scanning techniques of the finger-pads even in burn victims, that would be unsafe, so we will return his ashes instead.'

John swallowed. His throat felt so dry he doubted he would ever eat properly again. A lifetime's alcohol, and a dry throat, now. 'What about Spaccamonti's records? You don't have a corpse for him.'

Medina was untroubled. 'That is an Italian matter, and therefore unimportant. Cutullo's people will see to it. Just as they will see to the provision of legal papers attesting to your death. There is more than one corrupt judge in Italy. Welcome back from the grave, Mr Standing. In a few days we shall have to set to work providing you with a new personality. A new history.'

Standing rose, turning away from the old man. 'I have never believed in the resurrection of the dead,' he whispered. There was a long silence, then he spoke again, turning back to Medina.

'I am sorry,' he said simply. 'Betrayal hurts. Even betraying you. But you left me no choice. In the end, you wanted everything, and no one gets everything, David. Not even you. I did what I did so that no more innocent people should suffer. This was always only between me and you. I think you know that now.'

The cigarette he was holding was burnt down almost to the filter. A sudden breeze caught at the tip, which glowed a pale orange fire, a few sparks scattering, dead before they reached the grass. Standing spoke again.

'I can't work for you. I never could. I think you knew that, really, though you did not want to know it. I have accomplished what I came here for. This is the end.'

He turned his back on Medina again, and took a first hesitant step towards the cliff-face.

The old man's voice was gentle, distant, sad. 'Where are you going, John?'

Standing stopped, refusing to turn, refusing to look at Medina. He tried to swallow again, but the muscles of his mouth and throat refused to work. His voice was hoarse. 'I understand there are steps cut in that cliff-face, down to the landing stage. I'm going down those steps. I'm going to take the cigarette boat. I'm going home.'

There was still no anger in Medina's voice. John had counted on his rage. The old man's gentleness almost made him falter now. 'Oh, John,' he said, 'if you try to leave me now, you are going to die.'

Standing shook his head, still refusing to turn around. Instead he cast a glance to one side, where Marsha Morgan stood, a look of sorrow on her lovely face.

'All men die,' he half explained. 'And if I die, you will find it that much easier to settle this affair. Two dead bodies, for two dead men. And in the end, the difference between us is, I do not want to live for ever.'

He began to walk, unsteadily at first, but finally with purpose, the grass springy beneath his feet, the day's last light filling the lake before him, and told himself: *I will not be afraid. Not now. Though all things end, not all things fail.*

'John,' Medina whispered, almost pleading.

Standing ignored him, went on walking, thinking: *When all hope is gone, everything is simple. You do what you can. You leave the reckoning to others.*

He was almost at the cliff's edge, the fencing still torn from his first entrance, close by the steps which led to freedom or the grave. He wondered if there was any difference.

'Stop, John,' Medina called again. 'Stop, please. Stop *now*.'

John thought of Caro, broken by her final vision of the powers of this earth, and prayed she would be well. He thought of Oliver Ireton, who had come, as he had come, despite his fear, into the place of death. He thought of Mac-Kinnon, and almost smiled, knowing better than any the passion for truth and the inevitability of failure which animated the Scotsman's unforgiving soul. He thought of Robert, his brother, the best of men in the worst of trades, and wondered what the world was that it deserved such good men when it went so ill. He thought of Eleanor, and hoped she could be happy, hoped she could find for herself all the things he had failed as a father to provide. And he thought of the dead; of Tom Wellbeck and Alan Clarke, Ezzo Spaccamonti and Zara Francchetti, of the priests and the colonel, and the bankers. All mortal, all caught in humankind's uncertain state. And he thought at last of Emily, his dead, defeated, damaged daughter.

Then he heard the small steel slide of a gun-bolt pulling back, and he thought: *I will not die like this, cut down like a beast at slaughter. This is my life to dispose of, not his. At the end, the best thing we can hope for, is an instant to be free.*

Before him, the cliff-face fell away, down to the gold and black relentless waters of the Lake. Pale yellow light lay on the mountain-tops, a few miles, and a life, away.

Medina turned, back towards the house, his face set in a mask a stranger might have taken for grief, and whispered, without inflection or expression. 'Kill him. Now.'

And then John Standing jumped, outward, over the fencing, into the empty air. For an instant, diving from the wall, it looked as though he might, at long last, fly.

Marsha Morgan, with pity in her heart, and a knowledge of the way the world is in her head, and a pistol in her hands, fired, and fired, and fired again.

The gunfire cut through his body, snapping it almost in half, jacking it double, and Nature and Newton's laws asserted their uncompromising powers, and he fell.

And as he fell, diving away from light and life, the careless winds rushed past him, building to a scream, a scream like the wild hopeless whistle of trains at night, dragging him to his inevitable end on the rocks below, leaving him shattered on the remnants of his own bad dreams.